THE AMERICAN STORY

EDITED BY
MICHAEL M. REA

THE AMERICAN STORY

INTRODUCTION BY
CHARLES MCGRATH

*Short Stories from
The Rea Award*

SELECTED BY
*Ann Beattie • Stanley Elkin
Joyce Carol Oates • Cynthia Ozick
Shannon Ravenel • Joy Williams
Tobias Wolff*

THE ECCO PRESS

THE ECCO PRESS
100 West Broad Street
Hopewell, New Jersey 08525

Published simultaneously in Canada by
Penguin Books Canada Ltd., Ontario
Printed in the United States of America

Library of Congress Cataloging-in-Publication Data

The American story : a collection of short stories / selected by seven jurors for the Rea Award ;
    edited by Michael M. Rea ; introduced by Charles McGrath.
        p.   cm.
    "The jurors: Ann Beattie, Stanley Elkin, Joyce Carol Oates, Cynthia Ozick, Shannon
Ravenel, Joy Williams, Tobias Wolff."
        ISBN 0-88001-341-9
        ISBN 0-88001-435-0 (paperback)
        1. Short stories, American.   I. Rea, Michael M.
    PS648.S5A53   1993
    813'.0108—dc20   93-24178

Designed by Nick Mazzella

The text of this book is set in Bembo

9 8 7 6 5 4 3 2 1

FIRST PAPERBACK EDITION

CONTENTS

[v]

CONTENTS

PREFACE

The idea for this anthology emerged from the list of writers who have been nominated for the Rea Award for the Short Story over the past seven years. Since 1986 over forty writers have been nominated by juries of fellow writers and editors selected by the Dungannon Foundation, which oversees the running of the Rea Award. The past winners speak for themselves: Grace Paley, this year's winner, follows such major figures as Eudora Welty (1992), Paul Bowles (1991), and Joyce Carol Oates (1990). While each of the recipients has achieved notable success over a lifetime of work, *all* of the nominees illustrate what the Rea Award honors—writers who have made significant contributions to the short story. Unfortunately, in keeping this book to a manageable size, I have had to make difficult choices and leave out numerous important writers who were nominated. It is my hope to present these writers in a subsequent volume of the *American Story* Anthology.

It goes without saying that the jurors have been the key to the success of the award. In addition to all being writers themselves, they share a deep affection for and understanding of the art of the story. For this collection, we turned again to our jurors and asked them to select one representative sample from the rich collection of stories by their nominees. For example, Joy Williams, a juror in 1989, was asked to select a story from each of three nominees from that year—Tobias Wolff, Richard Ford, and Harold Brodkey. I believe the resulting collection of twenty-one stories well represents the diversity and ingeniousness of American short fiction over the last fifty years.

My thanks to Daniel Halpern and his staff at The Ecco Press, who displayed great patience in dealing with my occasionally overprotective indulgences. Also my deep appreciation to Chip McGrath, Deputy Editor of *The New Yorker* magazine, for his excellent introduction; his familiarity with the writers in this collection made his contribution very special. Finally, my gratitude to my friend Gary Millman who has advised me wisely through my literary projects.

—MICHAEL M. REA

CHARLES
McGRATH

INTRODUCTION

IT SEEMS like just a few years ago that we were promised a short-story "boom," or "renaissance," in America. The initial warning was issued, as I recall, back in the early eighties—following the unprecedented commercial and literary success of John Cheever's *Collected Stories* and Raymond Carver's *What We Talk About When We Talk About Love*—but anticipatory bulletins continued to be issued long afterward. The story, we were told, was the perfect medium for our sound-bite-and-infomercial era. Who had time to read novels? And with legions of young practitioners bursting forth yearly from the writing programs, eager to make their contribution to this most durable and quintessentially American genre, the art of the story is flourishing as never before. Publishers and booksellers were beginning to take notice, too (or so it was said) and it seemed only a matter of time before more and better story collections—handsomely printed, lavishly promoted, and generously advertised—would begin to turn up in the stores, where they would be snapped up by an insatiable public.

It never happened. The short story today is in exactly the same shape that it was in before the boom warnings, or perhaps a little worse. The number of magazines publishing short fiction has continued to dwindle, to the point where there are now only a handful that actually pay money—as opposed to free subscriptions or tearsheets—for stories; and though I haven't been keeping count, I suspect that the number of story collections published annually has undergone a similar shrinkage.

The reason the short-story boom never happened is in part that nobody really tried to make it happen. The publishers and the reviewers and the booksellers and the magazine editors talked a lot about stories, but they never changed their way of thinking about stories (which was, essentially, that stories weren't commercial) and they never did anything qualitatively different when it came to publishing them. But a more important reason the boom never happened was that it was based on a fallacy—the notion that because stories are shorter than novels they're less demanding to read. The truth is, stories aren't just *brief*, they're *different*; and they require of the reader something like the degree of concentration they require of the writer. William Maxwell, a great editor of stories and an equally great writer of them, believes that ideally a story should be written in a single sitting—by which he means a single, sustained, emotional moment, if not a single session in the chair. It seems to me that a story needs to be *read* in the same way. You can't skim or coast or leap ahead, and if you have to put a story down, it's not always easy to pick up—emotionally, that is—where you left off. You have to backtrack a little, or even start over. It's not enough to read a story the way you read a book or a newspaper. Stories ask of us that we surrender ourselves to them. It might even be argued that story collections are in some fundamental way unreadable as books—you can't just start at the beginning and plow straight through. You need time to recover. Good stories wear you out.

Contrary to what the boom predictors anticipated, then, it's more likely the novel that's the ideal form for our reduced attention spans, and it's certainly the novel that continues to hold out the possibility of monetary reward. The story market is now so diminished that, financially speaking, the lot of the story writer has probably never been more marginal. If the writing of stories were simply an economic proposition, in fact, most writers would no longer bother—and some, as it happens, do not. Many of us in the business of publishing magazine fiction have remarked in recent years on the increasing appearance of the "one-timer"—the young writer who publishes a story or two, parlays that into a book contract or a job in Hollywood, and is never heard from again. And yet there are probably more stories—maybe even more good stories—being written today than ever before, and it's not all because of the writing programs. Some writers just can't help themselves. It must be that there's something so alluring, so compelling and fulfilling about the short story that you can't put a price on it.

Unfortunately, it's not just a matter of economics. The story is essentially a popular form, and it owes its existence to the great burgeoning of popular magazines at the end of the last century. It's no accident that the golden age of the short story in this country coincides with the heyday of the great mass-circulation magazines, especially *Colliers* and *The Saturday Evening Post*. And the real danger of the current state of affairs—and especially of the near disappearance of fiction in large-circulation magazines—is not just that writers won't get *paid* but that they won't get *read*, except by a tiny group of adepts (most of whom are short-story writers themselves). The only way to keep up with short fiction in all its variety nowadays is to subscribe to dozens and dozens of literary quarterlies and reviews with odd and obscure names or else to rely on the people who make it their business to know what's going on: the anthologists, such as William Abrahams, with his yearly *O. Henry* collection; the roster of editors who assemble the annual *Best American Short Stories* volume; and the countless academics and literary entrepreneurs who package stories by theme or subject. Without this band of friendly and devoted readers, the story would be in considerably worse straits than it is.

To this essential list of experts may now be added the judges of the Rea Award. The collection of stories assembled here is a kind of anthology of anthologies. Most of the selections have already appeared in book form, and there are no newcomers among the authors. Neither are there any weak spots. The book is a long overdue acknowledgment of the award's distinguished winners and finalists, and it also happens to be as good an anthology as one could ask for of the best American short fiction right now. For completeness' sake, there are some writers who should be added—and no doubt will be in future years—but there's no one here who doesn't belong, and the volume as a whole is valuable both for its confirmations (the stories, like Cynthia Ozick's classic, "The Shawl," that you knew had to be here) and for the ones you had forgotten about, or somehow had missed. I thought I knew all of Coover, for example, but it turns out that there's a whole volume I'd overlooked—stunningly represented here by "You Must Remember This." I'm also happy to see that the list includes the first short story I ever read of my own free will and not because a teacher had assigned it (John Updike's "The Happiest I've Been," which appeared in *The New Yorker* in 1964) and a couple of stories that I personally worked on when—years later, and partly on the strength of my admiration for the work of Updike—I found myself editing fiction at the same magazine. These stories seem none the worse for my meddling, and, freed from the narrow gray columns of *The New Yorker*, have even acquired a welcome new expansiveness.

The arrangement of the collection—pairing judges and nominees—offers a number of incidental pleasures and surprises. Stanley Elkin and Joy Williams and Robert Coover, for example—that makes sense. Postmodernists all. But Elkin and Wright Morris? The champion of the extended riff and the master of understatement? Joy Williams and Harold Brodkey? It's like Ellington and Bach: surprising only until you think about it. The other revealing thing about the list of contributors is how many of them are exclusively, or almost exclusively, writers of stories; and even those who are not—Updike and Oates, that is—can hardly be said to be dabblers in the form. What this suggests is that real mastery of the story is a life's work, and not something that can be attained on a casual or part-time basis. It may even be that the story writer has little or no choice in the matter: This genre appears to select its own best practitioners, and not the other way around.

The contents of the collection are both surprising—the way good stories are surprising—and reassuringly familiar. Love. Family. The movies. The automobile. The city. The country. Distance. Closeness. The list of themes and settings and concerns is recognizably ours—recognizably American. So are the voices here. You couldn't mistake any of these for stories in translation. Reading through them, I was startled more than once to hear the echo of a slightly earlier voice—the plain, direct, unadorned cadence of Hemingway. It's a voice so natural to us now that we almost take it for granted, but if this collection is any indication, a lot of contemporary fiction would be unthinkable without it. And there's another, even older echo here: of the steady, authoritative voice at the edge of the pool of firelight, or by the bedside, or at the head of the lamplit table—the voice that begins "Once upon a time. . . ." Storytelling is an essential human attribute—it's the way we make sense of ourselves and of our times and of how we got to be the way we are.

In this country until not too long ago the storyteller tended to bring news from afar—from the worlds of the wealthy or of the downtrodden; news from wild and exotic territories, from that realm where the real consorts with the supernatural. That news is still available, but now, as these twenty-one stories suggest, the news is also from within: the news of the self, the kind of news that's singularly appropriate for the page—that private, solitary space where reader and writer connect. It's also news that seems unlikely ever to go out of fashion. The story doesn't need a renaissance. All it needs is listeners and tellers.

ACKNOWLEDGMENTS

"The Balloon" by Donald Barthelme © 1966 by Donald Barthelme, reprinted with the permission of Wylie, Aitken & Stone, Inc.

"Consolation" by Richard Bausch is reprinted by permission of Harriet Wasserman Literary Agency, Inc., agents for the author. Copyright © 1990 by Richard Bausch.

"Snow" is reprinted from *A Relative Stranger*, Stories by Charles Baxter, by permission of W. W. Norton & Company, Inc. Copyright © 1990 by Charles Baxter.

"A Vintage Thunderbird" is from *Distortions* by Ann Beattie. Reprinted by permission of the author.

"Verona: A Young Woman Speaks" is from *Stories in an Almost Classical Mode* by Harold Brodkey. Copyright © 1988 by Harold Brodkey. Reprinted by permission of Alfred A. Knopf, Inc.

ACKNOWLEDGMENTS

"The Cinema" is from *Dusk and Other Stories* by James Salter. Copyright © 1980 by James Salter. Reprinted by permission of North Point Press, a division of Farrar, Straus & Giroux, Inc.

"What You Hear From 'Em?" is from *The Collected Stories* by Peter Taylor. Copyright © 1951, 1969 by Peter Taylor. Reprinted by permission of Farrar, Straus & Giroux, Inc.

"The Happiest I've Been" is from *The Same Door* by John Updike. Copyright © 1959 by John Updike. Reprinted by permission of Alfred A. Knopf, Inc.

"No Place for You, My Love" is from *The Bride of the Innisfallen and Other Stories*, copyright 1952 and renewed 1980 by Eudora Welty, reprinted by permission of Harcourt Brace & Company.

"Escapes" is from the book *Escapes* by Joy Williams. Copyright © 1990 by Joy Williams. Used by permission of the Atlantic Monthly Press.

"Our Story Begins" is from *Back in the World* by Tobias Wolff. Copyright © 1985 by Tobias Wolff. Reprinted by permission of Houghton Mifflin Co. All rights reserved.

WINNERS OF THE REA AWARD

1993
Grace Paley

1992
Eudora Welty

1991
Paul Bowles

1990
Joyce Carol Oates

1989
Tobias Wolff

1988
Donald Barthelme

1987
Robert Coover

1986
Cynthia Ozick

THE AMERICAN STORY

ESCAPES

WHEN I WAS very small, my father said, "Lizzie, I want to tell you something about your grandfather. Just before he died, he was alive. Fifteen minutes before."

I had never known my grandfather. This was the most extraordinary thing I had ever heard about him.

Still, I said, No.

"No!" my father said. "What do you mean, 'No.' " He laughed. I shook my head.

"All right," my father said, "it was one minute before. I thought you were too little to know such things, but I see you're not. It was even less than a minute. It was one *moment* before."

"Oh stop teasing her," my mother said to my father.

"He's just teasing you, Lizzie," my mother said.

In warm weather once we drove up into the mountains, my mother, my father, and I, and stayed for several days at a resort lodge on a lake. In the afternoons, horse races took place in the lodge. The horses were blocks of wood with numbers painted on them, moved from one end of the room to the other by ladies in ball gowns. There was a long pier that led out into the lake and at the end of the pier was a nightclub that had a twenty-foot-tall champagne glass on the roof. At night, someone would pull a switch and neon bubbles would spring out from the lit glass into the black air. I very much wanted such a glass on the roof of our own house and I wanted to be the one who, every night, would turn on the switch. My mother always said about this, "We'll see."

I saw an odd thing once, there in the mountains. I saw my father, pretending to be lame. This was in the midst of strangers in the gift shop of the lodge. The shop sold hand-carved canes, among many other things, and when I came in to buy bubble gum in the shape of cigarettes, to which I was devoted, I saw my father, hobbling painfully down the aisle, leaning heavily on a dully gleaming yellow cane, his shoulders hunched, one leg turned out at a curious angle. My handsome, healthy father, his face drawn in dreams. He looked at me. And then he looked away as though he did not know me.

My mother was a drinker. Because my father left us, I assumed he was not a drinker, but this may not have been the case. My mother loved me and was always kind to me. We spent a great deal of time together, my mother and I. This was before I knew how to read. I suspected there was a trick to reading, but I did not know the trick. Written words were something between me and a place I could not go. My mother went back and forth to that place all the time, but couldn't explain to me exactly what it was like there. I imagined it to be a different place.

As a very young child, my mother had seen the magician Houdini. Houdini had made an elephant disappear. He had also made an orange tree grow from a seed right on the stage. Bright oranges hung from the tree and he had picked them and thrown them out into the audience. People could eat the oranges or take them home, whatever they wanted.

How did he make the elephant disappear, I asked.

"He disappeared in a puff of smoke," my mother said. "Houdini said that even the elephant didn't know how it was done."

Was it a baby elephant, I asked.

My mother sipped her drink. She said that Houdini was more than a magician, he was an escape artist. She said that he could escape from handcuffs and chains and ropes.

"They put him in straitjackets and locked him in trunks and threw him in swimming pools and rivers and oceans and he escaped," my mother said. "He escaped from water-filled vaults. He escaped from coffins."

I said that I wanted to see Houdini.

"Oh, Houdini's dead, Lizzie," my mother said. "He died a long time ago. A man punched him in the stomach three times and he died."

Dead. I asked if he couldn't get out of being dead.

"He met his match there," my mother said.

She said that he turned a bowl of flowers into a pony who cantered around the stage.

"He sawed a lady in half too, Lizzie." Oh, how I wanted to be that lady, sawed in half and then made whole again!

My mother spoke happily, laughing. We sat at the kitchen table and my mother was drinking from a small glass which rested snugly in her hand. It was my favorite glass too but she never let me drink from it. There were all kinds of glasses in our cupboard but this was the one we both liked. This was in Maine. Outside, in the yard, was our car which was an old blue convertible.

Was there blood, I asked.

"No, Lizzie, no. He was a magician!"

Did she cry, that lady, I wanted to know.

"I don't think so," my mother said. "Maybe he hypnotized her first."

It was winter. My father had never ridden in the blue convertible which my mother had bought after he had gone. The car was old then, and was rusted here and there. Beneath the rubber mat on my side, the passenger side, part of the floor had rusted through completely. When we went anywhere in the car, I would sometimes lift up the mat so I could see the road rushing past beneath us and feel the cold round air as it came up through the hole. I would pretend that the coldness was trying to speak to me, in the same way that words written down tried to speak. The air wanted to tell me something, but I didn't care about it, that's what I thought. Outside, the car stood in the snow.

I had a dream about the car. My mother and I were alone together as we always were, linked in our hopeless and uncomprehending love of one another, and we were driving to a house. It seemed to be our destination but we only arrived to move on. We drove again, always returning to the house which we would circle and leave, only to arrive at it again. As we drove, the inside of the car grew hair. The hair was gray and it grew and grew. I never told my mother about this dream just as I had never told her about my father leaning on the cane. I was a secretive person. In that way, I was like my mother.

I wanted to know more about Houdini. Was Houdini in love, did Houdini love someone, I asked.

"Rosabelle," my mother said. "He loved his wife, Rosabelle."

I went and got a glass and poured some ginger ale in it and I sipped my ginger ale slowly in the way that I had seen my mother sip her drink many, many times. Even then, I had the gestures down. I sat opposite her, very still and quiet, pretending.

But then I wanted to know was there magic in the way he loved her. Could he make her disappear. Could he make both of them disappear was the way I put my question.

"Rosabelle," my mother said. "No one knew anything about Rosabelle except that Houdini loved her. He never turned their love into loneliness, which would have been beneath him, of course."

We ate our supper and after supper my mother would have another little bit to drink. Then she would read articles from the newspaper aloud to me.

"My goodness," she said, "what a strange story. A hunter shot a bear who was carrying a woman's pocketbook in its mouth."

Oh, oh, I cried. I looked at the newspaper and struck it with my fingers. My mother read on, a little oblivious to me. The woman had lost her purse years before on a camping trip. Everything was still inside it, her wallet and her compact and her keys.

Oh, I cried. I thought this was terrible. I was frightened, thinking of my mother's pocketbook, the way she carried it always, and the poor bear too.

Why did the bear want to carry a pocketbook, I asked.

My mother looked up from the words in the newspaper. It was as though she had come back into the room I was in.

"Why, Lizzie," she said.

The poor bear, I said.

"Oh, the bear is all right," my mother said. "The bear got away."

I did not believe this was the case. She herself said the bear had been shot.

"The bear escaped," my mother said. "It says so right here," and she ran her finger along a line of words. "It ran back into the woods to its home." She stood up and came around the table and kissed me. She smelled then like the glass that was always in the sink in the morning, and the smell reminds me still of daring and deception, hopes and little lies.

I shut my eyes and in that way I felt I could not hear my mother. I saw the bear holding the pocketbook, walking through the woods with it, feeling fine in a different way and pretty too, then stopping to find something in it, wanting something, moving its big paw through the pocketbook's small things.

"Lizzie," my mother called to me. My mother did not know where I was which alarmed me. I opened my eyes.

"Don't cry, Lizzie," my mother said. She looked as though she were about to cry too. This was the way it often was at night, late in the kitchen, with my mother.

My mother returned to the newspaper and began to turn the

pages. She called my attention to the drawing of a man holding a hat with stars sprinkling out of it. It was an advertisement for a magician who would be performing not far away. We decided we would see him. My mother knew just the seats she wanted for us, good seats, on the aisle close to the stage. We might be called up on the stage, she said, to be part of the performance. Magicians often used people from the audience, particularly children. I might even be given a rabbit.

I wanted a rabbit.

I put my hands on the table and I could see the rabbit between them. He was solid white in the front and solid black in the back as though he were made up of two rabbits. There are rabbits like that. I saw him there, before me on the table, a nice rabbit.

My mother went to the phone and ordered two tickets, and not many days after that, we were in our car driving to Portland for the matinee performance. I very much liked the word *matinee*. Matinee, matinee, I said. There was a broad hump on the floor between our seats and it was here where my mother put her little glass, the glass often full, never, it seemed, more than half empty. We chatted together and I thought we must have appeared interesting to others as we passed by in our convertible in winter. My mother spoke about happiness. She told me that the happiness that comes out of nowhere, out of nothing, is the very best kind. We paid no attention to the coldness which was speaking in the way that it had, but enjoyed the sun which beat through the windshield upon our pale hands.

My mother said that Houdini had black eyes and that white doves flew from his fingertips. She said that he escaped from a block of ice.

Did he look like my father, Houdini, I asked. Did he have a mustache.

"Your father didn't have a mustache," my mother said, laughing. "Oh, I wish I could be more like you."

Later, she said, "Maybe he didn't escape from a block of ice, I'm not sure about that. Maybe he wanted to, but he never did."

We stopped for lunch somewhere, a dark little restaurant along the road. My mother had cocktails and I myself drank something cold and sweet. The restaurant was not very nice. It smelled of smoke and dampness as though once it had burned down, and it was so noisy that I could not hear my mother very well. My mother looked like a woman in a bar, pretty and disturbed, hunched forward saying, who do you think I look like, will you remember me? She was saying all matter of things. We lingered there, and then my mother asked the time of someone and seemed surprised. My mother was always surprised by time. Outside, there were woods of green fir trees whose lowest branches swept the ground, and as we were getting back into the car, I believed I saw something moving far back in the darkness of the woods beyond the slick, snowy square of the parking lot. It was the bear, I thought. Hurry, hurry, I thought. The hunter is playing with his children. He is making them something to play in as my father had once made a small playhouse for me. He is not the hunter yet. But in my heart I knew the bear was gone and the shape was just the shadow of something else in the afternoon.

My mother drove very fast but the performance had already begun when we arrived. My mother's face was damp and her good blouse had a spot on it. She went into the ladies' room and when she returned the spot was larger, but it was water now and not what it had been before. The usher assured us that we had not missed much. The usher said that the magician was not very good, that he talked and talked, he told a lot of jokes and then when you were bored and distracted, something would happen, something would have changed. The usher smiled at my mother. He seemed to like her, even know her in some way. He was a small man, like an old boy, balding. I did not care for him. He led us to our seats, but there were people sitting in them and there was a small disturbance as the strangers rearranged themselves. We were both expectant, my mother and I, and we watched the magician intently. My mother's lips were parted, and her eyes were bright. On the stage was a group of children about my age, each with a

[7]

hand on a small cage the magician was holding. In the cage was a tiny bird. The magician would ask the children to jostle the cage occasionally and the bird would flutter against the bars so that everyone would see it was a real thing with bones and breath and feelings too. Each child announced that they had a firm grip on the bars. Then the magician put a cloth over the cage, gave a quick tug, and cage and bird vanished. I was not surprised. It seemed just the kind of thing that was going to happen. I decided to withhold my applause when I saw that my mother's hands too were in her lap. There were several more tricks of the magician's invention, certainly nothing I would have asked him to do. Large constructions of many parts and colors were wheeled onto the stage. There were doors everywhere which the magician opened and slammed shut. Things came and went, all to the accompaniment of loud music. I was confused and grew hot. My mother too moved restlessly in the next seat. Then there was an intermission and we returned to the lobby.

"This man is a far, far cry from the great Houdini," my mother said.

What were his intentions exactly, I asked.

He had taken a watch from a man in the audience and smashed it for all to see with a hammer. Then the watch, unharmed, had reappeared behind the man's ear.

"A happy memory can be a very misleading thing," my mother said. "Would you like to go home?"

I did not want to leave really. I wanted to see it through. I held the glossy program in my hand and turned the pages. I stared hard at the print beneath the pictures and imagined all sorts of promises being made.

"Yes, we want to see how it's done, don't we, you and I," my mother said. "We want to get to the bottom of it."

I guessed we did.

"All right, Lizzie," my mother said, "but I have to get something out of the car. I'll be right back."

I waited for her in a corner of the lobby. Some children looked at me and I looked back. I had a package of gum cigarettes in my pocket and I extracted one carefully and placed the end in my mouth. I held the elbow of my right arm with my left hand and smoked the cigarette for a long time and then I folded it up in my mouth and I chewed it for a while. My mother had not yet returned when the performance began again. She was having a little drink, I knew, and she was where she went when she drank without me, somewhere in herself. It was not the place where words could take you but another place even. I stood alone in the lobby for a while, looking out into the street. On the sidewalk outside the theater, sand had been scattered and the sand ate through the ice in ugly holes. I saw no one like my mother who passed by. She was wearing a red coat. Once she had said to me, You've fallen out of love with me, haven't you, and I knew she was thinking I was someone else, but this had happened only once.

I heard the music from the stage and I finally returned to our seats. There were not as many people in the audience as before. On stage with the magician was a woman in a bathing suit and high-heeled shoes holding a chain saw. The magician demonstrated that the saw was real by cutting up several pieces of wood with it. There was the smell of torn wood for everyone to smell and sawdust on the floor for all to see. Then a table was wheeled out and the lady lay down on it in her bathing suit which was in two pieces. Her stomach was very white. The magician talked and waved the saw around. I suspected he was planning to cut the woman in half and I was eager to see this. I hadn't the slightest fear about this at all. I did wonder if he would be able to put her together again or if he would cut her in half only. The magician said that what was about to happen was too dreadful to be seen directly, that he did not want anyone to faint from the sight, so he brought out a small screen and placed it in front of the lady so that we could no longer see her white stomach, although everyone could still see her face and her shoes. The screen seemed unnecessary to me and I would have preferred to have been seated on the other side of it. Several people in the audience screamed. The lady who was about to be sawed in half began to chew on her lip and her face looked worried.

It was then that my mother appeared on the stage. She was crouched over a little, for she didn't have her balance back from having climbed up there. She looked large and strange in her red coat. The coat, which I knew very well, seemed the strangest thing. Someone screamed again, but more uncertainly. My mother moved toward the magician, smiling and speaking and gesturing with her hands, and the magician said, No, I can't of course, you should know better than this, this is a performance, you can't just appear like this, please sit down . . .

My mother said, But you don't understand I'm willing, though I know the hazards and it's not that I believe you, no one would believe you for a moment but you can trust me, that's right, your faith in me would be perfectly placed because I'm not part of this, that's why I can be trusted because I don't know how it's done . . .

Someone near me said, Is she kidding, that woman, what's her plan, she comes out of nowhere and wants to be cut in half . . .

Lady . . . the magician said, and I thought a dog might appear for I knew a dog named Lady who had a collection of colored balls.

My mother said, Most of us don't understand I know and it's just as well because the things we understand that's it for them, that's just the way we are . . .

She probably thought she was still in that place in herself, but everything she said were the words coming from her mouth. Her lipstick was gone. Did she think she was in disguise, I wondered.

But why not, my mother said, to go and come back, that's what we want, that's why we're here and why can't we expect something to be done you can't expect us every day we get tired of showing up every day you can't get away with this forever then it was different but you should be thinking about the children . . . She moved a little in a crooked fashion, speaking.

My God, said a voice, that woman's drunk. Sit down, please! someone said loudly.

My mother started to cry then and she stumbled and pushed her arms out before her as though she were pushing away someone who was trying to hold her, but no one was trying to hold her. The orchestra began to play and people began to clap. The usher ran out onto the stage and took my mother's hand. All this happened in an instant. He said something to her, he held her hand and she did not resist his holding it, then slowly the two of them moved down the few steps that led to the stage and up the aisle until they stopped beside me for the usher knew I was my mother's child. I followed them, of course, although in my mind I continued to sit in my seat. Everyone watched us leave. They did not notice that I remained there among them, watching too.

We went directly out of the theater and into the streets, my mother weeping on the little usher's arm. The shoulders of his jacket were of cardboard and there was gold braid looped around it. We were being taken away to be murdered, which seemed reasonable to me. The usher's ears were large and he had a bump on his neck above the collar of his shirt. As we walked he said little soft things to my mother which gradually seemed to be comforting her. I hated him. It was not easy to walk together along the frozen sidewalks of the city. There was a belt on my mother's coat and I hung on to that as we moved unevenly along.

Look, I've pulled myself through, he said. You can pull yourself through. He was speaking to my mother.

We went into a coffee shop and sat down in a booth. You can collect yourself in here, he said. You can sit here as long as you want and drink coffee and no one will make you leave. He asked me if I wanted a donut. I would not speak to him. If he addressed me again, I thought, I would bite him. On the wall over the counter were pictures of sandwiches and pies. I did not want to be there and I did not take off either my mittens or my coat. The little usher went up to the counter and brought back coffee for my mother and a donut on a plate for me. Oh, my mother said, what have I done, and she swung her head from side to side.

I could tell right away about you, the usher said. You've got to pull yourself together. It took jumping off a bridge for me and breaking both legs before I got turned around. You don't want to let it go that far.

My mother looked at him. I can't imagine, my mother said.

Outside, a child passed by, walking with her sled. She looked behind her often and you could tell she was admiring the way the sled followed her so quickly on its runners.

You're a mother, the usher said to my mother, you've got to pull yourself through.

His kindness made me feel he had tied us up with rope. At last he left us and my mother laid her head down upon the table and fell asleep. I had never seen my mother sleeping and I watched her as she must once have watched me, the same way everyone watches a sleeping thing, not knowing how it would turn out or when. Then slowly I began to eat the donut with my mittened hands. The sour hair of the wool mingled with the tasteless crumbs and this utterly absorbed my attention. I pretended someone was feeding me.

As it happened, my mother was not able to pull herself through, but this was later. At the time, it was not so near the end and when my mother woke we found the car and left Portland, my mother saying my name. Lizzie, she said. Lizzie. I felt as though I must be with her somewhere and that she knew that too, but not in that old blue convertible traveling home in the dark, the soft, stained roof ballooning up in the way I knew it looked from the outside. I got out of it, but it took me years.

ROBERT COOVER | # YOU MUST REMEMBER THIS

IT IS DARK in Rick's apartment. Black leader dark, heavy and abstract, silent but for a faint hoarse crackle like a voiceless plaint, and brief as sleep. Then Rick opens the door and the light from the hall scissors in like a bellboy to open up space, deposit surfaces (there is a figure in the room), harbinger event (it is Ilsa). Rick follows, too preoccupied to notice: his café is closed, people have been shot, he has troubles. But then, with a stroke, he lights a small lamp (such a glow! the shadows retreat, *everything* retreats: where are the walls?) and there she is, facing him, holding open the drapery at the far window like the front of a nightgown, the light flickering upon her white but determined face like static. Rick pauses for a moment in astonishment. Ilsa lets the drapery and its implications drop, takes a step forward into the strangely fretted light, her eyes searching his.

"How did you get in?" he asks, though this is probably not the question on his mind.

"The stairs from the street."

This answer seems to please him. He knows how vulnerable he is, after all, it's the way he lives—his doors are open, his head is bare, his tuxedo jacket is snowy white—that's not important. What matters is that by such a reply a kind of destiny is being fulfilled. Sam has a song about it. "I told you this morning you'd come around," he says, curling his lips as if to advertise his appetite for punishment, "but this is a little ahead of schedule." She faces him squarely, broad-shouldered and narrow-hipped, a sash around her waist like a gun belt, something shiny in her tensed left hand. He raises both of his own as if to show they are empty: "Well, won't you sit down?"

His offer, whether in mockery or no, releases her. Her shoulders dip in relief, her breasts; she sweeps forward (it is only a small purse she is carrying: a toothbrush perhaps, cosmetics, her hotel key), her face softening: "Richard!" He starts back in alarm, hands moving to his hips. "I had to see you!"

"So you use Richard again!" His snarling retreat throws up a barrier between them. She stops. He pushes his hands into his pockets as though to reach for the right riposte: "We're back in Paris!"

That probably wasn't it. Their song seems to be leaking into the room from somewhere out in the night, or perhaps it has been there all the time—Sam maybe, down in the darkened bar, sending out soft percussive warnings in the manner of his African race: "Think twice, boss. Hearts fulla passion, you c'n rely. Jealousy, boss, an' hate. Le's go fishin', Sam."

"Please!" she begs, staring at him intently, but he remains unmoved:

"Your unexpected visit isn't connected by any chance with the letters of transit?" He ducks his head, his upper lip swelling with bitterness and hurt. "It seems as long as I have those letters, I'll never be lonely."

Yet, needless to say, he will always be lonely—in fact, this is the confession ("You can ask any price you want," she is saying) only half-concealed in his muttered subjoinder. Rick Blaine is a loner, born and bred. Pity him. There is this lingering, almost primal image of him, sitting alone at a chessboard in his white tuxedo, smoking contemplatively in the midst of a raucous conniving crowd, a crowd he has himself assembled about him. He taps a pawn, moves a white knight, fondles a tall black queen while a sardonic smile plays on his lips. He seems to be toying, self-mockingly, with Fate itself, as indifferent toward Rick Blaine (never mind that he says—as he does now, turning away from her—that *"I'm* the only cause *I'm* interested in . . .") as toward the rest of the world. It's all shit, so who cares?

Ilsa is staring off into space, a space that a moment ago Rick filled. She seems to be thinking something out. The negotiations are going badly; perhaps it is this she is worried about. He has just refused her offer of "any price," ignored her ultimatum. ("You *must* giff me those letters!"), sneered at her husband's heroism, and scoffed at the very cause that first brought them together in Paris. How could he do that? And now he has abruptly turned his back on her (does he think it was just sex? what has happened to him since then?) and walked away toward the balcony door, meaning, apparently, to turn her out. She takes a deep breath, presses her lips together, and, clutching her tiny purse with both hands, wheels about to pursue him: "Richard!" This has worked before, it works again: he turns to face her new approach: "We luffed each other once . . ." Her voice catches in her throat, tears come to her eyes. She is beautiful there in the slatted shadows, her hair loosening around her ears, eyes glittering, throat bare and vulnerable in the open V neck of her ruffled blouse. She's a good dresser. Even that little purse she squeezes: so like the other one, so lovely, hidden away. She shakes her head slightly in wistful appeal: "If those days meant . . . anything at all to you . . ."

"I wouldn't bring up Paris if I were you," he says stonily. "It's poor salesmanship."

She gasps (*she* didn't bring it up: is he a madman?), tosses her head back: "Please! Please listen to me!" She closes her eyes, her lower lip pushed forward as though bruised. "If you knew what really happened, if you only knew the truth—."

He stands over this display, impassive as a Moorish executioner (that's it! he's turning into one of these bloody Arabs, she thinks). "I wouldn't believe you, no matter what you told me," he says. In Ethiopia, after an attempt on the life of an Italian officer he saw 1,600 Ethiopians get rounded up one night and shot in reprisal. Many were friends of his. Or clients anyway. But somehow her deceit is worse. "You'd say anything now, to get what you want." Again he turns his back on her, strides away.

She stares at him in shocked silence, as though all that had happened eighteen months ago in Paris were flashing suddenly before her eyes, now made ugly by some terrible revelation. An exaggerated gasp escapes her like the breaking of wind: his head snaps up and he turns sharply to the right. She chases him, dogging his heels. "You want to feel sorry for yourself, don't you?" she cries and, surprised (he was just reaching for something on an ornamental table, the humidor perhaps), he turns back to her. "With so much at stake, all you can think of is your own feeling," she rails. Her lips are drawn back, her breathing labored, her eyes watering in anger and frustration. "One woman has hurt you, and you take your reffenge on the rest off the world!" She is choking, she can hardly speak. Her accent seems to have got worse. "You're a coward, und veakling, und—"

She gasps. What is she saying? He watches her, as though faintly amused. "No. Richard, I'm sorry!" Tears are flowing in earnest now: she's gone too far! This is the expression on her face. She's in a corner, struggling to get out. "I'm sorry, but—" She wipes the tears from her cheek, and calls once again on her husband, that great and courageous man whom they both admire, whom the whole world admires: "—you're our last hope! If you don't help us, Victor Laszlo will die in Casablanca!"

"What of it?" he says. He has been waiting for this opportunity. He plays with it now, stretching it out. He turns, reaches for a cigarette, his head haloed in the light from an arched doorway. "I'm gonna die in Casablanca. It's a good spot for it." This line is meant to be amusing, but Ilsa reacts with horror. Her eyes widen.

She catches her breath, turns away. He lights up, pleased with himself, takes a practiced drag, blows smoke. "Now," he says, turning toward her, "if you'll—"

He pulls up short, squints: she has drawn a revolver on him. So much for toothbrushes and hotel keys. "All right. I tried to reason with you. I tried effrything. Now I want those letters." Distantly, a melodic line suggests a fight for love and glory, an ironic case of do or die. "Get them for me."

"I don't have to." He touches his jacket. "I got 'em right here."

"Put them on the table."

He smiles and shakes his head. "No." Smoke curls up from the cigarette he is holding at his side like the steam that enveloped the five o'clock train to Marseilles. Her eyes fill with tears. Even as she presses on ("For the last time . . . !"), she knows that "no" is final. There is, behind his ironic smile, a profound sadness, the fatalistic survivor's wistful acknowledgment that, in the end, the fundamental things apply. Time, going by, leaves nothing behind, not even moments like this. "If Laszlo and the cause mean so much," he says, taunting her with her own uncertainties, "you won't stop at anything . . ."

He seems almost to recede. The cigarette disappears, the smoke. His sorrow gives way to something not unlike eagerness. "All right, I'll make it easier for you," he says, and walks toward her. "Go ahead and shoot. You'll be doing me a favor."

She seems taken aback, her eyes damp, her lips swollen and parted. Light licks at her face. He gazes steadily at her from his superior moral position, smoke drifting up from his hand once more, his white tuxedo pressed against the revolver barrel. Her eyes close as the gun lowers, and she gasps his name: "Richard!" It is like an invocation. Or a profession of faith. "I tried to stay away," she sighs. She opens her eyes, peers up at him in abject surrender. A tear moves slowly down her cheek toward the corner of her mouth like secret writing. "I thought I would neffer see you again . . . that you were out off my life . . ." She blinks, cries out faintly—"Oh!"—and (he seems moved at last, his mask of disdain falling away like perspiration) turns away, her head wrenched to one side as though in pain.

Stricken with sudden concern, or what looks like concern, he steps up behind her, clasping her breasts with both hands, nuzzling in her hair. "The day you left Paris . . . !" she sobs, though she seems unsure of herself. One of his hands is already down between her legs, the other inside her blouse, pulling a breast out of its brassiere cup. "If you only knew . . . what I . . ." He is moaning, licking at one ear, the hand between her legs nearly lifting her off the floor, his pelvis bumping at her buttocks. "Is this . . . right?" she gasps.

"I—I don't know!" he groans, massaging her breast, the nipple between two fingers. "I can't think!"

"But . . . you *must* think!" she cries, squirming her hips. Tears are streaming down her cheeks now. "For . . . for . . ."

"What?" he gasps, tearing her blouse open, pulling on her breast as though to drag it over her shoulder where he might kiss it. Or eat it: he seems ravenous suddenly.

"I . . . I can't remember!" she sobs. She reaches behind to jerk at his fly (what else is she to do, for the love of Jesus?), then rips away her sash, unfastens her skirt, her fingers trembling.

"Holy shit!" he wheezes, pushing his hand inside her girdle as her skirt falls. His cheeks too are wet with tears. *"Ilsa!"*

"Richard!"

They fall to the floor, grabbing and pulling at each other's clothing. He's trying to get her bra off, which is tangled up now with her blouse, she's struggling with his belt, yanking at his black pants, wrenching them open. Buttons fly, straps pop, there's the soft unfocused rip of silk, the jingle of buckles and falling coins, grunts, gasps, whimpers of desire. He strips the tangled skein of underthings away (all these straps and stays—how does she get in and out of this crazy elastic?); she works his pants down past his bucking hips, fumbles with his shoes. *"Your elbow—!"*

"Mmmff!"

[18]

"Ah—!"

She pulls his pants and boxer shorts off, crawls round and (he strokes her shimmering buttocks, swept by the light from the airport tower, watching her full breasts sway above him: its all happening so fast, he'd like to slow it down, repeat some of the better bits—that view of her rippling haunches on her hands and knees just now, for example, like a twenty-two, his lucky number—but there's a great urgency on them, they can't wait) straddles him, easing him into her like a train being guided into a station. *"I luff you, Richard!"* she declares breathlessly, though she seems to be speaking, eyes squeezed shut and breasts heaving, not to him but to the ceiling, if there is one up there. His eyes too are closed now, his hands gripping her soft hips, pulling her down, his breath coming in short anguished snorts, his face puffy and damp with tears. There is, as always, something deeply wounded and vulnerable about the expression on his battered face, framed there against his Persian carpet: Rick Blaine, a man annealed by loneliness and betrayal, but flawed—hopelessly, it seems—by hope itself. He is, in the tragic sense, a true revolutionary: his gaping mouth bespeaks this, the spittle in the corners of his lips, his eyes, open now and staring into some infinite distance not unlike the future, his knitted brow. He heaves upward, impaling her to the very core: *"Oh, Gott!"* she screams, her back arching, mouth agape as though to commence "La Marseillaise."

Now, for a moment, they pause, feeling themselves thus conjoined, his organ luxuriating in the warm tub of her vagina, her enflamed womb closing around his pulsing penis like a mother embracing a lost child. "If you only knew . . . ," she seems to say, though perhaps she has said this before and only now it can be heard. He fondles her breasts; she rips his shirt open, strokes his chest, leans forward to kiss his lips, his nipples. This is not Victor inside her with his long thin rapier, all too rare in its embarrassed visits; this is not Yvonne with her cunning professional muscles, her hollow airy hole. This is love in all its clammy mystery, the ultimate connection, the squishy rub of truth, flesh as a self-consuming message. This is necessity, as in woman needs man, and man must have his mate. Even their identities seem to be dissolving; they have to whisper each other's name from time to time as though in recitative struggle against some ultimate enchantment from which there might be no return. Then slowly she begins to wriggle her hips above him, he to meet her gentle undulations with counterthrusts of his own. They hug each other close, panting, her breasts smashed against him, moving only from the waist down. She slides her thighs between his and squeezes his penis between them, as though to conceal it there, an underground member on the run, wounded but unbowed. He lifts his stockinged feet and plants them behind her knees as though in stirrups, her buttocks above pinching and opening, pinching and opening like a suction pump. And it is true about her vaunted radiance: she seems almost to glow from within, her flexing cheeks haloed in their own dazzling luster.

"It feels so good, Richard! In there . . . I've been so—ah!—so lonely . . . !"

"Yeah, me too, kid *Ngh*! Don't talk."

She slips her thighs back over his and draws them up beside his waist like a child curling around her teddy bear, knees against his ribs, her fanny gently hobbing on its pike like a mind caressing a cherished memory. He lies there passively for a moment, stretched out, eyes closed, accepting this warm rhythmical ablution as one might accept a nanny's teasing bath, a mother's care (a care, he's often said, denied him), in all its delicious innocence—or seemingly so: in fact, his whole body is faintly atremble, as though, with great difficulty, shedding the last of its pride and bitterness, its isolate neutrality. Then slowly his own hips begin to rock convulsively under hers, his knees to rise in involuntary surrender. She tongues his ear, her buttocks thumping more vigorously now, kisses his throat, his nose, his scarred lips, then rears up, arching her back, tossing her head back (her hair is looser now, wilder, a flush has crept into the distinctive pallor of her cheeks and throat, and what was before a fierce determination is now raw intensity, what vulnerability now a slack-jawed abandon), plunging him in more deeply than ever, his own buttocks bouncing up off the floor as though trying to take off like the next flight to Lisbon—"Gott in Himmel, *this is fonn!*" she cries. She reaches behind her back to clutch his testicles, he clasps her hand in both of his, his thighs spread, she falls forward, they roll over, he's pounding away now from above (he lacks her famous radiance: if anything his buttocks seem to suck in light, drawing a nostalgic murkiness around them like night fog, signaling a fundamental distance between them, and an irresistible attraction), she's clawing at his back under the white jacket, at his hips, his thighs, her voracious nether mouth leaping up at him from below and sliding back, over and over, like a frantic greased-pole climber. Faster and faster they slap their bodies together, submitting to this fierce rhythm as though to simplify themselves, emitting grunts and whinnies and helpless little farts, no longer Rick Blaine and Ilsa Lund, but some nameless conjunction somewhere between them, time, space, being itself getting redefined by the rapidly narrowing focus of their incandescent passion—then suddenly Rick rears back, his face seeming to puff out like a gourd, Ilsa cries out and kicks upward, crossing her ankles over Rick's clenched buttocks, for a moment they seem almost to float, suspended, unloosed from the earth's gravity, and then—*whumpf!*—they hit the floor again, their bodies continuing to hammer together, though less regularly, plunging, twitching, prolonging this exclamatory dialogue, drawing it out even as the intensity diminishes, even as it becomes more a declaration than a demand, more an inquiry than a declaration. Ilsa's feet uncross, slide slowly to the floor. "Fooff . . . *Gott!*" They lie there, cheek to cheek, clutching each other tightly, gasping for breath, their thighs quivering with the last involuntary spasms, the echoey reverberations, deep in their loins, of pleasure's fading blasts.

"Jesus," Rick wheezes, "I've been saving that one for a goddamn year and a half . . . !"

"It was the best fokk I effer haff," Ilsa replies with a tremulous sigh, and kisses his ear, runs her fingers in his hair. He starts to

ROBERT COOVER

roll off her, but she clasps him closely: "No . . . wait . . . !" A
deeper thicker pleasure, not so ecstatic, yet somehow more moving, seems to well up from far inside her to embrace the swollen
visitor snuggled moistly in her womb, once a familiar friend,
a comrade loved and trusted, now almost a stranger, like one
resurrected from the dead.

"Ah—!" he gasps. God, it's almost like she's milking it! Then
she lets go, surrounding him spongily with a kind of warm wet
pulsating gratitude. "Ah . . . !"

He lies there between Ilsa's damp silky thighs, feeling his weight
thicken, his mind soften and spread. His will drains away as if it
were some kind of morbid affection, lethargy overtaking him like
an invading army. Even his jaw goes slack, his fingers (three
sprawl idly on a dark-tipped breast) limp. He wears his snowy
white tuxedo jacket still, his shiny black socks, which, together
with the parentheses of Ilsa's white thighs, make his melancholy
buttocks—beaten in childhood, lashed at sea, run lean in union
skirmishes, sunburned in Ethiopia, and shot at in Spain—look
gloomier than ever, swarthy and self-pitying, agape now with a
kind of heroic sadness. A violent tenderness. These buttocks are,
it could be said, what the pose of isolation looks like at its best:
proud, bitter, mournful, and, as the prefect of police might have
put it, tremendously attractive. Though his penis has slipped out
of its vaginal pocket to lie limply like a fat little toe against her
slowly pursing lips, she clasps him close still, clinging to something she cannot quite define, something like a spacious dream of
freedom, or a monastery garden, or the discovery of electricity.
"Do you have a gramophone on, Richard?"

"What—?!" Her question has startled him. His haunches snap
shut, his head rears up, snorting, he seems to be reaching for the
letters of transit. "Ah . . . no . . ." He relaxes again, letting his
weight fall back, though sliding one thigh over hers now, stretching his arms out as though to unkink them, turning his face away.
His scrotum bulges up on her thigh like an emblem of his inner
serenity and generosity, all too often concealed, much as an au-

thentic decency might shine through a mask of cynicism and despair. He takes a deep breath. (A kiss is just a kiss is what the music is insinuating. A sigh . . .) "That's probably Sam . . ."

She sighs (. . . and so forth), gazing up at the ceiling above her, patterned with overlapping circles of light from the room's lamps and swept periodically by the wheeling airport beacon, coming and going impatiently, yet reliably, like desire itself. "He hates me, I think."

"Sam? No, he's a pal. What I think, he thinks."

"When we came into the bar last night, he started playing 'Luff for Sale.' Effryone turned and looked at me."

"It wasn't the song, sweetheart, it was the way you two were dressed. Nobody in Casablanca—"

"Then he tried to chase me away. He said I was bad luck to you." She can still see the way he rolled his white eyes at her, like some kind of crazy voodoo zombie.

Richard grunts ambiguously. "Maybe you should stop calling him 'boy.' "

Was that it? "But in all the moofies—" Well, a translation problem probably, a difficulty she has known often in her life. Language can sometimes be stiff as a board. Like what's under her now. She loves Richard's relaxed weight on her, the beat of his heart next to her breast, the soft lumpy pouch of his genitals squashed against her thigh, but the floor seems to be hardening under her like some kind of stern Calvinist rebuke and there is a disagreeable airy stickiness between her legs, now that he has slid away from there. "Do you haff a bidet, Richard?"

"Sure, kid." He slides to one side with a lazy grunt, rolls over. He's thinking vaguely about the pleasure he's just had, what it's likely to cost him (he doesn't care), and wondering where he'll find the strength to get up off his ass and go look for a cigarette. He stretches his shirttail down and wipes his crotch with it, nods back over the top of his head. "In there."

She is sitting up, peering between her spread legs. "I am afraid we haff stained your nice carpet, Richard."

"What of it? Put it down as a gesture to love. Want a drink?"

"Yes, that would be good." She leans over and kisses him, her face still flushed and eyes damp, but smiling now, then stands and gathers up an armload of tangled clothing. "Do I smell something burning?"

"What—?!" He rears up. "My goddamn cigarette! I musta dropped it on the couch!" He crawls over, brushes at it: it's gone out, but there's a big hole there now, dark-edged like ringworm. "Shit." He staggers to his feet, stumbles over to the humidor to light up a fresh smoke. Nothing's ever free, he thinks, feeling a bit light-headed. "What's your poison, kid?"

"I haff downstairs been drinking Cointreau," she calls out over the running water in the next room. He pours himself a large whiskey, tosses it down neat (light, sliding by, catches his furrowed brow as he tips his head back: what is wrong?), pours another, finds a decanter of Grand Marnier. She won't know the difference. In Paris she confused champagne with sparkling cider, ordered a Pommard thinking she was getting a rosé, drank gin because she couldn't taste it. He fits the half-burned cigarette between his lips, tucks a spare over his ear, then carries the drinks into the bathroom. She sits, straddling the bidet, churning water up between her legs like the wake of a pleasure boat. The beacon doesn't reach in here: it's as though he's stepped out of its line of sight, but that doesn't make him feel easier (something is nagging at him, has been for some time now). He holds the drink to her mouth for her, and she sips, looking mischievously up at him, one wet hand braced momentarily on his hipbone. Even in Paris she seemed to think drinking was naughtier than sex. Which made her on occasion something of a souse. She tips her chin, and he sets her drink down on the sink. "I wish I didn't luff you so much," she says casually, licking her lips, and commences to work up a lather between her legs with a bar of soap.

"Listen, what did you mean," he asks around the cigarette (this is it, or part of it: he glances back over his shoulder apprehensively, as though to find some answer to his question staring him in the face—or what, from the rear, is passing for his face), "when you said, 'Is this right?' "

"When . . . ?"

"A while ago, when I grabbed your, you know—"

"Oh, I don't know, darling. Yust a strange feeling, I don't exactly remember." She spreads the suds up her smooth belly and down the insides of her thighs, runs the soap up under her behind. "Like things were happening too fast or something."

He takes a contemplative drag on the cigarette, flips the butt into the toilet. "Yeah, that's it." Smoke curls out his nostrils like balloons of speech in a comic strip. "*All* this seems strange somehow. Like something that shouldn't have—"

"Well, I *am* a married woman, Richard."

"I don't mean that." But maybe he does mean that. She's rinsing now, her breasts flopping gaily above her splashing, it's hard to keep his mind on things. But he's not only been pronging some other guy's wife, this is the wife of Victor Laszlo of the International Underground, one of his goddamn heroes. One of the world's. Does that matter? He shoves his free hand in a jacket pocket, having no other, tosses back the drink. "Anyway," he wheezes, "from what you tell me, you were married already when we met in Paris, so that's not—"

"Come here, Richard," Ilsa interrupts with gentle but firm Teutonic insistence. *Komm' hier.* His back straightens, his eyes narrow, and for a moment the old Rick Blaine returns, the lonely American warrior, incorruptible, melancholy, master of his own fate, beholden to no one—but then she reaches forward and, like destiny, takes a hand. "Don't try to escape," she murmurs, pulling him up to the bidet between her knees. "You will neffer succeed."

She continues to hold him with one hand (he is growing there, stretching and filling in her hand with soft warm pulsations, and more than anything else that has happened to her since she came to Casablanca, more even than Sam's song, it is this sensation that takes her back to their days in Paris: wherever they went, from the circus to the movies, from excursion boats to dancehalls, it

[25]

swelled in her hand, just like this), while soaping him up with the other. "Why are you circumcised, Richard?" she asks, as the engorged head (when it flushes, it seems to flush blue) pushes out between her thumb and index finger. There was something he always said in Paris when it poked up at her like that. She peers wistfully at it, smiling to herself.

"My old man was a sawbones," he says, and takes a deep breath. He sets his empty glass down, reaches for the spare fag. It seems to have vanished. "He thought it was hygienic."

"Fictor still has his. Off course in Europe it is often important not to be mistaken for a Chew," She takes up the fragrant bar of soap (black market, the best, Ferrari gets it for him) and buffs the shaft with it, then thumbs the head with her sudsy hands as though, gently, trying to uncap it. The first day he met her, she opened his pants and jerked him off in his top-down convertible right under the Arc de Triomphe, then, almost without transition, or so it seemed to him, blew him spectacularly in the Bois de Boulogne. He remembers every detail, or anyway the best parts. And it was never—ever—any better than that. Until tonight.

She rinses the soap away, pours the rest of the Grand Marnier (she thinks: Cointreau) over his gleaming organ like a sort of libation, working the excess around as though lightly beating it (he thinks: priming it). A faint sad smile seems to be playing at the corners of her lips. "Say it once, Richard . . ."

"What—?"

She's smiling sweetly, but: is that a tear in her eye? "For old times' sake. Say it . . ."

"Ah." Yes, he'd forgotten. He's out of practice. He grunts, runs his hand down her damp cheek and behind her ear. "Here's lookin' at you, kid . . ."

She puckers her lips and kisses the tip, smiling cross-eyed at it, then, opening her mouth wide, takes it in, all of it at once. "Oh, Christ!" he groans, feeling himself awash in the thick muscular foam of her saliva, "I'm crazy about you, baby!"

"Mmmm!" she moans. He has said that to her before, more

than once no doubt (she wraps her arms around his hips under the jacket and hugs him close), but the time she is thinking about was at the cinema one afternoon in Paris. They had gone to see an American detective movie that was popular at the time, but there was a newsreel on before showing the Nazi conquests that month of Copenhagen, Oslo, Luxembourg, Amsterdam, and Brussels. *The Fall of Five Capitals*, it was called. And the scenes from Oslo, though brief, showing the Gestapo goose-stepping through the storied streets of her childhood filled her with such terror and nostalgia (something inside her was screaming, "Who *am* I?"), that she reached impulsively for Richard's hand, grabbing what Victor calls "the old fellow" instead. She started to pull her hand back, but he held it there, and the next thing she knew she had her head in his lap, weeping and sucking as though at her dead mother's breast, the terrible roar of the German blitzkrieg pounding in her ears, Richard kneading her nape as her father used to do before he died (and as Richard is doing now, his buttocks knotted up under her arms, his penis fluttering in her mouth like a frightened bird), the Frenchmen in the theater shouting out obscenities, her own heart pounding like cannon fire. "God! I'm crazy about you, baby!" Richard whinnied as he came (now, as his knees buckle against hers and her mouth fills with the shockingly familiar unfamiliarity of his spurting seed, it is just a desperate "Oh fuck! Don't let go . . . !"), and when she sat up, teary-eyed and drooling and gasping for breath (it is not all that easy to breathe now, as he clasps her face close to his hairy belly, whimpering gratefully, his body sagging, her mouth filling), what she saw on the screen were happy Germans, celebrating their victories, taking springtime strolls through overflowing flower and vegetable markets, going to the theater to see translations of Shakespeare, snapping photographs of their children. "Oh Gott," she sniffled then (now she swallows, sucks and swallows, as though to draw out from this almost impalpable essence some vast structure of recollection), "it's too much!" Whereupon the man behind them leaned over and said: "Then try mine, mademoiselle. As you can see, it is not so grand as your Nazi friend's, but here in France, we grow men not pricks!" Richard's French was terrible, but it was good enough to understand "your Nazi friend": he hadn't even put his penis back in his pants (now it slides greasily past her chin, flops down her chest, his buttocks in her hugging arms going soft as butter, like a delicious half-grasped memory losing its clear outlines, melting into mere sensation), but just leapt up and took a swing at the Frenchman. With that, the cinema broke into an uproar with everybody calling everyone else a fascist or a whore. They were thrown out of the theater of course, the police put Richard on their blacklist as an exhibitionist, and they never did get to see the detective movie. Ah well, they could laugh about it then . . .

He sits now on the front lip of the bidet, his knees knuckled under hers, shirttails in the water, his cheek fallen on her broad shoulder, arms loosely around her, feeling wonderfully unwound, mellow as an old tune (which is still there somewhere, moonlight and love songs, same old story—maybe it's coming up through the pipes), needing only a smoke to make things perfect. The one he stuck over his ear is floating in the scummy pool beneath them, he sees. Ilsa idly splashes his drooping organ as though christening it. Only one answer, she once said, peeling off that lovely satin gown of hers like a French letter, will take care of all our questions, and she was right. As always. He's the one who's made a balls-up of things with his complicated moral poses and insufferable pride—a diseased romantic, Louis once called him, and he didn't know the half of it. She's the only realist in town; he's got to start paying attention. Even now she's making sense: "My rump is getting dumb, Richard. Dry me off and let's go back in the other room."

But when he tries to stand, his knees feel like toothpaste, and he has to sit again. Right back in the bidet, as it turns out, dipping his ass like doughnuts in tea. She smiles understandingly, drapes a bath towel around her shoulders, pokes through the medicine cabinet until she finds a jar of Yvonne's cold cream, then takes him by the elbow. "Come on, Richard. You can do it, yust lean on me." Which reminds him (his mind at least is still working, more or less) of a night in Spain, halfway up (or down) Suicide Hill in the Jarama Valley, a night he thought was to be his last, when he said that to someone, or someone said it to him. God, what if he'd got it shot off there? And missed this? An expression compounded of hope and anguish, skepticism and awe, crosses his weary face (thirty-eight at Christmas, if Strasser is right—oh mother of God, it *is* going by!), picked up by the wheeling airport beacon. She removes his dripping jacket, his shirt as well, and towels his behind before letting him collapse onto the couch, then crosses to the ornamental table for a cigarette from the humidor. She wears the towel like a cape, her haunches under it glittering as though sequined. She is, as always, a kind of walking light show, no less spectacular from the front as she turns back now toward the sofa, the nubbly texture of the towel contrasting subtly with the soft glow of her throat and breast, the sleek wet gleam of her belly.

She fits two cigarettes in her lips, lights them both (there's a bit of fumbling with the lighter, she's not very mechanical), and gazing soulfully down at Rick, passes him one of them. He grins. "Hey, where'd you learn that, kid?" She shrugs enigmatically, hands him the towel, and steps up between his knees. As he rubs her breasts, her belly, her thighs with the towel, the cigarette dangling in his lips, she gazes around at the chalky rough-plastered walls of his apartment, the Moorish furniture with its filigrees and inlaid patterns, the little bits of erotic art (there is a statue of a camel on the sideboard that looks like a man's wet penis on legs, and a strange nude statuette that might be a boy, or a girl, or something in between), the alabaster lamps and potted plants, those slatted wooden blinds, so exotic to her Northern eyes: he has style, she thinks, rubbing cold cream into her neck and shoulder with her free hand, he always did have . . .

She lifts one leg for him to dry and then the other, gasping inwardly (outwardly, she chokes and wheezes, having inhaled the cigarette by mistake: he stubs out his own with a sympathetic grin, takes what is left of hers) when he rubs the towel briskly between them, then she turns and bends over, bracing herself on the coffee table. Rick, the towel in his hands, pauses a moment, gazing thoughtfully through the drifting cigarette haze at these luminous buttocks, finding something almost otherworldly about them, like archways to heaven or an image of eternity. Has he seen them like this earlier tonight? Maybe, he can't remember. Certainly now he's able to savor the sight, no longer crazed by rut. They are, quite literally, a dream come true: he has whacked off to their memory so often during the last year and a half that it almost feels more appropriate to touch himself than this present manifestation. As he reaches toward them with the towel, he seems to be crossing some strange threshold, as though passing from one medium into another. He senses the supple buoyancy of them bouncing back against his hand as he wipes them, yet, though flesh, they remain somehow immaterial, untouchable even when touched, objects whose very presence is a kind of absence. If Rick Blaine were to believe in angels, Ilsa's transcendent bottom is what they would look like.

"Is this how you, uh, imagined things turning out tonight?" he asks around the butt, smoke curling out his nose like thought's reek. Her cheeks seem to pop alight like his Café Américain sign each time the airport beacon sweeps past, shifting slightly like a sequence of film frames. Time itself may be like that, he knows: not a ceaseless flow, but a rapid series of electrical leaps across tiny gaps between discontinuous bits. It's what he likes to call his link-and-claw theory of time, though of course the theory is not his . . .

"Well, it may not be perfect, Richard, but it is better than if I haff shot you, isn't it?"

"No, I meant . . ." Well, let it be. She's right, it beats eating a goddamn bullet. In fact it beats anything he can imagine. He douses his cigarette in the wet towel, tosses it aside, wraps his arms around her thighs and pulls her buttocks (he is still thinking about time as a pulsing sequence of film frames, and not so much about the frames, their useless dated content, as the gaps between: infinitesimally small when looked at two-dimensionally, yet in their third dimension as deep and mysterious as the cosmos) toward his face, pressing against them like a child trying to see through a foggy window. He kisses and nibbles at each fresh-washed cheek (and what if one were to slip *between* two of those frames? he wonders—), runs his tongue into (—where would he be then?) her anus, kneading the flesh on her pubic knoll between his fingers all the while like little lumps of stiff taffy. She raises one knee up onto the cushions, then the other, lowering her elbows to the floor (oh! she thinks as the blood rushes in two directions at once, spreading into her head and sex as though filling empty frames, her heart the gap between: what a strange dizzying dream time is!), thus lifting to his contemplative scrutiny what looks like a clinging sea anemone between her thighs, a thick woolly pod, a cloven chinchilla, open purse, split fruit. But it is not the appearance of it that moves him (except to the invention of these fanciful catalogs), it is the smell. It is this which catapults him suddenly and wholly back to Paris, a Paris he'd lost until this moment (she is not in Paris, she is in some vast dimensionless region she associates with childhood, a nighttime glow in her midsummer room, feather bedding between her legs) but now has back again. Now and for all time. As he runs his tongue up and down the spongy groove, pinching the lips tenderly between his tongue and stiff upper lip (an old war wound), feeling it engorge, pulsate, almost pucker up to kiss him back, he seems to see—as thought it were fading in on the blank screen of her gently rolling bottom—that night at her apartment in Paris when she first asked him to "Kiss me, Richard, here. My other mouth wants to luff you, too . . ." He'd never done that before. He had been all over the world, had fought in wars, battled cops, been jailed and tortured, hid out in whorehouses, parachuted out of airplanes, had eaten and drunk just about everything, had been blown off the decks of ships, killed more men than he'd like to count, and had banged every kind and color of woman on earth, but he had never tasted one of these things before. Other women had sucked him off, of course, before Ilsa nearly caused him to wreck his car that day in the Bois de Boulogne, but he had always thought of that as a service due him, something he'd paid for in effect—he was the man, after all. But reciprocation, sucking back—well, that always struck him as vaguely queer, something guys, manly guys anyway, didn't do. That night, though, he'd had a lot of champagne and he was—this was the simple truth, and it was an experience as exotic to Rick Blaine as the taste of a cunt—madly in love. He had been an unhappy misfit all his life, at best a romantic drifter, at worst and in the eyes of most a sleazy gunrunner and chicken-shit mercenary (though God knows he'd hoped for more), a whoremonger and brawler and miserable gutter drunk: nothing like Ilsa Lund had ever happened to him, and he could hardly believe it was happening to him that night. His immediate reaction—he admits this, sucking greedily at it now (she is galloping her father's horse through the woods of the north, canopy-dark and sunlight-blinding at the same time, pushing the beast beneath her, racing toward what she believed to be God's truth, flushing through her from the saddle up as eternity might when the saints were called), while watching himself, on the cinescreen of her billowing behind, kneel to it that first time like an atheist falling squeamishly into conversion—was not instant rapture. No, like olives, home brew, and Arab cooking, it took a little getting used to. But she taught him how to stroke the vulva with his tongue, where to find the nun's cap ("my little sister," she called it, which struck him as odd) and how to draw it out, how to use his fingers, nose, chin, even his hair and ears, and the more he practiced for her sake, the more he liked it for his own, her pleasure (he could *see* it: it bloomed right under his nose, filling his grimy life with colors he'd never even thought of before!) augmenting his, until he found his appetite for it almost insatiable. God, the boys on the block back in New York would laugh their asses off to see how far he'd fallen! And though he has tried others since, it is still the only one he really likes. Yvonne's is terrible, bitter and pomaded (she seems to sense this, gets no pleasure from it at all, often turns fidgety and mean when he goes down on her, even had a kind of biting, scratching fit once: "Don' you lak to *fuck?*" she'd screamed), which is the main reason he's lost interest in her. That and her hairy legs.

His screen is shrinking (her knees have climbed to his shoulders, scrunching her hips into little bumps and bringing her shoulder-blades into view, down near the floor, where she is gasping and whimpering and sucking the carpet), but his vision of the past is expanding, as though her pumping cheeks were a chubby bellows, opening and closing, opening and closing, inflating his memories. Indeed, he no longer needs a screen for them, for it is not this or that conquest that he recalls now, this or that event, not what she wore or what she said, what he said, but something more profound than that, something experienced in the way that a blind man sees or an amputee touches. Texture returns to him, ambience, impressions of radiance, of coalescence, the foamy taste of the ineffable on his tongue, the downy nap of timelessness, the tooth of now. All this he finds in Ilsa's juicy bouncing cunt—and more: love's pungent illusions of consubstantiation and infinitude (oh, he knows what he lost that day in the rain in the Gare de Lyon!), the bittersweet fall into actuality, space's secret folds wherein one might lose one's ego, one's desperate sense of isolation, Paris, rediscovered here as pure aura, effervescent and allusive, La Belle Aurore as immanence's theater, sacred showplace—

Oh hell, he thinks as Ilsa's pounding hips drive him to his back on the couch, her thighs slapping against his ears (as she rises, her blood in riptide against her mounting excitement, the airport beacon touching her in its passing like bursts of inspiration, she thinks: childhood is a place apart, needing the adult world to exist at all: without Victor there could *be* no Rick—and then she cannot think at all), La Belle Aurore! She broke his goddamn heart at La Belle Aurore. "Kiss me," she said, holding herself with both hands as though to keep the pain from spilling out down there, "one last time," and he did, for her, Henri didn't care, *merde alors*, the Germans were coming anyway, and the other patrons thought it was just part of the entertainment; only Sam was offended and went off to the john till it was over. And then she left him. Forever. Or anyway until she turned up here a night ago with Laszlo. God, he remembers everything about that day in the Belle Aurore, what she was wearing, what the Germans were wearing, what Henri was wearing. It was not an easy day to forget. The Germans were at the very edge of the city, they were bombing the bejesus out of the place and everything was literally falling down around their ears (she's smothering him now with her bucking arse, her scissoring thighs: he heaves her over onto her back and pushes his arms between her thighs to spread them); they'd had to crawl over rubble and dead bodies, push through barricades, just to reach the damned café. No chance to get out by car, he was lucky there was enough left in his "F.Y. Fund" to buy them all train tickets. And then the betrayal: "I can' find her, Mr. Richard. She's checked outa de hotel. But dis note come jus' after you lef'!" Oh shit, even now it makes him cry. "I cannot go with you or ever see you again." In perfect Palmer Method handwriting, as though to exult in her power over him. He kicked poor Sam's ass up and down that train all the way to Marseilles, convinced it was somehow his fault. Even a hex maybe, that day he could have believed anything. Now, with her hips bouncing frantically up against his mouth, her bush grown to an astonishing size, the lips out and flapping like flags, the trench between them awash in a fragrant ooze like oily air, he lifts his head and asks: "Why weren't you honest with me? Why did you keep your marriage a secret?"

"Oh Gott, Richard! Not *now*—!"

She's right, it doesn't seem the right moment for it, but then nothing has seemed right since she turned up in this godforsaken town: it's almost as though two completely different places, two completely different times, are being forced to mesh, to intersect where no intersection is possible, causing a kind of warp in the universe. In his own private universe anyway. He gazes down on this lost love, this faithless wife, this trusting child, her own hands between her legs now, her hips still jerking out of control ("Please,

[34]

Richard!" she is begging softly through clenched teeth, tears in her eyes), thinking: It's still a story without an ending. But more than that: the beginning and middle bits aren't all there either. Her face is drained as though all the blood has rushed away to other parts, but her throat between the heaving white breasts is almost literally alight with its vivid blush. He touches it, strokes the soft bubbles to either side, watching the dark little nipples rise like patriots—and suddenly the answer to all his questions seems (yet another one, that is—answers, in the end, are easy) to suggest itself. "Listen kid, would it be all right if I—?"

"Oh yes! yes!—*but hurry!*"

He finds the cold cream (at last! he is so slow!), lathers it on, and slips into her cleavage, his knees over her shoulders like a yoke. She guides his head back into that tropical explosion between her legs, then clasps her arms around his hips, already beginning to thump at her chest like a resuscitator, popping little gasps from her throat. She tries to concentrate on his bouncing buttocks, but they communicate to her such a touching blend of cynicism and honesty, weariness and generosity, that they nearly break her heart, making her more light-headed than ever. The dark little hole between them bobs like a lonely survivor in a tragically divided world. It is he! "Oh Gott!" she whimpers. And she! The tension between her legs is almost unbearable. "I can't fight it anymore!" Everything starts to come apart. She feels herself falling as though through some rift in the universe (she cannot wait for him, and anyway, where she is going he cannot follow), out of time and matter into some wondrous radiance, the wheeling beacon flashing across her stricken vision new like intermittent star bursts, the music swelling, *everything* swelling, her eyes bursting, ears popping, teeth ringing in their sockets—"Oh Richard! Oh fokk! *I luff you so much!*"

He plunges his face deep into Ilsa's ambrosial pudding, lapping at its sweet sweat, feeling her loins snap and convulse violently around him, knowing that with a little inducement she can spasm like this for minutes on end, and meanwhile pumping away between her breasts now like a madman, no longer obliged to hold back, seeking purely his own pleasure. This pleasure is tempered only by (and maybe enhanced by as well) his pity for her husband, that heroic sonuvabitch. God, Victor Laszlo is almost a father figure to him, really. And while Laszlo is off at the underground meeting in the Caverne du Roi, no doubt getting his saintly ass shot to shit, here he is—Rick Blaine, the Yankee smart aleck and general jerk-off—safely closeted off in his rooms over the town saloon, tit-fucking the hero's wife, his callous nose up her own royal grotto like an advance scout for a squad of storm troopers. It's not fair, goddamn it, he thinks, and laughs at this even as he comes, squirting jism down her sleek belly and under his own, his head locked in her clamped thighs, her arms hugging him tightly as though to squeeze the juices out.

He is lying, completely still, his face between Ilsa's flaccid thighs, knees over her shoulders, arms around her lower body, which sprawls loosely now beneath him. He can feel her hands resting lightly on his hips, her warm breath against his leg. He doesn't remember when they stopped moving. Maybe he's been sleeping. Has he dreamt it all? No, he shifts slightly and feels the spill of semen, pooled gummily between their conjoined navels. His movement wakes Ilsa: she snorts faintly, sighs, kisses the inside of his leg, strokes one buttock idly. "That soap smells nice," she murmurs. "I bet effry girl in Casablanca wishes to haff a bath here."

"Yeah, well, I run it as a kind of public service," he grunts, chewing the words around a strand or two of pubic hair. He's always told Louis—and anyone else who wanted to know—that he sticks his neck out for nobody. But in the end, shit, he thinks, I stick it out for everybody. "I'm basically a civic-minded guy."

Cynic-minded, more like, she thinks, but keeps the thought to herself. She cannot risk offending him, not just now. She is still returning from wherever it is orgasm has taken her, and it has been an experience so profound and powerful, yet so remote from its immediate cause—his muscular tongue at the other end of this morosely puckered hole in front of her nose—that it has left her feeling very insecure, unsure of who or what she is, or even where. She knows of course that her role as the well-dressed wife of a courageous underground leader is just pretense, that beneath this charade she is certainly someone—or something—else. Richard's lover, for example. Or a little orphan girl who lost her mother, father, and adoptive aunt, all before she'd even started menstruating—that's who she often is, or feels like she is, especially at moments like this. But if her life as Victor Laszlo's wife is not real, are these others any more so? Is she one person, several—or no one at all? What was that thought she'd had about childhood? She lies there, hugging Richard's hairy cheeks (are they Richard's? are they cheeks?), her pale face framed by his spraddled legs, trying to puzzle it all out. Since the moment she arrived in Casablanca, she and Richard have been trying to tell each other stories, not very funny stories, as Richard has remarked, but maybe not very true ones either. Maybe memory itself is a kind of trick, something that turns illusion into reality and makes the real world vanish before everyone's eyes like magic. One can certainly sink away there and miss everything, she knows. Hasn't Victor, the wise one, often warned her of that? But Victor is a hero. Maybe the real world is too much for most people. Maybe making up stories is a way to keep them all from going insane. A tear forms in the corner of one eye. She blinks (and what are these unlikely configurations called "Paris" and "Casablanca," where in all the universe *is* she, and what is "where"?), and the tear trickles into the hollow between cheekbone and nose, then bends its course toward the middle of her cheek. There is a line in their song (yes, it is still there, tinkling away somewhere like mice in the walls: is someone trying to drive her crazy?) that goes, "This day and age we're living in gives cause for apprehension,/With speed and new invention and things like third dimension . . ." She always thought that was a stupid mistake of the lyricist, but now she is not so sure. For the real mystery—she sees this now, or *feels* it rather— is not the fourth dimension as she'd always supposed (the tear stops halfway down her cheek, begins to fade), or the third either for that matter . . . but the *first*.

"You never finished answering my question . . ."

There is a pause. Perhaps she is daydreaming. "What question, Richard?"

"A while ago. In the bathroom . . ." He, too, has been mulling over recent events, wondering not only about the events themselves (wondrous in their own right, of course: he's not enjoyed multiple orgasms like this since he hauled his broken-down blacklisted ass out of Paris a year and a half ago, and that's just for starters), but also about their "recentness": When did they really happen? Is *happen* the right word, or were they more like fleeting conjunctions with the Absolute, that *other* Other, boundless and immutable as number? And, if so, what now is "when"? How much time has elapsed, for example, since he opened the door and found her in this room? Has *any* time elapsed? "I asked you what you meant when you said, 'Is this right?' "

"Oh, Richard, I don't know what's right any longer." She lifts one thigh in front of his face, as though to erase his dark imaginings. He strokes it, thinking: well, what the hell, it probably doesn't amount to a hill of beans, anyway. "Do you think I can haff another drink now?"

"Sure, kid. Why not." He sits up beside her, shakes the butt out of the damp towel, wipes his belly off, hands the towel to her. "More of the same?"

"Champagne would be nice, if it is possible. It always makes me think of Paris . . . and you . . ."

"You got it, sweetheart." He pushes himself to his feet and thumps across the room, pausing at the humidor to light up a fresh smoke. "If there's any left. Your old man's been going through my stock like Vichy water." Not for the first time, he has the impression of being watched. Laszlo? Who knows, maybe the underground meeting was just a ruse; it certainly seemed like a dumb thing to do on the face of it, especially with Strasser in town. There's a bottle of champagne in his icebox, okay, but no ice. He touches the bottle: not cold, but cool enough. It occurs to him the sonuvabitch might be out on the balcony right now, taking it all in, he and all his goddamn underground. Europeans can be pretty screwy, especially these rich stiffs with titles. As he carries the champagne and glasses over to the coffee table, the cigarette like a dart between his lips, his bare ass feels suddenly both hot and chilly at the same time. "Does your husband ever get violent?" he asks around the smoke and snaps the metal clamp off the champagne bottle, takes a grip on the cork.

"No. He has killed some people, but he is not fiolent." She is rubbing her tummy off, smiling thoughtfully. The light from the airport beacon, wheeling past, picks up a varnishlike glaze still between her breasts, a tooth's wet twinkle in her open mouth, an unwonted shine on her nose. The cork pops, champagne spews out over the table top, some of it getting into the glasses. This seems to suggest somehow a revelation. Or another memory. The tune, as though released, rides up once more around them. "Gott, Richard," she sighs, pushing irritably to her feet. "That music is getting on my nerfs!"

"Yeah, I know." It's almost as bad in its way as the German blitzkrieg hammering in around their romance in Paris—sometimes it seemed to get right between their embraces. Gave him a goddamn headache. Now the music is doing much the same thing, even trying to tell them when to kiss and when not to. He can stand it, though, he thinks, tucking the cigarette back in his lips, if she can. He picks up the two champagne glasses, offers her one. "Forget it, kid. Drown it out with this." He raises his glass. "Uh, here's lookin'—"

She gulps it down absently, not waiting for his toast. "And that light from the airport," she goes on, batting at it as it passes as though to shoo it away. "How can you effer sleep here?"

"No one's supposed to sleep well in Casablanca," he replies with a worldly grimace. It's his best expression, he knows, but she isn't paying any attention. He stubs out the cigarette, refills her glass, blowing a melancholy whiff of smoke over it. "Hey, kid here's—"

"No, wait!" she insists, her ear cocked. "*Is* it?"

"Is what?" Ah well, forget the fancy stuff. He drinks off the champagne in his glass, reaches down for a refill.

"Time. Is it going by? Like the song is saying?"

He looks up, startled. "That's funny, I was just—!"

"What time do you haff, Richard?"

He sets the bottle down, glances at his empty wrist. "I dunno. My watch must have got torn off when we . . ."

"Mine is gone, too."

They stare at each other a moment, Rick scowling slightly in the old style, Ilsa's lips parted as though saying "story," or "glory." Then the airport beacon sweeps past like a prompter, and Rick, blinking, says: "Wait a minute—there's a clock down in the bar!" He strides purposefully over to the door in his stocking feet, pausing there a moment, one hand on the knob, to take a deep breath. "I'll be right back," he announces, then opens the door and (she seems about to call out to him) steps out on the landing. He steps right back in again. He pushes the door closed, leans against it, his face ashen. "They're all down there," he says.

"What? Who's down there?"

"Karl, Sam, Abdul, that Norwegian—"

"Fictor?!"

"Yes, everybody! Strasser, those goddamn Bulgarians, Sasha. Louis—"

"Yffonne?"

Why the hell did she ask about Yvonne? "I said everybody! They're just standing down there! Like they're waiting for something! But . . . for what?!" He can't seem to stop his goddamn voice from squeaking. He wants to remain cool and ironically detached, cynical even, because he knows it's expected of him, not least of all by himself, but he's still shaken by what he's seen down in the bar. Of course it might help if he had his pants on. At least he'd have some pockets to shove his hands into. For some reason, Ilsa is staring at his crotch, as though the real horror of it all were to be found there. Or maybe she's trying to see through to the silent crowd below. "It's, I dunno, like the place has sprung a goddamn leak or something!"

She crosses her hands to her shoulders, pinching her elbows in, hugging her breasts. She seems to have gone flat-footed, her feet splayed, her bottom, lost somewhat in the slatted shadows, drooping, her spine bent. "A leak?" she asks meaninglessly in her soft Scandinavian accent. She looks like a swimmer out of water in chilled air. Richard, slumping against the far door, stares at her as though at a total stranger. Or perhaps a mirror. He seems older somehow, tired, his chest sunken and belly out, legs bowed, his genitals shriveled up between them like dried fruit. It is not a beautiful sight. Of course Richard is not a beautiful man. He is short and bad-tempered and rather smashed up. Victor calls him riffraff. He says Richard makes him feel greasy. And it is true, there is something common about him. Around Victor she always feels crisp and white, but around Richard like a sweating pig. So how did she get mixed up with him, in the first place? Well, she was lonely, she had nothing, not even hope, and he seemed so happy when she took hold of his penis. As Victor has often said, each of us has a destiny, for good or for evil, and her destiny was Richard. Now that destiny seems confirmed—or sealed—by all those people downstairs. "They are not waiting for anything," she says, as the realization comes to her. It is over.

Richard grunts in reply. He probably hasn't heard her. She feels a terrible sense of loss. He shuffles in his black socks over to the humidor. "Shit, even the fags are gone," he mutters gloomily. "Why'd you have to come to Casablanca anyway, goddamn it; there are other places . . ." The airport beacon, sliding by, picks up an expression of intense concentration on his haggard face. She knows he is trying to understand what cannot be understood, to resolve what has no resolution. Americans are like that. In Paris he was always wondering how it was they kept getting from one place to another so quickly. "It's like everything is all speeded up," he would gasp, reaching deliriously between her legs as her apartment welled up around them. Now he is probably wondering why there seems to be no place to go and why time suddenly is just about all they have. He is an innocent man, after all; this is probably his first affair.

"I would not haff come if I haff known . . ." She releases her shoulders, picks up her ruffled blouse (the buttons are gone), pulls it on like a wrap. As the beacon wheels by, the room seems to expand with light as though it were breathing. "Do you see my skirt? It was here, but—is it getting dark or something?"

"I mean, of all the gin joints in all the towns in all the—!" He pauses, looks up. "What did you say?"

"I said, is it—?"

"Yeah, I know . . ."

They gaze about uneasily. "It seems like effry time that light goes past . . ."

"Yeah . . ." He stares at her, slumped there at the foot of the couch, working her garter belt like rosary beads, looking like somebody had just pulled her plug. "The world will always welcome lovers," the music is suggesting, not so much in mockery as in sorrow. He's thinking of all those people downstairs, so hushed, so motionless: it's almost how he feels inside. Like something dying. Or something dead revealed. Oh shit. Has this happened before? Ilsa seems almost wraithlike in the pale staticky light, as though she were wearing her own ghost on her skin. And which is it he's been in love with? he wonders. He sees she is trembling, and a tear slides down the side of her nose, or seems to, it's hard to tell. He feels like he's going blind. "Listen. Maybe if we started over . . ."

"I'm too tired, Richard . . ."

"No, I mean, go back to where you came in, see—the letters of transit and all that. Maybe we made some kinda mistake, I dunno, like when I put my hands on your jugs or something, and if—"

"A mistake? You think putting your hands on my yugs was a mistake—?"

"Don't get offended, sweetheart. I only meant—"

"Maybe my bringing my yugs *here* tonight was a mistake! Maybe my not shooting the *trigger* was a mistake!"

"Come on, don't get your tail in an uproar, goddamn it! I'm just trying to—"

"Oh, what a fool I was to fall . . . to fall . . ."

"Jesus, Ilsa, are you crying . . . ? Ilsa . . . ?" He sighs irritably. He is never going to understand women. Her head is bowed as though in resignation: one has seen her like this often when Laszlo is near. She seems to be staring at the empty buttonholes in her blouse. Maybe she's stupider than he thought. When the dimming light swings past, tears glint in the corners of her eyes, little points of light in the gathering shadows on her face. "Hey, dry up, kid! All I want you to do is go over there by the curtains where you were when I—"

"Can I tell you a . . . story, Richard?"

"Not *now*, Ilsa! Christ! The light's almost gone and—"

"Anyway, it wouldn't work."

"What?"

"Trying to do it all again. It wouldn't work. It wouldn't be the same. I won't even haff my girdle on."

"That doesn't matter. Who's gonna know? Come on, we can at least—"

"No, Richard. It is impossible. You are different, I am different. You haff cold cream on your penis—"

"But—"

"My makeup is gone, there are stains on the carpet. And I would need the pistol—how could we effer find it in the dark? No, it's useless, Richard. Belief me. Time goes by."

"But maybe that's just it . . ."

"Or what about your tsigarette? Eh? Can you imagine going through that without your tsigarette? Richard? I am laughing! Where are you, Richard . . . ?"

"Take it easy, I'm over here. By the balcony. Just lemme think."

"Efen the airport light has stopped."

"Yeah. I can't see a fucking thing out there."

"Well, you always said you wanted a wow finish . . . Maybe . . ."

"What?"

"What?"

"What did you say?"

"I said, maybe this is . . . you know, what we always wanted . . . Like a dream come true . . ."

"Speak up, kid. It's getting hard to hear you."

"I said, *when we are fokking*—"

"Nah, that won't do any good, sweetheart, I know that now. We gotta get back into the goddamn world somehow. If we don't, we'll regret it. Maybe not today—"

"What? We'll forget it?"

"No, I said—"

"What?"

"Never mind."

"Forget what, Richard?"

"I said I think I shoulda gone fishing with Sam when I had the chance."

"I can't seem to hear you . . ."

"No, wait a minute! Maybe you're right! Maybe going back isn't the right idea . . ."

"Richard . . . ?"

"Instead, maybe we gotta think ahead . . ."

"Richard, I am afraid . . ."

"Yeah, like you could sit there on the couch, see, we've been fucking, that's all right, who cares, now we're having some champagne—"

"I think I am *already* forgetting . . ."

"And you can tell me that story you've been wanting to tell—are you listening? A good story, that may do it—anything that *moves*! And meanwhile, lemme think, I'll, let's see, I'll sit down—

no, I'll sort of lean here in the doorway and—*oof!*—shit! I think they moved it!"

"Richard . . . ?"

"Who the hell rearranged the—*ungh!*—goddamn geography?"

"Richard, it's a crazy world . . ."

"Ah, here! this feels like it. Something like it. Now what was I—? Right! You're telling a story, so, uh, I'll say . . ."

"But wherever you are . . ."

"*And then*—? Yeah, that's good. It's almost like I'm remembering this. You've stopped, see, but I want you to go on, I want you to keep spilling what's on your mind, I'm filling in all the blanks . . ."

". . . whatever happens . . ."

"So I say: *And then*—? C'mon, kid, can you hear me? Remember all those people downstairs! They're depending on us! Just think it: if you think it, you'll do it! *And then*—?"

". . . I want you to know . . ."

"And then . . . ? Oh shit, Ilsa . . . ? Where are you? And then . . . ?"

". . . I luff you . . ."

"And then . . . ? Ilsa . . . ? And *then* . . . ?"

WRIGHT MORRIS | VICTROLA

"SIT!" said Bundy, although the dog already sat. His knowing what Bundy would say was one of the things people noticed about their close relationship. The dog sat—not erect, like most dogs, but off to one side, so that the short-haired pelt on one rump was always soiled. When Bundy attempted to clean it, as he once did, the spot no longer matched the rest of the dog, like a cleaned spot on an old rug. A second soiled spot was on his head, where children and strangers liked to pat him. Over his eyes the pelt was so thin his hide showed through. A third defacement had been caused by the leash in his younger years, when he had tugged at it harder, sometimes almost gagging as Bundy resisted.

Those days had been a strain on both of them. Bundy had developed a bad bursitis, and the crease of the leash could still be seen on the back of his hand. In the past year, over the last eight months, beginning with the cold spell in December, the dog was so slow to cross the street Bundy might have to drag him. That brought on spells of angina for Bundy, and they would both have to stand there until they felt better. At such moments the dog's slantwise gaze was one that Bundy avoided. "Sit!" he would say, no longer troubling to see if the dog did.

The dog leashed to a parking meter, Bundy walked through the drugstore to the prescription counter at the rear. The pharmacist, Mr. Avery, peered down from a platform two steps above floor level—the source of a customer's still pending lawsuit. His gaze to the front of the store, he said, "He still itching?"

Bundy nodded. Mr. Avery had recommended a vitamin supplement that some dogs found helpful. The scratching had been replaced by licking.

"You've got to remember," said Avery, "he's in his nineties. When you're in your nineties, you'll also do a little scratchin'!" Avery gave Bundy a challenging stare. If Avery reached his nineties, Bundy was certain Mrs. Avery would have to keep him on a leash or he would forget who he was. He had repeated this story about the dog's being ninety ever since Bundy had first met him and the dog was younger.

"I need your expertise," Bundy said. (Avery lapped up that sort of flattery.) "How does five cc's compare with five hundred mg's?"

"It doesn't. Five cc's is a liquid measure. It's a spoonful."

"What I want to know is, how much vitamin C am I getting in five cc's?"

"Might not be any. In a liquid solution, vitamin C deteriorates rapidly. You should get it in the tablet." It seemed clear he had expected more of Bundy.

"I see," said Bundy. "Could I have my prescription?"

Mr. Avery lowered his glasses to look for it on the counter. Bundy might have remarked that a man of Avery's age—and experience—ought to know enough to wear glasses he could both see and read through, but having to deal with him once a month dictated more discretion than valor.

Squinting to read the label, Avery said, "I see he's upped your dosage." On their first meeting, Bundy and Avery had had a sensible discussion about the wisdom of minimal medication, an attitude that Bundy thought was unusual to hear from a pharmacist.

"His point is," said Bundy, "since I like to be active, there's no reason I shouldn't enjoy it. He tells me the dosage is still pretty normal."

"Hmm," Avery said. He opened the door so Bundy could step behind the counter and up to the platform with his Blue Cross card. For the umpteenth time he told Bundy, "Pay the lady at the front. Watch your step as you leave."

As he walked toward the front Bundy reflected that he would rather be a little less active than forget what he had said two minutes earlier.

"We've nothing but trouble with dogs," the cashier said. "They're in and out every minute. They get at the bars of candy. But I can't ever remember trouble with your dog."

"He's on a leash," said Bundy.

"That's what I'm saying," she replied.

When Bundy came out of the store, the dog was lying down, but he made the effort to push up and sit.

"Look at you," Bundy said, and stooped to dust him off. The way he licked himself, he picked up dirt like a blotter. A shadow moved over them, and Bundy glanced up to see, at a respectful distance, a lady beaming on the dog like a healing heat lamp. Older than Bundy—much older, a wraithlike creature, more spirit than substance, her face crossed with wisps of hair like cobwebs—Mrs. Poole had known the dog as a pup; she had been a dear friend of its former owner, Miss Tyler, who had lived directly above Bundy. For years he had listened to his neighbor tease the dog to bark for pieces of liver, and heard the animal push his food dish around the kitchen.

"What ever will become of him?" Miss Tyler would whisper to Bundy, anxious that the dog shouldn't hear what she was saying. Bundy had tried to reassure her: look how spry she was at eighty! Look how the dog was overweight and asthmatic! But to ease her mind he had agreed to provide him with a home, if worst came to worst, as it did soon enough. So Bundy inherited the dog, three cases of dog food, balls and rubber bones in which the animal took no interest, along with an elegant cushioned sleeping basket he never used.

Actually, Bundy had never liked biggish dogs with very short pelts. Too much of everything, to his taste, was overexposed. The dog's long muzzle and small beady eyes put him in mind of something less than a dog. In the years with Miss Tyler, without provocation the animal would snarl at Bundy when they met on the stairs, or bark wildly when he opened his mailbox. The dog's one redeeming feature was that when he heard someone pronounce the word *sit* he would sit. That fact brought Bundy a certain distinction, and the gratitude of many shop owners. Bundy had once been a cat man. The lingering smell of cats in his apartment had led the dog to sneeze at most of the things he sniffed.

Two men, seated on stools in the corner tavern, had turned from the bar to gaze out into the sunlight. One of them was a clerk at the supermarket where Bundy bought his dog food. "Did he like it?" he called as Bundy came into view.

"Not particularly," Bundy replied. Without exception, the dog did not like anything he saw advertised on television. To that extent he was smarter than Bundy, who was partial to anything served with gravy.

The open doors of the bar looked out on the intersection, where an elderly woman, as if emerging from a package, unfolded her limbs through the door of a taxi. Sheets of plate glass on a passing truck reflected Bundy and the notice that was posted in the window of the bar, advising of a change of ownership. The former owner, an Irishman named Curran, had not been popular with the new crowd of wine and beer drinkers. Nor had he been popular with Bundy. A scornful man, Curran dipped the dirty glasses in tepid water, and poured drops of sherry back into the bottles. Two epidemics of hepatitis had been traced to him. Only when he was gone did Bundy realize how much the world had shrunk. To Curran, Bundy had confessed that he felt he was now living in another country. Even more he missed Curran's favorite expression, "Outlive the bastards!"

Two elderly men, indifferent to the screech of braking traffic, tottered toward each other to embrace near the center of the street. One was wearing shorts. A third party, a younger woman, escorted them both to the curb. Observing, an incident like this, Bundy might stand for several minutes as if he had witnessed something unusual. Under an awning, where the pair had been led, they shared the space with a woman whose gaze seemed to focus on infinity, several issues of the *Watchtower* gripped in her trembling hands.

At the corner of Sycamore and Poe streets—trees crossed poets, as a rule, at right angles—Bundy left the choice of the route up to the dog. Where the sidewalk narrowed, at the bend in the street, both man and dog prepared themselves for brief and unpredictable encounters. In the cities, people met and passed like sleepwalkers, or stared brazenly at each other, but along the sidewalks of small towns they felt the burden of their shared existence. To avoid rudeness, a lift of the eyes or a muttered greeting was necessary. This was often an annoyance for Bundy: the long approach by sidewalk, the absence of cover, the unavoidable moment of confrontation, then Bundy's abrupt greeting or a wag of his head, which occasionally startled the other person. To the young a quick "Hi!" was appropriate, but it was not at all suitable for elderly ladies, a few with pets as escorts. To avoid these encounters, Bundy might suddenly veer into the street or an alleyway, dragging the reluctant dog behind him. He liked to meet strangers, especially children, who would pause to stroke his bald spot. What kind of dog was he? Bundy was tactfully evasive; it had proved to be an unfruitful topic. He was equally noncommittal about the dog's ineffable name.

"Call him Sport," he would say, but this pleasantry was not

appreciated. A smart aleck's answer. Their sympathies were with the dog.

To delay what lay up ahead, whatever it was, they paused at the barnlike entrance of the local van-and-storage warehouse. The draft from inside smelled of burlap sacks full of fragrant pine kindling, and mattresses that were stored on boards above the rafters. The pair contemplated a barn full of junk being sold as antiques. Bundy's eyes grazed over familiar treasure and stopped at a morris chair with faded green corduroy cushions cradling a carton marked FREE KITTENS.

He did not approach to look. One thing having a dog had spared him was the torment of losing another cat. Music (surely Elgar, something awful!) from a facsimile edition of an Atwater Kent table-model radio bathed dressers and chairs, sofas, beds and love seats, man and dog impartially. As it ended the announcer suggested that Bundy stay tuned for a Musicdote.

Recently, in this very spot—as he sniffed similar air, having paused to take shelter from a drizzle—the revelation had come to Bundy that he no longer wanted other people's junk. Better yet (or was it worse?), he no longer *wanted*—with the possible exception of an English mint, difficult to find, described as curiously strong. He had a roof, a chair, a bed, and, through no fault of his own, he had a dog. What little he had assembled and hoarded (in the garage a German electric-train set with four locomotives, and three elegant humidors and a pouch of old pipes) would soon be gratifying the wants of others. Anything else of value? The cushioned sleeping basket from Abercrombie & Fitch that had come with the dog. That would sell first. Also two Italian raincoats in good condition, and a Borsalino hat—*Extra Extra Superiore*—bought from G. Colpo in Venice.

Two young women, in the rags of fashion but radiant and blooming as gift-packed fruit, brushed Bundy as they passed, the spoor of their perfume lingering. In the flush of this encounter, his freedom from want dismantled, he moved too fast, and the leash reined him in. Rather than be rushed, the dog had stopped to sniff a meter. He found meters more life-enhancing than trees now. It had not always been so: some years ago he would tug Bundy up the incline to the park, panting and hoarsely gagging, an object of compassionate glances from elderly women headed down the grade, carrying lapdogs. This period had come to a dramatic conclusion.

In the park, back in the deep shade of the redwoods, Bundy and the dog had had a confrontation. An old tree with exposed roots had suddenly attracted the dog's attention. Bundy could not re-strain him. A stream of dirt flew out between his legs to splatter Bundy's raincoat and fall into his shoes. There was something manic in the dog's excitement. In a few moments, he had franti-cally excavated a hole into which he could insert his head and shoulders. Bundy's tug on the leash had no effect on him. The sight of his soiled hairless bottom, his legs mechanically pumping, encouraged Bundy to give him a smart crack with the end of the leash. Not hard, but sharp, right on the button, and before he could move the dog had wheeled and the front end was barking at him savagely, the lips curled back. Dirt from the hole partially screened his muzzle, and he looked to Bundy like a maddened rodent. He was no longer a dog but some primitive, underground creature. Bundy lashed out at him, backing away, but they were joined by the leash. Unintentionally, Bundy stepped on the leash, which held the dog's snarling head to the ground. His slobbering jowls were bloody; the small veiled eyes peered up at him with hatred. Bundy had just enough presence of mind to stand there, unmoving, until they both grew calm.

Nobody had observed them. The children played and shrieked in the schoolyard as usual. The dog relaxed and lay flat on the ground, his tongue lolling in the dirt. Bundy breathed noisily, a film of perspiration cooling his face. When he stepped off the leash the dog did not move but continued to watch him warily, with bloodshot eyes. A slow burn of shame flushed Bundy's ears and cheeks, but he was reluctant to admit it. Another dog passed near them, but what he sniffed on the air kept him at a distance. In a tone of truce, if not reconciliation, Bundy said, "You had enough?"

When had he last said that? Seated on a school chum, whose face was red with Bundy's nosebleed. He bled too easily, but the boy beneath him had had enough.

"O.K.?" he said to the dog. The faintest tremor of acknowledgment stirred the dog's tail. He got to his feet, sneezed repeatedly, then splattered Bundy with dirt as he shook himself. Side by side, the leash slack between them, they left the park and walked down the grade. Bundy had never again struck the dog, nor had the dog ever again wheeled to snarl at him. Once the leash was snapped to the dog's collar a truce prevailed between them. In the apartment he had the floor of a closet all to himself.

At the Fixit Shop on the corner of Poplar, recently refaced with green asbestos shingles, Mr. Waller, the Fixit man, rapped on the glass with his wooden ruler. Both Bundy and the dog acknowledged his greeting. Waller had two cats, one asleep in the window, and a dog that liked to ride in his pickup. The two dogs had once been friends; they mauled each other a bit and horsed around like a couple of kids. Then suddenly it was over. Waller's dog would no longer trouble to leave the seat of the truck. Bundy had been so struck by this he had mentioned it to Waller. "Hell," Waller had said, "Gyp's a young dog. Your dog is old."

His saying that had shocked Bundy. There was the personal element, for one thing: Bundy was a good ten years older than Waller, and was he to read the remark to mean that Waller would soon ignore him? And were dogs—reasonably well bred, sensible chaps—so indifferent to the facts of a dog's life? They appeared to be. One by one, as Bundy's dog grew older, the younger ones ignored him. He might have been a stuffed animal leashed to a parking meter. The human parallel was too disturbing for Bundy to dwell on it.

Old men, in particular, were increasingly touchy if they confronted Bundy at the frozen-food lockers. Did they think he was spying on them? Did they think he looked *sharper* than they did? Elderly women, as a rule, were less suspicious, and grateful to exchange a bit of chitchat. Bundy found them more realistic: they knew they were mortal. To find Bundy still around, squeezing the avocados, piqued the old men who returned from their vacations. On the other hand, Dr. Biddle, a retired dentist with a glistening head like an egg in a basket of excelsior, would unfailingly greet Bundy with the words "I'm really going to miss that mutt, you know that?" but his glance betrayed that he feared Bundy would check out first.

Bundy and the dog used the underpass walkway to cross the supermarket parking area. Banners were flying to celebrate Whole Grains Cereal Week. In the old days, Bundy would leash the dog to a cart and they would proceed to do their shopping together, but now he had to be parked out front tied up to one of the bicycle racks. The dog didn't like it. The area was shaded and the cement was cold. Did he ever sense, however dimly, that Bundy too felt the chill? His hand brushed the coarse pelt as he fastened the leash.

"How about a new flea collar?" Bundy said, but the dog was not responsive. He sat, without being told to sit. Did it flatter the dog to leash him? Whatever Bundy would do if worst came to worst he had pondered, but had discussed with no one—his intent might be misconstrued. Of which one of them was he speaking? Impersonally appraised, in terms of survival the two of them were pretty much at a standoff: the dog was better fleshed out, but Bundy was the heartier eater.

Thinking of eating—of garlic-scented breadsticks, to be specific, dry but not dusty to the palate—Bundy entered the market to face a large display of odorless flowers and plants. The amplitude and bounty of the new market, at the point of entrance, before he selected a cart, always marked the high point of his expectations. Where else in the hungry world such a prospect? Barrels and baskets of wine, six packs of beer and bran muffins, still-warm sourdough bread that he would break and gnaw on as he shopped. Was this a cunning regression? As a child he had craved raw sugar cookies. But his euphoria sagged at the meat counter, as he studied the gray matter being sold as meat-loaf mix; it declined further at the dairy counter, where two cartons of yogurt had been sampled, and the low-fat cottage cheese was two days older than dated. By the time he entered the checkout lane, hemmed in by scandal sheets and romantic novels, the cashier's cheerfully inane "Have a good day!" would send him off forgetting his change in the machine. The girl who pursued him (always with pennies!) had been coached to say, "Thank you, sir!"

A special on avocados this week required that Bundy make a careful selection. Out in front, as usual, dogs were barking. On the airwaves, from the rear and side, the "Wang Wang Blues." Why wang wang, he wondered. Besides wang wang, how did it go? The music was interrupted by an announcement on the public-address system. Would the owner of the white dog leashed to the bike rack please come to the front? Was Bundy's dog white? The point was debatable. Nevertheless, he left his cart by the avocados and followed the vegetable display to the front. People were huddled to the right of the door. A clerk beckoned to Bundy through the window. Still leashed to the bike rack, the dog lay out on his side, as if sleeping. In the parking lot several dogs were yelping.

"I'm afraid he's a goner," said the clerk. "These other dogs rushed him. Scared him to death. He just keeled over before they got to him." The dog had pulled the leash taut, but there was no sign that anything had touched him. A small woman with a shopping cart thumped into Bundy.

"Is it Tiger?" she said. "I hope it's not Tiger." She stopped to see that it was not Tiger. "Whose dog was it?" she asked, peering around her. The clerk indicated Bundy. "Poor thing," she said. "What was his name?"

Just recently, watching the Royal Wedding, Bundy had noticed that his emotions were nearer the surface: on two occasions his eyes had filmed over. He didn't like the woman's speaking of the dog in the past tense. Did she think he had lost his name with his life?

"What was the poor thing's name?" she repeated.

Was the tremor in Bundy's limbs noticeable? "Victor," Bundy lied, since he could not bring himself to admit the dog's name was Victrola. It had always been a sore point, the dog being too old to be given a new one. Miss Tyler had felt that as a puppy he looked like the picture of the dog at the horn of the gramophone. The resemblance was feeble, at best. How could a person give a dog such a name?

"Let him sit," a voice said. A space was cleared on a bench for Bundy to sit, but at the sound of the word he could not bend his knees. He remained standing, gazing through the bright glare at the beacon revolving on the police car. One of those women who buy two frozen dinners and then go off with the shopping cart and leave it somewhere let the policeman at the crosswalk chaperon her across the street.

PAUL BOWLES # THE CIRCULAR VALLEY

THE ABANDONED MONASTERY stood on a slight emi-
nence of land in the middle of a vast clearing. On all sides the
ground sloped gently downward toward the tangled, hairy jungle
that filled the circular valley, ringed about by sheer, black cliffs.
There were a few trees in some of the courtyards, and the birds
used them as meeting places when they flew out of the rooms and
corridors where they had their nests. Long ago bandits had taken
whatever was removable out of the building. Soldiers had used it
once as headquarters, had, like the bandits, built fires in the great
windy rooms so that afterward they looked like ancient kitchens.
And now that everything was gone from within, it seemed that
never again would anyone come near the monastery. The vegeta-
tion had thrown up a protecting wall; the first story was soon
quite hidden from view by small trees which dripped vines to lasso
the cornices of the windows. The meadows roundabout grew dank
and lush; there was no path through them.

At the higher end of the circular valley a river fell off the cliffs
into a great cauldron of vapor and thunder below; after this it slid
along the base of the cliffs until it found a gap at the other end of

the valley, where it hurried discreetly through with no rapids, no cascades—a great thick black rope of water moving swiftly downhill between the polished flanks of the canyon. Beyond the gap the land opened out and became smiling; a village nestled on the side hill just outside. In the days of the monastery it was there that the friars had got their provisions, since the Indians would not enter the circular valley. Centuries ago when the building had been constructed the Church had imported the workmen from another part of the country. These were traditional enemies of the tribes thereabouts, and had another language; there was no danger that the inhabitants would communicate with them as they worked at setting up the mighty walls. Indeed, the construction had taken so long that before the east wing was completed the workmen had all died, one by one. Thus it was the friars themselves who had closed off the end of the wing with blank walls, leaving it that way, unfinished and blind-looking, facing the black cliffs.

Generation after generation, the friars came, fresh-cheeked boys who grew thin and gray, and finally died, to be buried in the garden beyond the courtyard with the fountain. One day not long ago they had all left the monastery; no one knew where they had gone, and no one thought to ask. It was shortly after this that the bandits and then the soldiers had come. And now, since the Indians do not change, still no one from the village went up through the gap to visit the monastery. The Atlájala lived there; the friars had not been able to kill it, had given up at last and gone away. No one was surprised, but the Atlájala gained in prestige by their departure. During the centuries the friars had been there in the monastery, the Indians had wondered why it allowed them to stay. Now, at last, it had driven them out. It always had lived there, they said, and would go on living there because the valley was its home, and it could never leave.

In the early morning the restless Atlájala would move through the halls of the monastery. The dark rooms sped past, one after the other. In a small patio, where eager young trees had pushed up the paving stones to reach the sun, it paused. The air was full of small sounds: the movements of butterflies, the falling to the ground of bits of leaves and flowers, the air following its myriad courses around the edges of things, the ants pursuing their endless labors in the hot dust. In the sun it waited, conscious of each gradation in sound and light and smell, living in the awareness of the slow, constant disintegration that attacked the morning and transformed it into afternoon. When evening came, it often slipped above the monastery roof and surveyed the darkening sky: the waterfall would roar distantly. Night after night, along the procession of years, it had hovered here above the valley, darting down to become a bat, a leopard, a moth for a few minutes or hours, returning to rest immobile in the center of the space enclosed by the cliffs. When the monastery had been built, it had taken to frequenting the rooms, where it had observed for the first time the meaningless gestures of human life.

And then one evening it had aimlessly become one of the young friars. This was a new sensation, strangely rich and complex, and at the same time unbearably stifling, as though every other possibility besides that of being enclosed in a tiny, isolated world of cause and effect had been removed forever. As the friar, it had gone and stood in the window, looking out at the sky, seeing for the first time, not the stars, but the space between and beyond them. Even at that moment it had felt the urge to leave, to step outside the little shell of anguish where it lodged for the moment, but a faint curiosity had impelled it to remain a little longer and partake a little further of the unaccustomed sensation. It held on; the friar raised his arms to the sky in an imploring gesture. For the first time the Atlájala sensed opposition, the thrill of a struggle. It was delicious to feel the young man striving to free himself of its presence, and it was immeasurably sweet to remain there. Then with a cry the friar had rushed to the other side of the room and seized a heavy leather whip hanging on the wall. Tearing off his clothing he had begun to carry out a ferocious self-beating. At the first blow of the lash the Atlájala had been on the point of letting go, but then it realized that the immediacy of that intriguing inner pain was only made more manifest by the impact of the blows from without, and so it stayed and felt the young man grow weak under his own lashing. When he had finished and said a prayer, he crawled to his pallet and fell asleep weeping, while the Atlájala slipped out obliquely and entered into a bird which passed the night sitting in a great tree on the edge of the jungle, listening intently to the night sounds, and uttering a scream from time to time.

Thereafter the Atlájala found it impossible to resist sliding inside the bodies of the friars; it visited one after the other, finding an astonishing variety of sensation in the process. Each was a separate world, a separate experience, because each had different reactions when he became conscious of the other being within him. One would sit and read or pray, one would go for a long troubled walk in the meadows, around and around the building, one would find a comrade and engage in an absurd but bitter quarrel, a few wept, some flagellated themselves or sought a friend to wield the lash for them. Always there was a rich profusion of perceptions for the Atlájala to enjoy, so that it no longer occurred to it to frequent the bodies of insects, birds, and furred animals, nor even to leave the monastery and move in the air above. Once it almost got into difficulties when an old friar it was occupying suddenly fell back dead. That was a hazard it ran in the frequenting of men: they seemed not to know when they were doomed, or if they did know, they pretended with such strength not to know, that it amounted to the same thing. The other beings knew beforehand, save when it was a question of being seized unawares and devoured. And that the Atlájala was able to prevent: a bird in which it was staying was always avoided by the hawks and eagles.

When the friars left the monastery, and, following the government's orders, doffed their robes, dispersed, and became workmen, the Atlájala was at a loss to know how to pass its days and nights. Now everything was as it had been before their arrival: there was no one but the creatures that always had lived in the circular valley. It tried a giant serpent, a deer, a bee: nothing had the savor it had grown to love. Everything was the same as before, but not for the Atlájala; it had known the existence of man, and now there were no men in the valley—only the abandoned building with its empty rooms to make man's absence more poignant.

Then one year bandits came, several hundred of them in one stormy afternoon. In delight it tried many of them as they sprawled about cleaning their guns and cursing, and it discovered still other facets of sensation: the hatred they felt for the world, the fear they had of the soldiers who were pursuing them, the strange gusts of desire that swept through them as they sprawled together drunk by the fire that smoldered in the center of the floor, and the insufferable pain of jealousy which the nightly orgies seem to awaken in some of them. But the bandits did not stay long. When they had left, the soldiers came in their wake. It felt very much the same way to be a soldier as to be a bandit. Missing were the strong fear and the hatred, but the rest was almost identical. Neither the bandits nor the soldiers appeared to be at all conscious of its presence in them; it could slip from one man to another without causing any change in their behavior. This surprised it, since its effect on the friars had been so definite, and it felt a certain disappointment at the impossibility of making its existence known to them.

Nevertheless, the Atlájala enjoyed both bandits and soldiers immensely, and was even more desolate when it was left alone once again. It would become one of the swallows that made their nests in the rocks beside the top of the waterfall. In the burning sunlight it would plunge again and again into the curtain of mist that rose from far below, sometimes uttering exultant cries. It would spend a day as a plant louse, crawling slowly along the underside of the leaves, living quietly in the huge green world down there which is forever hidden from the sky. Or at night, in the velvet body of a panther, it would know the pleasure of the kill. Once for a year it lived in an eel at the bottom of the pool below the waterfall, feeling the mud give slowly before it as it pushed ahead with its flat nose; that was a restful period, but afterward the desire to know again the mysterious life of man had returned—an obsession of which it was useless to try to rid itself. And now it moved restlessly through the ruined rooms, a mute presence, alone, and thirsting to be incarnate once again, but in man's flesh only. And with the building of highways through the country it was inevitable that people should come once again to the circular valley.

A man and a woman drove their automobile as far as a village down in a lower valley; hearing about the ruined monastery and the waterfall that dropped over the cliffs into the great amphitheater, they determined to see these things. They came on burros as far as the village outside the gap, but there the Indians they had hired to accompany them refused to go any farther, and so they continued alone, upward through the canyon and into the precinct of the Atlájala.

It was noon when they rode into the valley; the black ribs of the cliffs glistened like glass in the sun's blistering downward rays. They stopped the burros by a cluster of boulders at the edge of the sloping meadows. The man got down first, and reached up to help the woman off. She leaned forward, putting her hands on his face, and for a long moment the kissed. Then he lifted her to the ground and they climbed hand in hand up over the rocks. The Atlájala hovered near them, watching the woman closely: she was the first ever to have come into the valley. The two sat beneath a small tree on the grass, looking at one another, smiling. Out of habit, the Atlájala entered into the man. Immediately, instead of existing in the midst of the sunlit air, the bird calls and the plant odors, it was conscious only of the woman's beauty and her terrible imminence. The waterfall, the earth, and the sky itself receded, rushed into nothingness and there were only the woman's smile and her arms and her odor. It was a world more suffocating and painful than the Atlájala had thought possible. Still, while the man spoke and the woman answered, it remained within.

"Leave him. He doesn't love you."

"He would kill me."

"But I love you. I need you with me."

"I can't. I'm afraid of him."

The man reached out to pull her to him; she drew back slightly, but his eyes grew large.

"We have today," she murmured, turning her face toward the yellow walls of the monastery.

The man embraced her fiercely, crushing her against him as though the act would save his life. "No, no, no. It can't go on like this," he said. "No."

The pain of his suffering was too intense; gently the Atlájala left the man and slipped into the woman. And now it would have believed itself be housed in nothing, to be in its own spaceless self, so completely was it aware of the wandering wind, the small flutterings of the leaves, and the bright air that surrounded it. Yet there was a difference: each element was magnified in intensity, the whole sphere of being was immense, limitless. Now it understood what the man sought in the woman, and it knew that he suffered because he never would attain that sense of completion he sought. But the Atlájala, being one with the woman, had attained it, and being aware of possessing it, trembled with delight. The woman shuddered as her lips met those of the man. There on the grass in the shade of the tree their joy reached new heights, the Atlájala, knowing them both, formed a single channel between the secret springs of their desires. Throughout, it remained within the woman and began vaguely to devise ways of keeping her, if not inside the valley, at least nearby, so that she might return.

In the afternoon, with dreamlike motions, they walked to the burros and mounted them, driving them through the deep meadow grass to the monastery. Inside the great courtyard they halted, looking hesitantly at the ancient arches in the sunlight, and at the darkness inside the doorways.

"Shall we go in?" said the woman.

"We must get back."

"I want to go in," she said. (The Atlájala exulted.) A thin gray snake slid along the ground into the bushes. They did not see it.

The man looked at her perplexedly. "It's late," he said.

But she jumped down from her burro by herself and walked beneath the arches into the long corridor within. (Never had the rooms seemed so real as now when the Atlájala was seeing them through her eyes.)

They explored all the rooms. Then the woman wanted to climb up into the tower, but the man took a determined stand.

"We must go back now," he said firmly, putting his hand on her shoulder.

"This is our only day together, and you think of nothing but getting back."

"But the time . . ."

"There is a moon. We won't lose the way."

He would not change his mind. "No."

"As you like," she said. "I'm going up. You can go back alone if you like."

The man laughed uneasily. "You're mad." He tried to kiss her.

She turned away and did not answer for a moment. Then she said: "You want me to leave my husband for you. You ask everything from me, but what do you do for me in return? You refuse even to climb up into a little tower with me to see the view. Go back alone. Go!"

She sobbed and rushed toward the dark stairwell. Calling after her, he followed, but stumbled somewhere behind her. She was as sure of foot as if she had climbed the many stone steps a thousand times before, hurrying up through the darkness, around and around.

In the end she came out at the top and peered through the small apertures in the cracking walls. The beams which had supported the bell had rotted and fallen; the heavy bell lay on its side in the rubble, like a dead animal. The waterfall's sound was louder up here; the valley was nearly full of shadow. Below, the man called her name repeatedly. She did not answer. As she stood watching the shadow of the cliffs slowly overtake the farthest recesses of the valley and begin to climb the naked rocks to the east, an idea formed in her mind. It was not the kind of idea which she would have expected of herself, but it was there, growing and inescapable. When she felt it complete there inside her, she turned and went lightly back down. The man was sitting in the dark near the bottom of the stairs, groaning a little.

"What is it?" she said.

"I hurt my leg. Now are you ready to go or not?"

"Yes," she said simply. "I'm sorry you fell."

Without saying anything he rose and limped after her out into the courtyard where the burros stood. The cold mountain air was beginning to flow down from the tops of the cliffs. As they rode through the meadow she began to think of how she would broach the subject to him. (It must be done before they reached the gap. The Atlájala trembled.)

"Do you forgive me?" she asked him.

"Of course," he laughed.

"Do you love me?"

"More than anything in the world."

"Is that true?"

He glanced at her in the failing light, sitting erect on the jogging animal.

"You know it is," he said softly.

She hesitated.

"There is only one way, then," she said finally.

"But what?"

"I'm afraid of him. I won't go back to him. You go back. I'll stay in the village here." (Being that near, she would come each day to the monastery.) "When it is done, you will come and get me. Then we can go somewhere else. No one will find us."

The man's voice sounded strange. "I don't understand."

"You do understand. And that is the only way. Do it or not, as you like. It is the only way."

They trotted along for a while in silence. The canyon loomed ahead, black against the evening sky.

Then the man said, very clearly: "Never."

A moment later the trail led out into an open space high above the swift water below. The hollow sound of the river reached them faintly. The light in the sky was almost gone; in the dusk the landscape had taken on false contours. Everything was gray— the rocks, the bushes, the trail—and nothing had distance or scale. They slowed their pace.

His words still echoed in her ears.

"I won't go back to him!" she cried with sudden vehemence. "You can go back and play cards with him as usual. Be his good friend the same as always. I won't go. I can't go on with both of you in the town." (The plan was not working, the Atlájala saw it had lost her, yet it still could help her.)

"You're very tired," he said softly.

He was right. Almost as he said the words, that unaccustomed exhilaration and lightness she had felt ever since noon seemed to leave her; she hung her head wearily, and said: "Yes, I am."

At the same moment the man uttered a sharp, terrible cry; she looked up in time to see his burro plunge from the edge of the trail into the grayness below. There was a silence, and then the faraway sound of many stones sliding downward. She could not move or stop the burro; she sat dumbly, letting it carry her along, an inert weight on its back.

For one final instant, as she reached the pass which was the edge of its realm, the Atlájala alighted tremulously within her. She raised her head and a tiny exultant shiver passed through her; then she let it fall forward once again.

Hanging in the dim air above the trail, the Atlájala watched her indistinct figure grow invisible in the gathering night. (If it had not been able to hold her there, still it had been able to help her.)

A moment later it was in the tower, listening to the spiders mend their webs that she had damaged. It would be a long, long time before it would bestir itself to enter into another being's awareness. A long, long time—perhaps forever.

JOHN UPDIKE # THE HAPPIEST I'VE BEEN

NEIL HOVEY came for me wearing a good suit. He parked his father's blue Chrysler on the dirt ramp by our barn and got out and stood by the open car door in a double-breasted tan gabardine suit, his hands in his pockets and his hair combed with water, squinting up at a lightning rod an old hurricane had knocked crooked.

We were driving to Chicago, so I had dressed in worn-out slacks and an outgrown corduroy shirt. But Neil was the friend I had always been most relaxed with, so I wasn't very disturbed. My parents and I walked out from the house, across the low stretch of lawn that was mostly mud after the thaw that had come on Christmas Day, and my grandmother, though I had kissed her good-bye inside the house, came out onto the porch, stooped and rather angry-looking, her head haloed by wild old woman's white hair and the hand more severely afflicted by arthritis waggling at her breast in a worried way. It was growing dark and my grandfather had gone to bed. "Nev-er trust the man who wears the red necktie and parts his hair in the middle," had been his final advice to me.

We had expected Neil since middle afternoon. Nineteen almost twenty, I was a college sophomore home on vacation; that fall I had met in a fine arts course a girl I had fallen in love with, and she had invited me to the New Year's party her parents always gave and to stay at her house a few nights. She lived in Chicago and so did Neil now, though he had gone to our high school. His father did something—sell steel was my impression, a huge man opening a briefcase and saying "The I-beams are very good this year"—that required him to be always on the move, so that at about thirteen Neil had been boarded with Mrs. Hovey's parents, the Lancasters. They had lived in Olinger since the town was incorporated. Indeed, old Jesse Lancaster, whose sick larynx whistled when he breathed to us boys his shocking and uproarious thoughts on the girls that walked past his porch all day long, had twice been burgess. Meanwhile Neil's father got a stationary job, but he let Neil stay to graduate; after the night he graduated, Neil drove throughout the next day to join his parents. From Chicago to this part of Pennsylvania was seventeen hours. In the twenty months he had been gone Neil had come east fairly often; he loved driving and Olinger was the one thing he had that was close to a childhood home. In Chicago he was working in a garage and getting his teeth straightened by the Army so they could draft him. Korea was on. He had to go back, and I wanted to go, so it was a happy arrangement. "You're all dressed up," I accused him immediately.

"I've been saying good-bye." The knot of his necktie was loose and the corners of his mouth were rubbed with pink. Years later my mother recalled how that evening his breath to her stank so strongly of beer she was frightened to let me go with him. "*Your* grandfather always thought *his* grandfather was a very dubious character," she said then.

My father and Neil put my suitcases into the trunk; they contained all the clothes I had brought, for the girl and I were going to go back to college on the train together, and I would not see my home again until spring.

"Well, good-bye, boys," my mother said. "I think you're both very brave." In regard to me she meant the girl as much as the roads.

"Don't you worry, Mrs. Nordholm," Neil told her quickly. "He'll be safer than in his bed. I bet he sleeps from here to Indiana." He looked at me with an irritating imitation of her own fond gaze. When they shook hands good-bye it was with an equality established on the base of my helplessness. His being so slick startled me, but then you can have a friend for years and never see how he operates with adults.

I embraced my mother and over her shoulder with the camera of my head tried to take a snapshot I could keep of the house, the woods behind it and the sunset behind them, the bench beneath the walnut tree where my grandfather cut apples into skinless bits and fed them to himself, and the ruts in the soft lawn the bakery truck had made that morning.

We started down the half-mile of dirt road to the highway that, one way, went through Olinger to the city of Alton and, the other way, led through farmland to the Turnpike. It was luxurious, after the stress of farewell, to two-finger a cigarette out of the pack in my shirt pocket. My family knew I smoked but I didn't do it in front of them; we were all too sensitive to bear the awkwardness. I lit mine and held the match for Hovey. It was a relaxed friendship. We were about the same height and had the same degree of athletic incompetence and the same curious lack of whatever force it was that aroused loyalty and compliance in beautiful girls. There was his bad teeth and my skin allergy; these were being remedied now, when they mattered less. But it seemed to me the most important thing—about both our friendship and our failures to become, for all the love we felt for women, actual lovers—was that he and I lived with grandparents. This improved both our backward and forward vision; we knew about the bedside commodes and mid-night coughing fits that awaited most men, and we had a sense of childhoods before 1900, when the farmer ruled the land and America faced west. We had gained a humane dimension that made us gentle and humorous among peers but diffident at dances and hesitant in cars. Girls hate boys' doubts: they amount to insults. Gentleness is for married women to appreciate. (This is my thinking then.) A girl who has received out of nowhere a gift worth all Africa's ivory and Asia's gold wants more than just humanity to bestow it on.

Coming onto the highway, Neil turned right toward Olinger instead of left toward the Turnpike. My reaction was to twist and assure myself through the rear window that, though a pink triangle of sandstone stared through the bare treetops, nobody at my house could possibly see.

When he was again in third gear, Neil asked, "Are you in a hurry?"

"No. Not especially."

"Schuman's having his New Year's party two days early so we can go. I thought we'd go for a couple hours and miss the Friday night stuff on the Pike." His mouth moved and closed carefully over the dull, silver, painful braces.

"Sure," I said. "I don't care." In everything that followed there was this sensation of my being picked up and carried.

It was four miles from the farm to Olinger; we entered by Buchanan Road, driving past the tall white brick house I had lived in until I was fifteen. My grandfather had bought it before I was born and his stocks became bad, which had happened in the same year. The new owners had strung colored bulbs all along the front door frame and the edges of the porch roof. Downtown the cardboard Santa Claus still nodded in the drugstore window but the loudspeaker on the undertaker's lawn had stopped broadcasting carols. It was quite dark now, so the arches of red and green lights above Grand Avenue seemed miracles of lift; in daylight you saw the bulbs were just hung from a straight cable by cords of different lengths. Larry Schuman lived on the other side of town, the newer side. Lights ran all the way up the front edges of his house and across the rain gutter. The next-door neighbor had a plywood reindeer-and-sleigh floodlit on his front lawn and a snowman of papier-mâché leaning tipsily (his eyes were x's) against the corner of his house. No real snow had fallen yet that winter. The air this evening, though, hinted that harder weather was coming.

The Schuman's living room felt warm. In one corner a blue spruce drenched with tinsel reached to the ceiling; around its pot surged a drift of wrapping paper and ribbon and boxes, a few still containing presents, gloves and diaries and other small properties that hadn't yet been absorbed into the mainstream of affluence. The ornamental balls were big as baseballs and all either crimson or indigo; the tree was so well dressed I felt self-conscious in the same room with it, without a coat or tie and wearing an old green shirt too short in the sleeves. Everyone else was dressed for a party. Then Mr. Schuman stamped in comfortingly, crushing us all into one underneath his welcome, Neil and I and the three other boys who had showed up so far. He was dressed to go out on the town, in a vanilla topcoat and silvery silk muffler, smoking a cigar with the band still on. You could see in Mr. Schuman where Larry got the red hair and white eyelashes and the self-confidence, but what in the son was smirking and pushy was in the father shrewd and masterful. What the one used to make you nervous the other used to put you at ease. While Mr. was jollying us, Zoe Loessner, Larry's probable fiancée and the only other girl at the party so far, was talking nicely to Mrs., nodding with her entire neck and fingering her Kresge pearls and blowing cigarette smoke through the corners of her mouth, to keep it away from the middle-aged woman's face. Each time Zoe spat out a plume, the shelf of honey hair overhanging her temple bobbed. Mrs. Schuman beamed serenely above her mink coat and rhinestone pocketbook. It was odd to see her dressed in the trappings of the prosperity that usually supported her good nature invisibly, like a firm mattress under a bright homely quilt. Everybody loved her. She was a prime product of the country, a Pennsylvania Dutch woman with sons, who loved feeding her sons and who imagined that the entire world, like her life, was going well. I never saw her not smile, except at her husband. At last she moved him into the outdoors. He turned at the threshold and did a trick with his knees and called in to us, "Be good and if you can't be good, be careful."

With them out of the way, the next item was getting liquor. It was a familiar business. Did anybody have a forged driver's license? If not, who would dare to forge theirs? Larry could provide india ink. Then again, Larry's older brother Dale might be home and would go if it didn't take too much time. However, on weekends he often went straight from work to his fiancée's apartment and stayed until Sunday. If worse came to worse, Larry knew an illegal place in Alton, but they really soaked you. The problem was solved strangely. More people were arriving all the time and one of them, Cookie Behn, who had been held back one year and hence was deposited in our grade, announced that last November he had become in honest fact twenty-one. I at least gave Cookie my share of the money feeling a little queasy, vice had become so handy.

The party was the party I had been going to all my life, beginning with Ann Mahlon's first Hallowe en party, that I attended as a hot, lumbering, breathless, and blind Donald Duck. My mother had made the costume, and the eyes kept slipping, and were further apart than my eyes, so that even when the clouds of gauze parted, it was to reveal the frustrating depthless world seen with one eye. Ann, who because her mother loved her so much as a child had remained somewhat childish, and I and another boy and girl who were not involved in any romantic crisis went down into Schuman's basement to play circular Ping-Pong. Armed with paddles, we stood each at a side of the table and when the ball was stroked ran around it counterclockwise, slapping the ball and screaming. To run better the girls took off their heels and ruined their stockings on the cement floor. Their faces and arms and shoulder sections became flushed, and when a girl lunged forward toward the net the stiff neckline of her semiformal dress dropped away and the white arcs of her brassiere could be glimpsed cupping fat, and when she reached high her shaved armpit gleamed like a bit of chicken skin. An earring of Ann's flew off and the two connected rhinestones skidded to lie near the wall, among the Schumans' power mower and the badminton poles and empty bronze motor-oil cans twice punctured by triangles. All these images were immediately lost in the whirl of our running; we were dizzy before we stopped. Ann leaned on me getting back into her shoes.

When we pushed it open the door leading down into the cellar banged against the newel post of the carpeted stairs going to the second floor, a third of the way up these, a couple sat discussing. The girl, Jacky Iselin, cried without emotion—the tears and nothing else, like water flowing over wood. Some people were in the kitchen mixing drinks and making noise. In the living room others danced to records: 78s then, stiff discs stacked in a ponderous leaning cylinder on the spindle of the Schumans' console. Every three minutes with a click and a crash another dropped and the mood abruptly changed. One moment it would be "Stay as Sweet as You Are": Clarence Lang with the absolute expression of an idiot standing and rocking monotonously with June Kaufmann's boneless sad brown hand trapped in his and their faces, staring in the same direction, pasted together like the facets of an idol. The music stopped; when they parted, a big squarish dark patch stained the cheek of each. Then the next moment it would be Goodman's "Loch Lomond" or "Cherokee" and nobody but Margaret Lento wanted to jitterbug. Mad, she danced by herself, swinging her head recklessly and snapping her backside; a corner of her skirt flipped a Christmas ball onto the rug, where it collapsed into a hundred convex reflectors. Female shoes were scattered in innocent pairs about the room. Some were flats, resting under the sofa shyly toed in; others were high heels lying cockeyed, the spike of one thrust into its mate. Sitting alone and ignored in a great armchair, I experienced within a warm keen dishevelment, as if there were real tears in my eyes. Had things been less unchanged they would have seemed less tragic. But the girls who had stepped out of these shoes were with few exceptions the ones who had attended my life's party. The alterations were so small: a haircut, an engagement ring, a franker plumpness. While they wheeled above me I sometimes caught from their faces an unfamiliar glint, off of a hardness I did not remember, as if beneath their skins these girls were growing more dense. The brutality added to the features of the boys I knew seemed a more willed effect, more desired and so less grievous. Considering that there was a war, surprisingly many were present, 4-F or at college or simply waiting to be called. Shortly before midnight the door rattled and there, under the porchlight, looking forlorn and chilled in their brief athletic jackets, stood three members of the class ahead of ours who in the old days always tried to crash Schuman's parties. At Olinger High they had been sports stars, and they still stood with that well-coordinated looseness, a look of dangling from strings. The three of them had enrolled together at Melanchthon, a small Lutheran college on the edge of Alton, and in this season played on the Melanchthon basketball team. That is, two did; the third hadn't been good enough. Schuman, out of cowardice more than mercy, let them in, and they hid without hesitation in the basement, and didn't bother us, having brought their own bottle.

There was one novel awkwardness. Darryl Bechtel had married Emmy Johnson and the couple came. Darryl had worked in his father's greenhouse and was considered dull; it was Emmy that we knew. At first no one danced with her, and Darryl didn't know how, but then Schuman, perhaps as host, dared. Others followed, but Schuman had her in his arms most often, and at midnight, when we were pretending the new year began, he kissed her; a wave of kissing swept the room now, and everyone struggled to kiss Emmy. Even I did. There was something about her being married that made it extraordinary. Her cheeks in flame, she kept glancing around for rescue, but Darryl, embarrassed to see his wife dance, had gone into old man Schuman's den, where Neil sat brooding, sunk in mysterious sorrow.

When the kissing subsided and Darryl emerged, I went in to see Neil. He was holding his face in his hands and tapping his foot to a record playing on Mr. Schuman's private phonograph: Krupa's "Dark Eyes." The arrangement was droning and circular and Neil had kept the record going for hours. He loved saxophones; I guess all of us children of that Depression vintage did. I asked him, "Do you think the traffic on the Turnpike has died down by now?"

He took down the tall glass on the cabinet beside him and took a convincing swallow. His face from the side seemed lean and somewhat blue. "Maybe," he said, staring at the ice cubes submerged in the ochre liquid. "The girl in Chicago's expecting you?"

"Well, yeah, but we can call and let her know, once *we* know."

"You think she'll spoil?"

"How do you mean?"

"I mean, won't you be seeing her all the time after we get there? Aren't you going to marry her?"

"I have no idea. I might."

"Well then: you'll have the rest of Kingdom Come to see her." He looked directly at me, and it was plain in the blur of his eyes that he was sick-drunk. "The trouble with you guys that have all the luck," he said slowly, "is that you don't give a fuck about us that don't have any." Such melodramatic rudeness coming from Neil surprised me, as had his blarney with my mother hours before. In trying to evade his wounded stare, I discovered there was another person in the room: a girl sitting with her shoes on, reading *Holiday*. Though she held the magazine in front of her face I knew from her clothes and her unfamiliar legs that she was the girlfriend Margaret Lento had brought. Margaret didn't come from Olinger but from Riverside, a section of Alton, not a suburb. She had met Larry Schuman at a summer job in a restaurant and for the rest of high school they had more or less gone together. Since then, though, it had dawned on Mr. and Mrs. Schuman that even in a democracy distinctions exist, probably welcome news to Larry. In the cruelest and most stretched-out way he could manage he had been breaking off with her throughout the year now nearly ended. I had been surprised to find her at this party. Obviously she had felt shaky about attending and had brought the friend as the only kind of protection she could afford. The other girl was acting just like a hired guard.

There being no answer to Neil, I went into the living room, where Margaret, insanely drunk, was throwing herself around as if wanting to break a bone. Somewhat in time to the music she would run a few steps, then snap her body like a whip, her chin striking her chest and her hands flying backward, fingers fanned, as her shoulders pitched forward. In her state her body was childishly plastic; unharmed, she would bounce back from this jolt and begin to clap and kick and hum. Schuman stayed away from her. Margaret was small, not more than 5'3", with the smallness ripeness comes to early. She had bleached a section of her black hair platinum, cropped her head all over, and trained the stubble into short hyacinthine curls like those on antique statutes of boys. Her face seemed quite coarse from the front, so her profile was classical unexpectedly. She might have been Portia. When she was not putting on her savage pointless dance she was in the bathroom being sick. The pity and the vulgarity of her exhibition made everyone who was sober uncomfortable; our common guilt in witnessing this girl's rites brought us so close together in that room that it seemed never, not in all time, could we be parted. I myself was perfectly sober. I had the impression then that people only drank to stop being unhappy and I nearly always felt at least fairly happy.

Luckily, Margaret was in a sick phase around one o'clock, when the elder Schumans came home. They looked in at us briefly. It was a pleasant joke to see in their smiles that, however corrupt and unwinking we felt, to them we looked young and sleepy: Larry's friends. Things quieted after they went up the stairs. In half an hour people began coming out of the kitchen balancing cups of coffee. By two o'clock four girls stood in aprons at Mrs. Schuman's sink, and others were padding back and forth carrying glasses and ashtrays. Another blameless racket pierced the clatter in the kitchen. Out on the cold grass the three Melanchthon athletes had set up the badminton net and in the faint glow given off by the house were playing. The bird, ascending and descending through uneven bars of light, glimmered like a firefly. Now that the party was dying Neil's apathy seemed deliberately exasperating, even vindictive. For at least another hour he persisted in hearing "Dark Eyes" over and over again, holding his head and tapping his foot. The entire scene in the den had developed a fixity that was uncanny; the girl remained in the chair and read magazines, *Holiday* and *Esquire*, one after another. In the meantime, cars came and went and raced their motors out front; Schuman took Ann Mahlon off and didn't come back; and the athletes carried the neighbor's artificial snowman into the center of the street and disappeared. Somehow in the arrangements shuffled together at the end, Neil had contracted to drive Margaret and the other girl home. Margaret convalesced in the downstairs bathroom for most of that hour. I unlocked a little glass bookcase ornamenting a desk in the dark dining room and removed a volume of Thackeray's Works. It turned out to be volume II of *Henry Esmond*. I began it, rather than break another book out of the set, which had been squeezed in there so long the bindings had sort of interpenetrated.

Henry was going off to war again when Neil appeared in the archway and said, "O.K., Norseman. Let's go to Chicago." "Norseman" was a variant of my name he used only when feeling special affection.

We turned off all the lamps and left the hall bulb burning against Larry's return. Margaret Lento seemed chastened. Neil gave her his arm and led her into the backseat of his father's car; I stood aside to let the other girl get in with her, but Neil indicated that I should. I supposed he realized this left only the mute den-girl to go up front with him. She sat well over on her side, was all I noticed. Neil backed into the street and with unusual care steered past the snowman. Our headlights made vivid the fact that the snowman's back was a hollow right-angled gash; he had been built up against the corner of a house.

★ ★ ★

From Olinger, Riverside was diagonally across Alton. The city was sleeping as we drove through it. Most of the stoplights were blinking green. Among cities Alton had a bad reputation; its graft and gambling and easy juries and bawdy houses were supposedly notorious throughout the Middle Atlantic states. But to me it always presented an innocent face; row after row of houses built of a local dusty-red brick the shade of flowerpots, each house fortified with a tiny, intimate, balustraded porch, and nothing but the wealth of movie houses and beer signs along its main street to suggest that its citizens loved pleasure more than the run of mankind. Indeed, as we moved at moderate speed down these hushed streets bordered with parked cars, a limestone church bulking at every corner and the hooded street lamps keeping watch from above, Alton seemed less the ultimate center of an urban region than itself a suburb of some vast mythical metropolis, like Pandemonium or Paradise. I was conscious of evergreen wreaths on door after door and of fanlights of stained glass in which the house number was embedded. I was also conscious that every block was one block further from the Turnpike.

Riverside, fitted into the bends of the Schuylkill, was not so regularly laid out. Margaret's house was one of a short row, composition-shingled, which we approached from the rear, down a tiny cement alley speckled with drains. The porches were a few inches higher than the alley. Margaret asked us if we wanted to come in for a cup of coffee, since we were going to Chicago; Neil accepted by getting out of the car and slamming his door. The noise filled the alley, alarming me. I wondered at the easy social life that evidently existed among my friends at three-thirty in the morning. Margaret did, however, lead us in stealthily, and she turned on only the kitchen switch. The kitchen was divided from the living room by a large sofa, which faced into littered gloom where distant light from beyond the alley spilled over the window-sill and across the spines of a radiator. In one corner the glass of a television set showed; the screen would seem absurdly small now, but then it seemed disproportionately elegant. The shabbiness everywhere would not have struck me so definitely if I hadn't just come from Schuman's place. Neil and the other girl sat on the sofa; Margaret held a match to a gas burner and, as the blue flame licked an old kettle, doled instant coffee into four flowered cups.

Some man who had once lived in this house had built by the kitchen's one window a breakfast nook, nothing more than a booth, a table between two high-backed benches. I sat in it and read all the words I could see: "Salt," "Pepper," "Have Some Lumps," "December," "Mohn's Milk Inc.—A Very Merry Christmas and Joyous New Year—Mohn's Milk is *Safe* Milk— 'Mommy, Make It Mohn's!,' " "Matches," "Hotpoint," "press," Magee Stove Federal & Furnace Corp.," "God Is In This House," "Ave Maria Gratia Plena," "Shredded Wheat Benefits Exciting New Pattern Kungsholm." After serving the two on the sofa, Margaret came to me with coffee and sat down opposite me in the booth. Fatigue had raised two blue welts beneath her eyes.

"Well," I asked her, "did you have a good time?"

She smiled and glanced down and made the small sound "Ch," vestigial of "Jesus." With absentminded delicacy she stirred her coffee, lifting and replacing the spoon without a ripple.

"Rather odd at the end," I said, "not even the host there."

"He took Ann Mahlon home."

"I know." I was surprised that she knew, having been sick in the bathroom for that hour.

"You sound jealous," she added.

"Who does? I do? I don't."

"You like her, John, don't you?" Her using my first name and the quality of the question did not, although discounting parties we had just met, seem forward, considering the hour and that she had brought me coffee. There is very little further to go with a girl who has brought you coffee.

"Oh, I like everybody," I told her, "and the longer I've known them the more I like them, because the more they're me. The only people I like better are ones I've just met. Now Ann Mahlon I've known since kindergarten. Every day her mother used to bring her to the edge of the schoolyard for months after all the other mothers had stopped." I wanted to cut a figure in Margaret's eyes, but they were too dark. Stoically she had gotten on top of her weariness, but it was growing bigger under her.

"Did you like her then?"

"I felt sorry for her being embarrassed by her mother."

She asked me, "What was Larry like when he was little?"

"Oh, bright. Kind of mean."

"Was he mean?"

"I'd say so. Yes. In some grade or other he and I began to play chess together. I always won until secretly he took lessons from a man his parents knew and read strategy books."

Margaret laughed, genuinely pleased. "Then did he win?"

"Once. After that I really tried, and after *that* he decided chess was kid stuff. Besides, I was used up. He'd have these runs on people where you'd be down at his house every afternoon, then in a couple months he'd get a new pet and that'd be that."

"He's funny," she said. "He has a kind of cold mind. He decides on what he wants, then he does what he has to do, you know, and nothing anybody says can change him."

"He does tend to get what he wants," I admitted guardedly, realizing that to her this meant her. Poor bruised little girl, in her mind he was all the time cleaving with rare cunning through his parents' objections straight to her.

My coffee was nearly gone, so I glanced toward the sofa in the other room. Neil and the girl had sunk out of sight behind its back. Before this it had honestly not occurred to me that they had a relationship, but now that I saw, it seemed plausible and, at this time of night, good news, though it meant we would not be going to Chicago yet.

So I talked to Margaret about Larry, and she responded, show-ing really quite an acute sense of him. To me, considering so seriously the personality of a childhood friend, as if overnight he had become a factor in the world, seemed disproportionate; I couldn't deeply believe that even in her world he mattered much. Larry Schuman, in little more than a year, had become nothing to me. The important thing, rather than the subject, was the conversation itself, the quick agreements, the slow nods, the weave of different memories; it was like one of those Panama baskets shaped underwater around a worthless stone.

She offered me more coffee. When she returned with it, she sat down, not opposite, but beside me, lifting me to such a pitch of gratitude and affection the only way I could think to express it was by *not* kissing her, as if a kiss were another piece of abuse women suffered. She said, "Cold. Cheap bastard turns the thermostat down to sixty," meaning her father. She drew my arm around her shoulders and folded my hand around her bare forearm, to warm it. The back of my thumb fitted against the curve of one breast. Her head went into the hollow where my arm and chest joined; she was terribly small, measured against your own body. Perhaps she weighed a hundred pounds. Her lids lowered and I kissed her two beautiful eyebrows and then the spaces of skin between the rough curls, some black and some bleached, that fringed her forehead. Other than this I tried to keep as still as a bed would be. It *had* grown cold. A shiver starting on the side away from her would twitch my shoulders when I tried to repress it; she would frown and unconsciously draw my arm tighter. No one had switched the kitchen light off. On Margaret's foreshortened upper lip there seemed to be two pencil marks; the length of wrist my badly fitting sleeve exposed looked pale and naked against the spiraling down of the smaller arm held beneath it.

Outside on the street the house faced there was no motion. Only once did a car go by: around five o'clock, with twin mufflers, the radio on and a boy yelling. Neil and the girl murmured together incessantly; some of what they said I could overhear.

"No. Which?" she asked.

"I don't care."

"Wouldn't you want a boy?"

"I'd be happy whatever I got."

"I know, but which would you *rather* have? Don't men want boys?"

"I don't care. You."

Somewhat later, Mohn's truck passed on the other side of the street. The milkman, well bundled, sat behind headlights in a warm orange volume the size of a phone booth, steering one-handed and smoking a cigar that he set on the edge of the dashboard when, his wire carrier vibrant, he ran out of the truck with bottles. His passing led Neil to decide the time had come. Margaret woke up frightened of her father; we hissed our farewells and thanks to her quickly. Neil dropped the other girl off at her house a few blocks away; he knew where it was. Sometime during that night I must have seen this girl's face, but I have no memory of it. She is always behind a magazine or in the dark or with her back turned. Neil married her years later, I know, but after we arrived in Chicago I never saw him again either.

Red dawn light touched the clouds above the black slate roofs as, with a few other cars, we drove through Alton. The moon-sized clock of a beer billboard said ten after six. Olinger was deathly still. The air brightened as we moved along the highway; the glowing wall of my home hung above the woods as we rounded the long curve by the Mennonite dairy. With a .22 I could have had a pane of my parents' bedroom window, and they were dreaming I was in Indiana. My grandfather would be up, stamping around in the kitchen for my grandmother to make him breakfast, or outside, walking to see if any ice had formed on the brook. For an instant I genuinely feared he might hail me from the peak of the barn roof. Then trees interceded and we were safe in a landscape where no one cared.

At the entrance to the Turnpike Neil did a strange thing, stopped the car and had me take the wheel. He had never trusted me to drive his father's car before; he had believed my not knowing where the crankshaft and fuel pump were handicapped my competence to steer. But now he was quite complacent. He hunched under an old mackinaw and leaned his head against the metal of the window frame and soon was asleep. We crossed the Susquehanna on a long smooth bridge below Harrisburg, then began climbing toward the Alleghenies. In the mountains there was snow, a dry dusting like sand, that waved back and forth on the road surface. Further along there had been a fresh fall that night, about two inches, and the plows had not yet cleared all the lanes. I was passing a Sunoco truck on a high curve when without warning the scraped section gave out and I realized I might skid into the fence if not over the edge. The radio was singing "Carpets of clover, I'll lay right at your feet," and the speedometer said eighty-five. Nothing happened; the car stayed firm in the snow and Neil slept through the danger, his face turned skyward and his breath struggling in his nose. It was the first time I heard a contemporary of mine snore.

When we came into tunnel country the flicker and hollow amplification stirred Neil awake. He sat up, the mackinaw dropping to his lap, and lit a cigarette. A second after the scratch of his match occurred the moment of which each following moment was a slight diminution, as we made the long irregular descent toward Pittsburgh. There were many reasons for my feeling so happy. We were on our way. I had seen a dawn. This far, Neil could appreciate, I had brought us safely. Ahead, a girl waited who, if I asked, would marry me, but first there was a vast trip: many hours and towns interceded between me and that encounter. There was the quality of the 10 A.M. sunlight as it existed in the air ahead of the windshield, filtered by the thin overcast, blessing irresponsibility—you felt you could slice forever through such a cool pure element—and springing, by implying how high these hills had become, a widespreading pride: Pennsylvania, your state—as if you had made your life. And there was knowing that twice since midnight a person had trusted me enough to fall asleep beside me.

ANDRE DUBUS | # KILLINGS

ON THE AUGUST morning when Matt Fowler buried his
youngest son, Frank, who had lived for twenty-one years, eight
months, and four days, Matt's older son, Steve, turned to him as
the family left the grave and walked between their friends, and
said "I should kill him." He was twenty-eight, his brown hair
starting to thin in front where he used to have a cowlick. He bit
his lower lip, wiped his eyes, then said it again. Ruth's arm, linked
with Matt's, tightened; he looked at her. Beneath her eyes there
was swelling from the three days she had suffered. At the limousine
Matt stopped and looked back at the grave, the casket, and the
Congregationalist minister who he thought had probably had a
difficult job with the eulogy though he hadn't seemed to, and the
old funeral director who was saying something to the six young
pallbearers. The grave was on a hill and overlooked the Merrimack, which he could not see from where he stood; he looked at
the opposite bank, at the apple orchard with its symmetrically
planted trees going up a hill.

Next day Steve drove with his wife back to Baltimore, where
he managed the branch office of a bank, and Cathleen, the middle

child, drove with her husband back to Syracuse. They had left the grandchildren with friends. A month after the funeral Matt played poker at Willis Trottier's because Ruth, who knew this was the second time he had been invited, told him to go, he couldn't sit home with her for the rest of her life, she was all right. After the game Willis went outside to tell everyone good night and, when the others had driven away, he walked with Matt to his car. Willis was a short, silver-haired man who had opened a diner after World War II, his trade then mostly very early breakfast, which he cooked, and then lunch for the men who worked at the leather and shoe factories. He now owned a large restaurant.

"He walks the Goddamn streets," Matt said.

"I know. He was in my place last night, at the bar. With a girl."

"I don't see him. I'm in the store all the time. Ruth sees him. She sees him too much. She was at Sunnyhurst today getting cigarettes and aspirin, and there he was. She can't even go out for cigarettes and aspirin. It's killing her."

"Come back in for a drink."

Matt looked at his watch. Ruth would be asleep. He walked with Willis back into the house, pausing at the steps to look at the starlit sky. It was a cool summer night; he thought vaguely of the Red Sox, did not even know if they were at home tonight; since it happened he had not been able to think about any of the small pleasures he believed he had earned, as he had earned also what was shattered now forever: the quietly harried and quietly pleasurable days of fatherhood. They went inside. Willis's wife, Martha, had gone to bed hours ago, in the rear of the large house which was rigged with burglar and fire alarms. They went downstairs to the game room: the television set suspended from the ceiling, the pool table, the poker table with beer cans, cards, chips, filled ashtrays, and the six chairs where Matt and his friends had sat, the friends picking up the old banter as though he had only been away on vacation; but he could see the affection and courtesy in their eyes. Willis went behind the bar and mixed them each a scotch and soda; he stayed behind the bar and looked at Matt sitting on the stool.

"How often have you thought about it?" Willis said.

"Every day since he got out. I didn't think about bail. I thought I wouldn't have to worry about him for years. She sees him all the time. It makes her cry."

"He was in my place a long time last night. He'll be back."

"Maybe he won't."

"The band. He likes the band."

"What's he doing now?"

"He's tending bar up to Hampton Beach. For a friend. Ever notice even the worst bastard always has friends? He couldn't get work in town. It's just tourists and kids up to Hampton. Nobody knows him. If they do, they don't care. They drink what he mixes."

"Nobody tells me about him."

"I hate him, Matt. My boys went to school with him. He was the same then. Know what he'll do? Five at the most. Remember that woman about seven years ago? Shot her husband and dropped him off the bridge in the Merrimack with a hundred pound sack of cement and said all the way through it that nobody helped her. Know where she is now? She's in Lawrence now, a secretary. And whoever helped her, where the hell is he?"

"I've got a .38 I've had for years. I take it to the store now. I tell Ruth it's for the night deposits. I tell her things have changed: we got junkies here now too. Lots of people without jobs. She knows though."

"What does she know?"

"She knows I started carrying it after the first time she saw him in town. She knows it's in case I see him, and there's some kind of a situation—"

He stopped, looked at Willis, and finished his drink. Willis mixed him another.

"What kind of a situation?"

"Where he did something to me. Where I could get away with it."

"How does Ruth feel about that?"

"She doesn't know."

"You said she does, she's got it figured out."

He thought of her that afternoon: when she went into Sunnyhurst, Strout was waiting at the counter while the clerk bagged the things he had bought; she turned down an aisle and looked at soup cans until he left.

"Ruth would shoot him herself, if she thought she could hit him."

"You got a permit?"

"No."

"I do. You could get a year for that."

"Maybe I'll get one. Or maybe I won't. Maybe I'll just stop bringing it to the store."

Richard Strout was twenty-six years old, a high school athlete, football scholarship to the University of Massachusetts, where he lasted for almost two semesters before quitting in advance of the final grades that would have forced him not to return. People then said: Dickie can do the work; he just doesn't want to. He came home and did construction work for his father but refused his father's offer to learn the business; his two older brothers had learned it, so that Strout and Sons trucks going about town, and signs on construction sites, now slashed wounds into Matt Fowler's life. Then Richard married a young girl and became a bartender, his salary and tips augmented and perhaps sometimes matched by his father, who also posted his bond. So his friends, his enemies (he had those: fistfights or, more often, boys and then young men who had not fought him when they thought they should have), and those who simply knew him by face and name, had a series of images of him which they recalled when they heard of the killing: the high school running back, the young drunk in bars, the oblivious hard-hatted young man eating lunch at a counter, the bartender who could perhaps be called courteous but not more than that: as he tended bar, his dark eyes and dark, wide-jawed face appeared less sullen, near blank.

One night he beat Frank. Frank was living at home and waiting for September, for graduate school in economics, and working as a lifeguard at Salisbury Beach, where he met Mary Ann Strout, in her first month of separation. She spent most days at the beach with her two sons. Before ten o'clock one night Frank came home; he had driven to the hospital first, and he walked into the living room with stitches over his right eye and both lips bright and swollen.

"I'm all right," he said, when Matt and Ruth stood up, and Matt turned off the television, letting Ruth get to him first: the tall, muscled but slender suntanned boy. Frank tried to smile at them but couldn't because of his lips.

"It was her husband, wasn't it?" Ruth said.

"Ex," Frank said. "He dropped in."

Matt gently held Frank's jaw and turned his face to the light, looked at the stitches, the blood under the white of the eye, the bruised flesh.

"Press charges," Matt said.

"No."

"What's to stop him from doing it again? Did you hit him at all? Enough so he won't want to next time?"

"I don't think I touched him."

"So what are you going to do?"

"Take karate," Frank said, and tried again to smile.

"That's not the problem," Ruth said.

"You know you like her," Frank said.

"I like a lot of people. What about the boys? Did they see it?"

"They were asleep."

"Did you leave her alone with him?"

"He left first. She was yelling at him. I believe she had a skillet in her hand."

"Oh for God's sake," Ruth said.

Matt had been dealing with that too: at the dinner table on evenings when Frank wasn't home, was eating with Mary Ann; or, on the other nights—and Frank was with her every night—he talked with Ruth while they watched television, or lay in bed with the windows open and he smelled the night air and imagined, with both pride and muted sorrow, Frank in Mary Ann's arms. Ruth didn't like it because Mary Ann was in the process of divorce, because she had two children, because she was four years older than Frank, and finally—she told this in bed, where she had during all of their marriage told him of her deepest feelings: of love, of passion, of fears about one of the children, of pain Matt had caused her or she had caused him—she was against it because of what she had heard: that the marriage had gone bad early, and for most of it Richard and Mary Ann had both played around.

"That can't be true," Matt said. "Strout wouldn't have stood for it."

"Maybe he loves her."

"He's too hot-tempered. He couldn't have taken that."

But Matt knew Strout had taken it, for he had heard the stories too. He wondered who had told them to Ruth; and he felt vaguely annoyed and isolated: living with her for thirty-one years and still not knowing what she talked about with her friends. On these summer nights he did not so much argue with her as try to comfort her, but finally there was no difference between the two: she had concrete objections, which he tried to overcome. And in his attempt to do this, he neglected his own objections, which were the same as hers, so that as he spoke to her he felt as disembodied as he sometimes did in the store when he helped a man choose a blouse or dress or piece of costume jewelry for his wife.

"The divorce doesn't mean anything," he said. "She was young and maybe she liked his looks and then after a while she realized she was living with a bastard. I see it as a positive thing."

"She's not divorced yet."

"It's the same thing. Massachusetts has crazy laws, that's all.

Her age is no problem. What's it matter when she was born? And that other business: even if it's true, which it probably isn't, it's got nothing to do with Frank, it's in the past. And the kids are no problem. She's been married six years; she ought to have kids. Frank likes them. He plays with them. And he's not going to marry her anyway, so it's not a problem of money."

"Then what's he doing with her?"

"She probably loves him, Ruth. Girls always have. Why can't we just leave it at that?"

"He got home at six o'clock Tuesday morning."

"I didn't know you knew. I've already talked to him about it."

Which he had: since he believed almost nothing he told Ruth, he went to Frank with what he believed. The night before, he had followed Frank to the car after dinner.

"You wouldn't make much of a burglar," he said.

"How's that?"

Matt was looking up at him; Frank was six feet tall, an inch and a half taller than Matt, who had been proud when Frank at seventeen outgrew him; he had only felt uncomfortable when he had to reprimand or caution him. He touched Frank's bicep, thought of the young taut passionate body, believed he could sense the desire, and again he felt the pride and sorrow and envy too, not knowing whether he was envious of Frank or Mary Ann.

"When you came in yesterday morning, I woke up. One of these mornings your mother will. And I'm the one who'll have to talk to her. She won't interfere with you. Okay? I know it means—" But he stopped, thinking: I know it means getting up and leaving that suntanned girl and going sleepy to the car, I know—

"Okay," Frank said, and touched Matt's shoulder and got into the car.

There had been other talks, but the only long one was their first one: a night driving to Fenway Park, Matt having ordered the tickets so they could talk, and knowing when Frank said yes, he would go, that he knew the talk was coming too. It took them forty minutes to get to Boston, and they talked about Mary Ann until they joined the city traffic along the Charles River, blue in the late sun. Frank told him all the things that Matt would later pretend to believe when he told them to Ruth.

"It seems like a lot for a young guy to take on," Matt finally said.

"Sometimes it is. But she's worth it."

"Are you thinking about getting married?"

"We haven't talked about it. She can't for over a year. I've got school."

"I *do* like her," Matt said.

He did. Some evenings, when the long summer sun was still low in the sky, Frank brought her home; they came into the house smelling of suntan lotion and the sea, and Matt gave them gin and tonics and started the charcoal in the backyard, and looked at Mary Ann in the lawn chair: long and very light brown hair (Matt thinking that twenty years ago she would have dyed it blonde), and the long brown legs he loved to look at; her face was pretty; she had probably never in her adult life gone unnoticed into a public place. It was in her wide brown eyes that she looked older than Frank; after a few drinks Matt thought what he saw in her eyes was something erotic, testament to the rumors about her; but he knew it wasn't that, or all that: she had, very young, been through a sort of pain that his children, and he and Ruth, had been spared. In the moments of his recognizing that pain, he wanted to tenderly touch her hair, wanted with some gesture to give her solace and hope. And he would glance at Frank, and hope they would love each other, hope Frank would soothe that pain in her heart, take it from her eyes; and her divorce, her age, and her children did not matter at all. On the first two evenings she did not bring her boys, and then Ruth asked her to bring them next time. In bed that night Ruth said, "She hasn't brought them because she's embarrassed. She shouldn't feel embarrassed."

Richard Strout shot Frank in front of the boys. They were sitting on the living room floor watching television, Frank sitting on the couch, and Mary Ann just returning from the kitchen with a tray of sandwiches. Strout came in the front door and shot Frank twice in the chest and once in the face with a 9 mm. automatic. Then he looked at the boys and Mary Ann, and went home to wait for the police.

It seemed to Matt that from the time Mary Ann called weeping to tell him until now, a Saturday night in September, sitting in the car with Willis, parked beside Strout's car, waiting for the bar to close, that he had not so much moved through his life as wandered through it, his spirit like a dazed body bumping into furniture and corners. He had always been a fearful father: when his children were young, at the start of each summer he thought of them drowning in a pond or the sea, and he was relieved when he came home in the evenings and they were there; usually that relief was his only acknowledgment of his fear, which he never spoke of, and which he controlled within his heart. As he had when they were very young and all of them in turn, Cathleen too, were drawn to the high oak in the backyard, and had to climb it. Smiling, he watched them, imagining the fall: and he was poised to catch the small body before it hit the earth. Or his legs were poised; his hands were in his pockets or his arms were folded and, for the child looking down, he appeared relaxed and confident while his heart beat with the two words he wanted to call out but did not: *Don't fall.* In winter he was less afraid: he made sure the ice would hold him before they skated, and he brought or sent them to places where they could sled without ending in the street. So he and his children had survived their childhood, and he only worried about them when he knew they were driving a long distance, and then he lost Frank in a way no father expected to lose his son, and he felt that all the fears he had borne while they were growing up, and all the grief he had been afraid of, had backed up like a huge wave and struck him on the beach and swept him out to sea. Each day he felt the same and when he was able to forget how he felt, when he was able to force himself not to feel that way, the eyes of his clerks and customers defeated him. He wished those eyes were oblivious, even cold; he felt he was withering in their tenderness. And beneath his listless wandering, every day in his soul he shot Richard Strout in the face; while Ruth, going about town on errands, kept seeing him. And at nights in bed she would hold Matt and cry, or sometimes she was silent and Matt would touch her tightening arm, her clenched fist.

As his own right fist was now, squeezing the butt of the revolver, the last of the drinkers having left the bar, talking to each other, going to their separate cars which were in the lot in front of the bar, out of Matt's vision. He heard their voices, their cars, and then the ocean again, across the street. The tide was in and sometimes it smacked the sea wall. Through the windshield he looked at the dark red side wall of the bar, and then to his left, past Willis, at Strout's car, and through its windows he could see the now-emptied parking lot, the road, the sea wall. He could smell the sea.

The front door of the bar opened and closed again and Willis looked at Matt then at the corner of the building; when Strout came around it alone Matt got out of the car, giving up the hope he had kept all night (and for the past week) that Strout would come out with friends, and Willis would simply drive away; thinking: *All right then. All right*; and he went around the front of Willis's car, and at Strout's he stopped and aimed over the hood at Strout's blue shirt ten feet away. Willis was aiming too, crouched on Matt's left, his elbow resting on the hood.

"Mr. Fowler," Strout said. He looked at each of them, and at the guns. "Mr. Trottier."

Then Matt, watching the parking lot and the road, walked quickly between the car and the building and stood behind Strout. He took one leather glove from his pocket and put it on his left hand.

"Don't talk. Unlock the front and back and get in."

Strout unlocked the front door, reached in and unlocked the

back, then got in, and Matt slid into the backseat, closed the door with his gloved hand, and touched Strout's head once with the muzzle.

"It's cocked. Drive to your house."

When Strout looked over his shoulder to back the car, Matt aimed at his temple and did not look at his eyes.

"Drive slowly," he said. "Don't try to get stopped."

They drove across the empty front lot and onto the road, Willis's headlights shining into the car; then back through town, the sea wall on the left hiding the beach, though far out Matt could see the ocean; he uncocked the revolver; on the right were the places, most with their neon signs off, that did so much business in summer: the lounges and cafés and pizza houses, the street itself empty of traffic, the way he and Willis had known it would be when they decided to take Strout at the bar rather than knock on his door at two o'clock one morning and risk that one insomniac neighbor. Matt had not told Willis he was afraid he could not be alone with Strout for very long, smell his smells, feel the presence of his flesh, hear his voice, and then shoot him. They left the beach town and then were on the high bridge over the channel: to the left the smacking curling white at the breakwater and beyond that the dark sea and the full moon, and down to his right the small fishing boats bobbing at anchor in the cove. When they left the bridge, the sea was blocked by abandoned beach cottages, and Matt's left hand was sweating in the glove. Out here in the dark in the car he believed Ruth knew. Willis had come to his house at eleven and asked if he wanted a nightcap; Matt went to the bedroom for his wallet, put the gloves in one trouser pocket and the .38 in the other and went back to the living room, his hand in his pocket covering the bulge of the cool cylinder pressed against his fingers, the butt against his palm. When Ruth said good night she looked at his face, and he felt she could see in his eyes the gun, and the night he was going to. But he knew he couldn't trust what he saw. Willis's wife had taken her sleeping pill, which gave her eight hours—the reason, Willis had told Matt, he had the alarms installed, for nights when he was late at the restaurant—and when it was all done and Willis got home he would leave ice and a trace of scotch and soda in two glasses in the game room and tell Martha in the morning that he had left the restaurant early and brought Matt home for a drink.

"He was making it with my wife." Strout's voice was careful, not pleading.

Matt pressed the muzzle against Strout's head, pressed it harder than he wanted to, feeling through the gun Strout's head flinching and moving forward; then he lowered the gun to his lap.

"Don't talk," he said.

Strout did not speak again. They turned west, drove past the Dairy Queen closed until spring, and the two lobster restaurants that faced each other and were crowded all summer and were now also closed, onto the short bridge crossing the tidal stream, and over the engine Matt could hear through his open window the water rushing inland under the bridge; looking to his left he saw its swift moonlit current going back into the marsh which, leaving the bridge, they entered: the salt marsh stretching out on both sides, the grass tall in patches but mostly low and leaning earth-ward as though windblown, a large dark rock sitting as though it rested on nothing but itself, and shallow pools reflecting the bright moon.

Beyond the marsh they drove through woods, Matt thinking now of the hole he and Willis had dug last Sunday afternoon after telling their wives they were going to Fenway Park. They listened to the game on a transistor radio, but heard none of it as they dug into the soft earth on the knoll they had chosen because elms and maples sheltered it. Already some leaves had fallen. When the hole was deep enough they covered it and the piled earth with dead branches, then cleaned their shoes and pants and went to a restau-rant farther up in New Hampshire where they ate sandwiches and drank beer and watched the rest of the game on television. Looking at the back of Strout's head he thought of Frank's grave; he had not been back to it; but he would go before winter, and its second burial of snow.

He thought of Frank sitting on the couch and perhaps talking to the children as they watched television, imagined him feeling young and strong, still warmed from the sun at the beach, and feeling loved, hearing Mary Ann moving about in the kitchen, hearing her walking into the living room; maybe he looked up at her and maybe she said something, looking at him over the tray of sandwiches, smiling at him, saying something the way women do when they offer food as a gift, then the front door opening and this son of a bitch coming in and Frank seeing that he meant the gun in his hand, this son of a bitch and his gun the last person and thing Frank saw on earth.

When they drove into town the streets were nearly empty: a few slow cars, a policeman walking his beat past the darkened fronts of stores. Strout and Matt both glanced at him as they drove by. They were on the main street, and all the stoplights were blinking yellow. Willis and Matt had talked about that too: the lights changed at midnight, so there would be no place Strout had to stop and where he might try to run. Strout turned down the block where he lived and Willis's headlights were no longer with Matt in the backseat. They had planned that too, had decided it was best for just the one car to go to the house, and again Matt had said nothing about his fear of being alone with Strout, especially in his house: a duplex, dark as all the houses on the street were, the street itself lit at the corner of each block. As Strout turned into the driveway Matt thought of the one insomniac neighbor, thought of some man or woman sitting alone in the dark living room, watching the all-night channel from Boston. When Strout stopped the car near the front of the house, Matt said: "Drive it to the back."

He touched Strout's head with the muzzle.

"You wouldn't have it cocked, would you? For when I put on the brakes."

Matt cocked it, and said: "It is now."

Strout waited a moment, then he eased the car forward, the engine doing little more than idling, and as they approached the garage he gently braked. Matt opened the door, then took off the glove and put it in his pocket. He stepped out and shut the door with his hip and said: "All right."

Strout looked at the gun, then got out, and Matt followed him across the grass, and as Strout unlocked the door Matt looked quickly at the row of small backyards on either side, and scattered tall trees, some evergreens, others not, and he thought of the red and yellow leaves on the trees over the hole, saw them falling soon, probably in two weeks, dropping slowly, covering. Strout stepped into the kitchen.

"Turn on the light."

Strout reached to the wall switch, and in the light Matt looked at his wide back, the dark blue shirt, the white belt, the red plaid pants.

"Where's your suitcase?"

"My suitcase?"

"Where is it."

"In the bedroom closet."

"That's where we're going then. When we get to a door you stop and turn on the light."

They crossed the kitchen, Matt glancing at the sink and stove and refrigerator: no dishes in the sink or even the dish rack beside it, no grease splashings on the stove, the refrigerator door clean and white. He did not want to look at any more but he looked quickly at all he could see: in the living room magazines and newspapers in a wicker basket, clean ashtrays, a record player, the records shelved next to it, then down the hall where, near the bedroom door, hung a color photograph of Mary Ann and the two boys sitting on a lawn—there was no house in the picture— Mary Ann smiling at the camera or Strout or whoever held the camera, smiling as she had on Matt's lawn this summer while he waited for the charcoal and they all talked and he looked at her brown legs and at Frank touching her arm, her shoulder, her hair;

he moved down the hall with her smile in his mind, wondering: was that when they were both playing around and she was smiling like that at him and they were happy, even sometimes, making it worth it? He recalled her eyes, the pain in them, and he was conscious of the circles of love he was touching with the hand that held the revolver so tightly now as Strout stopped at the door at the end of the hall.

"There's no wall switch."

"Where's the light?"

"By the bed."

"Let's go."

Matt stayed a pace behind, then Strout leaned over and the room was lighted: the bed, a double one, was neatly made; the ashtray on the bedside table clean, the bureau top dustless, and no photographs; probably so the girl—who *was* she?—would not have to see Mary Ann in the bedroom she believed was theirs. But because Matt was a father and a husband, though never an ex-husband, he knew (and did not want to know) that this bedroom had never been theirs alone. Strout turned around; Matt looked at his lips, his wide jaw, and thought of Frank's doomed and fearful eyes looking up from the couch.

"Where's Mr. Trottier?"

"He's waiting. Pack clothes for warm weather."

"What's going on?"

"You're jumping bail."

"Mr. Fowler—"

He pointed the cocked revolver at Strout's face. The barrel trembled but not much, not as much as he had expected. Strout went to the closet and got the suitcase from the floor and opened it on the bed. As he went to the bureau, he said: "He was making it with my wife. I'd go pick up my kids and he'd be there. Sometimes he spent the night. My boys told me."

He did not look at Matt as he spoke. He opened the top drawer and Matt stepped closer so he could see Strout's hands: underwear and socks, the socks rolled, the underwear folded and stacked. He took them back to the bed, arranged them neatly in the suitcase, then from the closet he was taking shirts and trousers and a jacket; he laid them on the bed and Matt followed him to the bathroom and watched from the door while he packed his shaving kit; watched in the bedroom as he folded and packed those things a person accumulated and that became part of him so that at times in the store Matt felt he was selling more than clothes.

"I wanted to try to get together with her again." He was bent over the suitcase. "I couldn't even talk to her. He was always with her. I'm going to jail for it; if I ever get out I'll be an old man. Isn't that enough?"

"You're not going to jail."

Strout closed the suitcase and faced Matt, looking at the gun. Matt went to his rear, so Strout was between him and the lighted hall; then using his handkerchief he turned off the lamp and said: "Let's go."

They went down the hall, Matt looking again at the photograph, and through the living room and kitchen, Matt turning off the lights and talking, frightened that he was talking, that he was telling this lie he had not planned: "It's the trial. We can't go through that, my wife and me. So you're leaving. We've got you a ticket, and a job. A friend of Mr. Trottier's. Out west. My wife keeps seeing you. We can't have that anymore."

Matt turned out the kitchen light and put the handkerchief in his pocket, and they went down the two brick steps and across the lawn. Strout put the suitcase on the floor of the backseat, then got into the front seat and Matt got in the back and put on his glove and shut the door.

"They'll catch me: They'll check passenger lists."

"We didn't use your name."

"They'll figure that out too. You think I wouldn't have done it myself if it was that easy?"

He backed into the street, Matt looking down the gun barrel but not at the profiled face beyond it.

"You were alone," Matt said. "We've got it worked out."

"There's no planes this time of night, Mr. Fowler."

"Go back through town. Then north on 125."

They came to the corner and turned, and now Willis's headlights were in the car with Matt.

"Why north, Mr. Fowler?"

"Somebody's going to keep you for a while. They'll take you to the airport." He uncocked the hammer and lowered the revolver to his lap and said wearily: "No more talking."

As they drove back through town, Matt's body sagged, going limp with his spirit and its new and false bond with Strout, the hope his lie had given Strout. He had grown up in this town whose streets had become places of apprehension and pain for Ruth as she drove and walked, doing what she had to do; and for him too, if only in his mind as he worked and chatted six days a week in his store; he wondered now if his lie would have worked, if sending Strout away would have been enough; but then he knew that just thinking of Strout in Montana or whatever place lay at the end of the lie he had told, thinking of him walking the streets there, loving a girl there (who *was* she?) would be enough to slowly rot the rest of his days. And Ruth's. Again he was certain that she knew, that she was waiting for him.

They were in New Hampshire now, on the narrow highway, passing the shopping center at the state line, and then houses and small stores and sandwich shops. There were few cars on the road. After ten minutes he raised his trembling hand, touched Strout's neck with the gun, and said: "Turn in up here. At the dirt road."

Strout flicked on the indicator and slowed.

"Mr. Fowler?"

"They're waiting here."

Strout turned very slowly, easing his neck away from the gun. In the moonlight the road was light brown, lighter and yellowed where the headlights shone; weeds and a few trees grew on either side of it, and ahead of them were the woods.

"There's nothing back here, Mr. Fowler."

"It's for your car. You don't think we'd leave it at the airport, do you?"

He watched Strout's large, big-knuckled hands tighten on the wheel, saw Frank's face that night: not the stitches and bruised eye and swollen lips, but his own hand gently touching Frank's jaw, turning his wounds to the light. They rounded a bend in the road and were out of sight of the highway: tall trees all around them now, hiding the moon. When they reached the abandoned gravel pit on the left, the bare flat earth and steep pale embankment behind it, and the black crowns of trees at its top, Matt said: "Stop here."

Strout stopped but did not turn off the engine. Matt pressed the gun hard against his neck, and he straightened in the seat and looked in the rearview mirror, Matt's eyes meeting his in the glass for an instant before looking at the hair at the end of the gun barrel.

"Turn it off."

Strout did, then held the wheel with two hands, and looked in the mirror.

"I'll do twenty years, Mr. Fowler; at least. I'll be forty-six years old."

"That's nine years younger than I am," Matt said, and got out and took off the glove and kicked the door shut. He aimed at Strout's ear and pulled back the hammer. Willis's headlights were off and Matt heard him walking on the soft thin layer of dust, the hard earth beneath it. Strout opened the door, sat for a moment in the interior light, then stepped out onto the road. Now his face was pleading. Matt did not look at his eyes, but he could see it in the lips.

"Just get the suitcase. They're right up the road."

Willis was beside him now, to his left. Strout looked at both guns. Then he opened the back door, leaned in, and with a jerk brought the suitcase out. He was turning to face them when Matt said: "Just walk up the road. Just ahead."

Strout turned to walk, the suitcase in his right hand, and Matt and Willis followed; as Strout cleared the front of his car he dropped the suitcase and, ducking, took one step that was the beginning of a sprint to his right. The gun kicked in Matt's hand, and the explosion of the shot surrounded him, isolated him in a nimbus of sound that cut him off from all his time, all his history, isolated him standing absolutely still on the dirt road with the gun in his hand, looking down at Richard Strout squirming on his belly, kicking one leg behind him, pushing himself forward, toward the woods. Then Matt went to him and shot him once in the back of the head.

Driving south to Boston, wearing both gloves now, staying in the middle lane and looking often in the rearview mirror at Willis's headlights, he relived the suitcase dropping, the quick dip and turn of Strout's back, and the kick of the gun, the sound of the shot. When he walked to Strout, he still existed within the first shot, still trembled and breathed with it. The second shot and the burial seemed to be happening to someone else, someone he was watching. He and Willis each held an arm and pulled Strout facedown off the road and into the woods, his bouncing sliding belt white under the trees where it was so dark that when they stopped at the top of the knoll, panting and sweating, Matt could not see where Strout's blue shirt ended and the earth began. They pulled off the branches then dragged Strout to the edge of the hole and went behind him and lifted his legs and pushed him in. They stood still for a moment. The woods were quiet save for their breathing, and Matt remembered hearing the movements of birds and small animals after the first shot. Or maybe he had not heard them. Willis went down to the road. Matt could see him clearly out on the tan dirt, could see the glint of Strout's car and, beyond the road, the gravel pit. Willis came back up the knoll with the suitcase. He dropped it in the hole and took off his gloves and they went down to his car for the spades. They worked quietly. Sometimes they paused to listen to the woods. When they were finished Willis turned on his flashlight and they covered the earth with leaves and branches and then went down to the spot in front of the car, and while Matt held the light Willis crouched and sprinkled dust on the blood, backing up till he reached the grass and leaves, then he used leaves until they had worked up to the grave again. They did not stop. They walked around the grave and through the woods, using the light on the ground, looking up through the trees to where they ended at the lake. Neither of them spoke above the sounds of their heavy and clumsy strides through low brush and over fallen branches. Then they reached it: wide and dark, lapping softly at the bank, pine needles smooth under Matt's feet, moon-light on the lake, a small island near its middle, with black, tall evergreens. He took out the gun and threw for the island: taking two steps back on the pine needles, striding with the throw and going to one knee as he followed through, looking up to see the dark shapeless object arcing downward, splashing.

They left Strout's car in Boston, in front of an apartment building on Commonwealth Avenue. When they got back to town Willis drove slowly over the bridge and Matt threw the keys into the Merrimack. The sky was turning light. Willis let him out a block from his house, and walking home he listened for sounds from the houses he passed. They were quiet. A light was on in his living room. He turned it off and undressed in there, and went softly toward the bedroom; in the hall he smelled the smoke, and he stood in the bedroom doorway and looked at the orange of her cigarette in the dark. The curtains were closed. He went to the closet and put his shoes on the floor and felt for a hanger.

"Did you do it?" she said.

He went down the hall to the bathroom and in the dark he washed his hands and face. Then he went to her, lay on his back, and pulled the sheet up to his throat.

"Are you all right?" she said.

"I think so."

Now she touched him, lying on her side, her hand on his belly, his thigh.

"Tell me," she said.

He started from the beginning, in the parking lot at the bar; but soon with his eyes closed and Ruth petting him, he spoke of Strout's house: the order, the woman presence, the picture on the wall.

"The way she was smiling," he said.

"What about it?"

"I don't know. Did you ever see Strout's girl? When you saw him in town?"

"No."

"I wonder who she was."

Then he thought: *not was: is. Sleeping now she is his girl.* He opened his eyes, then closed them again. There was more light beyond the curtains. With Ruth now he left Strout's house and told again his lie to Strout, gave him again that hope that Strout must have for a while believed, else he would have to believe only the gun pointed at him for the last two hours of his life. And with Ruth he saw again the dropping suitcase, the darting move to the right: and he told of the first shot, feeling her hand on him but his heart isolated still, beating on the road still in that explosion like thunder. He told her the rest, but the words had no images for him, he did not see himself doing what the words said he had done; he only saw himself on that road.

"We can't tell the other kids," she said. "It'll hurt them, thinking he got away. But we mustn't."

"No."

She was holding him, wanting him, and he wished he could make love with her but he could not. He saw Frank and Mary Ann making love in her bed, their eyes closed, their bodies brown and smelling of the sea; the other girl was faceless, bodiless, but he felt her sleeping now; and he saw Frank and Strout, their faces alive; he saw red and yellow leaves falling to the earth, then snow: falling and freezing and falling; and holding Ruth, his cheek touching her breast, he shuddered with a sob that he kept silent in his heart.

GRACE PALEY # FRIENDS

TO PUT US at our ease, to quiet our hearts as she lay dying, our dear friend Selena said, Life, after all, has not been an unrelieved horror—you know, I *did* have many wonderful years with her.

She pointed to a child who leaned out of a portrait on the wall—long brown hair, white pinafore, head and shoulders forward.

Eagerness, said Susan. Ann closed her eyes.

On the same wall three little girls were photographed in a schoolyard. They were in furious discussion; they were holding hands. Right in the middle of the coffee table, framed, in autumn colors, a handsome young woman of eighteen sat on an enormous horse—aloof, disinterested, a rider. One night this young woman, Selena's child, was found in a rooming house in a distant city, dead. The police called. They said, Do you have a daughter named Abby?

And with *him*, too, our friend Selena said. We had good times, Max and I. You know that.

There were no photographs of *him*. He was married to another woman and had a new, stalwart girl of about six, to whom no harm would ever come, her mother believed.

Our dear Selena had gotten out of bed. Heavily but with a comic dance, she soft-shoed to the bathroom, singing, "Those were the days, my friend . . ."

Later that evening, Ann, Susan, and I were enduring our five-hour train ride to home. After one hour of silence and one hour of coffee and the sandwiches Selena had given us (she actually stood, leaned her big soft excavated body against the kitchen table to make those sandwiches), Ann said, Well, we'll never see *her* again.

Who says? Anyway, listen, said Susan. Think of it. Abby isn't the only kid who died. What about that great guy, remember Bill Dalrymple—he was a noncooperator or a deserter? And Bob Simon. They were killed in automobile accidents. Matthew, Jeannie, Mike. Remember Al Lurie—he was murdered on Sixth Street—and that little kid Brenda, who O.D.'d on your roof, Ann? The tendency, I suppose, is to forget. You people don't remember them.

What do you mean, "you people"? Ann asked. You're talking to *us*.

I began to apologize for not knowing them all. Most of them were older than my kids, I said.

Of course, the child Abby was exactly in my time of knowing and in all my places of paying attention—the park, the school, our street. But oh! It's true! Selena's Abby was not the only one of that beloved generation of our children murdered by cars, lost to war, to drugs, to madness.

Selena's main problem, Ann said—you know, she didn't tell the truth.

What?

A few hot human truthful words are powerful enough, Ann thinks, to steam all God's chemical mistakes and society's slimy lies out of her life. We all believe in that power, my friends and I, but sometimes . . . the heat.

Anyway, I always thought Selena had told us a lot. For instance, we knew she was an orphan. There were six, seven other children.

She was the youngest. She was forty-two years old before someone informed her that her mother had *not* died in childbirthing her. It was some terrible sickness. And she had lived close to her mother's body—at her breast, in fact—until she was eight months old. Whew! said Selena. What a relief! I'd always felt I was the one who'd killed her.

Your family stinks, we told her. They really held you up for grief.

Oh, people, she said. Forget it. They did a lot of nice things for me too. Me and Abby. Forget it. Who has the time?

That's what I mean, said Ann. Selena should have gone after them with an ax.

More information: Selena's two sisters brought her to a Home. They were ashamed that at sixteen and nineteen they could not take care of her. They kept hugging her. They were sure she'd cry. They took her to her room—not a room, a dormitory with about eight beds. This is your bed, Lena. This is your table for your things. This little drawer is for your toothbrush. All for me? she asked. No one else can use it? Only me. That's all? Artie can't come? Franky can't come? Right?

Believe me, Selena said, those were happy days at Home.

Facts, said Ann, just facts. Not necessarily the *truth*.

I don't think it's right to complain about the character of the dying or start hustling all their motives into the spotlight like that. Isn't it amazing enough, the bravery of that private inclusive intentional community?

It wouldn't help not to be brave, said Selena. You'll see.

She wanted to get back to bed. Susan moved to help her.

Thanks, our Selena said, leaning on another person for the first time in her entire life. The trouble is, when I stand, it hurts me here all down my back. Nothing they can do about it. All the chemotherapy. No more chemistry left in me to therapeut. Ha! Did you know before I came to New York and met you I used to work in that hospital? I was supervisor in gynecology. Nursing. They were my friends, the doctors. They weren't so snotty then.

David Clark, big surgeon. He couldn't look at me last week. He kept saying, Lena . . . Lena . . . Like that. We were in North Africa the same year—'44, I think. I told him, Davy, I've been around a long enough time. I haven't missed too much. He knows it. But I didn't want to make him look at me. Ugh, my damn feet are a pain in the neck.

Recent research, said Susan, tells us that it's the neck that's a pain in the feet.

Always something new, said Selena, our dear friend.

On the way back to the bed, she stopped at her desk. There were about twenty snapshots scattered across it—the baby, the child, the young woman. Here, she said to me, take this one. It's a shot of Abby and your Richard in front of the school—third grade? What a day! The show those kids put on! What a bunch of kids! What's Richard doing now?

Oh, who knows? Horsing around someplace. Spain. These days, it's Spain. Who knows where he is? They're all the same.

Why did I say that? I knew exactly where he was. He writes. In fact, he found a broken phone and was able to call every day for a week—mostly to give orders to his brother but also to say, Are you O.K., Ma? How's your new boyfriend, did he smile yet?

The kids, they're all the same, I said.

It was only politeness, I think, not to pour my boy's light, noisy face into that dark afternoon. Richard used to say in his early mean teens, You'd sell us down the river to keep Selena happy and innocent. It's true. Whenever Selena would say, I don't know, Abby has some peculiar friends, I'd answer for stupid comfort, You should see Richard's.

Still, he's in Spain, Selena said. At least you know that. It's probably interesting. He'll learn a lot. Richard is a wonderful boy, Faith. He acts like a wise guy but he's not. You know the night Abby died, when the police called me and told me? That was my first night's sleep in two years. I *knew* where she was.

Selena said this very matter-of-factly—just offering a few informative sentences.

But Ann, listening, said, Oh!—she called out to us all, Oh!—
and began to sob. Her straightforwardness had become an arrow
and gone right into her own heart.

Then a deep tear-drying breath: I want a picture too, she said.

Yes. Yes, wait, I have one here someplace. Abby and Judy and
that Spanish kid Victor. Where is it? Ah. Here!

Three nine-year-old children sat high on that long-armed sycamore in the park, dangling their legs on someone's patient head—
smooth dark hair, parted in the middle. Was that head Kitty's?

Our dear friend laughed. Another great day, she said. Wasn't
it? I remember you two sizing up the men. I *had* one at the time—
I thought. Some joke. Here, take it. I have two copies. But you
ought to get it enlarged. When this you see, remember me. Ha-
ha. Well, girls—excuse me, I mean ladies—it's time for me to rest.

She took Susan's arm and continued that awful walk to her bed.

We didn't move. We had a long journey ahead of us and had
expected a little more comforting before we set off.

No, she said. You'll only miss the express. I'm not in much
pain. I've got lots of painkiller. See?

The tabletop was full of little bottles.

I just want to lie down and think of Abby.

It was true, the local could cost us an extra two hours at least.
I looked at Ann. It had been hard for her to come at all. Still, we
couldn't move. We stood there before Selena in a row. Three old
friends. Selena pressed her lips together, ordered her eyes into cold
distance.

I know that face. Once, years ago, when the children were
children, it had been placed modestly in front of J. Hoffner, the
principal of the elementary school.

He'd said, No! Without training you cannot tutor these kids.
There are real problems. You have to know *how to teach*.

Our P.T.A. had decided to offer some one-to-one tutorial help
for the Spanish kids, who were stuck in crowded classrooms with
exhausted teachers among little middle-class achievers. He had
said, in a written communication to show seriousness and then in

personal confrontation to *prove* seriousness, that he could not allow it. And the board of ed itself had said no. (All this no-ness was to lead to some terrible events in the schools and neighborhoods of our poor yes-requiring city.) But most of the women in our P.T.A. were independent—by necessity and disposition. We were, in fact, the soft-speaking tough souls of anarchy.

I had Fridays off that year. At about 11 A.M. I'd bypass the principal's office and run up to the fourth floor. I'd take Robert Figueroa to the end of the hall, and we'd work away at storytelling for about twenty minutes. Then we would write the beautiful letters of the alphabet invented by smart foreigners long ago to fool time and distance.

That day, Selena and her stubborn face remained in the office for at least two hours. Finally, Mr. Hoffner, besieged, said that because she was a nurse, she would be allowed to help out by taking the littlest children to the modern difficult toilet. Some of them, he said, had just come from the barbarous hills beyond Maricao. Selena said O.K., she'd do that. In the toilet she taught the little girls which way to wipe, as she had taught her own little girl a couple of years earlier. At three o'clock she brought them home for cookies and milk. The children of that year ate cookies in her kitchen until the end of the sixth grade.

Now, what did we learn in that year of my Friday afternoons off? The following: Though the world cannot be changed by talking to one child at a time, it may at least be known.

Anyway, Selena placed into our eyes for long remembrance that useful stubborn face. She said, No. Listen to me, you people. Please. I don't have lots of time. What I want . . . I want to lie down and think about Abby. Nothing special. Just think about her, you know.

In the train Susan fell asleep immediately. She woke up from time to time, because the speed of the new wheels and the resistance of the old track gave us some terrible jolts. Once, she opened her eyes wide and said, You know, Ann's right. You don't get sick like that for nothing. I mean, she didn't even mention him.

Why should she? She hasn't even seen him, I said. Susan, you still have him-itis, the dread disease of females.

Yeah? And you don't? Anyway, he *was* around quite a bit. He was there every day, nearly, when the kid died.

Abby. I didn't like to hear "the kid." I wanted to say "Abby" the way I've said "Selena"—so those names can take thickness and strength and fall back into the world with their weight.

Abby, you know, was a wonderful child. She was in Richard's classes every class till high school. Good-hearted little girl from the beginning, noticeably kind—for a kid, I mean. Smart.

That's true, said Ann, very kind. She'd give away Selena's last shirt. Oh yes, they were all wonderful little girls and wonderful little boys.

Chrissy *is* wonderful, Susan said.

She *is*, I said.

Middle kids aren't supposed to be, but she is. She put herself through college—I didn't have a cent—and now she has this fellowship. And, you know, she never did take any crap from boys. She's something.

Ann went swaying up the aisle to the bathroom. First she said, Oh, all of them—just wohunderful.

I loved Selena, Susan said, but she never talked to me enough. Maybe she talked to you women more, about things. Men.

Then Susan fell asleep.

Ann sat down opposite me. She looked straight into my eyes with a narrow squint. It often connotes accusation.

Be careful—you're wrecking your laugh lines, I said.

Screw you, she said. You're kidding around. Do you realize I don't know where Mickey is? You know, you've been lucky. You always have been. Since you were a little kid. Papa and Mama's darling.

As is usual in conversations, I said a couple of things out loud and kept a few structured remarks for interior mulling and righteousness. I thought: She's never even met my folks. I thought: What a rotten thing to say. Luck—isn't it something like an insult?

I said, Annie, I'm only forty-eight. There's lots of time for me to be totally wrecked—if I live, I mean.

Then I tried to knock wood, but we were sitting in plush and leaning on plastic. Wood! I shouted. Please, some wood! Anybody here have a matchstick?

Oh, shut up, she said. Anyway, death doesn't count.

I tried to think of a couple of sorrows as irreversible as death. But truthfully nothing in my life can compare to hers: a son, a boy of fifteen, who disappears before your very eyes into a darkness or a light behind his own, from which neither hugging nor hitting can bring him. If you shout, Come back, come back, he won't come. Mickey, Mickey, Mickey, we once screamed, as though he were twenty miles away instead of right in front of us in a kitchen chair; but he refused to return. And when he did, twelve hours later, he left immediately for California.

Well, some bad things have happened in my life, I said.

What? You were born a woman? Is that it?

She was, of course, mocking me this time, referring to an old discussion about feminism and Judaism. Actually, on the prism of isms, both of those do have to be looked at together once in a while.

Well, I said, my mother died a couple of years ago and I still feel it. I think *Ma* sometimes and I lose my breath. I miss her. You understand that. Your mother's seventy-six. You have to admit it's nice still having her.

She's very sick, Ann said. Half the time she's out of it.

I decided not to describe my mother's death. I could have done so and made Ann even more miserable. But I thought I'd save that for her next attack on me. These constrictions of her spirit were coming closer and closer together. Probably a great anxiety was about to be born.

Susan's eyes opened. The death or dying of someone near or

dear often makes people irritable, she stated. (She's been taking a course in relationships *and* interrelationships.) The real name of my seminar is Skills: Personal Friendship and Community. It's a very good course despite your snide remarks.

While we talked, a number of cities passed us, going in the opposite direction. I had tried to look at New London through the dusk of the windows. Now I was missing New Haven. The conductor explained, smiling: Lady, if the windows were clean, half of you'd be dead. The tracks are lined with sharpshooters.

Do you believe that? I hate people to talk that way.

He may be exaggerating, Susan said, but don't wash the window.

A man leaned across the aisle. Ladies, he said, I do believe it. According to what I hear of this part of the country, it don't seem unplausible.

Susan turned to see if he was worth engaging in political dialogue.

You've forgotten Selena already, Ann said. All of us have. Then you'll make this nice memorial service for her and everyone will stand up and say a few words and then we'll forget her again— for good. What'll you say at the memorial, Faith?

It's not right to talk like that. She's not dead yet, Annie.

Yes, she is, said Ann.

We discovered the next day that give or take an hour or two, Ann had been correct. It was a combination—David Clark, surgeon, said—of being sick unto real death and having a tabletop full of little bottles.

Now, why are you taking all those hormones? Susan had asked Selena a couple of years earlier. They were visiting New Orleans. It was Mardi Gras.

Oh, they're mostly vitamins, Selena said. Besides, I want to be young and beautiful. She made a joking pirouette.

Susan said, That's absolutely ridiculous.

But Susan's seven or eight years younger than Selena. What did she know? Because: People *do* want to be young and beautiful. When they meet in the street, male or female, if they're getting older they look at each other's face a little ashamed. It's clear they want to say, Excuse me, I didn't mean to draw attention to mortality and gravity all at once. I didn't want to remind you, my dear friend, of our coming eviction, first from liveliness, then from life. To which, most of the time, the friend's eyes will courteously reply, My dear, it's nothing at all. I hardly noticed.

Luckily, I learned recently how to get out of that deep well of melancholy. Anyone can do it. You grab at roots of the littlest future, sometimes just stubs of conversation. Though some believe you miss a great deal of depth by not sinking down down down.

Susan, I asked, you still seeing Ed Flores?

Went back to his wife.

Lucky she didn't kill you, said Ann. I'd never fool around with a Spanish guy. They all have tough ladies back in the barrio.

No, said Susan, she's unusual. I met her at a meeting. We had an amazing talk. Luisa is a very fine woman. She's one of the office-worker organizers I told you about. She only needs him two more years, she says. Because the kids—they're girls—need to be watched a little in their neighborhood. The neighborhood is definitely not good. He's a good father but not such a great husband.

I'd call that a word to the wise.

Well, you know me—I don't want a husband. I like a male person around. I hate to do without. Anyway, listen to this. She, Luisa, whispers in my ear the other day, she whispers, Suzie, in two years you still want him, I promise you, you got him. Really, I may still want him then. He's only about forty-five now. Still got a lot of spunk. I'll have my degree in two years. Chrissy will be out of the house.

Two years! In two years we'll all be dead, said Ann.

I know she didn't mean all of us. She meant Mickey. That boy of hers would surely be killed in one of the drugstores or whorehouses of Chicago, New Orleans, San Francisco. I'm in a big beautiful city, he said when he called last month. Makes New York look like a garbage tank.

Mickey! Where?

Ha-ha, he said, and hung up.

Soon he'd be picked up for vagrancy, dealing, small thievery, or simply screaming dirty words at night under a citizen's window. Then Ann would fly to the town or not fly to the town to disentangle him, depending on a confluence of financial reality and psychiatric advice.

How *is* Mickey? Selena had said. In fact, that was her first sentence when we came, solemn and embarrassed, into her sunny front room that was full of the light and shadow of windy courtyard trees. We said, each in her own way, How are you feeling, Selena? She said, O.K., first things first. Let's talk about important things. How's Richard? How's Tonto? How's John? How's Chrissy? How's Judy? How's Mickey?

I don't want to talk about Mickey, said Ann.

Oh, let's talk about him, talk about him, Selena said, taking Ann's hand. Let's all think before it's too late. How did it start? Oh, for godsake talk about him.

Susan and I were smart enough to keep our mouths shut.

Nobody knows, nobody knows anything. Why? Where? Everybody has an idea, theories, and writes articles. Nobody knows.

Ann said this sternly. She didn't whine. She wouldn't lean too far into Selena's softness, but listening to Selena speak Mickey's name, she could sit in her chair more easily. I watched. It was interesting. Ann breathed deeply in and out the way we've learned in our Thursday-night yoga class. She was able to rest her body a little bit.

We were riding the rails of the trough called Park-Avenue-in-the-Bronx. Susan had turned from us to talk to the man across the aisle. She was explaining that the war in Vietnam was not yet over and would not be, as far as she was concerned, until we repaired the dikes we'd bombed and paid for some of the hopeless ecological damage. He didn't see it that way. Fifty thousand American lives, our own boys—we'd paid, he said. He asked us if we agreed with Susan. Every word, we said.

You don't look like hippies. He laughed. Then his face changed. As the resident face-reader, I decided he was thinking: Adventure. He may have hit a mother lode of late counterculture in three opinionated left-wing ladies. That was the nice part of his face. The other part was the sly out-of-town-husband-in-New-York look.

I'd like to see you again, he said to Susan.

Oh? Well, come to dinner day after tomorrow. Only two of my kids will be home. You ought to have at least one decent meal in New York.

Kids? His face thought it over. Thanks. Sure, he said. I'll come.

Ann muttered, She's impossible. She did it again.

Oh, Susan's O.K., I said. She's just right in there. Isn't that good?

This is a long ride, said Ann.

Then we were in the darkness that precedes Grand Central.

We're irritable, Susan explained to her new pal. We're angry with our friend Selena for dying. The reason is, we want her to be present when we're dying. We all require a mother or mother-surrogate to fix our pillows on that final occasion, and we were counting on her to be that person.

I know just what you mean, he said. You'd like to have someone around. A little fuss, maybe.

Something like that. Right, Faith?

It always takes me a minute to slide under the style of her public-address system. I agreed. Yes.

The train stopped hard, in a grinding agony of opposing technologies.

Right. Wrong. Who cares? Ann said. She didn't have to die. She really wrecked everything.

Oh, Annie, I said.

Shut up, will you? Both of you, said Ann, nearly breaking our knees as she jammed past us and out of the train.

Then Susan, like a New York hostess, began to tell that man all our private troubles—the mistake of the World Trade Center,

Westway, the decay of the South Bronx, the rage in Williamsburg. She rose with him on the escalator, gabbing into evening friendship and, hopefully, a happy night.

At home Anthony, my youngest son, said, Hello, you just missed Richard. He's in Paris now. He had to call collect.

Collect? From Paris?

He saw my sad face and made one of the herb teas used by his peer group to calm their overwrought natures. He does want to improve my pretty good health and spirits. His friends have a book that says a person should, if properly nutritioned, live forever. He wants me to give it a try. He also believes that the human race, its brains and good looks, will end in his time.

At about 11:30 he went out to live the pleasures of his eighteen-year-old nighttime life.

At 3 A.M. he found me washing the floors and making little apartment repairs.

More tea, Mom? he asked. He sat down to keep me company. O.K., Faith. I know you feel terrible. But how come Selena never realized about Abby?

Anthony, what the hell do I realize about you?

Come on, you had to be blind. I was just a little kid, and *I* saw. Honest to God, Ma.

Listen, Tonto. Basically Abby was O.K. She was. You don't know yet what their times can do to a person.

Here she goes with her goody-goodies—everything is so groovy wonderful far-out terrific. Next thing, you'll say people are darling and the world is *so* nice and round that Union Carbide will never blow it up.

I have never said anything as hopeful as that. And why to all our knowledge of that sad day did Tonto at 3 A.M. have to add the fact of the world?

The next night Max called from North Carolina. How's Selena? I'm flying up, he said. I have one early morning appointment. Then I'm canceling everything.

At 7 A.M. Annie called. I had barely brushed my morning teeth. It was hard, she said. The whole damn thing. I don't mean Selena. All of us. In the train. None of you seemed real to me.

Real? Reality, huh? Listen, how about coming over for breakfast?—I don't have to get going until after nine. I have this neat sourdough rye?

No, she said. Oh Christ, no. No!

I remember Ann's eyes and the hat she wore the day we first looked at each other. Our babies had just stepped howling out of the sandbox on their new walking legs. We picked them up. Over their sandy heads we smiled. I think a bond was sealed then, at least as useful as the vow we'd all sworn with husbands to whom we're no longer married. Hindsight, usually looked down upon, is probably as valuable as foresight, since it does include a few facts.

Meanwhile, Anthony's world—poor, dense, defenseless thing—rolls round and round. Living and dying are fastened to its surface and stuffed into its softer parts.

He was right to call my attention to its suffering and danger. He was right to harass my responsible nature. But I was right to invent for my friends and our children a report on these private deaths and the condition of our lifelong attachments.

CYNTHIA OZICK | # THE SHAWL

STELLA, cold, cold, the coldness of hell. How they walked on the roads together, Rosa with Magda curled up between sore breasts, Magda wound up in the shawl. Sometimes Stella carried Magda. But she was jealous of Magda. A thin girl of fourteen, too small, with thin breasts of her own, Stella wanted to be wrapped in a shawl, hidden away, asleep, rocked by the march, a baby, a round infant in arms. Magda took Rosa's nipple, and Rosa never stopped walking, a walking cradle. There was not enough milk; sometimes Magda sucked air; then she screamed. Stella was ravenous. Her knees were tumors on sticks, her elbows chicken bones.

Rosa did not feel hunger; she felt light, not like someone walking but like someone in a faint, in trance, arrested in a fit, someone who is already a floating angel, alert and seeing everything, but in the air, not there, not touching the road. As if teetering on the tips of her fingernails. She looked into Magda's face through a gap in the shawl; a squirrel in a nest, safe, no one could reach her inside the little house of the shawl's windings. The face, very round, a pocket mirror of a face: but it was not Rosa's bleak complexion, dark like cholera, it was another kind of face altogether, eyes blue as air, smooth feathers of hair nearly as yellow as the Star sewn into Rosa's coat. You could think she was one of *their* babies.

Rosa, floating, dreamed of giving Magda away in one of the villages. She could leave the line for a minute and push Magda into the hands of any woman on the side of the road. But if she moved out of line they might shoot. And even if she fled the line for half a second and pushed the shawl-bundle at a stranger, would the woman take it? She might be surprised, or afraid; she might drop the shawl, and Magda would fall out and strike her head and die. The little round head. Such a good child, she gave up screaming, and sucked now only for the taste of the drying nipple itself. The neat grip of the tiny gums. One mite of a tooth tip sticking up in the bottom gum, how shining, an elfin tombstone of white marble gleaming there. Without complaining, Magda relinquished Rosa's teats, first the left, then the right; both were cracked, not a sniff of milk. The duct-crevice extinct, a dead volcano, blind eye, chill hole, so Magda took the corner of the shawl and milked it instead. She sucked and sucked, flooding the threads with wetness. The shawl's good flavor, milk of linen.

It was a magic shawl, it could nourish an infant for three days and three nights. Magda did not die, she stayed alive, although very quiet. A peculiar smell, of cinnamon and almonds, lifted out of her mouth. She held her eyes open every moment, forgetting how to blink or nap, and Rosa and sometimes Stella studied their blueness. On the road they raised one burden of a leg after another and studied Magda's face. "Aryan," Stella said, in a voice grown as thin as a string; and Rosa thought how Stella gazed at Magda like a young cannibal. And the time that Stella said "Aryan," it sounded to Rosa as if Stella had really said "Let us devour her."

But Magda lived to walk. She lived that long, but she did not walk very well, partly because she was only fifteen months old, and partly because the spindles of her legs could not hold up her fat belly. It was fat with air, full and round. Rosa gave almost all her food to Magda, Stella gave nothing; Stella was ravenous, a growing child herself, but not growing much. Stella did not menstruate. Rosa did not menstruate. Rosa was ravenous, but also not, she learned from Magda how to drink the taste of a finger in one's mouth. They were in a place without pity, all pity was annihilated in Rosa, she looked at Stella's bones without pity. She was sure that Stella was waiting for Magda to die so she could put her teeth into the little thighs.

Rosa knew Magda was going to die very soon; she should have been dead already, but she had been buried away deep inside the magic shawl, mistaken there for the shivering mound of Rosa's breasts; Rosa clung to the shawl as if it covered only herself. No one took it away from her. Magda was mute. She never cried. Rosa hid her in the barracks, under the shawl, but she knew that one day someone would inform; or one day someone, not even Stella, would steal Magda to eat her. When Magda began to walk Rosa knew that Magda was going to die very soon, something would happen. She was afraid to fall asleep; she slept with the weight of her thigh on Magda's body; she was afraid she would smother Magda under her thigh. The weight of Rosa was becoming less and less; Rosa and Stella were slowly turning into air.

Magda was quiet, but her eyes were horribly alive, like blue tigers. She watched. Sometimes she laughed—it seemed a laugh, but how could it be? Magda had never seen anyone laugh. Still, Magda laughed at her shawl when the wind blew its corners, the bad wind with pieces of black in it, that made Stella's and Rosa's eyes tear. Magda's eyes were always clear and tearless. She watched like a tiger. She guarded her shawl. No one could touch it; only Rosa could touch it. Stella was not allowed. The shawl was Magda's own baby, her pet, her little sister. She tangled herself up in it and sucked on one of the corners when she wanted to be very still.

Then Stella took the shawl away and made Magda die.

Afterward Stella said: "I was cold."

And afterward she was always cold, always. The cold went into her heart: Rosa saw that Stella's heart was cold. Magda flopped onward with her little pencil legs scribbling this way and that, in search of the shawl; the pencils faltered at the barracks opening, where the light began. Rosa saw and pursued. But already Magda was in the square outside the barracks, in the jolly light. It was the roll-call arena. Every morning Rosa had to conceal Magda under the shawl against a wall of the barracks and go out and stand in the arena with Stella and hundreds of others, sometimes for hours, and Magda, deserted, was quiet under the shawl, sucking on her corner. Every day Magda was silent, and so she did not die. Rosa saw that today Magda was going to die, and at the same time a fearful joy ran in Rosa's two palms, her fingers were on fire, she was astonished, febrile: Magda, in the sunlight, swaying on her pencil legs, was howling. Ever since the drying up of Rosa's nipples, ever since Magda's last scream on the road, Magda had been devoid of any syllable; Magda was a mute. Rosa believed that something had gone wrong with her vocal cords, with her windpipe, with the cave of her larynx; Magda was defective, without a voice; perhaps she was deaf; there might be something amiss with her intelligence; Magda was dumb. Even the laugh that came when the ash-stippled wind made a clown out of Magda's shawl was only the air-blown showing of her teeth. Even when the lice, head lice and body lice, crazed her so that she became as wild as one of the big rats that plundered the barracks at daybreak looking for carrion, she rubbed and scratched and kicked and bit and rolled without a whimper. But now Magda's mouth was spilling a long viscous rope of clamor.

"Maaaa—"

It was the first noise Magda had ever sent out from her throat since the drying up of Rosa's nipples.

"Maaaa . . . aaa!"

Again! Magda was wavering in the perilous sunlight of the arena, scribbling on such pitiful little bent shins. Rosa saw. She saw that Magda was grieving for the loss of her shawl, she saw that Magda was going to die. A tide of commands hammered in Rosa's nipples: Fetch, get, bring! But she did not know which to go after first, Magda or the shawl. If she jumped out into the arena to snatch Magda up, the howling would not stop, because Magda would still not have the shawl; but if she ran back into the barracks to find the shawl, and if she found it, and if she came after Magda holding it and shaking it, then she would get Magda back, Magda would put the shawl in her mouth and turn dumb again.

Rosa entered the dark. It was easy to discover the shawl. Stella was heaped under it, asleep in her thin bones. Rosa tore the shawl free and flew—she could fly, she was only air—into the arena. The sunheat murmured of another life, of butterflies in summer. The light was placid, mellow. On the other side of the steel fence, far away, there were green meadows speckled with dandelions and deep-colored violets; beyond them, even farther, innocent tiger lilies, tall, lifting their orange bonnets. In the barracks they spoke of "flowers," of "rain": excrement, thick turd-braids, and the slow stinking maroon waterfall that slunk down from the upper bunks, the stink mixed with a bitter fatty floating smoke that greased Rosa's skin. She stood for an instant at the margin of the arena. Sometimes the electricity inside the fence would seem to hum; even Stella said it was only an imagining, but Rosa heard real sounds in the wire: grainy sad voices. The farther she was from the fence, the more clearly the voices crowded at her. The lamenting voices strummed so convincingly, so passionately, it was impossible to suspect them of being phantoms. The voices told her to hold up the shawl, high; the voices told her to shake it, to whip with it, to unfurl it like a flag. Rosa lifted, shook, whipped, unfurled. Far off, very far, Magda leaned across her air-fed belly, reaching out with the rods of her arms. She was high up, elevated, riding someone's shoulder. But the shoulder that carried Magda was not coming toward Rosa and the shawl, it was drifting away, the speck of Magda was moving more and more into the smoky distance. Above the shoulder a helmet glinted. The light tapped the helmet and sparkled it into a goblet. Below the helmet a black body like a domino and a pair of black boots hurled themselves in the direction of the electrified fence. The electric voices began to chatter wildly. "Maamaa, maaamaaa," they all hummed together.

How far Magda was from Rosa now, across the whole square, past a dozen barracks, all the way on the other side! She was no bigger than a moth.

All at once Magda was swimming through the air. The whole of Magda traveled through loftiness. She looked like a butterfly touching a silver vine. And the moment Magda's feathered round head and her pencil legs and balloonish belly and zigzag arms splashed against the fence, the steel voices went mad in their growling, urging Rosa to run and run to the spot where Magda had fallen from her flight against the electrified fence; but of course Rosa did not obey them. She only stood, because if she ran they would shoot, and if she tried to pick up the sticks of Magda's body they would shoot, and if she let the wolf's screech ascending now through the ladder of her skeleton break out, they would shoot; so she took Magda's shawl and filled her own mouth with it, stuffed it in and stuffed it in, until she was swallowing up the wolf's screech and tasting the cinnamon and almond depth of Magda's saliva; and Rosa drank Magda's shawl until it dried.

PETER TAYLOR | # WHAT YOU HEAR FROM 'EM?

SOMETIMES people misunderstood Aunt Munsie's question, but she wouldn't bother to clarify it. She might repeat it two or three times, in order to drown out some fool answer she was getting from some fool white woman, or man, either. "What you hear from 'em?" she would ask. And, then, louder and louder: "What you hear from 'em? *What you hear from 'em?*" She was so deaf that anyone whom she thoroughly drowned out only laughed and said Aunt Munsie had got so deaf she couldn't hear it thunder.

It was, of course, only the most utterly fool answers that ever received Aunt Munsie's drowning-out treatment. She was, for a number of years at least, willing to listen to those who mistook her " 'em" to mean any and all of the Dr. Tolliver children. And for more years than that she was willing to listen to those who thought she wanted just *any* news of her two favorites among the Tolliver children—Thad and Will. But later on she stopped putting the question to all insensitive and frivolous souls who didn't understand that what she was interested in hearing—and *all* she was interested in hearing—was when Mr. Thad Tolliver and Mr. Will

Tolliver were going to pack up their families and come back to Thornton for good.

They had always promised her to come back—to come back sure enough, once and for all. On separate occasions, both Thad and Will had actually given her their word. She had not seen them together for ten years, but each of them had made visits to Thornton now and then with his own family. She would see a big car stopping in front of her house on a Sunday afternoon and see either Will or Thad with his wife and children piling out into the dusty street—it was nearly always summer when they came— and then see them filing across the street, jumping the ditch, and unlatching the gate to her yard. She always met them in that pen of a yard, but long before they had jumped the ditch she was clapping her hands and calling out, "Hai-ee! Hai-ee, now! Look-a-here! Whee! Whee! Look-a-here!" She had got so blind that she was never sure whether it was Mr. Thad or Mr. Will until she had her arms around his waist. They had always looked a good deal alike, and their city clothes made them look even more alike nowadays. Aunt Munsie's eyes were so bad, besides being so full of moisture on those occasions, that she really recognized them by their girth. Will had grown a regular wash pot of a stomach and Thad was still thin as a rail. They would sit on her porch for twenty or thirty minutes—whichever one it was and his family— and then they would be gone again.

Aunt Munsie would never try to detain them—not seriously. Those short little old visits didn't mean a thing to her. He—Thad or Will—would lean against the banister rail and tell her how well his children were doing in school or college, and she would make each child in turn come and sit beside her on the swing for a minute and receive a hug around the waist or shoulders. They were timid with her, not seeing her any more than they did, but she could tell from their big Tolliver smiles that they liked her to hug them and make over them. Usually, she would lead them all out to her backyard and show them her pigs and dogs and chickens. (She always had at least one frizzly chicken to show the children.) They would traipse through her house to the backyard and then traipse through again to the front porch. It would be time for them to go when they came back, and Aunt Munsie would look up at *him*— Mr. Thad or Mr. Will (she had begun calling them "Mr." the day they married)—and say, "Now, look-a-here. When you comin' back?"

Both Thad and Will knew what she meant, of course, and whichever it was would tell her he was making definite plans to wind up his business and that he was going to buy a certain piece of property, "a mile north of town" or "on the old River Road," and build a jim-dandy house there. He would say, too, how good Aunt Munsie's own house was looking, and his wife would say how grand the zinnias and cannas looked in the yard. (The yard was all flowers—not a blade of grass, and the ground packed hard in little paths between the flower beds.) The visit was almost over then. There remained only the exchange of presents. One of the children would hand Aunt Munsie a paper bag containing a pint of whiskey or a carton of cigarettes. Aunt Munsie would go to her back porch or to the pit in the yard and get a fern or a wandering Jew, potted in a rusty lard bucket, and make Mrs. Thad or Mrs. Will take it along. Then the visit was over, and they would leave. From the porch Aunt Munsie would wave good-bye with one hand and lay the other hand, trembling slightly, on the banister rail. And sometimes her departing guests, looking back from the yard, would observe that the banisters themselves were trembling under her hand—so insecurely were those knobby banisters attached to the knobby porch pillars. Often as not Thad or Will, observing this, would remind his wife that Aunt Munsie's porch banisters and pillars had come off a porch of the house where he had grown up. (Their father, Dr. Tolliver, had been one of the first to widen his porches and remove the gingerbread from his house.) The children and their mother would wave to Aunt Munsie from the street. Their father would close the gate, resting his hand a moment on its familiar wrought-iron frame, and wave to her before he jumped the ditch. If the children had not gone too far ahead, he might even draw their attention to the iron fence which, with its iron gate, had been around the yard at the Tolliver place till Dr. Tolliver took it down and set out a hedge, just a few weeks before he died.

But such paltry little visits meant nothing to Aunt Munsie. No more did the letters that came with "her things" at Christmas. She was supposed to get her daughter, Lucrecie, who lived next door, to read the letters, but in late years she had taken to putting them away unopened, and some of the presents, too. All she wanted to hear from *them* was when they were coming back for good, and she had learned that the Christmas letters never told her that. On her daily route with her slop wagon through the square, up Jackson Street, and down Jefferson, there were only four or five houses left where she asked her question. These were houses where the amount of pig slop was not worth stopping for, houses where one old maid, or maybe two, lived, or a widow with one old bachelor son who had never amounted to anything and ate no more than a woman. And so—in the summertime, anyway—she took to calling out at the top of her lungs, when she approached the house of one of the elect, "What you hear from 'em?" Sometimes a Miss Patty or a Miss Lucille or a Mr. Ralph would get up out of a porch chair and come down the brick walk to converse with Aunt Munsie. Or sometimes one of them would just lean out over the shrubbery planted around the porch and call, "Not a thing, Munsie. Not a thing lately."

She would shake her head and call back, "Naw. Naw. Not a thing. Nobody don't hear from 'em. Too busy, they be."

Aunt Munsie's skin was the color of a faded tow sack. She was hardly four feet tall. She was generally believed to be totally bald, and on her head she always wore a white dust cap with an elastic band. She wore an apron, too, while making her rounds with her slop wagon. Even when the weather got bad and she tied a wool scarf about her head and wore an overcoat, she put on an apron over the coat. Her hands and feet were delicately small, which made the old-timers sure she was of Guinea stock that had come

to Tennessee out of South Carolina. What most touched the hearts
of old ladies on Jackson and Jefferson streets were her little feet.
The sight of her feet "took them back to the old days," they said,
because Aunt Munsie still wore flat-heeled, high-button shoes.
Where ever did Munsie find such shoes any more?

She walked down the street, down the very center of the street,
with a spry step, and she was continually turning her head from
side to side, as though looking at the old houses and trees for the
first time. If her sight was as bad as she sometimes let on it was,
she probably recognized the houses only by their roof lines against
the Thornton sky. Since this was nearly thirty years ago, most of
the big Victorian and antebellum houses were still standing,
though with their lovely gingerbread work beginning to go. (It
went first from houses where there was someone, like Dr. Tolliver, with a special eye for style and for keeping up with the
times.) The streets hadn't yet been broadened—or only Nashville
Street had—and the maples and elms met above the streets. In the
autumn, their leaves covered the high banks and filled the deep
ditches on either side. The dark macadam surfacing itself was
barely wide enough for two automobiles to pass. Aunt Munsie,
pulling her slop wagon, which was a long, low, four-wheeled
vehicle about the size and shape of a coffin, paraded down the
center of the street without any regard for, if with any awareness
of, the traffic problems she sometimes made. Seizing the wagon's
heavy, sawed-off-looking tongue, she hauled it after her with a
series of impatient jerks, just as though that tongue were the arm
of some very stubborn, overgrown white child she had to nurse
in her old age. Strangers in town or trifling high-school boys
would blow their horns at her, but she was never known to so
much as glance over her shoulder at the sound of a horn. Now
and then a pedestrian on the sidewalk would call out to the driver
of an automobile, "She's so deaf she can't hear it thunder."

It wouldn't have occurred to anyone in Thornton—not in those
days—that something ought to be done about Aunt Munsie and
her wagon for the sake of the public good. In those days, everyone

[129]

had equal rights on the streets of Thornton. A vehicle was a vehicle, and a person was a person, each with the right to move as slowly as he pleased and to stop where and as often as he pleased. In the Thornton mind, there was no imaginary line down the middle of the street, and, indeed, no one there at that time had heard of drawing a real line on *any* street. It was merely out of politeness that you made room for others to pass. Nobody would have blown a horn at an old colored woman with her slop wagon—nobody but some Yankee stranger or a trifling high-school boy or maybe old Mr. Ralph Hadley in a special fit of temper. When citizens of Thornton were in a particular hurry and got caught behind Aunt Munsie, they leaned out their car windows and shouted: "Aunt Munsie, can you make a little room?" And Aunt Munsie didn't fail to hear *them*. She would holler, "Hai-ee, now! Whee! Look-a-here!" and jerk her wagon to one side. As they passed her, she would wave her little hand and grin a toothless, pink-gummed grin.

Yet, without any concern for the public good, Aunt Munsie's friends and connections among the white women began to worry more and more about the danger of her being run down by an automobile. They talked among themselves and they talked to her about it. They wanted her to give up collecting slop, now she had got so blind and deaf. "Pshaw," said Aunt Munsie, closing her eyes contemptuously. "Not me." She meant by that that no one would dare run into her or her wagon. Sometimes when she crossed the square on a busy Saturday morning or on a first Monday, she would hold up one hand with the palm turned outward and stop all traffic until she was safely across and in the alley beside the hotel.

Thornton wasn't even then what it had been before the Great World War. In every other house there was a stranger or a mill hand who had moved up from factory town. Some of the biggest old places stood empty, the way Dr. Tolliver's had until it burned. They stood empty not because nobody wanted to rent them or buy them but because the heirs who had gone off somewhere making money could never be got to part with "the home place." The story was that Thad Tolliver nearly went crazy when he heard their old house had burned, and wanted to sue the town, and even said he was going to help get the Republicans into office. Yet Thad had hardly put foot in the house since the day his daddy died. It was said the Tolliver house had caught fire from the Major Pettigru house, which had burned two nights before. And no doubt it had. Sparks could have smoldered in that roof of rotten shingles for a long time before bursting into flame. Some even said the Pettigru house might have caught from the Johnston house, which had burned earlier that same fall. But Thad knew and Will knew and everybody knew the town wasn't to blame, and knew there was no firebug. Why, those old houses stood there empty year after year, and in the fall the leaves fell from the trees and settled around the porches and stoops, and who was there to rake the leaves? Maybe it was a good thing those houses burned, and maybe it would have been as well if some of the houses that still had people in them burned, too. There were houses in Thornton the heirs had never left that looked far worse than the Tolliver or the Pettigru or the Johnston house ever had. The people who lived in them were the ones who gave Aunt Munsie the biggest fool answers to her question, the people whom she soon quit asking her question of or even passing the time of day with, except when she couldn't help it, out of politeness. For, truly, to Aunt Munsie there were things under the sun worse than going off and getting rich in Nashville or in Memphis or even in Washington, D.C. It was a subject she and her daughter Lucrecie sometimes mouthed at each other about across their back fence. Lucrecie was shiftless, and she liked shiftless white people like the ones who didn't have the ambition to leave Thornton. She thought their shiftlessness showed they were *quality*. "Quality?" Aunt Munsie would echo, her voice full of sarcasm. "Whee! Hai-ee! You talk like *you* was *my* mammy, Crecie. Well, if there be quality, there be quality *and* quality. There's quality and there's *has-been* quality, Crecie." There was no end to that argument Aunt Munsie had with Crecie, and it wasn't at all important to Aunt Munsie. The people who still lived in those houses—the ones she called has-been quality— meant little more to her than the mill hands, or the strangers from up North who ran the Piggly Wiggly, the five-and-ten-cent store, and the roller-skating rink.

There was this to be said, though, for the has-been quality: they knew *who* Aunt Munsie was, and in a limited, literal way they understood what she said. But those *others*—why, they thought Aunt Munsie a beggar, and she knew they did. They spoke of her as Old What You Have for Mom, because that's what they thought she was saying when she called out, "What you hear from 'em?" Their ears were not attuned to that soft *r* she put in "from" or the elision that made "from 'em" sound to them like "for Mom." Many's the time Aunt Munsie had seen or sensed the presence of one of those *other* people, watching from next door, when Miss Leonora Lovell, say, came down her front walk and handed her a little parcel of scraps across the ditch. Aunt Munsie knew what they thought of her—how they laughed at her and felt sorry for her and despised her all at once. But, like the has-been quality, they didn't matter, never had, never would. Not ever.

Oh, they mattered in a way to Lucrecie. Lucrecie thought about them and talked about them a lot. She called them "white trash" and even "radical Republicans." It made Aunt Munsie grin to hear Crecie go on, because she knew Crecie got all her notions from her own has-been-quality people. And so it didn't matter, except that Aunt Munsie knew that Crecie truly had all sorts of good sense and had only been carried away and spoiled by such folks as she had worked for, such folks as had really raised Crecie from the time she was big enough to run errands for them, fifty years back. In her heart, Aunt Munsie knew that even Lucrecie didn't matter to her the way a daughter might. It was because while Aunt Munsie had been raising a family of white children, a different sort of white people from hers had been raising her own child, Crecie. Sometimes, if Aunt Munsie was in her chicken yard or out in her little patch of cotton when Mr. Thad or Mr. Will arrived, Crecie would come out to the fence and say, "Mama, some of your chillun's out front."

Miss Leonora Lovell and Miss Patty Bean, and especially Miss Lucille Satterfield, were all the time after Aunt Munsie to give up collecting slop. "You're going to get run over by one of those crazy drivers, Munsie," they said. Miss Lucille was the widow of old Judge Satterfield. "If the Judge were alive, Munsie," she said, "I'd make him find a way to stop you. But the men down at the courthouse don't listen to the women in this town any more. Not since we got the vote. And I think they'd be most too scared of you to do what I want them to do." Aunt Munsie wouldn't listen to any of that. She knew that if Miss Lucille had come out there to her gate, she must have *something* she was going to say about Mr. Thad or Mr. Will. Miss Lucille had two brothers and a son of her own who were lawyers in Memphis, and who lived in style down there and kept Miss Lucille in style here in Thornton. Memphis was where Thad Tolliver had his Ford and Lincoln agency, and so Miss Lucille always had news about Thad, and indirectly about Will, too.

"Is they doin' any good? What you hear from 'em?" Aunt Munsie asked Miss Lucille one afternoon in early spring. She had come along just when Miss Lucille was out picking some of the jonquils that grew in profusion on the steep bank between the sidewalk and the ditch in front of her house.

"Mr. Thad and his folks will be up one day in April, Munsie," Miss Lucille said in her pleasantly hoarse voice. "I understand Mr. Will and his crowd may come for Easter Sunday."

"One day, and gone again!" said Aunt Munsie.

"We always try to get them to stay at least one night, but they're busy folks, Munsie."

"When they comin' back sure enough, Miss Lucille?"

"Goodness knows, Munsie. Goodness knows. Goodness knows when any of them are coming back to stay." Miss Lucille took three quick little steps down the bank and hopped lightly across the ditch. "They're prospering so, Munsie," she said, throwing her chin up and smiling proudly. This fragile lady, this daughter, wife, sister, mother of lawyers (and, of course, the darling of all their hearts), stood there in the street with her pretty little feet and shapely ankles close together, and holding a handful of jonquils before her as if it were her bridal bouquet. "They're *all* prospering so, Munsie. Mine *and* yours. You ought to go down to Memphis to see them now and then, the way I do. Or go up to Nashville to see Mr. Will. I understand he's got an even finer establishment than Thad. They've done well, Munsie—yours *and* mine—and we can be proud of them. You owe it to yourself to go and see how well they're fixed. They're rich men by our standards in Thornton, and they're going farther—*all* of them."

Aunt Munsie dropped the tongue of her wagon noisily on the pavement. "What I want to go see 'em for?" she said angrily and with a lowering brow. Then she stooped and, picking up the wagon tongue again, she wheeled her vehicle toward the middle of the street, to get by Miss Lucille, and started off toward the square. As she turned out into the street, the brakes of a car, as so often, screeched behind her. Presently everyone in the neighborhood could hear Mr. Ralph Hadley tooting the insignificant little horn on his mama's coupé and shouting at Aunt Munsie in his own tooty voice, above the sound of the horn. Aunt Munsie pulled over, making just enough room to let poor old Mr. Ralph get by but without once looking back at him. Then, before Mr. Ralph could get his car started again, Miss Lucille was running along beside Aunt Munsie, saying, "Munsie, you be careful! You're going to meet your death on the streets of Thornton, Tennessee!"

"Let 'em," said Aunt Munsie.

Miss Lucille didn't know whether Munsie meant "Let 'em run over me; I don't care" or meant "Let 'em just dare!" Miss Lucille soon turned back, without Aunt Munsie's ever looking at her. And when Mr. Ralph Hadley did get his motor started, and sailed past in his mama's coupé, Aunt Munsie didn't give him a look, either. Nor did Mr. Ralph bother to turn his face to look at Aunt Munsie. He was on his way to the drugstore, to pick up his mama's prescriptions, and he was too entirely put out, peeved, and upset to endure even the briefest exchange with that ugly, uppity old Munsie of the Tollivers.

Aunt Munsie continued to tug her slop wagon on toward the square. There was a more animated expression on her face than usual, and every so often her lips would move rapidly and emphatically over a phrase or sentence. Why should she go to Memphis and Nashville and see how rich they were? No matter how rich they were, what difference did it make; they didn't own any land, did they? Or at least none in Cameron County. She had heard the old Doctor tell them—tell his boys and tell his girls, and tell the old lady, too, in her day—that nobody was rich who didn't own land, and nobody stayed rich who didn't see after his land firsthand. But of course Aunt Munsie had herself mocked the old Doctor to his face for going on about land so much. She knew it was only something he had heard his own daddy go on about. She would say right to his face that she hadn't ever seen *him* behind a plow. And was there ever anybody more scared of a mule than Dr. Tolliver was? Mules or horses, either? Aunt Munsie had heard him say that the happiest day of his life was the day he first learned that the horseless carriage was a reality.

No, it was not really to own land that Thad and Will ought to come back to Thornton. It was more that if they were going to be rich, they ought to come home, where their granddaddy had owned land and where their money counted for something. How could they ever be rich anywhere else? They could have a lot of money in the bank and a fine house, that was all—like that mill manager from Chi. The mill manager could have a yard full of big cars and a stucco house as big as you like, but who would ever take him for rich? Aunt Munsie would sometimes say all these things to Crecie, or something as nearly like them as she could find words for. Crecie might nod her head in agreement or she might be in a mood to say being rich wasn't any good for anybody and didn't matter, and that you could live on just being quality better than on being rich in Thornton. "Quality's better than land or better than money in the bank here," Crecie would say.

Aunt Munsie would sneer at her and say, "It never were."

Lucrecie could talk all she wanted about the old times! Aunt Munsie knew too much about what they were like, for both the richest white folks and the blackest field hands. Nothing about the old times was as good as these days, and there were going to be better times yet when Mr. Thad and Mr. Will Tolliver came back. Everybody lived easier now than they used to, and were better off. She could never be got to reminisce about her childhood in slavery, or her life with her husband, or even about those halcyon days after the old Mizziz had died and Aunt Munsie's word had become law in the Tolliver household. Without being able to book read or even to make numbers, she had finished raising the whole pack of towheaded Tollivers just as the Mizziz would have wanted it done. The Doctor told her she *had* to—he didn't ever once think about getting another wife, or taking in some cousin, not after his "Molly darling"—and Aunt Munsie *did*. But, as Crecie said, when a time was past in her mama's life, it seemed to be gone and done with in her head, too.

Lucrecie would say frankly she thought her mama was "hard about people and things in the world." She talked about her mama not only to the Blalocks, for whom she had worked all her life, but to anybody else who gave her an opening. It wasn't just about her mama, though, that she would talk to anybody. She liked to talk, and she talked about Aunt Munsie not in any ugly, resentful way but as she would about when the sheep-rains would begin or where the fire was last night. (Crecie was twice the size of her mama, and black the way her old daddy had been, and loud and good-natured the way he was—or at least the way Aunt Munsie wasn't. You wouldn't have known they were mother and daughter, and not many of the young people in town did realize it. Only by accident did they live next door to each other; Mr. Thad and

Mr. Will had bought Munsie her house, and Crecie had heired hers from her second husband.) *That* was how she talked about her mama—as she would have about any lonely, eccentric, harmless neighbor. "I may be dead wrong, but I think Mama's kind of hard-hearted," she would say. "Mama's a good old soul, I reckon, but when something's past, it's gone and done with for Mama. She don't think about day before yestiddy—yestiddy, either. I don't know, maybe that's the way to be. Maybe that's why the old soul's gonna outlive us all." Then, obviously thinking about what a picture of health she herself was at sixty, Crecie would toss her head about and laugh so loud you might hear her all the way out to the fairgrounds.

Crecie, however, knew her mama was not honest-to-God mean and hadn't ever been mean to the Tolliver children, the way the Blalocks liked to make out she had. All the Tolliver children but Mr. Thad and Mr. Will had quarreled with her for good by the time they were grown, but they had quarreled with the old Doctor, too (and as if they were the only ones who shook off their old folks this day and time). When Crecie talked about her mama, she didn't spare her anything, but she was fair to her, too. And it was in no hateful or disloyal spirit that she took part in the conspiracy that finally got Aunt Munsie and her slop wagon off the streets of Thornton. Crecie would have done the same for any neighbor. She had small part enough, actually, in that conspiracy. Her part was merely to break the news to Aunt Munsie that there was now a law against keeping pigs within the city limits. It was a small part but one that no one else quite dared to take.

"They ain't no such law!" Aunt Munsie roared back at Crecie. She was slopping her pigs when Crecie came to the fence and told her about the law. It had seemed the most appropriate time to Lucrecie. "They ain't never been such a law, Crecie," Aunt Munsie said. "Every house on Jackson and Jefferson used to keep pigs."

"It's a brand-new law, Mama."

Aunt Munsie finished bailing out the last of the slop from her wagon. It was just before twilight. The last, weak rays of the sun colored the clouds behind the mock orange tree in Crecie's yard. When Aunt Munsie turned around from the sky, she pretended that that little bit of light in the clouds hurt her eyes, and turned away her head. And when Lucrecie said that everybody had until the first of the year to get rid of their pigs, Aunt Munsie was in a spell of deafness. She headed out toward the crib to get some corn for the chickens. She was trying to think whether anybody else inside the town still kept pigs. Herb Mallory did—two doors beyond Crecie. Then Aunt Munsie remembered Herb didn't pay town taxes. The town line ran between him and Shad Willis.

That was sometime in June, and before July came, Aunt Munsie knew all there was worth knowing about the conspiracy. Mr. Thad and Mr. Will had each been in town for a day during the spring. They and their families had been to her house and sat on the porch; the children had gone back to look at her half-grown collie dog and the two hounds, at the old sow and her farrow of new pigs, and at the frizzliest frizzly chicken Aunt Munsie had ever had. And on those visits to Thornton, Mr. Thad and Mr. Will had also made their usual round among their distant kin and close friends. Everywhere they went, they had heard of the near-accidents Aunt Munsie was causing with her slop wagon and the real danger there was of her being run over. Miss Lucille Satterfield and Miss Patty Bean had both been to the mayor's office and also to see Judge Lawrence to try to get Aunt Munsie "ruled" off the streets, but the men in the courthouse and in the mayor's office didn't listen to the women in Thornton any more. And so either Mr. Thad or Mr. Will—how would which one of them it was matter to Munsie?—had been prevailed upon to stop by Mayor Lunt's office, and in a few seconds' time had set the wheels of conspiracy in motion. Soon a general inquiry had been made in the town as to how many citizens still kept pigs. Only two property owners besides Aunt Munsie had been found to have pigs on their premises, and they, being men, had been docile and reasonable enough to sell what they had on hand to Mr. Will or Mr.

Thad Tolliver. Immediately afterward—within a matter of weeks, that is—a town ordinance had been passed forbidding the possession of swine within the corporate limits of Thornton. Aunt Munsie had got the story bit by bit from Miss Leonora and Miss Patty and Miss Lucille and others, including the constable himself, whom she did not hesitate to stop right in the middle of the square on a Saturday noon. Whether it was Mr. Thad or Mr. Will who had been prevailed upon by the ladies she never ferreted out, but that was only because she did not wish to do so.

The constable's word was the last word for her. The constable said yes, it was the law, and he admitted yes, he had sold his own pigs—for the constable was one of those two reasonable souls— to Mr. Thad or Mr. Will. He didn't say which of them it was, or if he did, Aunt Munsie didn't bother to remember it. And after her interview with the constable, Aunt Munsie never again exchanged words with any human being about the ordinance against pigs. That afternoon, she took a fishing pole from under her house and drove the old sow and the nine shoats down to Herb Mallory's, on the outside of town. They were his, she said, if he wanted them, and he could pay her at killing time.

It was literally true that Aunt Munsie never again exchanged words with anyone about the ordinance against pigs or about the conspiracy she had discovered against herself. But her daughter Lucrecie had a tale to tell about what Aunt Munsie did that afternoon after she had seen the constable and before she drove the pigs over to Herb Mallory's. It was mostly a tale of what Aunt Munsie said to her pigs and to her dogs and her chickens.

Crecie was in her own backyard washing her hair when her mama came down the rickety porch steps and into the yard next door. Crecie had her head in the pot of suds, and so she couldn't look up, but she knew by the way Mama flew down the steps that there was trouble. "She come down them steps like she was wasp-nest bit, or like some young'on who's got hisself wasp-nest bit— and her all of eighty, I reckon!" Then, as Crecie told it, her mama scurried around in the yard for a minute or so like she thought Judgment was about to catch up with her, and pretty soon she commenced slamming at something. Crecie wrapped a towel about her soapy head, squatted low, and edged over toward the plank fence. She peered between the planks and saw what her mama was up to. Since there never had been a gate to the fence around the pigsty, Mama had taken the wood ax and was knocking a hole in it. But directly, just after Crecie had taken her place by the plank fence, her mama had left off her slamming at the sty and turned about so quickly and so exactly toward Crecie that Crecie thought the poor, blind old soul had managed to spy her squatting there. Right away, though, Crecie realized it was not *her* that Mama was staring at. She saw that all Aunt Munsie's chickens and those three dogs of hers had come up behind her, and were all clucking and whining to know why she didn't stop that infernal racket and put out some feed for them.

Crecie's mama set one hand on her hip and rested the ax on the ground. "Just look at yuh!" she said, and then she let the chickens and the dogs—and the pigs, too—have it. She told them what a miserable bunch of creatures they were, and asked them what right they had to always be looking for handouts from her. She sounded like the boss-man who's caught all his pickers laying off before sundown, and she sounded, too, like the preacher giving his sinners Hail Columbia at camp meeting. Finally, shouting at the top of her voice and swinging the ax wide and broad above their heads, she sent the dogs howling under the house and the chickens scattering in every direction. "Now, g'wine! G'wine widja!" she shouted after them. Only the collie pup, of the three dogs, didn't scamper to the farthest corner underneath the house. He stopped under the porch steps, and not two seconds later he was poking his long head out again and showing the whites of his doleful brown eyes. Crecie's mama took a step toward him and then she halted. "You want to know what's the commotion about? I reckoned you would," she said with profound contempt, as though the collie were a more reasonable soul than the other animals, and as though there were nothing she held in such thorough disrespect as reason. "I tell you what the commotion's about," she said. "They *ain't* comin' back. They ain't never comin' back. They ain't never had no notion of comin' back." She turned her head to one side, and the only explanation Crecie could find for her mama's next words was that that collie pup did look so much like Miss Lucille Satterfield.

"Why don't I go down to Memphis or up to Nashville and see 'em sometime, like *you* does?" Aunt Munsie asked the collie. "I tell you why. Becaze I ain't nothin' to 'em in Memphis, and they ain't nothin' to me in Nashville. *You* can go!" she said, advancing and shaking the big ax at the dog. "A collie dog's a collie dog anywhar. But Aunt Munsie, she's just their Aunt Munsie here in Thornton. I got mind enough to see *that*." The collie slowly pulled his head back under the steps, and Aunt Munsie watched for a minute to see if he would show himself again. When he didn't, she went and jerked the fishing pole out from under the house and headed toward the pigsty. Crecie remained squatting beside the fence until her mama and the pigs were out in the street and on their way to Herb Mallory's.

That was the end of Aunt Munsie's keeping pigs and the end of her daily rounds with her slop wagon, but it was not the end of Aunt Munsie. She lived on for nearly twenty years after that, till long after Lucrecie had been put away, in fine style, by the Blalocks. Ever afterward, though, Aunt Munsie seemed different to people. They said she softened, and everybody said it was a change for the better. She would take paper money from under her carpet, or out of the chinks in her walls, and buy things for up at the church, or buy her own whiskey when she got sick, instead of making somebody bring her a hip. On the square she would laugh and holler with the white folks the way they liked her to and the way Crecie and all the other old-timers did, and she even took to tying a bandanna about her head—took to talking old-nigger foolishness, too, about the Bell Witch, and claiming she remembered the day General N. B. Forrest rode into town and saved all the cotton from the Yankees at the depot. When Mr. Will and Mr. Thad came to see her with their families, she got so she would reminisce with them about their daddy and tease them about all the silly little things they had done when they were growing up: "Mr. Thad—him still in kilts, too—he says, 'Aunt Munsie, reach down in yo' stockin' and git me a copper cent. I want some store candy.' " She told them about how Miss Yola Ewing, the sewing woman, heard her threatening to bust Will's back wide open when he broke the lamp chimney, and how Miss Yola went to the Doctor and told him he ought to run Aunt Munsie off. Then Aunt Munsie and the Doctor had had a big laugh about it out in the kitchen, and Miss Yola must have eavesdropped on them, because she left without finishing the girls' Easter dresses.

Indeed, these visits from Mr. Thad and Mr. Will continued as long as Aunt Munsie lived, but she never asked them any more about when they were sure enough coming back. And the children, though she hugged them more than ever—and, toward the last, there were the children's children to be hugged—never again set foot in her backyard. Aunt Munsie lived on for nearly twenty years, and when they finally buried her, they put on her tombstone that she was aged one hundred years, though nobody knew how old she was. There was no record of when she was born. All anyone knew was that in her last years she had said she was a girl helping about the big house when freedom came. That would have made her probably about twelve years old in 1865, according to her statements and depictions. But all agreed that in her extreme old age Aunt Munsie, like other old darkies, was not very reliable about dates and such things. Her spirit softened, even her voice lost some of the rasping quality that it had always had, and in general she became not very reliable about facts.

TOBIAS WOLFF | # OUR STORY BEGINS

THE FOG blew in early again. This was the tenth straight day of it. The waiters and waitresses gathered along the window to watch, and Charlie pushed his cart across the dining room so that he could watch with them as he filled the water glasses. Boats were beating in ahead of the fog, which loomed behind them like a tall rolling breaker. Gulls glided from the sky to the pylons along the wharf, where they shook out their feathers and rocked from side to side and glared at the tourists passing by.

The fog covered the stanchions of the bridge. The bridge appeared to be floating free as the fog billowed into the harbor and began to overtake the boats. One by one they were swallowed up in it.

"Now that's what I call hairy," one of the waiters said. "You couldn't get me out there for love or money."

A waitress said something and the rest of them laughed.

"Nice talk," the waiter said.

The maître d' came out of the kitchen and snapped his fingers. "Busboy!" he called. One of the waitresses turned and looked at Charlie, who put down the pitcher he was pouring from and pushed his cart back across the dining room to its assigned place. For the next half hour, until the first customer came in, Charlie folded napkins and laid out squares of butter in little bowls filled with crushed ice, and thought of the things he would do to the maître d' if he ever got the maître d' in his power.

But this was a diversion; he didn't really hate the maître d'. He hated his meaningless work and his fear of being fired from it, and most of all he hated being called a busboy because being called a busboy made it harder for him to think of himself as a man, which he was just learning to do.

Only a few tourists came into the restaurant that night. All of them were alone, and plainly disappointed. They sat by them-selves, across from their shopping bags, and stared morosely in the direction of the Golden Gate though there was nothing to see but the fog pressing up against the windows and greasy drops of water running down the glass. Like most people who ate alone they ordered the bargain items, scampi or cod or the Cap'n's Plate, and maybe a small carafe of the house wine. The waiters neglected them. The tourists dawdled over their food, overtipped the wait-ers, and left more deeply sunk in disappointment than before.

At nine o'clock the maître d' sent all but three of the waiters home, then went home himself. Charlie hoped he'd be given the nod too, but he was left standing by his cart, where he folded more napkins and replaced the ice as it melted in the water glasses and under the squares of butter. The three waiters kept going back to the storeroom to smoke dope. By the time the restaurant closed they were so wrecked they could hardly stand.

Charlie started home the long way, up Columbus Avenue, because Columbus Avenue had the brightest streetlights. But in this fog the lights were only a presence, a milky blotch here and there in the vapor above. Charlie walked slowly and kept to the walls. He met no one on his way; but once, as he paused to wipe the damp-ness from his face, he heard strange ticking steps behind him and turned to see a three-legged dog appear out of the mist. It moved past in a series of lurches and was gone. "Christ," Charlie said. Then he laughed to himself, but the sound was unconvincing and he decided to get off the street for a while.

Just around the corner on Vallejo there was a coffeehouse where Charlie sometimes went on his nights off. Jack Kerouac had mentioned this particular coffeehouse in *The Subterraneans*. These days the patrons were mostly Italian people who came to listen to the jukebox, which was filled with music from Italian operas, but Charlie always looked up when someone came in the door; it might be Ginsberg or Corso, stopping by for old times' sake. He liked sitting there with an open book on the table, listening to music that he thought of as being classical. He liked to imagine that the rude, sluggish woman who brought him his cappuccino had once been Neil Cassady's lover. It was possible.

When Charlie came into the coffeehouse the only other customers were four old men sitting by the door. He took a table across the room. Someone had left an Italian movie magazine on the chair next to his. Charlie looked through the photographs, keeping time with his fingers to "The Anvil Chorus" while the waitress made up his cappuccino. The coffee machine hissed as she worked the handle. The room filled with the sweet smell of coffee. Charlie also caught the smell of fish and realized that it came from him, that he was reeking of it. His fingers fell still on the table.

Charlie paid the waitress when she served him. He intended to drink up and get out. While he was waiting for the coffee to cool, a woman came in the door with two men. They looked around, held a conference, and finally sat down at the table next to Charlie's. As soon as they were seated they began to talk without regard for whether Charlie could hear them. He listened, and after a time he began to glance over at them. Either they didn't notice or they didn't care. They were indifferent to his presence.

Charlie gathered from their conversation that they were members of a church choir, making the rounds after choir practice. The woman's name was Audrey. Her lipstick was smeared, making her mouth look a little crooked. She had a sharp face with thick black brows that she raised skeptically whenever her husband spoke. Audrey's husband was tall and heavy. He shifted constantly, scraping his chair as he did so, and moved his hat back and forth from one knee to the other. Big as he was, the green suit he wore fitted him perfectly. His name was Truman, and the other man's name was George. George had a calm, reedy voice that he enjoyed using; Charlie could see him listening to it as he talked. He was a teacher of some kind, which did not surprise Charlie. George looked to him like the young professors he'd had during his three years of college: rimless spectacles, turtleneck sweater, the ghost of a smile always on his lips. But George wasn't really young. His thick hair, parted in the middle, had begun to turn gray.

No—it seemed that only Audrey and George sang in the choir. They were telling Truman about a trip the choir had just made to Los Angeles, to a festival of choirs. Truman looked from his wife to George as each of them spoke, and shook his head as they described the sorry characters of the other members of the choir and the eccentricities of the choir director.

"Of course Father Wes is nothing compared to Monsignor Strauss," George said. "Monsignor Strauss was positively certifiable."

"Strauss?" Truman said. "Which one is Strauss? The only Strauss I know is Johann." Truman looked at his wife and laughed.

"Forgive me," George said. "I was being cryptic. George sometimes forgets the basics. When you've met someone like Monsignor Strauss, you naturally assume that everyone else has heard of him. The monsignor was our director for five years, prior to Father Wes's tenure. He got religion and left for the subcontinent just before Audrey joined us, so of course you wouldn't recognize the name."

"The subcontinent," Truman said. "What's that? Atlantis?"

"For God's sake, Truman," Audrey said. "Sometimes you embarrass me."

"India," George said. "Calcutta. Mother Teresa and all that."

Audrey put her hand on George's arm. "George," she said, "tell Truman that marvelous story you told me about Monsignor Strauss and the Filipino."

George smiled to himself. "Ah yes," he said. "Miguel. That's a long story, Audrey. Perhaps another night would be better."

"Oh no," Audrey said. "Tonight would be perfect."

Truman said, "If it's that long . . ."

"It's not," Audrey said. She knocked on the table with her knuckles. "Tell the story, George."

George looked over at Truman and shrugged. "Don't blame George," he said. He drank off the last of his brandy. "All right then. Our story begins. Monsignor Strauss had some money from somewhere, and every year he made a journey to points exotic. When he came home he always had some unusual souvenir that he'd picked up on his travels. From Argentina he brought everyone seeds which grew into plants whose flowers smelled like, excuse me, *merde*. He got them in an Argentine joke shop, if you can imagine such a thing. When he came back from Kenya he smuggled in a lizard that could pick off flies with its tongue from a distance of six feet. The monsignor carried this lizard around on his finger and whenever a fly came within range he would say, 'Watch this!' and aim the lizard like a pistol, and *poof*— no more fly."

Audrey pointed her finger at Truman and said, "Poof." Truman just looked at her. "I need another drink," Audrey said, and signaled the waitress.

George ran his finger around the rim of his snifter. "After the lizard," he said, "there was a large Australian rodent that ended up in the zoo, and after the rodent came a nineteen-year-old human being from the Philippines. His name was Miguel Lopez de Constanza, and he was a cabdriver from Manila the monsignor had hired as a chauffeur during his stay there and taken a liking to. When the monsignor got back he pulled some strings at Immigration, and a few weeks later Miguel showed up. He spoke no English, really—only a few buzz words for tourists in Manila.

The first month or so he stayed with Monsignor Strauss in the rectory, then he found a room in the Hotel Overland and moved in there."

"The Hotel Overland," Truman said. "That's that druggy hangout on upper Grant."

"The Hotel Overdose," Audrey said. When Truman looked at her she said, "That's what they call it."

"You seem to be up on all the nomenclature," Truman said.

The waitress came with their drinks. When her tray was empty she stood behind Truman and began to write in a notebook she carried. Charlie hoped she wouldn't come over to his table. He did not want the others to notice him. They would guess that he'd been listening to them, and they might not like it. They might stop talking. But the waitress finished making her entries and moved back to the bar without a glance at Charlie.

The old men by the door were arguing in Italian. The window above them was all steamed up, and Charlie could feel the closeness of the fog outside. The jukebox glowed in the corner. The song that was playing ended abruptly, the machinery whirred, and "The Anvil Chorus" came on again.

"So why the Hotel Overland?" Truman asked.

"Truman prefers the Fairmont," Audrey said. "Truman thinks everyone should stay at the Fairmont."

"Miguel had no money," George said. "Only what the monsignor gave him. The idea was that he would stay there just long enough to learn English and pick up a trade. Then he could get a job. Take care of himself."

"Sounds reasonable," Truman said.

Audrey laughed. "Truman, you slay me. That is *exactly* what I thought you would say. Now let's just turn things around for a minute. Let's say that for some reason you, Truman, find yourself in Manila dead broke. You don't know anybody, you don't understand anything anyone says, and you wind up in a hotel where people are sticking needles into themselves and nodding out on the stairs and setting their rooms on fire all the time. How much Spanish are you going to learn living like that? What kind of trade are you going to pick up? Get real," Audrey said. "That's not a reasonable existence."

"San Francisco isn't Manila," Truman said. "Believe me—I've been there. At least here you've got a chance. And it isn't true that he didn't know anybody. What about the monsignor?"

"Terrific," Audrey said. "A priest who walks around with a lizard on his finger. Great friend. Or, as you would say, great connection."

"I have never, to my knowledge, used the word *connection* in that way," Truman said.

George had been staring into his brandy snifter, which he held cupped in both hands. He looked up at Audrey. "Actually," he said, "Miguel was not entirely at a loss. In fact he managed pretty well for a time. Monsignor Strauss got him into a training course for mechanics at the Porsche-Audi place on Van Ness, and he picked up English at a terrific rate. It's amazing, isn't it, what one can do if one has no choice." George rolled the snifter back and forth between his palms. "The druggies left him completely alone, incredible as that may seem. No hassles in the hallways, nothing. It was as if Miguel lived in a different dimension from them, and in a way he did. He went to Mass every day, and sang in the choir. That's where I made his acquaintance. Miguel had a gorgeous baritone, truly gorgeous. He was extremely proud of his voice. He was proud of his body, too. Ate precisely so much of this, so much of that. Did elaborate exercises every day. He even gave himself facial massages to keep from getting a double chin."

"There you are," Truman said to Audrey. "There is such a thing as character." When she didn't answer he added, "What I'm getting at is that people are not necessarily limited by their circumstances."

"I know what you're getting at," Audrey said. "The story isn't over yet."

★ ★ ★

Truman moved his hat from his knee to the table. He folded his arms across his chest. "I've got a full day ahead of me," he said to Audrey. She nodded but did not look at him.

George took a sip of his brandy. He closed his eyes afterward and ran the tip of his tongue around his lips. Then he lowered his head again and stared back into the snifter. "Miguel met a woman," he said, "as do we all. Her name was Senga. My guess is that she had originally been called Agnes, and that she turned her name around in hopes of making herself more interesting to people of the male persuasion. Senga was older than Miguel by at least ten years, maybe more. She had a daughter in, I believe, fifth grade. Senga was a finance officer at B of A. I don't remember how they met. They went out for a while, then Senga broke it off. I suppose it was a casual thing for her, but for Miguel it was serious. He worshiped Senga, and I use that word advisedly. He set up a little shrine to her in his room. A high school graduation picture of Senga surrounded by different objects that she had worn or used. Combs. Handkerchiefs. Empty perfume bottles. A whole pile of things. How he got them I have no idea—whether she gave them to him or whether he just took them. The odd thing is, he only went out with her a few times. I very much doubt that they ever reached the point of sleeping together."

"They didn't," Truman said.

George looked up at him.

"If he'd slept with her," Truman said, "he wouldn't have built a shrine to her."

Audrey shook her head. "Pure Truman," she said. "Vintage Truman."

He patted her arm. "No offense," he told her.

"Be that as it may," George said, "Miguel wouldn't give up, and that's what caused all the trouble. First he wrote her letters, long mushy letters in broken English. He gave me one to read through for spelling and so on, but it was utterly hopeless. All fragments and run-ons. No paragraphs. I just gave it back after a few days and said it was fine. Miguel thought that the letters would bring Senga around, but she never answered and after a while he began calling her at all hours. She wouldn't talk to him. As soon as she heard his voice she hung up. Eventually she got an unlisted number. She wouldn't talk to Miguel, but Miguel thought that she would listen to yours truly. He wanted me to go down to B of A and plead his cause. Act as a kind of character witness. Which, after some reflection, I agreed to do."

"Oho," Truman said. "The plot thickens. Enter Miles Standish."

"I *knew* you would say that," Audrey said. She finished her drink and looked around, but the waitress was sitting at the bar with her back to the room, smoking a cigarette.

George took his glasses off, held them up to the light, and put them on again. "So," he said, "George sallies forth to meet Senga. Senga—doesn't it make you think of a jungle queen, that name? Flashing eyes, dagger at the hip, breasts bulging over a leopard-skin halter? Such was not the case. This Senga was still an Agnes. Thin. Businesslike. And *very* grouchy. No sooner did I mention Miguel's name than I was shown the door, with a message for Miguel: if he bothered her again she would set the police on him.

" 'Set the police on him.' Those were her words, and she meant them. A week or so later Miguel followed her home from work and she forthwith got a lawyer on the case. The upshot of it was that Miguel had to sign a paper saying that he understood he would be arrested if he wrote, called, or followed Senga again. He signed, but with his fingers crossed, as it were. He told me, 'Horhay, I sign—but I do not accept.' 'Nobly spoken,' I told him, 'but you'd damn well better accept or that woman will have you locked up.' Miguel said that prison did not frighten him, that in his country all the best people were in prison. Sure enough, a few days later he followed Senga home again and she did it—she had him locked up."

"Poor kid," Audrey said.

Truman had been trying to get the attention of the waitress, who wouldn't look at him. He turned to Audrey. "What do you mean, 'Poor kid'? What about the girl? Senga? She's trying to hold down a job and feed her daughter and meanwhile she has this Filipino stalking her all over the city. If you want to feel sorry for someone, feel sorry for her."

"I do," Audrey said.

"All right then." Truman looked back toward the waitress again, and as he did so Audrey picked up George's snifter and took a drink from it. George smiled at her. "What's wrong with that woman?" Truman said. He shook his head. "I give up."

"George, go on," Audrey said.

George nodded. "In brief," he said, "it was a serious mess. *Très sérieux.* They set bail at twenty thousand dollars, which Monsignor Strauss could not raise. Nor, it goes without saying, could yours truly. So Miguel remained in jail. Senga's lawyer was out for blood, and he got Immigration into the act. They were threatening to revoke Miguel's visa and throw him out of the country. Monsignor Strauss finally got him off, but it was, as the Duke said, a damn close-run thing. It turned out that Senga was going to be transferred to Portland in a month or so, and the monsignor persuaded her to drop charges with the understanding that Miguel would not come within ten miles of the city limits as long as she lived there. Until she left, Miguel would stay with Monsignor Strauss at the rectory, under his personal supervision. The monsignor also agreed to pay Senga for her lawyer's fees, which were outrageous. Absolutely outrageous."

"So what was the bottom line?" Truman asked.

"Simplicity itself," George said. "If Miguel messed up, they'd throw him on the first plane to Manila."

"Sounds illegal," Truman said.

"Perhaps. But that was the arrangement."

A new song began on the jukebox. The men by the door stopped arguing, and each of them seemed all at once to draw into himself.

"Listen," Audrey said. "It's him. Caruso."

The record was worn and gave the effect of static behind Ca-

ruso's voice. The music coming through the static made Charlie
think of the cultural broadcasts from Europe his parents had listened to so gravely when he was a boy. At times Caruso's voice
was almost lost, and then it would swell again. The old men were
still. One of them began to weep. The tears fell freely from his
open eyes, down his shining cheeks.

"So that was Caruso," Truman said when it ended. "I always
wondered what all the fuss was about. Now I know. That's what
I call singing." Truman took out his wallet and put some money
on the table. He examined the money left in the wallet before
putting it away. "Ready?" he said to Audrey.

"No," Audrey said. "Finish the story, George."

George took his glasses off and laid them next to his snifter. He
rubbed his eyes. "All right," he said. "Back to Miguel. As per the
agreement, he lived in the rectory until Senga moved to Portland.
Behaved himself, too. No letters, no calls, no following her
around. In his pajamas every night by ten. Then Senga left town
and Miguel went back to his room at the Overland. For a while
there he looked pretty desperate, but after a few weeks he seemed
to come out of it.

"I say 'seemed.' There was in fact more going on than met the
eye. My eye, anyway. One night I am sitting at home and listening, believe it or not, to *Tristan*, when the telephone rings.
At first no one says anything; then this voice comes on the line
whispering, 'Help me, Horhay, help me,' and of course I know
who it is. He says he needs to see me right away. No explanation.
He doesn't even tell me where he is. I just have to assume he's at
the Overland, and that's where I find him, in the lobby."

George gave a little laugh. "Actually," he said, "I almost missed
him. His face was all bandaged up, from his nose to the top of his
forehead. If I hadn't been looking for him I never would have
recognized him. Never. He was sitting there with his suitcases all
around him and a white cane across his knees. When I made my
presence known to him he said, 'Horhay, I am blind.' How, I
asked him, had this come to pass? He would not say. Instead he

gave me a piece of paper with a telephone number on it and asked me to call Senga and tell her that he had gone blind, and that he would be arriving in Portland by Trailways at eleven o'clock the next morning."

"Great Scott," Truman said. "He was faking it, wasn't he? I mean he wasn't really blind, was he?"

"Now that is an interesting question," George said. "Because, while I would have to say that Miguel was not really blind, I would also have to say that he was not really faking it, either. But to go on. Senga was unmoved. She instructed me to tell Miguel that not she but the police would be waiting to meet his bus. Miguel didn't believe her. 'Horhay,' he said, 'she will be there,' and that was that. End of discussion."

"Did he go?" Truman asked.

"Of course he went," Audrey said. "He loved her."

George nodded. "I put him on the bus myself. Led him to his seat, in fact."

"So he still had the bandages on," Truman said.

"Oh yes. Yes, he still had them on."

"But that's a twelve-, thirteen-hour ride. If there wasn't anything wrong with his eyes, why didn't he just take the bandages off and put them on again when the bus reached Portland?"

Audrey put her hand on Truman's. "Truman," she said. "We have to talk about something."

"I don't get it," Truman went on. "Why would he travel blind like that? Why would he go all that way in the dark?"

"Truman, listen," Audrey said. But when Truman turned to her she took her hand away from his and looked across the table at George. George's eyes were closed. His fingers were folded together as if in prayer.

"George," Audrey said. "Please. I can't."

George opened his eyes.

"Tell him," Audrey said.

Truman looked back and forth between them. "Now just wait a minute," he said.

"I'm sorry," George said. "This is not easy for me."

Truman was staring at Audrey. "Hey," he said.

She pushed her empty glass back and forth. "We have to talk," she said.

He brought his face close to hers. "Do you think that just because I make a lot of money I don't have feelings?"

"We have to talk," she repeated.

"Indeed," George said.

The three of them sat there for a while. Then Truman said, "This takes the cake," and put his hat on. A few minutes later they all got up and left the coffeehouse.

The waitress sat by herself at the bar, motionless except when she raised her head to blow smoke at the ceiling. Over by the door the Italians were throwing dice for toothpicks. "The Anvil Chorus" was playing on the jukebox. It was the first piece of classical music Charlie had heard often enough to get sick of, and he was sick of it now. He closed the magazine he'd been pretending to read, dropped it on the table, and went outside.

It was still foggy, and colder than before. Charlie's father had warned him about moving here in the middle of the summer. He had even quoted Mark Twain at Charlie, to the effect that the coldest winter Mark Twain ever endured was the summer he spent in San Francisco. This had been a particularly bad one; even the natives said so. In truth it was beginning to get to Charlie. But he had not admitted this to his father, any more than he had admitted that his job was wearing him out and paying him barely enough to keep alive on, or that the friends he wrote home about did not exist, or that the editors to whom he'd submitted his novel had sent it back without comment—all but one, who had scrawled in pencil across the title page, "Are you kidding?"

Charlie's room was on Broadway, at the crest of the hill. The hill was so steep they'd had to carve steps into the sidewalk and block the street with a cement wall because of the cars that had lost their brakes going down. Sometimes, at night, Charlie would sit on that wall and look out over the lights of North Beach and think of all the writers out there, bent over their desks, steadily filling pages with well-chosen words. He thought of these writers gathering together in the small hours to drink wine, and read each other's work, and talk about the things that weighed on their hearts. These were the brilliant men and women, the deep conversations Charlie wrote home about.

He was close to giving up. He didn't even know how close to giving up he was until he walked out of the coffeehouse that night and felt himself deciding that he would go on after all. He stood there and listened to the foghorn blowing out upon the Bay. The sadness of that sound, the idea of himself stopping to hear it, the thickness of the fog all gave him pleasure.

Charlie heard violins behind him as the coffeehouse door opened; then it banged shut and the violins were gone. A deep voice said something in Italian. A higher voice answered, and the two voices floated away together down the street.

Charlie turned and started up the hill, picking his way past lampposts that glistened with running beads of water, past sweating walls and dim windows. A Chinese woman appeared beside him. She held before her a lobster that was waving its pincers back and forth as if conducting music. The woman hurried past and vanished. The hill began to steepen under Charlie's feet. He stopped to catch his breath, and listened again to the foghorn. He knew that somewhere out there a boat was making its way home in spite of the solemn warning, and as he walked on Charlie imagined himself kneeling in the prow of that boat, lamp in hand, intent on the light shining just before him. All distraction gone. Too watchful to be afraid. Tongue wetting the lips and eyes wide open, ready to call out in this shifting fog where at any moment anything might be revealed.

RICHARD FORD | # WINTERKILL

I HAD NOT been back in town long. Maybe a month was all. The work had finally given out for me down at Silver Bow, and I had quit staying down there when the weather turned cold, and come back to my mother's, on the Bitterroot, to lay up and set my benefits aside for when things got worse.

My mother had her boyfriend then, an old wildcatter named Harley Reeves. And Harley and I did not get along, though I don't blame him for that. He had been laid off himself down near Gillette, Wyoming, where the boom was finished. And he was just doing what I was doing and had arrived there first. Everyone was laid off then. It was not a good time in that part of Montana, nor was it going to be. The two of them were just giving it a final try, both of them in their sixties, strangers together in the little house my father had left her.

So in a week I moved up to town, into a little misery flat across from the Burlington Northern yards, and began to wait. There was nothing to do. Watch TV. Stop in a bar. Walk down to the Clark Fork and fish where they had built a little park. Just find a way to spend the time. You think you'd like to have all the time be your own, but that is a fantasy. I was feeling my back to the wall then, and didn't know what would happen to me in a week's time, which is a feeling to stay with you and make being cheerful hard. And no one can like that.

I was at the Top Hat having a drink with Little Troy Burnham, talking about the deer season, when a woman who had been sitting at the front of the bar got up and came over to us. I had seen this woman other times in other bars in town. She would be there in the afternoons around three, and then sometimes late at night when I would be cruising back. She danced with some men from the air base, then sat drinking and talking late. I suppose she left with someone finally. She wasn't a bad-looking woman at all—blond, with wide, dark eyes set out, wide hips and dark eyebrows. She could've been thirty-four years old, although she could've been forty-four or twenty-four, because she was drinking steady, and steady drink can do both to you, especially to women. But I had thought the first time I saw her: Here's one on the way down. A miner's wife drifted up from Butte, or a rancher's daughter just suddenly run off, which can happen. Or worse. And I hadn't been tempted. Trouble comes cheap and leaves expensive, is a way of thinking about that.

"Do you suppose you could give me a light?" the woman said to us. She was standing at our table. Nola was her name. Nola Foster. I'd heard that around. She wasn't drunk. It was four o'clock in the afternoon, and no one was there but Troy Burnham and me.

"If you'll tell me a love story, I'd do anything in the world for you," Troy said. It was what he always said to women. He'd do anything in the world for something. Troy sits in a wheelchair due to a smoke jumper's injury, and can't do very much. We had been friends since high school and before. He was always short, and I was tall. But Troy had been an excellent wrestler and won awards in Montana, and I had done little of that—some boxing once was all. We had been living, recently, in the same apartments

[158]

on Ryman Street, though Troy lived there permanently and drove a Checker cab to earn a living, and I was hoping to pass on to something better. "I *would* like a little love story," Troy said, and called out for whatever Nola Foster was drinking.

"Nola, Troy. Troy, Nola," I said and lit her cigarette.

"Have we met?" Nola said, taking a seat and glancing at me.

"At the East Gate. Some time ago," I said.

"That's a very nice bar," she said in a cool way. "But I hear it's changed hands."

"I'm glad to make an acquaintance," Troy said, grinning and adjusting his glasses. "Now let's hear that love story." He pulled up close to the table so that his head and his big shoulders were above the tabletop. Troy's injury had caused him not to have any hips left. There is something there, but not hips. He needs bars and a special seat in his cab. He is both frail and strong at once, though in most ways he gets on like everybody else.

"I *was* in love," Nola said quietly as the bartender set her drink down and she took a sip. "And now I'm not."

"That's a short love story," I said.

"There's more to it," Troy said, grinning. "Am I right about that? Here's cheers to you," he said, and raised his glass.

Nola glanced at me again. "All right. Cheers," she said and took another drink.

Two men had started playing a pool game at the far end of the room. They had turned on the table light, and I could hear the balls click and someone say, "Bust 'em up, Craft." And then the smack.

"You don't want to hear about that," Nola said. "You're drunk men, that's all."

"We do too," Troy said. Troy always has enthusiasm. He could very easily complain, but I have never heard it come up. And I believe he has a good heart.

"What about you? What's your name?" Nola said to me.

"Les," I said.

"Les, then," she said. "You don't want to hear this, Les."

"Yes he does," Troy said, putting his elbows on the table and raising himself. Troy was a little drunk. Maybe we all were a little.

"Why not?" I said.

"See? Sure. Les wants more. He's like me."

Nola was actually a pretty woman, with a kind of dignity to her that wasn't at once so noticeable, and Troy was thrilled by her.

"All right," Nola said, taking another sip.

"What'd I tell you?" Troy said.

"I had really thought he was dying," Nola said.

"Who?" I said.

"My husband. Harry Lyons. I don't use that name now. Someone's told you this story before, haven't they?"

"Not me. Goddamn!" Troy said. "I *want* to hear this story."

I said I hadn't heard it either, though I had heard there was a story.

She had a puff on her cigarette and gave us both a look that said she didn't believe us. But she went on. Maybe she'd thought about another drink by then.

"He had this death look. Ca-shit-ic, they call it. He was pale, and his mouth turned down like he could see death. His heart had already gone out once in June, and I had the feeling I'd come in the kitchen some morning and he'd be slumped on his toast."

"How old was this Harry?" Troy said.

"Fifty-three years old. Older than me by a lot."

"That's cardiac alley there," Troy said and nodded at me. Troy has trouble with his own organs now and then. I think they all moved lower when he hit the ground.

"A man gets strange when he's going to die," Nola said in a quiet voice. "Like he's watching it come. Though Harry was still going to work out at Champion's every day. He was an estimator. Plus he watched *me* all the time. Watched to see if I was getting ready, I guess. Checking the insurance, balancing the checkbook, locating the safe-deposit key. All that. Though I would, too. Who wouldn't?"

"Bet your ass," Troy said and nodded again. Troy was taking this all in, I could see that.

"And I admit it, I *was*," Nola said. "I loved Harry. But if he died, where was I going? Was I supposed to die, too? I had to make some plans for myself. I had to think Harry was expendable at some point. To *my* life, anyway."

"Probably that's why he was watching you," I said. "He might not have felt expendable in *his* life."

"I know." Nola looked at me seriously and smoked her cigarette. "But I had a friend whose husband killed himself. Went into the garage and left the motor running. And his wife was *not* ready. Not in her mind. She thought he was out putting on brakeshoes. And there he was dead when she went out there. She ended up having to move to Washington, D.C. Lost her balance completely over it. Lost her house, too."

"All bad things," Troy agreed.

"And that just wasn't going to be me, I thought. And if Harry had to get wind of it, well, so be it. Some days I'd wake up and look at him in bed and I'd think, Die, Harry, quit worrying about it."

"I thought this was a love story," I said. I looked down at where the two men were playing an eight-ball rack. One man was chalking a cue while the other man was leaning over to shoot.

"It's coming," Troy said. "Just be patient, Les."

Nola drained her drink. "I'll guarantee it is."

"Then let's hear it," I said. "Get on to the love part."

Nola looked at me strangely then, as if I really did know what she was going to tell, and thought maybe I might tell it first myself. She raised her chin at me. "Harry came home one evening from work, right?" she said. "Just death as usual. Only he said to me, 'Nola, I've invited some friends over, sweetheart. Why don't you go out and get a flank steak at Albertson's.' I asked when were they coming? He said, in an hour. And I thought, An hour! Because he never brought people home. We went to bars, you know. We didn't entertain. But I said, 'All right. I'll go get a flank steak.' And I got in the car and went out and bought a flank steak. I thought Harry ought to have what he wants. If he wants to have friends and steak he ought to be able to. Men, before they die, will want strange things."

"That's a fact, too," Troy said seriously. "I was full dead all of four minutes when I hit. And I dreamed about nothing but lobster the whole time. And I'd never even seen a lobster, though I have now. Maybe that's what they serve in heaven." Troy grinned at both of us.

"Well, this wasn't heaven," Nola said and signaled for another drink. "So when I got back, there was Harry with three Crow Indians, in my house, sitting in the living room drinking mai tais. A man and two women. His *friends*, he said. From the mill. He wanted to have his friends over, he said. And Harry was raised a strict Mormon. Not that it matters."

"I guess he had a change of heart," I said.

"That'll happen, too," Troy said gravely. "LDS's aren't like they used to be. They used to be bad, but that's all changed. Though I guess coloreds still can't get inside the temple all the way."

"These three were inside my house, though. I'll just say that. And I'm not prejudiced about it. Leopards with spots, leopards without. All the same to me. But I was nice. I went right in the kitchen and put the flank steak in the oven, put some potatoes in water, got out some frozen peas. And went back in to have a drink. And we sat around and talked for half an hour. Talked about the mill. Talked about Marlon Brando. The man and one of the women were married. He worked with Harry. And the other woman was her sister, Winona. There's a town in Mississippi with the same name. I looked it up. So after a while—all nice and friends—I went in to peel my potatoes. And this other woman, Bernie, came in with me to help, I guess. And I was standing there cooking over a little range, and this Bernie said to me, 'I don't know how you do it, Nola.' 'Do what, Bernie?' I said. 'Let Harry go with my sister like he does and you stay so happy about it. I couldn't ever stand that with Claude.' And I just turned around and looked at her. *Winona is what?* I thought. That name seemed so unusual for an Indian. And I just started yelling it. 'Winona, Winona,' at the top of my lungs right at the stove. I just went crazy a minute, I guess. Screaming, holding a potato in my hand, hot. The man came running into the kitchen. Claude Smart Enemy. Claude was awfully nice. He kept me from harming myself. But when I started yelling, Harry, I guess, figured everything was all up. And he and his Winona woman went right out the door. And he didn't get even to the car when his heart went. He had a myocardial infarction right out on the sidewalk at this Winona's feet. I guess he thought everything was going to be just great. We'd all have dinner together. And I'd never know what was what. Except he didn't count on Bernie saying something."

"Maybe he was trying to make you appreciate him more," I said. "Maybe he didn't like being expendable and was sending you a message."

Nola looked at me seriously again. "I thought of that," she said. "I thought about that more than once. But that would've been hurtful. And Harry Lyons wasn't a man to hurt you. He was more of a sneak. I just think he wanted us all to be friends."

"That makes sense." Troy nodded and looked at me.

"What happened to Winona," I asked.

"What happened to Winona?" Nola took a drink and gave me a hard look. "Winona moved herself to Spokane. What happened to me is a better question."

"Why? You're here with us," Troy said enthusiastically. "You're doing great. Les and me ought to do as well as you're doing. Les is out of work. And I'm out of luck. You're doing the best of the three of us, I'd say."

"I wouldn't," Nola said frankly, then turned and stared down at the men playing pool.

"What'd he leave you?" I said. "Harry."

"Two thousand," Nola said coldly.

"That's a small amount," I said.

"And it's a sad love story, too," Troy said, shaking his head. "You loved him and it ended rotten. That's like Shakespeare."

"I loved him enough," Nola said.

"How about sports. Do you like sports?" Troy said.

Nola looked at Troy oddly then. In his chair Troy doesn't look exactly like a whole man, and sometimes simple things he'll say will seem surprising. And what he'd said then surprised Nola. I've gotten used to it, myself, after all these years.

"Did you want to try skiing?" Nola said and glanced at me.

"Fishing," Troy said, up on his elbows again. "Let's all of us go fishing. Put an end to old gloomy." Troy seemed like he wanted to pound the table. And I wondered when was the last time he had slept with a woman. Fifteen years ago, maybe. And now that was all over for him. But he was excited just to be here and get to talk to Nola Foster, and I wasn't going to be in his way. "No one'll be there now," he said. "We'll catch a fish and cheer ourselves up. Ask Les. He caught a fish."

I had been going mornings in those days, when the "Today" show got over. Just to kill an hour. The river runs through the middle of town, and I could walk over in five minutes and fish downstream below the motels that are there, and could look up at the blue and white mountains up the Bitterroot, toward my mother's house, and sometimes see the geese coming back up their flyway. It was a strange winter. January was like a spring day, and the Chinook blew down over us a warm wind from the eastern slopes. Some days were cool or cold, but many days were warm, and the only ice you'd see was in the lows where the sun didn't reach. You could walk right out to the river and make a long cast to where the fish were deep down in the cold pools. And you could even think things might turn out better.

Nola turned and looked at me. The thought of fishing was seeming like a joke to her, I know. Though maybe she didn't have money for a meal and thought we might buy her one. Or maybe she'd never even been fishing. Or maybe she knew that she was on her way to the bottom, where everything is the same, and here was this something different being offered, and it was worth a try.

"Did you catch a big fish, Les?" she asked.

"Yes," I said.

"See?" Troy said. "Am I a liar? Or am I not?"

"You might be." Nola looked at me oddly then, but I thought sweetly, too. "What kind of fish was it?"

"A brown trout. Caught deep, on a hare's ear," I said.

"I don't know what that is," Nola said and smiled. I could see that she wasn't minding any of this because her face was flushed, and she looked pretty.

"Which," I asked. "A brown trout? Or a hare's ear?"

"That's it," she said.

"A hare's ear is a kind of fly," I said.

"I see," Nola said.

"Let's get out of the bar for once," Troy said loudly, running his chair backward and forward. "We'll go fish, then we'll have chicken-in-the-ruff. Troy's paying."

"What'll I lose?" Nola said and shook her head. She looked at both of us, smiling as though she could think of something that might be lost.

"You got it all to win," Troy said. "Let's go."

"Whatever," Nola said. "Sure."

And we went out of the Top Hat, with Nola pushing Troy in his chair and me coming on behind.

On Front Street the evening was as warm as May, though the sun had gone behind the peaks already, and it was nearly dark. The sky was deep blue in the east behind the Sapphires, where the darkness was, but salmon pink above the sun. And we were in the middle of it. Half-drunk, trying to be imaginative in how we killed our time.

Troy's Checker was parked in front, and Troy rolled over to it and spun around.

"Let me show you this great trick," he said and grinned. "Get in and drive, Les. Stay there, sweetheart, and watch me."

Nola had kept her drink in her hand, and she stood by the door of the Top Hat. Troy lifted himself off his chair onto the concrete. I got in beside Troy's bars and his raised seat, and started the cab with my left hand.

"Ready," Troy shouted. "Ease forward. Ease up."

And I eased the car up.

"Oh my God," I heard Nola say and saw her put her palm to her forehead and look away.

"Yaah. Ya-hah," Troy yelled.

"Your poor foot," Nola said.

"It doesn't hurt me," Troy yelled. "It's just like a pressure." I couldn't see him from where I was.

"Now I know I've seen it all," Nola said. She was smiling.

"Back up, Les. Just ease it back again," Troy called out.

"Don't do it again," Nola said.

"One time's enough, Troy," I said. No one else was in the street. I thought how odd it would be for anyone to see that, without knowing something in advance. A man running over another man's foot for fun. Just drunks, you'd think, and be right.

"Sure. Okay," Troy said. I still couldn't see him. But I put the cab back in park and waited. "Help me, sweetheart, now," I heard Troy say to Nola. "It's easy getting down, but old Troy can't get up again by himself. You have to help him."

And Nola looked at me in the cab, the glass still in her hand. It was a peculiar look she gave me, a look that seemed to ask something of me, but I did not know what it was and couldn't answer. And then she put her glass on the pavement and went to put Troy back in his chair.

When we got to the river it was as good as dark, and the river was only a big space you could hear, with the south-of-town lights up behind it and the three bridges and Champion's Paper downstream a mile. And it was cold with the sun gone, and I thought there would be fog in before morning.

Troy had insisted on driving with us in the back, as if we'd hired a cab to take us fishing. On the way down he sang a smoke jumper's song, and Nola sat close to me and let her leg be beside mine. And by the time we stopped by the river, below the Lion's Head motel, I had kissed her twice, and knew all that I could do.

"I think I'll go fishing," Troy said from his little raised-up seat in front. "I'm going night fishing. And I'm going to get my own chair out and my rod and all I need. I'll have a time."

"How do you ever change a tire?" Nola said. She was not moving. It was just a question she had. People say all kinds of things to cripples.

Troy whipped around suddenly, though, and looked back at us where we sat on the cab seat. I had put my arm around Nola, and we sat there looking at his big head and big shoulders, below which there was only half a body any good to anyone. "Trust Mr. Wheels," Troy said. "Mr. Wheels can do anything a whole man can." And he smiled at us a crazy man's smile.

"I think I'll just stay in the car," Nola said. "I'll wait for chicken-in-the-ruff. That'll be my fishing."

"It's too cold for ladies now anyway," Troy said gruffly. "Only men. Only men in wheelchairs is the new rule."

I got out of the cab with Troy then and set up his chair and put him in it. I got his fishing gear out of the trunk and strung it up. Troy was not a man to fish flies, and I put a silver dace on his spin line and told him to hurl it far out and let it flow for a time into the deep current and then to work it, and work it all the way in. I said he would catch a fish with that strategy in five minutes, or ten.

"Les," Troy said to me in the cold dark behind the cab.

"What?" I said.

"Do you ever just think of just doing a criminal thing sometime? Just do something terrible. Change everything."

"Yes," I said. "I think about that."

Troy had his fishing rod across his chair now, and he was gripping it and looking down the sandy bank toward the dark and sparkling water.

"Why don't you do it?" he said.

"I don't know what I'd choose to do," I said.

"Mayhem," Troy said. "Commit mayhem."

"And go to Deer Lodge forever," I said. "Or maybe they'd hang me and let me dangle. That would be worse than this."

"Okay, that's right," Troy said, still staring. "But *I* should do it, shouldn't I? I should do the worst thing there is."

"No, you shouldn't," I said.

And then he laughed. "Hah. Right. Never do that," he said. And he wheeled himself down toward the river into the darkness, laughing all the way.

In the cold cab, after that, I held Nola Foster for a long time. Just held her with my arms around her, breathing and waiting. From the back window I could see the Lion's Head motel, see the restaurant there that faces the river and that is lighted with candles, and where people were eating. I could see the WELCOME out front, though not who was welcomed. I could see cars on the bridge going home for the night. And it made me think of Harley Reeves in my father's little house on the Bitterroot. I thought about him in bed with my mother. Warm. I thought about the faded old tattoo on Harley's shoulder. VICTORY, that said. And I could not connect it easily with what I knew about Harley Reeves, though I thought possibly that he had won a victory of kinds over me just by being where he was.

"A man who isn't trusted is the worst thing," Nola Foster said. "You know that, don't you?" I suppose her mind was wandering. She was cold, I could tell by the way she held me. Troy was gone out in the dark now. We were alone, and her skirt had come up a good ways.

"Yes, that's bad," I said, though I couldn't think at that moment of what trust could mean to me. It was not an issue in my life, and I hoped it never would be. "You're right," I said to make her happy.

"What was your name again?"

"Les," I said. "Lester Snow. Call me Les."

"Les Snow," Nola said. "Do you like less snow?"

"Usually I do." And I put my hand then where I wanted it most.

"How old are you, Les?" she said.

"Thirty-seven."

"You're an old man."

"How old are you?" I said.

"It's my business, isn't it?"

"I guess it is," I said.

"I'll do this, you know," Nola said, "and not even care about it. Just do a thing. It means nothing more than how I feel at this time. You know? Do you know what I mean, Les?"

"I know it," I said.

"But *you* need to be trusted. Or you aren't anything. Do you know that too?"

We were close to each other. I couldn't see the lights of town or the motel or anything more. Nothing moved.

"I know that, I guess," I said. It was whiskey talking.

"Warm me up then, Les," Nola said. "Warm. Warm."

"You'll get warm," I said.

"I'll think about Florida."

"I'll make you warm," I said.

What I thought I heard at first was a train. So many things can sound like a train when you live near trains. This was a *woo* sound, you would say. Like a train. And I lay and listened for a long time, thinking about a train and its light shining through the darkness along the side of some mountain pass north of there and about something else I don't even remember now. And then Troy came around to my thinking, and I knew then that the *woo* sound had been him.

Nola Foster said, "It's Mr. Wheels. He's caught a fish, maybe. Or else drowned."

"Yes," I said. I sat up and looked out the window but could see nothing. It had become foggy in just that little time, and tomorrow, I thought, would be warm again, though it was cold now. Nola and I had not even taken off our clothes to do what we'd done.

"Let me see," I said.

I got out and walked into the fog to where I could only see fog and hear the river running. Troy had not made a *woo*-ing sound again, and I thought to myself, There is no trouble here. Nothing's wrong.

Though when I walked a ways up the sandy bank, I saw Troy's chair come visible in the fog. And he was not in it, and I couldn't see him. And my heart went then. I heard it go click in my chest. And I thought: This is the worst. What's happened here will be the worst. And I called out, "Troy. Where are you? Call out now."

And Troy called out, "Here I am, here."

I went for the sound, ahead of me, which was not out in the river but on the bank. And when I had gone farther, I saw him, out of his chair, of course, on his belly, holding on to his fishing rod with both hands, the line out into the river as though it meant to drag him to the water.

"Help me!" he yelled. "I've got a huge fish. Do something to help me."

"I will," I said. Though I didn't see what I could do. I would not dare to take the rod, and it would only have been a mistake to take the line. Never give a straight pull to the fish, is an old rule. So that my only choice was to grab Troy and hold him until the fish was either in or lost, just as if Troy was a part of a rod *I* was fishing with.

I squatted in the cold sand behind him, put my heels down and took up his legs, which felt like matchsticks, and began to hold him there away from the water.

But Troy suddenly twisted toward me. "Turn me loose, Les. Don't be here. Go out. It's snagged. You've got to go out."

"That's crazy," I said. "It's too deep there."

"It's not deep," Troy yelled. "I've got it in close now."

"You're crazy," I said.

"Oh, Christ, Les, go get it. I don't want to lose it."

I looked a moment at Troy's face then, in the dark. His glasses were gone off of him. His face was wet. And he had the look of a desperate man, a man who has nothing to hope for but, in some strange way, everything in the world to lose.

"Stupid. This is stupid," I said, because it seemed to me to be. But I got up, walked to the edge and stepped out into the cold water.

Then, it was at least a month before the runoff would begin in the mountains, and the water I stepped in was cold and painful as broken glass, though the wet parts of me numbed at once, and my feet felt like bricks bumping the bottom.

Troy had been wrong all the way about the depth. Because when I stepped out ten yards, keeping touch of his line with the back of my hand, I had already gone above my knees, and on the bottom I felt large rocks, and there was a loud rushing around me that suddenly made me afraid.

But when I had gone five more yards, and the water was on my thighs and hurting, I hit the snag Troy's fish was hooked to, and I realized then I had no way at all to hold a fish or catch it with my numbed hands. And that all I could really hope for was to break the snag and let the fish slip down into the current and hope Troy could bring it in, or that I could go back and beach it.

"Can you see it, Les?" Troy yelled out of the dark. "God-damn it."

"It isn't easy," I said, and I had to hold the snag then to keep my balance. My legs were numb. And I thought: This might be the time and the place I die. What an odd place it is. And what an odd reason for it to happen.

"Hurry up," Troy yelled.

And I wanted to hurry. Except when I ran the line as far as where the snag was, I felt something there that was not a fish and not the snag but something else entirely, some thing I thought I recognized, though I am not sure why. A man, I thought. This is a man.

Though when I reached farther into the snag branches and woods scruff, deeper into the water, what I felt was an animal. With my fingers I touched its hard rib-side, its legs, its short slick coat. I felt to its neck and head and touched its nose and teeth, and it was a deer, though not a big deer, not even a yearling. And I knew when I found where Troy's dace had gone up in the neck flesh, that he had hooked a deer already snagged here, and that he had pulled himself out of his chair trying to work it free.

"What is it? I know it's a big *Brown*. Don't tell me, Les, don't even tell me."

"I've got it," I said. "I'll bring it in."

"Sure, hell yes," Troy said out of the fog.

It was not so hard to work the deer off the snag brush and float it up free. Though once I did, it was dangerous to get turned in the current on numb legs, and hard to keep from going down, and I had to hold on to the deer to keep balance enough to heave myself into the slower water. And as I did that, I thought: In the Clark Fork many people drown doing less dangerous things than I am doing.

"Throw it way far up," Troy shouted when he could see me. He had righted himself on the sand and was sitting up like a little doll. "Get it way up safe."

"It's safe," I said. I had the deer beside me, floating, but I knew Troy couldn't see it.

"What did I catch?" Troy yelled.

"Something unusual," I said, and with effort I hauled the little deer a foot up onto the sand, dropped it, and put my cold hands under my arms. I heard a car door close back where I had come from, up the riverbank.

"What *is* that?" Troy said and put his hand out to touch the deer's side. He looked up at me. "I can't see without my glasses."

"It's a deer," I said.

Troy moved his hand around on the deer, then looked at me again in a painful way.

"What is it?" he said.

"A deer," I said. "You caught a dead deer."

Troy looked back at the little deer for a moment, and stared as if he did not know what to say about it. And sitting on the wet sand, in the foggy night, he all at once looked scary to me, as though it was him who had washed up there and was finished. "I don't see it," he said and sat there.

"It's what you caught," I said. "I thought you'd want to see it."

"It's crazy, Les," he said. "Isn't it?" And he smiled at me in a wild, blind-eyed way.

"It's unusual," I said.

"I never shot a deer before."

"I don't believe you shot this one," I said.

He smiled at me again, but then suddenly he gasped back a sob, something I had never seen before. "Goddamn it," he said. "Just goddamn it."

"It's an odd thing to catch," I said, standing above him in the grimy fog.

"I can't change a fucking tire," he said and sobbed. "But I'll catch a fucking deer with my fucking fishing rod."

"Not everyone can say that," I said.

"Why would they want to?" He looked up at me crazy again, and broke his spinning rod into two pieces with only his hands. And I knew he must've been drunk still, because I was still drunk a little, and that by itself made me want to cry. And we were there for a time just silent.

"Who killed a deer?" Nola said. She had come behind me in the cold and was looking. I had not known, when I heard the car door, if she wasn't starting back up to town. But it was too cold for that, and I put my arm around her because she was shivering. "Did Mr. Wheels kill it?"

"It drowned," Troy said.

"And why is that?" Nola said and pushed closer to me to be warm, though that was all.

"They get weak and they fall over," I said. "It happens in the mountains. This one fell in the water and couldn't get up."

"So a gimp man can catch it on a fishing rod in a shitty town," Troy said and gasped with bitterness. Real bitterness. The worst I have ever heard from any man, and I have heard bitterness voiced, though it was a union matter then.

"Maybe it isn't so bad," Nola said.

"Hah!" Troy said from the wet ground. "Hah, hah, hah." And I wished that I had never shown him the deer, wished I had spared him that, though the river's rushing came up then and snuffed his sound right out of hearing, and drew it away from us into the foggy night beyond all accounting.

Nola and I pushed the deer back into the river while Troy watched, and then we all three drove up into town and ate chicken-in-the-ruff at the Two Fronts, where the lights were bright and they cooked the chicken fresh for you. I bought a jug of wine and we drank that while we ate, though no one talked. Each of us had done something that night. Something different. That was plain enough. And there was nothing more to talk about.

When we were finished we walked outside, and I asked Nola where she'd like to go. It was only eight o'clock, and there was no place to go but to my little room. She said she wanted to go back to the Top Hat, that she had someone to meet there later, and there was something about the band that night that she liked. She said she wanted to dance.

I told her I was not much for dancing, and she said fine. And when Troy came out from paying, we said good-bye, and she shook my hand and said that she would see me again. Then she and Troy got in the Checker and drove away together down the foggy street, leaving me alone, where I didn't mind being at all.

For a long time I just walked then. My clothes were wet, but it wasn't so cold if you kept moving, though it stayed foggy. I walked to the river again and across on the bridge and a long way down into the south part of town on a wide avenue where there were houses with little porches and little yards, all the way, until it became commercial, and bright lights lit the drive-ins and car lots. I could've walked then, I thought, clear to my mother's house twenty miles away. But I turned back, and walked the same way, only on the other side of the street. Though when I got near the bridge, I came past the Senior Citizen Recreation, where there were soft lights on inside a big room, and I could see through a window in the pinkish glow, old people dancing across the floor to a record player that played in the corner. It was a rumba or something like a rumba that was being played, and the old people were dancing the box step, smooth and graceful and courteous, moving across the linoleum like real dancers, their arms on each other's shoulders like husbands and wives. And it pleased me to see that. And I thought that it was too bad my mother and father could not be here now, too bad they couldn't come up and dance and go home happy, and have me to watch them. Or even for my mother and Harley Reeves to do that. It didn't seem like too much to wish for. Just a normal life other people had.

I stood and watched them a while, then I walked back home across the river. Though for some reason I could not sleep that night, and simply lay in bed with the radio turned on to Denver, and smoked cigarettes until it was light. Of course I thought about Nola Foster, that I didn't know where she lived, though for some reason I thought she might live in Frenchtown, near the pulp plant. Not far. Never-never land, they called that. And I thought about my father, who had once gone to Deer Lodge prison for stealing hay from a friend, and had never recovered from it, though that meant little to me now.

And I thought about the matter of trust. That I would always lie if it would save someone an unhappiness. That was easy. And that I would rather a person mistrust me than dislike me. Though I thought you could always trust me to act a certain way, to be a place, or to say a thing if it ever were to matter. You could predict within human reason what I'd do—that I would not, for example, commit a vicious crime—trust that I would risk my own life for you if I knew it meant enough. And as I lay in the gray light, smoking, while the refrigerator clicked and the switches in the Burlington Northern yard shunted cars and made their couplings, I thought that though my life at that moment seemed to have taken a bad turn and paused, it still meant something to me as a life, and that before long it would start again in some promising way.

I know I must've dozed a little, because I woke suddenly and there was the light. Earl Nightingale was on the radio, and I heard a door close. It was that that woke me.

I knew it would be Troy, and I thought I would step out and meet him, fix coffee for us before he went to bed and slept all day, the way he always did. But when I stood up I heard Nola Foster's voice. I could not mistake that. She was drunk, and laughing about something. "Mr. Wheels," she said. Mr. Wheels this, Mr. Wheels that. Troy was laughing. And I heard them come in the little entry, heard Troy's chair bump the sill. And I waited to see if they would knock on my door. And when they didn't, and I heard Troy's door shut and the chain go up, I thought that we had all had a good night finally. Nothing had happened that hadn't turned out all right. None of us had been harmed. And I put on my pants, then my shirt and shoes, turned off my radio, went into the kitchen where I kept my fishing rod, and with it went out into the warm, foggy morning, using just this once the back door, the quiet way, so as not to see or be seen by anyone.

HAROLD BRODKEY | # VERONA: A YOUNG WOMAN SPEAKS

I KNOW a lot! I know about happiness! I don't mean the love of God, either: I mean I know the human happiness with the crimes in it.

Even the happiness of childhood.

I think of it now as a cruel, middle-class happiness.

Let me describe one time—one day, one night.

I was quite young, and my parents and I—there were just the three of us—were traveling from Rome to Salzburg, journeying across a quarter of Europe to be in Salzburg for Christmas, for the music and the snow. We went by train because planes were erratic, and my father wanted us to stop in half a dozen Italian towns and see paintings and buy things. It was absurd, but we were all three drunk with this; it was very strange; we woke every morning in a strange hotel, in a strange city. I would be the first one to wake; and I would go to the window and see some tower or palace; and then I would wake my mother and be justified in my sense of wildness and belief and adventure by the way she acted, her sense of romance at being in a city as strange as I had thought it was when I had looked out the window and seen the palace or the tower.

We had to change trains in Verona, a darkish, smallish city at the edge of the Alps. By the time we got there, we'd bought and bought our way up the Italian peninsula: I was dizzy with shopping and new possessions: I hardly knew who I was, I owned so many new things: my reflection in any mirror or shop window was resplendently fresh and new, disguised even, glittering, I thought. I was seven or eight years old. It seemed to me we were almost in a movie or in the pages of a book: only the simplest and most light-filled words and images can suggest what I thought we were then. We went around shiningly: we shone everywhere. *Those clothes.* It's easy to buy a child. I had a new dress, knitted, blue and red, expensive as hell, I think; leggings, also red; a red loden-cloth coat with a hood and a knitted cap for under the hood; marvelous lined gloves; fur-lined boots and a fur purse or carryall, and a tartan skirt—and shirts and a scarf, and there was even more; a watch, a bracelet: more and more.

On the trains we had private rooms, and Momma carried games in her purse and things to eat, and Daddy sang carols off-key to me; and sometimes I became so intent on my happiness I would suddenly be in real danger of wetting myself; and Momma, who understood such emergencies, would catch the urgency in my voice and see my twisted face; and she—a large, good-looking woman—would whisk me to a toilet with amazing competence and unstoppability, murmuring to me, "Just hold on for a while," and she would hold my hand while I did it.

So we came to Verona, where it was snowing, and the people had stern, sad faces, beautiful, unlaughing faces. But if they looked at me, those serious faces would lighten, they would smile at me in my splendor. Strangers offered me candy, sometimes with the most excruciating sadness, kneeling or stopping to look directly into my face, into my eyes; and Momma or Papa would judge them, the people, and say in Italian we were late, we had to hurry, or pause and let the stranger touch me, talk to me, look into my face for a while. I would see myself in the eyes of some strange man or woman; sometimes they stared so gently I would want to touch their eyelashes, stroke those strange, large, glistening eyes. I knew I decorated life. I took my duties with great seriousness. An Italian count in Siena said I had the manners of an English princess—at times—and then he laughed because it was true I would be quite lurid: I ran shouting in his *galleria*, a long room, hung with pictures, and with a frescoed ceiling: and I sat on his lap and wriggled: I was a wicked child, and I liked myself very much; and almost everywhere, almost every day, there was someone new to love me, briefly, while we traveled.

I understood I was special. I understood it *then*.

I knew that what we were doing, everything we did, involved money. I did not know if it involved mind or not, or style. But I knew about money somehow, checks and traveler's checks and the clink of coins. Daddy was a fountain of money: he said it was a spree; he meant for us to be amazed; he had saved money—we weren't really rich but we were to be for this trip. I remember a conservatory in a large house outside Florence and orange trees in tubs; and I ran there, too. A servant, a man dressed in black, a very old man, mean-faced—he did not like being a servant anymore after the days of servants were over—and he scowled—but he smiled at me, and at my mother, and even once at my father: we were clearly so separate from the griefs and weariness and cruelties of the world. We were at play, we were at our joys, and Momma was glad, with a terrible and naive inner gladness, and she relied on Daddy to make it work: oh, she worked, too, but she didn't know the secret of such—unreality: is that what I want to say? Of such a game, of such an extraordinary game.

There was a picture in Verona Daddy wanted to see: a painting; I remember the painter because the name Pisanello reminded me I had to go to the bathroom when we were in the museum, which was an old castle, Guelph or Ghibelline, I don't remember which; and I also remember the painting because it showed the hind end of the horse, and I thought that was not nice and rather funny, but Daddy was admiring; and so I said nothing.

He held my hand and told me a story so I wouldn't be bored as we walked from room to room in the museum/castle, and then we went outside into the snow, into the soft light when it snows, light coming through snow; and I was dressed in red and had on boots, and my parents were young and pretty and had on boots, too; and we could stay out in the snow if we wanted; and we did. We went to a square, a piazza—the Scaligera, I think; I don't remember—and just as we got there, the snowing began to bellow and then subside, to fall heavily and then sparsely, and then it stopped: and it was very cold, and there were pigeons everywhere in the piazza, on every cornice and roof, and all over the snow on the ground, leaving little tracks as they walked, while the air trembled in its just-after-snow and just-before-snow weight and thickness and gray seriousness of purpose. I had never seen so many pigeons or such a private and haunted place as that piazza, me in my new coat at the far rim of the world, the far rim of who knew what story, the rim of foreign beauty and Daddy's games, the edge, the white border of a season.

I was half mad with pleasure anyway, and now Daddy brought five or six cones made of newspaper, wrapped, twisted; and they held grains of something like corn, yellow and white kernels of something; and he poured some on my hand and told me to hold my hand out; and then he backed away.

At first, there was nothing, but I trusted him and I waited; and then the pigeons came. On heavy wings. Clumsy pigeony bodies. And red, unreal birds' feet. They flew at me, slowing at the last minute; they lit on my arm and fed from my hand. I wanted to flinch, but I didn't. I closed my eyes and held my arm stiffly; and felt them peck and eat—from my hand, these free creatures, these flying things. I liked that moment. I liked my happiness. If I was mistaken about life and pigeons and my own nature, it didn't matter *then*.

The piazza was very silent, with snow; and Daddy poured grains on both my hands and then on the sleeves of my coat and on the shoulders of the coat, and I was entranced with yet more stillness, with this idea of his. The pigeons fluttered heavily in the heavy air, more and more of them, and sat on my arms and on my shoulders; and I looked at Momma and then at my father and then at the birds on me.

Oh, I'm sick of everything as I talk. There is happiness. It always makes me slightly ill. I lose my balance because of it.

The heavy birds, and the strange buildings, and Momma near, and Daddy, too: Momma is pleased that I am happy and she is a little jealous; she is jealous of everything Daddy does; she is a woman of enormous spirit; life is hardly big enough for her; she is drenched in wastefulness and prettiness. She knows things. She gets inflexible, though, and foolish at times, and temperamental; but she is a somebody, and she gets away with a lot, and if she is near, you can feel her, you can't escape her, she's that important, that echoing, her spirit is that powerful in the space around her.

If she weren't restrained by Daddy, if she weren't in love with him, there is no knowing what she might do: she does not know. But she manages almost to be gentle because of him; he is incredibly watchful and changeable and he gets tired; he talks and charms people; sometimes, then, Momma and I stand nearby, like moons; we brighten and wane; and after a while, he comes to us, to the moons, the big one and the little one, and we welcome him, and he is always, to my surprise, he is always surprised, as if he didn't deserve to be loved, as if it were time he was found out.

Daddy is very tall, and Momma is watching us, and Daddy anoints me again and again with the grain. I cannot bear it much longer. I feel joy or amusement or I don't know what; it is all through me, like a nausea—I am ready to scream and laugh, that laughter that comes out like magical, drunken, awful, and yet pure spit or vomit or God knows what, makes me a child mad with laughter. I become brilliant, gleaming, soft: an angel, a great bird-child of laughter.

I am ready to be like that, but I hold myself back.

There are more and more birds near me. They march around my feet and peck at falling and fallen grains. One is on my head. Of those on my arms, some move their wings, fluff those frail, feather-loaded wings, stretch them. I cannot bear it, they are so frail, and I am, at the moment, the kindness of the world that feeds them in the snow.

All at once, I let out a splurt of laughter: I can't stop myself and the birds fly away but not far; they circle around me, above me; some wheel high in the air and drop as they return; they all returned, some in clouds and clusters driftingly, some alone and angry, pecking at others; some with a blind, animal-strutting abruptness. They gripped my coat and fed themselves. It started to snow again.

I was there in my kindness, in that piazza, within reach of my mother and father.

Oh, how will the world continue? Daddy suddenly understood I'd had enough, I was at the end of my strength—Christ, he was alert—and he picked me up, and I went limp, my arm around his neck, and the snow fell. Momma came near and pulled the hood lower and said there were snowflakes in my eyelashes. She knew he had understood, and she wasn't sure she had; she wasn't sure he ever watched her so carefully. She became slightly unhappy, and so she walked like a clumsy boy beside us, but she was so pretty: she had powers anyway.

We went to a restaurant, and I behaved very well, but I couldn't eat, and then we went to the train and people looked at us, but I couldn't smile; I was too dignified, too sated; some leftover— pleasure, let's call it—made my dignity very deep; I could not stop remembering the pigeons, or that Daddy loved me in a way he did not love Momma; and Daddy was alert, watching the luggage, watching strangers for assassination attempts or whatever; he was on duty; and Momma was pretty and alone and *happy*, defiant in that way.

And then, you see, what she did was wake me in the middle of the night when the train was chugging up a very steep mountain-side; and outside the window, visible because our compartment was dark and the sky was clear and there was a full moon, were mountains, a landscape of mountains everywhere, big mountains, huge ones, impossible, all slanted and pointed and white with snow, and absurd, sticking up into an ink blue sky and down into blue, blue shadows, miraculously deep. I don't know how to say what it was like: they were not like anything I knew: they were high things: and we were up high in the train and we were climbing higher, and it was not at all true, but it was, you see. I put my hands on the window and stared at the wild, slanting, unlikely marvels, whiteness and dizziness and moonlight and shadows cast by moonlight, not real, not familiar, not pigeons, but a clean world.

We sat a long time, Momma and I, and stared, and then Daddy woke up and came and looked, too. "It's pretty," he said, but he didn't really understand. Only Momma and I did. She said to him, "When I was a child, I was bored all the time, my love—I thought nothing would ever happen to me—and now these things are happening—and you have happened." I think he was flabbergasted by her love in the middle of the night; he smiled at her, oh, so swiftly that I was jealous, but I stayed quiet, and after a while, in his silence and amazement at her, at us, he began to seem different from us, from Momma and me; and then he fell asleep again; Momma and I didn't; we sat at the window and watched all night, watched the mountains and the moon, the clean world. We watched together.

Momma was the winner.

We were silent, and in silence we spoke of how we loved men and how dangerous men were and how they stole everything from you no matter how much you gave—but we didn't say it aloud.

We looked at mountains until dawn, and then when dawn came, it was too pretty for me—there was pink and blue and gold in the sky, and on icy places, brilliant pink and gold flashes, and the snow was colored, too, and I said, "Oh," and sighed; and each moment was more beautiful than the one before; and I said, "I love you, Momma." Then I fell asleep in her arms.

That was happiness then.

THE CINEMA

I

AT TEN-THIRTY then, she arrived. They were waiting. The door at the far end opened and somewhat shyly, trying to see in the dimness if anyone was there, her long hair hanging like a schoolgirl's, everyone watching, she slowly, almost reluctantly approached . . . . Behind her came the young woman who was her secretary.

Great faces cannot be explained. She had a long nose, a mouth, a curious distance between the eyes. It was a face open and unknowable. It pronounced itself somehow indifferent to life.

When he was introduced to her, Guivi, the leading man, smiled. His teeth were large and there existed a space between the incisors. On his chin was a mole. These defects at that time were revered. He'd had only four or five roles, his discovery was sudden, the shot in which he appeared for the first time was often called one of the most memorable introductions in all of film. It was true. There is sometimes one image which outlasts everything, even the names are forgotten. He held her chair. She acknowledged the introductions faintly, one could hardly hear her voice.

THE CINEMA

The director leaned forward and began to talk. They would rehearse for ten days in this bare hall. Anna's face was buried in her collar as he spoke. The director was new to her. He was a small man known as a hard worker. The saliva flew from his mouth as he talked. She had never rehearsed a film before, not for Fellini, not for Chabrol. She was trying to listen to what he said. She felt strongly the presence of others around her. Guivi sat calmly, smoking a cigarette. She glanced at him unseen.

They began to read, sitting at the table together. Make no attempt to find meaning, Iles told them, not so soon, this was only the first step. There were no windows. There was neither day nor night. Their words seemed to rise, to vanish like smoke above them. Guivi read his lines as if laying down cards of no particular importance. Bridge was his passion. He gave it all his nights. Halfway through, he touched her shoulder lightly as he was doing an intimate part. She seemed not to notice. She was like a lizard, only her throat was beating. The next time he touched her hair. That single gesture, so natural as to be almost unintended, made her quiet, stilled her fears.

She fled afterward. She went directly back to the Hotel de Ville. Her room was filled with objects. On the desk were books still wrapped in brown paper, magazines in various languages, letters hastily read. There was a small anteroom, not regularly shaped, and a bedroom beyond. The bed was large. In the manner of a sequence when the camera carefully, increasing our apprehension, moves from detail to detail, the bathroom door, half-open, revealed a vast array of bottles, of dark perfumes, medicines, things unknown. Far below on Via Sistina was the sound of traffic.

The next day she was better, she was like a woman ready to work. She brushed her hair back with her hand as she read. She was attentive, once she even laughed.

They were brought small cups of coffee from across the courtyard.

"How does it sound to you?" she asked the writer.

"Well . . ." he hesitated.

He was a wavering man named Peter Lang, at one time Leng-sner. He had seen her in all her sacred life, a figure of lights, he had read the article, the love letter written to her in *Bazaar*. It described her perfect modesty, her instinct, the shape of her face. On the opposite page was the photograph he cut out and placed in his journal. This film he had written, this important work of the newest of the arts, already existed complete in his mind. Its power came from its chasteness, the discipline of its images. It was a film of indirection, the surface was calm with the calm of daily life. That was not to say still. Beneath the visible were emotions more potent for their concealment. Only occasionally, like the head of an iceberg ominously rising from nowhere and then drop-ping from sight did the terror come into view.

When she turned to him then, he was overwhelmed, he couldn't think of what to say. It didn't matter. Guivi gave an answer.

"I think we're still a little afraid of some of the lines," he said. "You know, you've written some difficult things."

"Ah, well . . ."

"Almost impossible. Don't misunderstand, they're good, ex-cept they have to be perfectly done."

She had already turned away and was talking to the director.

"Shakespeare is filled with lines like this," Guivi continued. He began to quote Othello.

It was now Iles's turn, the time to expose his ideas. He plunged in. He was like a kind of crazy schoolmaster as he described the work, part Freud, part lovelorn columnist, tracing interior lines and motives deep as rivers. Members of the crew had sneaked in to stand near the door. Guivi jotted something in his script.

"Yes, notes, make notes," Iles told him, "I am saying some brilliant things."

A performance was built up in layers, like a painting, that was his method, to start with this, add this, then this, and so forth. It expanded, became rich, developed depths and undercurrents. Then in the end they would cut it back, reduce it to half its size. That was what he meant by good acting.

He confided to Lang, "I never tell them everything. I'll give you an example: the scene in the clinic. I tell Guivi he's going to pieces, he thinks he's going to scream, actually scream. He has to stuff a towel in his mouth to prevent it. Then, just before we shoot, I tell him: Do it without the towel. Do you see?"

His energy began to infect the performers. A mood of excitement, even fever came over them. He was thrilling them, it was their world he was describing and then taking to pieces to reveal its marvelous intricacies.

If he was a genius, he would be crowned in the end because, like Balzac, his work was so vast. He, too, was filling page after page, unending, crowded with the sublime and the ordinary, fantastic characters, insights, human frailty, trash. If I make two films a year for thirty years, he said . . . The project was his life.

At six the limousines were waiting. The sky still had light, the cold of autumn was in the air. They stood near the door and talked. They parted reluctantly. He had converted them, he was their master. They drove off separately with a little wave. Lang was left standing in the dusk.

There were dinners. Guivi sat with Anna beside him. It was the fourth day. She leaned her head against his shoulder. He was discussing the foolishness of women. They were not genuinely intelligent, he said, that was a myth of Western society.

"I'm going to surprise you," Iles said. "Do you know what I believe? I believe they're not as intelligent as men. They are *more* intelligent."

Anna shook her head very slightly.

"They're not logical," Guivi said. "It's not their way. A woman's whole essence is here." He indicated down near his stomach. "The womb," he said. "Nowhere else. Do you realize there are no great women bridge players?"

It was as if she had submitted to all his ideas. She ate without speaking. She barely touched dessert. She was content to be what he admired in a woman. She was aware of her power, he knelt to it nightly, his mind wandering. He was already becoming indifferent to her. He performed the act as one plays a losing hand, he did the best he could with it. The cloud of white leapt from him. She moaned.

"I am really a romantic and a classicist," he said. "I have *almost* been in love twice."

Her glance fell, he told her something in a whisper.

"But never really," he said, "never deeply. No, I long for that. I am ready for it."

Beneath the table her hand discovered this. The waiters were brushing away the crumbs.

Lang was staying at the Inghilterra in a small room on the side. Long after the evening was over he still swam in thoughts of it. He washed his underwear distractedly. Somewhere in the shuttered city, the river black with fall, he knew they were together, he did not resent it. He lay in bed like a poor student—how little life changes from the first to the last—and fell asleep clutching his dreams. The windows were open. The cold air poured over him like sea on a blind sailor, drenching him, filling the room. He lay with his legs crossed at the ankle like a martyr, his face turned to God.

Iles was at the Grand in a suite with tall doors and floors that creaked. He could hear chambermaids pass in the hall. He had a cold and could not sleep. He called his wife in America, it was just evening there, and they talked for a long time. He was depressed: Guivi was no actor.

"What's wrong with him?"

"Oh, he has nothing, no depth, no emotion."

"Can't you get someone else?"

"It's too late."

They would have to work around it, he said. He had the telephone propped on the pillow, his eyes were drifting aimlessly around the room. They would have to change the character somehow, make the falseness a part of it. Anna was all right. He was pleased with Anna. Well, they would do something, pump life into it somehow, make dead birds fly.

By the end of the week they were rehearsing on their feet. It was cold. They wore their coats as they moved from one place to another. Anna stood near Guivi. She took the cigarette from his fingers and smoked it. Sometimes they laughed.

Iles was alive with work. His hair fell in his face, he was explaining actions, details. He didn't rely on their knowledge, he arranged it all. Often he tied a line to an action, that is to say the words were keyed by it: Guivi touched Anna's elbow, without looking she said, "Go away."

Lang sat and watched. Sometimes they were working very close to him, just in front of where he was. He couldn't really pay attention. She was speaking *his* lines, things he had invented. They were like shoes. She tried them on, they were nice, she never thought who had made them.

"Anna has a limited range," Guivi confided.

Lang said yes. He wanted to learn more about acting, this secret world.

"But what a face," Guivi said.

"Her eyes!"

"There is a little touch of the idiot in them, isn't there?" Guivi said.

She could see them talking. Afterward she sent someone to Lang. Whatever he had told Guivi, she wanted to know, too. Lang looked over at her. She was ignoring him.

He was confused, he did not know if it was serious. The minor actors with nothing to do were sitting on two old sofas. The floor was chalky, dust covered their shoes. Iles was following the scenes closely, nodding his approval, yes, yes, good, excellent. The script girl walked behind him, a stopwatch around her neck. She was forty-five, her legs ached at night. She went along noting everything, careful not to step on any of the half-driven nails.

"My love," Iles turned to her, he had forgotten her name. "How long was it?"

They always took too much time. He had to hurry them, force them to be economical.

At the end, like school, there was the final test. They seemed to do it all perfectly, the gestures, the cadences he had devised. He was timing them like runners. Two hours and twenty minutes.

"Marvelous," he told them.

That night Lang was drunk at the party the producer gave. It was in a small restaurant. The entry was filled with odors and displays of food, the cooks nodded from the kitchen. Fifty people were there, a hundred, crowded together and speaking different languages. Among them Anna shone like a queen. On her wrist was a new bracelet from Bulgari's, she had coolly demanded a discount, the clerk hadn't known what to say. She was in a slim gold suit that showed her breasts. Her strange, flat face seemed to float without expression among the others, sometimes she wore a faint, a drifting smile.

Lang felt depressed. He did not understand what they had been doing, the exaggerations dismayed him, he didn't believe in Iles, his energies, his insight, he didn't believe in any of it. He tried to calm himself. He saw them at the biggest table, the producer at Anna's elbow. They were talking, why was she so animated? They always come alive when the lights are on, someone said.

He watched Guivi. He could see Anna leaning across to him, her long hair, her throat.

"It's stupid to be making it in color," Lang said to the man beside him.

"What?" He was a film company executive. He had a face like a fish, a bass, that had gone bad. "What do you mean, not in color?"

"Black and white," Lang told him.

"What are you talking about? You can't sell a black and white film. Life is in color."

"Life?"

"Color is real," the man said. He was from New York. The ten greatest films of all time, the twenty greatest, were in color, he said.

"What about . . ." Lang tried to concentrate, his elbow slipped, *"The Bicycle Thief?"*

"I'm talking about modern films."

II

Today was sunny. He was writing in brief, disconsolate phrases. *Yesterday it rained, it was dark until late afternoon, the day before was the same.* The corridors of the Inghilterra were vaulted like a convent, the doors set deep in the walls. Still, he thought, it was comfortable. He gave his shirts to the maid in the morning, they were back the next day. She did them at home. He had seen her bending over to take linen from a cabinet. The tops of her stockings showed—it was classic Buñuel—the mysterious white of a leg.

The girl from publicity called. They needed information for his biography.

"What information?"

"We'll send a car for you," she said.

It never came. He went the next day by taxi and waited thirty minutes in her office, she was in seeing the producer. Finally she returned, a thin girl with damp spots under the arms of her dress.

"You called me?" Lang said.

She did not know who he was.

"You were going to send a car for me."

"Mr. Lang," she suddenly cried. "Oh, I'm sorry."

The desk was covered with photos, the chairs with newspapers and magazines. She was an assistant, she had worked on *Cleopatra, The Bible, The Longest Day.* There was money to be earned in American films.

"They've put me in this little room," she apologized.

Her name was Eva. She lived at home. Her family ate without speaking, four of them in the sadness of bourgeois surroundings, the radio which didn't work, thin rugs on the floor. When he was finished, her father cleared his throat. The meat was better the last time, he said. The *last* time? her mother asked.

"Yes, it was better," he said.

"The last time it was tasteless."

"Ah, well, two times ago," he said.

They fell into silence again. There was only the sound of forks, an occasional glass. Suddenly her brother rose from the table and left the room. No one looked up.

He was crazy, this brother, well, perhaps not crazy but enough to make them weep. He would remain for days in his room, the door locked. He was a writer. There was one difficulty, everything worthwhile had already been written. He had gone through a period when he devoured books, three and four a day, and could quote vast sections of them afterward, but the fever had passed. He lay on his bed now and looked at the ceiling.

Eva was nervous, people said. Of course, she was nervous. She was thirty. She had black hair, small teeth, and a life in which she had already given up hope. They had nothing for his biography, she told Lang. They had to have a biography for everybody. She suggested finally he write it himself. Yes, of course, he imagined it would be something like that.

Her closest friend—like all Italians she was alert to friends and enemies—her most useful friend was an hysterical woman named Mirella Ricci who had a large apartment and aristocratic longings, also the fears and illnesses of women who live alone. Mirella's friends were homosexuals and women who were separated. She had dinner with them in the evening, she telephoned them several times a day. She was a woman with large nostrils and white skin, pale as paper, but she was still able to see white spots on it. Her doctor said they were a circulatory condition.

She was working on the film, like Eva. They talked of everyone. Iles: he knew actors, Mirella said. Whichever ones were brought in, he chose the best, well, he had made one or two mistakes. They were eating at Otello's, tortoises crawled on the floor. The script was interesting, Mirella said, but she didn't like the writer, he was cold. He was also a *frocio*, she knew the signs. As for the producer . . . she made a disgusted sound. He dyed his hair, she said. He looked thirty-nine but he was really fifty. He had already tried to seduce her.

"When?" Eva said.

They knew everything. They were like nurses whose tenderness was dead. It was they who ran the sickhouse. They knew how much money everyone was getting, who was not to be trusted.

The producer: first of all he was impotent, Mirella said. When he wasn't impotent, he was unwilling, the rest of the time he didn't know how to go about it and when he did, it was unsatisfactory. On top of that, he was a man who was always without a girl.

Her nostrils had darkness in them. She expected waiters to treat her well.

"How is your brother?" she said.

"Oh, the same."

"He still isn't working?"

"He has a job in a record shop but he won't be there long. They'll fire him."

"What is wrong with men?" she said.

"I'm exhausted," Eva sighed. She was haggard from late hours. She had to type letters for the producer because one of his secretaries was sick.

"He tried to make love to me, too," she admitted.

"Tell me," Mirella said.

"At his hotel . . ."

Mirella waited.

"I brought him some letters. He insisted I stay and talk. He wanted to give me a drink. Finally he tried to kiss me. He fell on his knees—I was cowering on the divan—and said, Eva, you smell so sweet. I tried to pretend it was all a joke."

The joys of rectitude. They drove around in little Fiats. They paid attention to their clothes.

The film was going well, a day ahead of schedule. Iles was working with a kind of vast assurance. He roamed around the great, black Mitchell in tennis shoes, he ate no lunch. The rushes were said to be extraordinary. Guivi never went to see them. Anna asked Lang about them, what did he think? He tried to decide. She was beautiful in them, he told her—it was true—there was a quality in her face which illuminated the entire film . . . he never finished. As usual, she was disinterested. She had already turned to someone else, the cameraman.

"Did you see them?" she said.

Iles wore an old sweater, the hair hung in his face. Two films a year, he repeated . . . that was the keystone of all his belief. Eisenstein only made six altogether, but he didn't work under the American system. Anyway, Iles had no confidence when he was at rest.

Whatever his weaknesses, his act of grandeur was in concealing the knowledge that the film was already wreckage: Guivi was simply not good enough, he worked without thinking, he worked as one eats a meal. Iles knew actors.

Farewell, Guivi. It was the announcement of death. He was already beginning to enter the past. He signed autographs, the space showing between his teeth. He charmed journalists. The perfect victim, he suspected nothing. The glory of his life had blinded him. He dined at the best tables, a bottle of fine Bordeaux before him. He mimicked the foolishness of Iles.

"Guivi, my love," he imitated, "the trouble is you are Russian, you are moody and violent. He's telling me what it is to be Russian. Next he'll start describing life under communism."

Anna was eating with very slow bites.

"Do you know something?" she said calmly.

He waited.

"I've never been so happy."

"Really?"

"Not in my whole life," she said.

He smiled. His smile was opera.

"With you I am the woman everyone believes I am," she said.

He looked at her long and deeply. His eyes were dark, the pupils invisible. Love scenes during the day, he thought wearily, love scenes at night. People were watching them from all around the room. When they rose to go, the waiters crowded near the door.

Within three years his career would be over. He would see himself in the flickering television as if it were some curious dream. He invested in apartment houses, he owned land in Spain. He would become like a woman, jealous, unforgiving, and perhaps one day in a restaurant even see Iles with a young actor, explaining with the heat of a fanatic some very ordinary idea. Guivi was thirty-seven. He had a moment on the screen that would never be forgotten. Tinted posters of him would peel from the sides of buildings more and more remote, the resemblance fading, his name becoming stale. He would smile across alleys, into the sour darkness. Far-off dogs were barking. The streets smelled of the poor.

III

There was a party for Anna's birthday at a restaurant in the outskirts, the restaurant in which Farouk, falling backward from the table, had died. Not everyone was invited. It was meant to be a surprise.

She arrived with Guivi. She was not a woman, she was a minor deity, she was some beautiful animal innocent of its grace. It was February, the night was cold. The chauffeurs waited inside the cars. Later they gathered quietly in the cloakroom.

"My love," Iles said to her, "you are going to be very, very happy."

"Really?"

He put his arm around her without replying; he nodded. The shooting was almost over. The rushes, he said, were the best he had ever seen. Ever.

"As for this fellow . . ." he said, reaching for Guivi.

The producer joined them.

"I want you for my next picture, both of you," he announced. He was wearing a suit a size too small, a velvet suit bought on Via Borgognona.

"Where did you get it?" Guivi said. "It's fantastic. Who is supposed to be the star here anyway?"

Posener looked down at himself. He smiled like a guilty boy.

"Do you like it?" he said. "Really?"

"No, where did you get it?"

"I'll send you one tomorrow."

"No, no . . ."

"Guivi, please," he begged, "I want to."

He was filled with goodwill, the worst was past. The actors had not run away or refused to work, he was overcome with love for them, as for a bad child who unexpectedly does something good. He felt he must do something in return.

"Waiter!" he cried. He looked around, his gestures always seemed wasted, vanished in empty air.

"Waiter," he called, "champagne!"

There were twenty or so people in the room, other actors, the American wife of a count. At the table Guivi told stories. He drank like a Georgian prince, he had plans for Geneva, Gstaad. There was the Italian producer, he said, who had an actress under contract, she was a second Sophia Loren. He had made a fortune with her. Her films were only shown in Italy, but everyone went to them, the money was pouring in. He always kept the journalists away, however, he never let them talk to her alone.

"Sellerio," someone guessed.

"Yes," said Guivi, "that's right. Do you know the rest of the story?"

"He sold her."

But half the contract only, Guivi said. Her popularity was fading, he wanted to get everything he could. There was a big ceremony, they invited all the press. She was going to sign. She picked up the pen and leaned forward a little for the photographers, you know, she had these enormous, eh . . . well, anyway, on the paper she wrote: with his finger Guivi made a large *X*. The newsmen all looked at each other. Then Sellerio took the pen and very grandly, just below her name: Guivi made one *X* and next to it, carefully, another. Illiterate. That's the truth. They asked him, look, what is the second *X* for? You know what he told them? *Dottore.*

They laughed. He told them about shooting in Naples with a producer so cheap he threw a cable across the trolley wires to steal power. He was clever, Guivi, he was a storyteller in the tradition of the east, he could speak three languages. Later, when she finally understood what had happened, Anna remembered how happy he seemed this night.

"Shall we go on to the Hostaria?" the producer said.

"What?" Guivi asked.

"The Hostaria . . ." As with the waiters, it seemed no one heard him. "The Blue Bar. Come on, we're going to the Blue Bar," he announced.

Outside the Botanical Gardens, parked in the cold, the small windows of the car frosted, Lang sat. His clothing was open. His flesh was pale in the refracted light. He had eaten dinner with Eva. She had talked for hours in a low, uncertain voice, it was a night for stories, she had told him everything, about Coleman the head of publicity, Mirella, her brother, Sicily, life. On the road to the mountains which overlooked Palermo there were cars parked at five in the afternoon. In each one was a couple, the man with a handkerchief spread in his lap.

"I am so lonely," she said suddenly.

She had only three friends, she saw them all the time. They went to the theater together, the ballet. One was an actress. One was married. She was silent, she seemed to wait. The cold was everywhere, it covered the glass. Her breath was in crystals, visible in the dark.

"Can I kiss it?" she said.

She began to moan then, as if it were holy. She touched it with her forehead. She was murmuring. The nape of her neck was bare.

She called the next morning. It was eight o'clock.

"I want to read something to you," she said.

He was half-asleep, the racket was already drifting up from the street. The room was chill and unlighted. Within it, distant as an old record, her voice was playing. It entered his body, it commanded his blood.

"I found this," she said. "Are you there?"

"Yes."

"I thought you would like it."

It was from an article. She began to read.

In February of 1868, in Milan, Prince Umberto had given a splendid ball. *In a room which blazed with light the young bride who was one day to be queen of Italy was introduced. It was the event of the year, crowded and gay, and while the world of fashion amused itself thus, at the same hour and in the same city a lone astronomer was discovering a new planet, the ninety-seventh on Chacornac's chart . . . .*

Silence. *A new planet.*

In his mind, still warmed by the pillow, it seemed a sacred calm had descended. He lay like a saint. He was naked, his ankles, his hipbones, his throat.

He heard her call his name. He said nothing. He lay there becoming small, smaller, vanishing. The room became a window, a facade, a group of buildings, squares and sections, in the end all of Rome. His ecstasy was beyond knowing. The roofs of the great cathedrals shone in the winter air.

JOYCE CAROL OATES | # HEAT

IT WAS midsummer, the heat rippling above the macadam roads, cicadas screaming out of the trees, and the sky like pewter, glaring.

The days were the same day, like the shallow mud brown river moving always in the same direction but so slow you couldn't see it. Except for Sunday: church in the morning, then the fat Sunday newspaper, the color comics, and newsprint on your fingers.

Rhea and Rhoda Kunkel went flying on their rusted old bicycles, down the long hill toward the railroad yard, Whipple's Ice, the scrubby pastureland where dairy cows grazed. They'd stolen six dollars from their own grandmother who loved them. They were eleven years old; they were identical twins; they basked in their power.

Rhea and Rhoda Kunkel: it was always Rhea-and-Rhoda, never Rhoda-and-Rhea, I couldn't say why. You just wouldn't say the names that way. Not even the teachers at school would say them that way.

We went to see them in the funeral parlor where they were waked; we were made to. The twins in twin caskets, white,

smooth, gleaming, perfect as plastic, with white satin lining puckered like the inside of a fancy candy box. And the waxy white
lilies, and the smell of talcum powder and perfume. The room
was crowded; there was only one way in and out.

Rhea and Rhoda were the same girl; they'd wanted it that way.
Only looking from one to the other could you see they were two.

The heat was gauzy; you had to push your way through like
swimming. On their bicycles Rhea and Rhoda flew through it
hardly noticing, from their grandmother's place on Main Street to
the end of South Main where the paved road turned to gravel
leaving town. That was the summer before seventh grade, when
they died. Death was coming for them, but they didn't know.

They thought the same thoughts sometimes at the same moment, had the same dream and went all day trying to remember
it, bringing it back like something you'd be hauling out of the
water on a tangled line. We watched them; we were jealous. None
of us had a twin. Sometimes they were serious and sometimes,
remembering, they shrieked and laughed like they were being
killed. They stole things out of desks and lockers but if you caught
them they'd hand them right back; it was like a game.

There were three floor fans in the funeral parlor that I could see,
tall whirring fans with propeller blades turning fast to keep the
warm air moving. Strange little gusts came from all directions,
making your eyes water. By this time Roger Whipple was arrested,
taken into police custody. No one had hurt him. He would never
stand trial; he was ruled mentally unfit and would never be released
from confinement.

He died there, in the state psychiatric hospital, years later, and
was brought back home to be buried—the body of him, I mean.
His earthly remains.

Rhea and Rhoda Kunkel were buried in the same cemetery, the
First Methodist. The cemetery is just a field behind the church.

In the caskets the dead girls did not look like anyone we knew,
really. They were placed on their backs with their eyes closed, and

their mouths, the way you don't always look in life when you're sleeping. Their faces were too small. Every eyelash showed, too perfect. Like angels, everyone was saying, and it was strange it was *so*. I stared and stared.

What had been done to them, the lower parts of them, didn't show in the caskets.

Roger Whipple worked for his father at Whipple's Ice. In the newspaper it stated he was nineteen. He'd gone to DeWitt Clinton until he was sixteen; my mother's friend Sadie taught there and remembered him from the special education class. A big slow sweet-faced boy with these big hands and feet, thighs like hams. A shy gentle boy with good manners and a hushed voice.

He wasn't simpleminded exactly, like the others in that class. He was watchful, he held back.

Roger Whipple in overalls squatting in the rear of his father's truck, one of his older brothers driving. There would come the sound of the truck in the driveway, the heavy block of ice smelling of cold, ice tongs over his shoulder. He was strong, round-shouldered like an older man. Never staggered or grunted. Never dropped anything. Pale washed-looking eyes lifting out of a big face, a soft mouth wanting to smile. We giggled and looked away. They said he'd never been the kind to hurt even an animal; all the Whipples swore.

Sucking ice, the cold goes straight into your jaws and deep into the bone.

People spoke of them as the Kunkel twins. Mostly nobody tried to tell them apart: homely corkscrew-twisty girls you wouldn't know would turn up so quiet and solemn and almost beautiful, perfect little dolls' faces with the freckles powdered over, touches of rouge on the cheeks and mouths. I was tempted to whisper to them, kneeling by the coffins, *Hey, Rhea! Hey, Rhoda! Wake up!*

They had loud slip-sliding voices that were the same voice. They weren't shy. They were always first in line. One behind you and one in front of you and you'd better be wary of some trick.

Flamey orange hair and the bleached-out skin that goes with it, freckles like dirty raindrops splashed on their faces. Sharp green eyes they'd bug out until you begged them to stop.

Places meant to be serious, Rhea and Rhoda had a hard time sitting still. In church, in school, a sideways glance between them could do it. Jamming their knuckles into their mouths, choking back giggles. Sometimes laughter escaped through their fingers like steam hissing. Sometimes it came out like snorting and then none of us could hold back. The worst time was in assembly, the principal up there telling us that Miss Flagler had died, we would all miss her. Tears shining in the woman's eyes behind her goggle glasses and one of the twins gave a breathless little snort you could feel it like flames running down the whole row of girls, none of us could hold back.

Sometimes the word *tickle* was enough to get us going, just that word.

I never dreamt about Rhea and Rhoda so strange in their caskets sleeping out in the middle of a room where people could stare at them, shed tears, and pray over them. I never dream about actual things, only things I don't know. Places I've never been, people I've never seen. Sometimes the person I am in the dream isn't me. Who it is, I don't know.

Rhea and Rhoda bounced up the drive on their bicycles behind Whipple's Ice. They were laughing like crazy and didn't mind the potholes jarring their teeth or the clouds of dust. If they'd had the same dream the night before, the hot sunlight erased it entirely.

When death comes for you, you sometimes know and sometimes don't.

Roger Whipple was by himself in the barn, working. Kids went down there to beg him for ice to suck or throw around or they'd tease him, not out of meanness but for something to do. It was slow, the days not changing in the summer, heat sometimes all night long. He was happy with children that age, he was that age himself in his head—sixth-grade learning abilities, as the newspaper stated, though he could add and subtract quickly. Other kinds of arithmetic gave him trouble.

People were saying afterward he'd always been strange. Watchful like he was, those thick soft lips. The Whipples did wrong to let him run loose.

They said he'd always been a good gentle boy, went to Sunday school and sat still there and never gave anybody any trouble. He collected Bible cards; he hid them away under his mattress for safekeeping. Mr. Whipple started in early disciplining him the way you might discipline a big dog or a horse. Not letting the creature know he has any power to be himself exactly. Not giving him the opportunity to test his will.

Neighbors said the Whipples worked him like a horse, in fact. The older brothers were the most merciless. And why they all wore coveralls, heavy denim and long legs on days so hot, nobody knew. The thermometer above the First Midland Bank read 98 degrees F. on noon of that day, my mother said.

Nights afterward my mother would hug me before I went to bed. Pressing my face hard against her breasts and whispering things I didn't hear, like praying to Jesus to love and protect her little girl and keep her from harm, but I didn't hear; I shut my eyes tight and endured it. Sometimes we prayed together, all of us or just my mother and me kneeling by my bed. Even then I knew she was a good mother, there was this girl she loved as her daughter that was me and loved more than that girl deserved. There was nothing I could do about it.

Mrs. Kunkel would laugh and roll her eyes over the twins. In that house they were "double trouble"—you'd hear it all the time like a joke on the radio that keeps coming back. I wonder did she pray with them too. I wonder would they let her.

In the long night you forget about the day; it's like the other side of the world. Then the sun is there, and the heat. You forget.

We were running through the field behind school, a place where people dumped things sometimes, and there was a dead dog there, a collie with beautiful fur, but his eyes were gone from the sockets and the maggots had got him where somebody tried to lift him with her foot, and when Rhea and Rhoda saw they screamed a single scream and hid their eyes.

They did nice things—gave their friends candy bars, nail polish, some novelty key chains they'd taken from somewhere, movie stars' pictures framed in plastic. In the movies they'd share a box of popcorn, not noticing where one or the other of them left off and a girl who wasn't any sister of theirs sat.

Once they made me strip off my clothes where we'd crawled under the Kunkels' veranda. This was a large hollowed-out space where the earth dropped away at one end and you could sit without bumping your head; it was cool and smelled of dirt and stone. Rhea said all of a sudden, *Strip!* and Rhoda said at once, *Strip! Come on!* So it happened. They wouldn't let me out unless I took off my clothes, my shirt and shorts, yes, and my panties too. *Come on*, they said, whispering and giggling; they were blocking the way out so I had no choice. I was scared but I was laughing too. This is to show our power over you, they said. But they stripped too just like me.

You have power over others you don't realize until you test it.

Under the Kunkels' veranda we stared at each other but we didn't touch each other. My teeth chattered, because what if somebody saw us, some boy, or Mrs. Kunkel herself? I was scared but I was happy too. Except for our faces, their face and mine, we could all be the same girl.

The Kunkel family lived in one side of a big old clapboard house by the river; you could hear the trucks rattling on the bridge, shifting their noisy gears on the hill. Mrs. Kunkel had eight children. Rhea and Rhoda were the youngest. Our mothers wondered why Mrs. Kunkel had let herself go: she had a moon-shaped pretty face but her hair was frizzed ratty; she must have weighed two hundred pounds, sweated and breathed so hard in the warm weather. They'd known her in school. Mr. Kunkel worked construction for the county. Summer evenings after work he'd be sitting on the veranda drinking beer, flicking cigarette butts out into the yard; you'd be fooled, almost thinking they were fireflies. He went bare-chested in the heat, his upper body dark like stained wood. Flat little purplish nipples inside his chest hair the girls giggled to see. Mr. Kunkel teased us all; he'd mix Rhea and Rhoda up the way he'd mix the rest of us up, like it was too much trouble to keep names straight.

Mr. Kunkel was in police custody; he didn't even come to the wake. Mrs. Kunkel was there in rolls of chin fat that glistened with sweat and tears, the makeup on her face so caked and discolored you were embarrassed to look. It scared me, the way she grabbed me as soon as my parents and I came in, hugging me against her big balloon breasts, sobbing. All the strength went out of me; I couldn't push away.

The police had Mr. Kunkel for his own good, they said. He'd gone to the Whipples, though the murderer had been taken away, saying he would kill anybody he could get his hands on: the old man, the brothers. They were all responsible, he said; his little girls were dead. Tear them apart with his bare hands, he said, but he had a tire iron.

Did it mean anything special, or was it just an accident Rhea and Rhoda had taken six dollars from their grandmother an hour before? Because death was coming for them; it had to happen one way or another.

If you believe in God you believe that. And if you don't believe in God it's obvious.

Their grandmother lived upstairs over a shoe store downtown, an apartment looking out on Main Street. They'd bicycle down there for something to do and she'd give them grape juice or lemonade and try to keep them a while, a lonely old lady but she was nice, she was always nice to me; it was kind of nasty of Rhea and Rhoda to steal from her but they were like that. One was in the kitchen talking with her and without any plan or anything the other went to use the bathroom, then slipped into her bedroom, got the money out of her purse like it was something she did every day of the week, that easy. On the stairs going down to the street Rhoda whispered to Rhea, What did you *do*? knowing Rhea had done something she hadn't ought to have done but not knowing what it was or anyway how much money it was. They started in poking each other, trying to hold the giggles back until they were safe away.

On their bicycles they stood high on the pedals, coasting, going down the hill but not using their brakes. *What did you do! Oh, what did you do!*

Rhea and Rhoda always said they could never be apart. If one didn't know exactly where the other was that one could die. Or the other could die. Or both.

Once they'd gotten some money from somewhere, they wouldn't say where, and paid for us all to go to the movies. And ice cream afterward too.

You could read the newspaper articles twice through and still not know what he did. Adults talked about it for a long time but not so we could hear. I thought probably he'd used an ice pick. Or maybe I heard somebody guess who didn't know any more than me.

We liked it that Rhea and Rhoda had been killed, and all the stuff in the paper, and everybody talking about it, but we didn't like it that they were dead; we missed them.

Later, in tenth grade, the Kaufmann twins moved into our school district: Doris and Diane. But it wasn't the same thing.

Roger Whipple said he didn't remember any of it. Whatever he did, he didn't remember. At first everybody thought he was lying; then they had to accept it as true, or true in some way: doctors from the state hospital examined him. He said over and over he hadn't done anything and he didn't remember the twins there that afternoon, but he couldn't explain why their bicycles were at the foot of his stairway and he couldn't explain why he'd taken a bath in the middle of the day. The Whipples admitted that wasn't a practice of Roger's or of any of them, ever, a bath in the middle of the day.

Roger Whipple was a clean boy, though. His hands always scrubbed so you actually noticed, swinging the block of ice off the truck and, inside the kitchen, helping to set it in the icebox. They said he'd go crazy if he got bits of straw under his nails from the icehouse or inside his clothes. He'd been taught to shave and he shaved every morning without fail; they said the sight of the beard growing in, the scratchy feel of it, seemed to scare him.

A few years later his sister Linda told us how Roger was built like a horse. She was our age, a lot younger than him; she made a gesture toward her crotch so we'd know what she meant. She'd happened to see him a few times, she said, by accident.

There he was squatting in the dust laughing, his head lowered, watching Rhea and Rhoda circle him on their bicycles. It was a rough game where the twins saw how close they could come to hitting him, brushing him with their bike fenders, and he'd lunge out, not seeming to notice if his fingers hit the spokes, it was all happening so fast you maybe wouldn't feel pain. Out back of the icehouse, the yard blended in with the yard of the old railroad depot next door that wasn't used any more. It was burning hot in the sun; dust rose in clouds behind the girls. Pretty soon they got bored with the game, though Roger Whipple even in his heavy overalls wanted to keep going. He was red-faced with all the excitement, he was a boy who loved to laugh and didn't have much chance. Rhea said she was thirsty, she wanted some ice, so Roger Whipple scrambled right up and went to get a big bag of ice cubes! He hadn't any more sense than that.

They sucked on the ice cubes and fooled around with them. He was panting and lolling his tongue pretending to be a dog, and Rhea and Rhoda cried. Here doggie! Here, doggie-doggie! tossing ice cubes at Roger Whipple he tried to catch in his mouth. That went on for a while. In the end the twins just dumped the rest of the ice onto the dirt, then Roger Whipple was saying he had some secret things that belonged to his brother Eamon he could show them, hidden under his bed mattress; would they like to see what the things were?

He wasn't one who could tell Rhea from Rhoda or Rhoda from Rhea. There was a way some of us knew: the freckles on Rhea's face were a little darker than Rhoda's, and Rhea's eyes were just a little darker than Rhoda's. But you'd have to see the two side by side with no clowning around to know.

Rhea said OK, she'd like to see the secret things. She let her bike fall where she was straddling it.

Roger Whipple said he could only take one of them upstairs to his room at a time, he didn't say why.

OK, said Rhea. Of the Kunkel twins, Rhea always had to be first.

She'd been born first, she said. Weighed a pound or two more.

Roger Whipple's room was in a strange place: on the second floor of the Whipple house above an unheated storage space that had been added after the main part of the house was built. There was a way of getting to the room from the outside, up a flight of rickety wooden stairs. That way Roger could get in and out of his room without going through the rest of the house. People said the Whipples had him live there like some animal, they didn't want him tramping through the house, but they denied it. The room had an inside door too.

Roger Whipple weighed about one hundred ninety pounds that day. In the hospital he swelled up like a balloon, people said, bloated from the drugs his skin was soft and white as bread dough and his hair fell out. He was an old man when he died aged thirty-one.

Exactly why he died, the Whipples never knew. The hospital just told them his heart had stopped in his sleep.

Rhoda shaded her eyes, watching her sister running up the stairs with Roger Whipple behind her, and felt the first pinch of fear, that something was wrong or was going to be wrong. She called after them in a whining voice that she wanted to come along too, she didn't want to wait down there all alone, But Rhea just called back to her to be quiet and wait her turn, so Rhoda waited, kicking at the ice cubes melting in the dirt, and after a while she got restless and shouted up to them—the door was shut, the shade on the window was drawn—saying she was going home, damn them, she was sick of waiting, she said, and she was going home. But nobody came to the door or looked out the window; it was like the place was empty. Wasps had built one of those nests that look like mud in layers under the eaves, and the only sound was wasps.

Rhoda bicycled toward the road so anybody who was watching would think she was going home; she was thinking she hated Rhea! hated her damn twin sister! wished she was dead and gone, God damn her! She was going home, and the first thing she'd tell their mother was that Rhea had stolen six dollars from Grandma: she had it in her pocket right that moment.

The Whipple house was an old farmhouse they'd tried to modernize by putting on red asphalt siding meant to look like brick. Downstairs the rooms were big and drafty; upstairs they were small, some of them unfinished and with bare floorboards, like Roger Whipple's room, which people would afterward say based on what the police said was like an animal's pen, nothing in it but a bed shoved into a corner and some furniture and boxes and things Mrs. Whipple stored there.

Of the Whipples—there were seven in the family still living at home—only Mrs. Whipple and her daughter Iris were home that afternoon. They said they hadn't heard a sound except for kids playing in the back; they swore it.

Rhoda was bent on going home and leaving Rhea behind, but at the end of the driveway something made her turn her bicycle wheel back . . . so if you were watching you'd think she was just cruising around for something to do, a red-haired girl with whitish skin and freckles, skinny little body, pedaling fast, then slow, then coasting, then fast again, turning and dipping and crisscrossing her path, talking to herself as if she was angry. She hated Rhea! She was furious at Rhea! But feeling sort of scared too and sickish in the pit of her belly, knowing that she and Rhea shouldn't be in two places; something might happen to one of them or to both. Some things you know.

So she pedaled back to the house. Laid her bike down in the dirt next to Rhea's. The bikes were old hand-me-downs, the kickstands were broken. But their daddy had put on new Goodyear tires for them at the start of the summer, and he'd oiled them too.

You never would see just one of the twins' bicycles anywhere, you always saw both of them laid down on the ground and facing in the same direction with the pedals in about the same position.

Rhoda peered up at the second floor of the house, the shade drawn over the window, the door still closed. She called out, Rhea? Hey, Rhea? starting up the stairs, making a lot of noise so they'd hear her, pulling on the railing as if to break it the way a boy would. Still she was scared. But making noise like that and feeling so disgusted and mad helped her get stronger, and there was Roger Whipple with the door open staring down at her flush-faced and sweaty as if he was scared too. He seemed to have forgotten her. He was wiping his hands on his overalls. He just stared, a lemony light coming up in his eyes.

Aftrward he would say he didn't remember anything. Just didn't remember anything. The size of a grown man but round-shouldered so it was hard to judge how tall he was, or how old. His straw-colored hair falling in his eyes and his fingers twined together as if he was praying or trying with all the strength in him to keep his hands still. He didn't remember the twins in his room and couldn't explain the blood but he cried a lot, acted scared and guilty and sorry like a dog that's done bad, so they decided he shouldn't be made to stand trial; there was no point to it.

Afterward Mrs. Whipple kept to the house, never went out, not even to church or grocery shopping. She died of cancer just a few months before Roger died; she'd loved her boy, she always said; she said none of it was his fault in his heart, he wasn't the kind of boy to injure an animal; he loved kittens especially and was a good sweet obedient boy and religious too and Jesus was looking after him and whatever happened it must have been those girls teasing him; everybody knew what the Kunkel twins were like. Roger had had a lifetime of being teased and taunted by children, his heart broken by all the abuse, and something must have snapped that day, that was all.

The Whipples were the ones, though, who called the police. Mr. Whipple found the girls' bodies back in the icehouse hidden under some straw and canvas. Those two look-alike girls, side by side.

He found them around 9 P.M. that night. He knew, he said. Oh, he knew.

The way Roger was acting, and the fact that the Kunkel girls were missing: word had gotten around town. Roger taking a bath like that in the middle of the day and washing his hair too and not answering when anyone said his name, just sitting there staring at the floor. So they went up to his room and saw the blood. So they knew.

The hardest minute of his life, Mr. Whipple said, was in the icehouse lifting that canvas to see what was under it.

He took it hard too; he never recovered. He hadn't any choice but to think what a lot of people thought—it had been his fault. He was an old-time Methodist, he took all that seriously, but none of it helped him. Believed Jesus Christ was his personal savior and He never stopped loving Roger or turned His face from him, and if Roger did truly repent in his heart he would be saved and they would be reunited in Heaven, all the Whipples reunited. He believed, but none of it helped in his life.

The icehouse is still there but boarded up and derelict, the Whipples' ice business ended long ago. Strangers live in the house, and the yard is littered with rusting hulks of cars and pickup trucks. Some Whipples live scattered around the county but none in town. The old train depot is still there too.

After I'd been married some years I got involved with this man, I won't say his name, his name is not a name I say, but we would meet back there sometimes, back in that old lot that's all weeds and scrub trees. Wild as kids and on the edge of being drunk. I was crazy for this guy, I mean crazy like I could hardly think of anybody but him or anything but the two of us making love the way we did; with him deep inside me I wanted it never to stop. Just fuck and fuck and fuck, I'd whisper to him, and this went on for a long time, two or three years, then ended the way these things do and looking back on it I'm not able to recognize that woman, as if she was someone not even not-me but a crazy woman I would despise, making so much of such a thing, risking her marriage and her kids finding out and her life being ruined for such a thing, my God. The things people do.

It's like living out a story that has to go its own way.

Behind the icehouse in his car I'd think of Rhea and Rhoda and what happened that day upstairs in Roger Whipple's room. And the funeral parlor with the twins like dolls laid out and their eyes like dolls' eyes too that shut when you tilt them back. One night when I wasn't asleep but wasn't awake either I saw my parents standing in the doorway of my bedroom watching me and I knew their thoughts, how they were thinking of Rhea and Rhoda and of me their daughter wondering how they could keep me from harm, and there was no clear answer.

In his car in his arms I'd feel my mind drift, after we'd made love or at least after the first time. And I saw Rhoda Kunkel hesitating on the stairs a few steps down from Roger Whipple. I saw her white-faced and scared but deciding to keep going anyway, pushing by Roger Whipple to get inside the room, to find Rhea; she had to brush against him where he was standing as if he meant to block her but not having the nerve exactly to block her and he was smelling of his body and breathing hard but not in imitation of any dog now, not with his tongue flopping and lolling to make them laugh. Rhoda was asking where was Rhea? She couldn't see well at first in the dark little cubbyhole of a room because the sunshine had been so bright outside.

Roger Whipple said Rhea had gone home. His voice sounded scratchy as if it hadn't been used in some time. She'd gone home, he said, and Rhoda said right away that Rhea wouldn't go home without her and Roger Whipple came toward her saying, Yes she did, yes she *did*, as if he was getting angry she wouldn't believe him. Rhoda was calling, *Rhea, where are you?* Stumbling against something on the floor tangled with the bedclothes.

Behind her was this big boy saying again and again, Yes she did, yes she *did*, his voice rising, but it would never get loud enough so that anyone would hear and come save her.

I wasn't there, but some things you know.

ANN BEATTIE | # A VINTAGE THUNDERBIRD

NICK AND KAREN had driven from Virginia to New York in a little under six hours. They had made good time, keeping ahead of the rain all the way, and it was only now, while they were in the restaurant, that the rain began. It had been a nice summer weekend in the country with their friends Stephanie and Sammy, but all the time he was there Nick had worried that Karen had consented to go with him only out of pity; she had been dating another man, and when Nick suggested the weekend she had been reluctant. When she said she would go, he decided that she had given in for old time's sake.

The car they drove was here—a white Thunderbird convertible. Every time he drove the car, he admired it more. She owned many things that he admired: a squirrel coat with a black taffeta lining, a pair of carved soapstone bookends that held some books of poetry on her night table, her collection of Louis Armstrong 78s. He loved to go to her apartment and look at her things. He was excited by them, the way he had been spellbound, as a child, exploring the playrooms of schoolmates.

He had met Karen several years before, soon after he came to

New York. Her brother had lived in the same building he lived in then, and the three of them met on the volleyball courts adjacent to the building. Her brother moved across town within a few months, but by then Nick knew Karen's telephone number. At her suggestion, they had started running in Central Park on Sundays. It was something he looked forward to all week. When they left the park, his elation was always mixed with a little embarrassment over his panting and his being sweaty on the street, but she had no self-consciousness. She didn't care if her shirt stuck to her body, or if she looked unattractive with her wet, matted hair. Or perhaps she knew that she never looked really unattractive; men always looked at her. One time, on Forty-second Street, during a light rain, Nick stopped to read a movie marquee, and when he turned back to Karen she was laughing and protesting that she couldn't take the umbrella that a man was offering her. It was only when Nick came to her side that the man stopped insisting—a nicely dressed man who was only offering her his big black umbrella, and not trying to pick her up. Things like this were hard for Nick to accept, but Karen was not flirtatious, and he could see that it was not her fault that men looked at her and made gestures.

It became a routine that on Sundays they jogged or went to a basketball court. One time, when she got frustrated because she hadn't been able to do a simple hook shot—hadn't made a basket that way all morning—he lifted her to his shoulders and charged the backboard so fast that she almost missed the basket from there too. After playing basketball, they would go to her apartment and she would make dinner. He would collapse, but she was full of energy and she would poke fun at him while she studied a cookbook, staring at it until she knew enough of a recipe to begin preparing the food. His two cookbooks were dog-eared and sauce-stained, but Karen's were perfectly clean. She looked at recipes, but never followed them exactly. He admired this—her creativity, her energy. It took him a long while to accept that she thought he was special, and later, when she began to date other men, it took him a long while to realize that she did not mean to shut him out of her life. The first time she went away with a man for the weekend—about a year after he first met her—she stopped by his apartment on her way to Pennsylvania and gave him the keys to her Thunderbird. She left so quickly—the man was downstairs in his car, waiting—that as he watched her go he could feel the warmth of the keys from her hand.

Just recently Nick had met the man she was dating now: a gaunt psychology professor, with a black-and-white tweed cap and a thick mustache that made him look like a sad-mouthed clown. Nick had gone to her apartment not knowing for certain that the man would be there—actually, it was Friday night, the beginning of the weekend, and he had gone on the hunch that he finally would meet him—and had drunk a vodka collins that the man mixed for him. He remembered that the man had complained tediously that Paul McCartney had stolen words from Thomas Dekker for a song on the "Abbey Road" album, and that the man said he got hives from eating shellfish.

In the restaurant now, Nick looked across the table at Karen and said, "That man you're dating is a real bore. What is he—a scholar?"

He fumbled for a cigarette and then remembered that he no longer smoked. He had given it up a year before, when he went to visit an old girlfriend in New Haven. Things had gone badly, they had quarreled, and he had left her to go to a bar. Coming out, he was approached by a tall black round-faced teenager and told to hand over his wallet, and he had mutely reached inside his coat and pulled it out and given it to the boy. A couple of people came out of the bar, took in the situation, and walked away quickly, pretending not to notice. The boy had a small penknife in his hand. "And your cigarettes," the boy said. Nick had reached inside his jacket pocket and handed over the cigarettes. The boy pocketed them. Then the boy smiled and cocked his head and held up the wallet, like a hypnotist dangling a pocket watch. Nick stared dumbly at his own wallet. Then, before he knew what was happening, the boy turned into a blur of motion: he grabbed his arm and yanked hard, like a judo wrestler, and threw him across the sidewalk. Nick fell against a car that was parked at the curb. He was so frightened that his legs buckled and he went down. The boy watched him fall. The he nodded and walked down the sidewalk past the bar. When the boy was out of sight, Nick got up and went into the bar to tell his story. He let the bartender give him a beer and call the police. He declined the bartender's offer of a cigarette, and had never smoked since.

His thoughts were drifting, and Karen still had not answered his question. He knew that he had already angered her once that day, and that it had been a mistake to speak of the man again. Just an hour or so earlier, when they got back to the city, he had been abrupt with her friend Kirby. She kept her car in Kirby's garage, and in exchange for the privilege she moved into his brownstone whenever he went out of town and took care of his six declawed chocolate-point cats. Actually, Kirby's psychiatrist, a Dr. Kellogg, lived in the same house, but the doctor had made it clear he did not live there to take care of cats.

From his seat Nick could see the sign of the restaurant hanging outside the front window. Star Thrower Café, it said, in lavender neon. He got depressed thinking that if she became more serious about the professor—he had lasted longer than any of the others— he would only be able to see her by pretending to run into her at places like the Star Thrower. He had also begun to think that he had driven the Thunderbird for the last time. She had almost refused to let him drive it again after the time, two weeks earlier, when he tapped a car in front of them on Sixth Avenue, making a dent above their left headlight. Long ago she had stopped letting him use her squirrel coat as a kind of blanket. He used to like to lie naked on the tiny balcony outside her apartment in the autumn, with the Sunday *Times* arranged under him for padding and the coat spread on top of him. Now he counted back and came up with the figure: he had known Karen for seven years.

"What are you thinking?" he said to her.

"That I'm glad I'm not thirty-eight years old, with a man putting pressure on me to have a baby." She was talking about Stephanie and Sammy.

Her hand was on the table. He cupped his hand over it just as the waiter came with the plates.

"What are *you* thinking?" she said, withdrawing her hand.

"At least Stephanie has the sense not to do it," he said. He picked up his fork and put it down. "Do you really love that man?"

"If I loved him, I suppose I'd be at my apartment, where he's been waiting for over an hour. If he waited."

When they finished she ordered espresso. He ordered it also. He had half expected her to say at some point that the trip with him was the end, and he still thought she might say that. Part of the problem was that she had money and he didn't. She had had money since she was twenty-one, when she got control of a fifty-thousand-dollar trust fund her grandfather had left her. He remembered the day she had bought the Thunderbird. It was the day after her birthday, five years ago. That night, laughing, they had driven the car through the Lincoln Tunnel and then down the back roads in Jersey, with a stream of orange crepe paper blowing from the radio antenna, until the wind ripped it off.

"Am I still going to see you?" Nick said.

"I suppose," Karen said. "Although things have changed between us."

"I've known you for seven years. You're my oldest friend."

She did not react to what he said, but much later, around midnight, she called him at his apartment. "Was what you said at the Star Thrower calculated to make me feel bad?" she said. "When you said that I was your oldest friend?"

"No," he said. "You are my oldest friend."

"You must know somebody longer than you've known me."

"You're the only person I've seen regularly for seven years." She sighed.

"Professor go home?" he asked.

"No. He's here."

"You're saying all this in front of him?"

"I don't see why there has to be any secret about this."

"You could put an announcement in the paper," Nick said. "Run a little picture of me with it."

"Why are you so sarcastic?"

"It's embarrassing. It's embarrassing that you'd say this in front of that man."

He was sitting in the dark, in a chair by the phone. He had wanted to call her ever since he got back from the restaurant. The long day of driving had finally caught up with him, and his shoulders ached. He felt the black man's hands on his shoulders, felt his own body folding up, felt himself flying backward. He had lost sixty-five dollars that night. The day she bought the Thunderbird, he had driven it through the tunnel into New Jersey. He had driven, then she had driven, and then he had driven again. Once he had pulled into the parking lot of a shopping center and told her to wait, and had come back with the orange crepe paper. Years later he had looked for the road they had been on that night, but he could never find it.

The next time Nick heard from her was almost three weeks after the trip to Virginia. Since he didn't have the courage to call her, and since he expected not to hear from her at all, he was surprised to pick up the phone and hear her voice. Petra had been in his apartment a woman at his office whom he had always wanted to date and who had just broken off an unhappy engagement. As he held the phone clamped between his ear and shoulder, he looked admiringly at Petra's profile.

"What's up?" he said to Karen, trying to sound very casual for Petra.

"Get ready," Karen said. "Stephanie called and said that she was going to have a baby."

"What do you mean? I thought she told you in Virginia that she thought Sammy was crazy to want a kid."

"It happened by accident. She missed her period just after we left."

Petra shifted on the couch and began leafing through *Newsweek*.

"Can I call you back?" he said.

"Throw whatever woman is there out of your apartment and talk to me now," Karen said. "I'm about to go out."

He looked at Petra, who was sipping her drink. "I can't do that," he said.

"Then call me when you can. But call back tonight."

When he hung up, he took Petra's glass but found that he had run out of scotch. He suggested that they go to a bar on West Tenth Street.

When they got to the bar, he excused himself almost immediately. Karen had sounded depressed, and he could not enjoy his evening with Petra until he made sure everything was all right. Once he heard her voice, he knew he was going to come to her apartment when he had finished having a drink, and she said that he should come over immediately or not at all, because she was about to go to the professor's. She was so abrupt that he wondered if she could be jealous.

He went back to the bar and sat on the stool next to Petra and picked up his scotch and water and took a big drink. It was so cold that it made his teeth ache. Petra had on blue slacks and a white blouse. He rubbed his hand up and down her back, just below the shoulders. She was not wearing a brassiere.

"I have to leave," he said.

"You have to leave? Are you coming back?"

He started to speak, but she put up her hand. "Never mind," she said. "I don't want you to come back." She sipped her margarita. "Whoever the woman is you just called, I hope the two of you have a splendid evening."

Petra gave him a hard look, and he knew that she really wanted him to go. He stared at her—at the little crust of salt on her bottom lip—and then she turned away from him.

He hesitated for just a second before he left the bar. He went outside and walked about ten steps, and then he was jumped. They got him from behind, and in his shock and confusion he thought that he had been hit by a car. He lost sense of where he was, and although it was a dull blow, he thought that somehow a car had hit him. Looking up from the sidewalk, he saw them—two men, younger than he was, picking at him like vultures, pushing him, rummaging through his jacket and his pockets. The crazy thing was he was on West Tenth Street; there should have been other people on the street, but there were not. His clothes were tearing. His right hand was wet with blood. They had cut his arm, the shirt was bloodstained, he saw his own blood spreading out into a little puddle. He stared at it and was afraid to move his hand out of it. Then the men were gone and he was left half sitting, propped up against a building where they had dragged him. He was able to push himself up, but the man he began telling the story to, a passerby, kept coming into focus and fading out again. The man had on a sombrero, and he was pulling him up but pulling too hard. His legs didn't have the power to support him—something had happened to his legs—so that when the man loosened his grip he went down on his knees. He kept blinking to stay conscious. He blacked out before he could stand again.

Back in his apartment, later that night, with his arm in a cast, he felt confused and ashamed—ashamed for the way he had treated Petra, and ashamed for having been mugged. He wanted to call Karen, but he was too embarrassed. He sat in the chair by the phone, willing her to call him. At midnight the phone rang, and he picked it up at once, sure that his telepathic message had worked. The phone call was from Stephanie, at La Guardia. She had been trying to reach Karen and couldn't. She wanted to know if she could come to his apartment.

"I'm not going through with it," Stephanie said, her voice wavering. "I'm thirty-eight years old, and this was a goddamn accident."

"Calm down," he said. "We can get you an abortion."

"I don't know if I could take a human life," she said, and she began to cry.

"Stephanie?" he said. "You okay? Are you going to get a cab?" More crying, no answer.

"Because it would be silly for me to get a cab just to come get you. You can make it here okay, can't you, Steph?"

The cabdriver who took him to La Guardia was named Arthur Shales. A small pink baby shoe was glued to the dashboard of the cab. Arthur Shales chainsmoked Picayunes. "Woman I took to Bendel's today, I'm still trying to get over it," he said. "I picked her up at Madison and Seventy-fifth. Took her to Bendel's and pulled up in front and she said, 'Oh, screw Bendel's.' I took her back to Madison and Seventy-fifth."

Going across the bridge, Nick said to Arthur Shales that the woman he was going to pick up was going to be very upset.

"Upset? What do I care? Neither of you are gonna hold a gun to my head, I can take anything. You're my last fares of the night. Take you back where you came from, then I'm heading home myself."

When they were almost at the airport exit, Arthur Shales snorted and said, "Home is a room over an Italian grocery. Guy who runs it woke me up at six this morning, yelling so loud at his supplier. 'You call these tomatoes?' he was saying. 'I could take these out and bat them on the tennis court.' Guy is always griping about tomatoes being so unripe."

Stephanie was standing on the walkway, right where she had said she would be. She looked haggard, and Nick was not sure that he could cope with her. He raised his hand to his shirt pocket for cigarettes, forgetting once again that he had given up smoking. He also forgot that he couldn't grab anything with his right hand because it was in a cast.

"You know who I had in my cab the other day?" Arthur Shales said, coasting to a stop in front of the terminal. "You're not going to believe it. Al Pacino."

★ ★ ★

For more than a week, Nick and Stephanie tried to reach Karen. Stephanie began to think that Karen was dead. And although Nick chided her for calling Karen's number so often, he began to worry too. Once he went to her apartment on his lunch hour and listened at the door. He heard nothing, but he put his mouth close to the door and asked her to please open the door, if she was there, because there was trouble with Stephanie. As he left the building he had to laugh at what it would have looked like if someone had seen him—a nicely dressed man, with his hands on either side of his mouth, leaning into a door and talking to it. And one of the hands in a cast.

For a week he came straight home from work, to keep Stephanie company. Then he asked Petra if she would have dinner with him. She said no. As he was leaving the office, he passed by her desk without looking at her. She got up and followed him down the hall and said, "I'm having a drink with somebody after work, but I could meet you for a drink around seven o'clock."

He went home to see if Stephanie was all right. She said that she had been sick in the morning, but after the card came in the mail—she held out a postcard to him—she felt much better. The card was addressed to him; it was from Karen, in Bermuda. She said she had spent the afternoon in a sailboat. No explanation. He read the message several times. He felt very relieved. He asked Stephanie if she wanted to go out for a drink with him and Petra. She said no, as he had known she would.

At seven he sat alone at a table in the Blue Bar, with the postcard in his inside pocket. There was a folded newspaper on the little round table where he sat, and his broken right wrist rested on it. He sipped a beer. At seven-thirty he opened the paper and looked through the theater section. At quarter to eight he got up and left. He walked over to Fifth Avenue and began to walk downtown. In one of the store windows there was a poster for Bermuda tourism. A woman in a turquoise blue bathing suit was rising out of blue waves, her mouth in an unnaturally wide smile. She seemed oblivious of the little boy next to her who was tossing a ball into the sky. Standing there, looking at the poster, Nick began a mental game that he had sometimes played in college. He invented a cartoon about Bermuda. It was a split-frame drawing. Half of it showed a beautiful girl, in the arms of her lover, on the pink sandy beach of Bermuda, with the caption: "It's glorious to be here in Bermuda." The other half of the frame showed a tall tired man looking into the window of a travel agency at a picture of the lady and her lover. He would have no lines, but in a balloon above his head he would be wondering if, when he went home, it was the right time to urge an abortion to the friend who had moved into his apartment.

When he got home, Stephanie was not there. She had said that if she felt better, she would go out to eat. He sat down and took off his shoes and socks and hung forward, with his head almost touching his knees, like a droopy doll. Then he went into the bedroom, carrying the shoes and socks, and took off his clothes and put on jeans. The phone rang and he picked it up just as he heard Stephanie's key in the door.

"I'm sorry," Petra said, "I've never stood anybody up before in my life."

"Never mind," he said. "I'm not mad."

"I'm very sorry," she said.

"I drank a beer and read the paper. After what I did to you the other night, I don't blame you."

"I like you," she said. "That was why I didn't come. Because I knew I wouldn't say what I wanted to say, I got as far as Forty-eighth Street and turned around."

"What did you want to say?"

"That I like you. That I like you and that it's a mistake, because I'm always letting myself in for it, agreeing to see men who treat me badly. I wasn't very flattered the other night."

"I know, I apologize, Look, why don't you meet me at that bar now and let me not walk out on you. Okay?"

"No," she said, her voice changing. "That wasn't why I called.

I called to say I was sorry, but I know I did the right thing. I have to hang up now."

He put the phone back and continued to look at the floor. He knew that Stephanie was not even pretending not to have heard. He took a step forward and ripped the phone out of the wall. It was not a very successful dramatic gesture. The phone just popped out of the jack, and he stood there, holding it in his good hand.

"Would you think it was awful if I offered to go to bed with you?" Stephanie asked.

"No." he said. "I think it would be very nice."

Two days later he left work early in the afternoon and went to Kirby's. Dr. Kellogg opened the door and then pointed toward the back of the house and said, "The man you're looking for is reading." He was wearing baggy white pants and a Japanese kimono.

Nick almost had to push through the half-open door because the psychiatrist was so intent on holding the cats back with one foot. In the kitchen Kirby was indeed reading—he was looking at a Bermuda travel brochure and listening to Karen.

She looked sheepish when she saw him. Her face was tan, and her eyes, which were always beautiful, looked startlingly blue now that her face was so dark. She had lavender-tinted sunglasses pushed on top of her head. She and Kirby seemed happy and comfortable in the elegant, air-conditioned house.

"When did you get back?" Nick said.

"A couple of days ago," she said. "The night I last talked to you, I went over to the professor's apartment, and in the morning we went to Bermuda."

Nick had come to Kirby's to get the car keys and borrow the Thunderbird—to go for a ride and be by himself for a while—and for a moment now he thought of asking her for the keys anyway. He sat down at the table.

"Stephanie is in town." he said. "I think we ought to get a cup of coffee and talk about it."

[225]

ANN BEATTIE

Her key ring was on the table. If he had the keys, he could be heading for the Lincoln Tunnel. Years ago, they would be walking to the car hand in hand, in love. It would be her birthday. The car's odometer would have five miles on it.

One of Kirby's cats jumped up on the table and began to sniff at the butter dish there.

"Would you like to walk over to the Star Thrower and get a cup of coffee?" Nick said.

She got up slowly.

"Don't mind me," Kirby said.

"Would you like to come, Kirby?" she asked.

"Not me. No, no."

She patted Kirby's shoulder, and they went out.

"What happened?" she said, pointing to his hand.

"It's broken."

"How did you break it?"

"Never mind," he said. "I'll tell you when we get there."

When they got there it was not yet four o'clock, and the Star Thrower was closed.

"Well, just tell me what's happening with Stephanie," Karen said impatiently. "I don't really feel like sitting around talking because I haven't even unpacked yet."

"She's at my apartment, and she's pregnant, and she doesn't even talk about Sammy."

She shook her head sadly. "How did you break your hand?" she said.

"I was mugged. After our last pleasant conversation on the phone—the time you told me to come over immediately or not at all. I didn't make it because I was in the emergency room."

"Oh, Christ," she said. "Why didn't you call me?"

"I was embarrassed to call you."

"Why? Why didn't you call?"

"You wouldn't have been there anyway." He took her arm. "Let's find some place to go," he said.

Two young men came up to the door of the Star Thrower,

"Isn't this where David had that great Armenian dinner?" one of them said.

"I *told* you it wasn't," the other said, looking at the menu posted to the right of the door.

"I didn't really think this was the place. *You* said it was on this street."

They continued to quarrel as Nick and Karen walked away.

"Why do you think Stephanie came here to the city?" Karen said.

"Because we're her friends," Nick said.

"But she has lots of friends."

"Maybe she thought we were more dependable."

"Why do you say that in that tone of voice? I don't have to tell you every move I'm making. Things went very well in Bermuda. He almost lured me to London."

"Look," he said. "Can't we go somewhere where you can call her?"

He looked at her, shocked because she didn't understand that Stephanie had come to see her, not him. He had seen for a long time that it didn't matter to her how much she meant to him, but he had never realized that she didn't know how much she meant to Stephanie. She didn't understand people. When he found out she had another man, he should have dropped out of her life. She did not deserve her good looks and her fine car and all her money. He turned to face her on the street, ready to tell her what he thought.

"You know what happened there?" she said. "I got sunburned and had a terrible time. He went on to London without me."

He took her arm again and they stood side by side and looked at some sweaters hanging in the window of Countdown.

"So going to Virginia wasn't the answer for them," she said. "Remember when Sammy and Stephanie left town and we told each other what a stupid idea it was—that it would never work out? Do you think we jinxed them?"

They walked down the street again, saying nothing.

"It would kill me if I had to be a good conversationalist with you," she said at last. "You're the only person I can rattle on with," She stopped and leaned into him. "I had a rotten time in Bermuda," she said. "Nobody should go to a beach but a sand flea."

"You don't have to make clever conversation with me," he said.

"I know," she said. "It just happened."

Late in the afternoon of the day that Stephanie had her abortion, Nick called Sammy from a street phone near his apartment. Karen and Stephanie were in the apartment, but he had to get out for a while. Stephanie had seemed pretty cheerful, but perhaps it was just an act for his benefit. With him gone, she might talk to Karen about it. All she had told was that it felt like she had caught an ice pick in the stomach.

"Sammy?" Nick said into the phone. "How are you? It just dawned on me that I ought to call and let you know that Stephanie is all right."

"She has called me herself, several times," Sammy said. "Collect. From your phone. But thank you for your concern, Nick." He sounded brusque.

"Oh," Nick said, taken aback. "Just so you know where she is."

"I could name you as corespondent in the divorce case, you know?"

"What would you do that for?" Nick said.

"I wouldn't. I just wanted you to know what I could do."

"Sammy—I don't get it. I didn't ask for any of this, you know."

"Poor Nick. My wife gets pregnant, leaves without a word, calls from New York with a story about how you had a broken hand and were having bad luck with women, so she went to bed with you. Two weeks later I get a phone call from you, all concern, wanting me to know where Stephanie is."

Nick waited for Sammy to hang up on him.

"You know what happened to you?" Sammy said. "You got eaten up by New York."

"What kind of dumb thing is that to say?" Nick said. "Are you trying to get even or something?"

"If I wanted to do that, I could tell you that you have bad teeth. Or that Stephanie said you were a lousy lover. What I was trying to do was tell you something important, for a change. Stephanie ran away when I tried to tell it to her, you'll probably hang up on me when I say the same thing to you: you can be happy. For instance, you can get out of New York and get away from Karen. Stephanie could have settled down with a baby."

"This doesn't sound like you, Sammy, to give advice."

He waited for Sammy's answer.

"You think I ought to leave New York?" Nick said.

"Both. Karen *and* New York. Do you know that your normal expression shows pain? Do you know how much scotch you drank the weekend you visited?"

Nick stared through the grimy plastic window of the phone booth.

"What you just said about my hanging up on you," Nick said. "I was thinking that you were going to hang up on me. When I talk to people, they hang up on me. The conversation just ends that way."

"Why haven't you figured out that you don't know the right kind of people?"

"They're the only people I know."

"Does that seem like any reason for tolerating that sort of rudeness?"

"I guess not."

"Another thing," Sammy went on. "Have you figured out that I'm saying these things to you because when you called I was already drunk? I'm telling you all this because I think you're so numbed out by your lousy life that you probably even don't know I'm not in my right mind."

The operator came on, demanding more money. Nick clattered quarters into the phone. He realized that he was not going to hang up on Sammy, and Sammy was not going to hang up on him. He would have to think of something else to say.

"Give yourself a break," Sammy said. "Boot them out. Stephanie included. She'll see the light eventually and come back to the farm."

"Should I tell her you'll be there? I don't know if—"

"I told her I'd be here when she called. All the times she called. I just told her that I had no idea of coming to get her. I'll tell you another thing. I'll be—I'll *bet*—that when she first turned up there she called you from the airport, and she wanted you to come for her, didn't she?"

"Sammy," Nick said, staring around him, wild to get off the phone. "I want to thank you for saying what you think. I'm going to hang up now."

"Forget it," Sammy said. "I'm not in my right mind. Good-bye."

"Good-bye," Nick said.

He hung up and started back to his apartment. He realized that he hadn't told Sammy that Stephanie had had the abortion. On the street he said hello to a little boy—one of the neighborhood children he knew.

He went up the stairs and up to his floor. Some people downstairs were listening to Beethoven. He lingered in the hallway, not wanting to go back to Stephanie and Karen. He took a deep breath and opened the door. Neither of them looked too bad. They said hello silently, each raising one hand.

It had been a hard day. Stephanie's appointment at the abortion clinic had been at eight in the morning, Karen had slept in the apartment with them the night before, on the sofa. Stephanie slept in his bed, and he slept on the floor. None of them had slept much. In the morning they all went to the abortion clinic. Nick had intended to go to work in the afternoon, but when they got back to the apartment he didn't think it was right for him to leave Stephanie. She went back to the bedroom, and he stretched out on the sofa and fell asleep. Before he slept, Karen sat on the sofa with him for a while, and he told her the story of his second mugging. When he woke up, it was four o'clock. He called his office and told them he was sick. Later they all watched the television news together. After that, he offered to go out and get some food, but nobody was hungry. That's when he went out and called Sammy.

Now Stephanie went back into the bedroom. She said she was tired and she was going to work on a crossword puzzle in bed. The phone rang. It was Petra. She and Nick talked a little about a new apartment she was thinking of moving into. "I'm sorry for being so cold-blooded the other night," she said. "The reason I'm calling is to invite myself to your place for a drink, if that's all right with you."

"It's not all right," he said. "I'm sorry. There are some people here now."

"I get it," she said. "Okay. I won't bother you any more."

"You don't understand," he said. He knew he had not explained things well, but the thought of adding Petra to the scene at his apartment was more than he could bear, and he had been too abrupt.

She said good-bye coldly, and he went back to his chair and fell in it, exhausted.

"A girl?" Karen said.

He nodded.

"Not a girl you wanted to hear from."

He shook his head no. He got up and pulled up the blind and looked out to the street. The boy he had said hello to was playing with a Hula Hoop. The Hula Hoop was bright blue in the twilight. The kid rotated his hips and kept the hoop spinning perfectly. Karen came to the window and stood next to him. He turned to her, wanting to say that they should go and get the Thunderbird, and as the night air cooled, drive out of the city, smell honeysuckle in the fields, feel the wind blowing.

But the Thunderbird was sold. She had told him the news while they were sitting in the waiting room of the abortion clinic. The car had needed a valve job, and a man she met in Bermuda who knew all about cars had advised her to sell it. Coincidentally, the man—a New York architect—wanted to buy it. Even as Karen told him, he knew she had been set up. If she had been more careful, they could have been in the car now, with the key in the ignition, the radio playing. He stood at the window for a long time. She had been conned, and he was more angry than he could tell her. She had no conception—she had somehow never understood—that Thunderbirds of that year, in good condition, would someday be worth a fortune. She had told him this way: "Don't be upset, because I'm sure I made the right decision. I sold the car as soon as I got back from Bermuda. I'm going to get a new car." He had moved in his chair, there in the clinic. He had had an impulse to get up and hit her. He remembered the scene in New Haven outside the bar, and he understood now that it was as simple as this: he had money that the black man wanted.

Down the street the boy picked up his Hula Hoop and disappeared around the corner.

"Say you were kidding about selling the car," Nick said.

"When are you going to stop making such a big thing over it?" Karen said.

"That creep cheated you. He talked you into selling it when nothing was wrong with it."

"Stop it," she said. "How come your judgments are always right and my judgments are always wrong?"

"I don't want to fight," he said. "I'm sorry I said anything."

"Okay," she said and leaned her head against him. He draped his right arm over her shoulder. The fingers sticking out of the cast rested a little above her breast.

"I just want to ask one thing," he said, "and then I'll never mention it again. Are you sure the deal is final?"

Karen pushed his hand off her shoulder and walked away. But it was his apartment, and she couldn't go slamming around in it. She sat on the sofa and picked up the newspaper. He watched her. Soon she put it down and stared across the room and into the dark bedroom, where Stephanie had turned off the light. He looked at her sadly for a long time, until she looked up at him with tears in her eyes.

"Do you think maybe we could get it back if I offered him more than he paid me for it?" she said. "You probably don't think that's a sensible suggestion, but at least that way we could get it back."

CHARLES BAXTER | SNOW

TWELVE years old, and I was so bored I was combing my hair just for the hell of it. This particular Saturday afternoon, time was stretching out unpleasantly in front of me. I held the comb under the tap and then stared into the bathroom mirror as I raked the wave at the front of my scalp upward so that it would look casual and sharp and perfect. For inspiration I had my transistor radio, balanced on the doorknob, tuned to an AM Top Forty station. But the music was making me jumpy, and instead of looking casual my hair, soaking wet, had the metallic curve of the rear fins of a De Soto. I looked aerodynamic but not handsome. I dropped the comb into the sink and went down the hallway to my brother's room.

Ben was sitting at his desk, crumpling up papers and tossing them into a wastebasket near the window. He was a great shot, particularly when he was throwing away his homework. His stainless-steel sword, a souvenir of military school, was leaning against the bookcase, and I could see my pencil-thin reflection in it as I stood in his doorway. "Did you hear about the car?" Ben asked, not bothering to look at me. He was gazing through his window at Five Oaks Lake.

"What car?"

"The car that went through the ice two nights ago. Thursday. Look. You can see the pressure ridge near Eagle Island."

I couldn't see any pressure ridge; it was too far away. Cars belonging to ice fishermen were always breaking through the ice, but swallowing up a car was a slow process in January, though not in March or April, and the drivers usually got out safely. The clear lake ice reflected perfectly the flat gray sky this drought winter, and we could still see the spiky brown grass on our back lawn. It crackled and crunched whenever I walked on it.

"I don't see it," I said. "I can't see the hole. Where did you hear about this car? Did Pop tell you?"

"No," Ben said. "Other sources." Ben's sources, his network of friends and enemies, were always calling him on the telephone to tell him things. He basked in information. Now he gave me a quick glance. "Holy smoke," he said. "What did you do to your hair?"

"Nothing," I said. "I was just combing it."

"You look like that guy," he said. "The one in the movies."

"Which guy?"

"That Harvey guy."

"Jimmy Stewart?"

"Of course not," he said. "You know the one I mean. Everybody knows that guy. The Harvey guy." When I looked blank, he said, "Never mind. Let's go down to the lake and look at that car. You'd better tell them we're going." He gestured toward the other end of the house.

In the kitchen I informed my parents that I was headed somewhere with my brother, and my mother, chopping carrots for one of her stews, looked up at me and my hair. "Be back by five," she said. "Where did you say you were off to?"

"We're driving to Navarre," I said. "Ben has to get his skates sharpened."

My stepfather's eyebrows started to go up; he exchanged a glance with my mother—the usual pantomime of skepticism. I turned around and ran out of the kitchen before they could stop me. I put on my boots, overcoat, and gloves, and hurried outside to my brother's car, a 1952 Rocket 88. He was already inside. The motor roared.

The interior of the car smelled of gum, cigarettes, wet wool, analgesic balm, and after-shave. "What'd you tell them?" my brother asked.

"I said you were going to Navarre to get your skates sharpened."

He put the car into first gear, then sighed. "Why'd you do that? I have to explain everything to you. Number one: my skates aren't in the car. What if they ask to see them when we get home? I won't have them. That's a problem, isn't it? Number two: when you lie about being somewhere, you make sure you have a friend who's there who can say you *were* there, even if you weren't. Unfortunately, we don't have any friends in Navarre."

"Then we're safe," I said. "No one will say we *weren't* there."

He shook his head. Then he took off his glasses and examined them as if my odd ideas were visible right there on the frames. I was just doing my job, being his private fool, but I knew he liked me and liked to have me around. My unworldliness amused him; it gave him a chance to lecture me. But now, tired of wasting words on me, he turned on the radio. Pulling out onto the highway, he steered the car in his customary way. He had explained to me that only very old or very sick people actually grip steering wheels. You didn't have to hold the wheel to drive a car. Resting your arm over the top of the wheel gave a better appearance. You dangled your hand down, preferably with a cigarette in it, so that the car, the entire car, responded to the mere pressure of your wrist.

"Hey," I said. "Where are we going? This isn't the way to the lake."

"We're not going there first. We're going there second."

"Where are we going first?"

"We're going to Five Oaks. We're going to get Stephanie. Then we'll see the car."

"How come we're getting her?"

"Because she wants to see it. She's never seen a car underneath the ice before. She'll be impressed."

"Does she know we're coming?"

He gave me that look again. "What do they teach you at that school you go to? Of course she knows. We have a date."

"A date? It's three o'clock in the afternoon," I said. "You can't have a date at three in the afternoon. Besides, I'm along."

"Don't argue," Ben said. "Pay attention."

By the time we reached Five Oaks, the heater in my brother's car was blowing out warm air in tentative gusts. If we were going to get Stephanie, his current girlfriend, it was fine with me. I liked her smile—she had an overbite, the same as I did, but she didn't seem self-conscious about it—and I liked the way she shut her eyes when she laughed. She had listened to my crystal radio set and admired my collection of igneous rocks on one of her two visits to our house. My brother liked to bring his girlfriends over to our house because the house was old and large and, my brother said, they would be impressed by the empty rooms and the long hallways and the laundry chutes that dropped down into nowhere. They'd be snowed. Snowing girls was something I knew better than to ask my brother about. You had to learn about it by watching and listening. That's why he had brought me along.

Ben parked outside Stephanie's house and told me to wait in the car. I had nothing to do but look at houses and telephone poles. Stephanie's front-porch swing had rusted chains, and the paint around her house seemed to have blistered in cobweb patterns. One drab lamp with a low-wattage bulb was on near an upstairs window. I could see the lampshade: birds—I couldn't tell what kind—had been painted on it. I adjusted the dashboard clock. It didn't run, but I liked to have it seem accurate. My brother had said that anyone who invented a clock that would really work in a car would become a multimillionaire. Clocks in cars never work, he said, because the mainsprings can't stand the shook of potholes. I checked my wristwatch and yawned. The inside of the front window began to frost over with my breath. I decided that when I grew up I would invent a new kind of timepiece for cars, without springs or gears. At three-twenty I adjusted the clock again. One minute later, my brother came out of the house with Stephanie. She saw me in the car, and she smiled.

I opened the door and got out. "Hi, Steph," I said. "I'll get in the backseat."

"That's okay, Russell," she said, smiling, showing her overbite. "Sit up in front with us."

"Really?"

She nodded. "Yeah. Keep us warm."

She scuttled in next to my brother, and I squeezed in on her right side, with my shoulder against the door. As soon as the car started, she and my brother began to hold hands: he steered with his left wrist over the steering wheel, and she held his right hand. I watched all this, and Stephanie noticed me watching. "Do you want one?" she asked me.

"What?"

"A hand." She gazed at me, perfectly serious. "My other hand."

"Sure," I said.

"Well, take my glove off," she said. "I can't do it by myself." My brother started chuckling, but she stopped him with a look. I took Stephanie's wrist in my left hand and removed her glove, finger by finger. I hadn't held hands with anyone since second grade. Her hand was not much larger than mine, but holding it gave me an odd sensation, because it was a woman's hand, and where my fingers were bony, hers were soft. She was wearing a bright green cap, and when I glanced up at it she said, "I like your hair, Russell. It's kind of slummy. You're getting to look dangerous. Is there any gum?"

I figured she meant in the car. "There's some up there on the dashboard," Ben said. His car always had gum in it. It was a museum of gum. The ashtrays were full of cigarette butts and gum, mixed together, and the floor was flecked silver from the foil wrappers.

"I can't reach it," Stephanie said. "You two have both my hands tied down."

"Okay," I said. I reached up with my free hand and took a piece of gum and unwrapped it. The gum was light pink, a sunburn color.

"Now what?" I asked.

"What do you think?" She looked down at me, smiled again, then opened her mouth. I suddenly felt shy. "Come on, Russell," she said. "Haven't you ever given gum to a girl before?" I raised my hand with the gum in it. She kept her eyes open and on me. I reached forward, and just as I got the gum close to her mouth she opened wider, and I slid the gum in over her tongue without even brushing it against her lipstick. She closed and began chewing.

"Thank you," she said. Stephanie and my brother nudged each other. Then they broke out in short quick laughs—vacation laughter. I knew that what had happened hinged on my ignorance, but that I wasn't exactly the butt of the joke and could laugh, too, if I wanted. My palm was sweaty, and she could probably feel it. The sky had turned darker, and I wondered whether, if I was still alive fifty years from now, I would remember any of this. I saw an old house on the side of the highway with a cracked upstairs window, and I thought, that's what I'll remember from this whole day when I'm old—that one cracked window.

Stephanie was looking out at the dry winter fields and suddenly said, "The state of Michigan. You know who this state is for? You know who's really happy in this state?"

"No," I said. "Who?"

"Chickens and squirrels," she said. "They love it here."

★ ★ ★

My brother parked the car on the driveway down by our dock, and we walked out onto the ice on the bay. Stephanie was stepping awkwardly, a high-center-of-gravity shuffle. "Is it safe?" she asked.

"Sure, it's safe," my brother said. "Look." He began to jump up and down. Ben was heavy enough to be a tackle on his high-school football team, and sounds of ice cracking reverberated all through the bay and beyond into the center of the lake, a deep echo. Already, four ice fishermen's houses had been set up on the ice two hundred feet out—four brightly painted shacks, male hideaways—and I could see tire tracks over the thin layer of sprinkled snow. "Clear the snow and look down into it," he said.

After lowering herself to her knees, Stephanie dusted the snow away. She held her hands to the side of her head and looked. "It's real thick," she said. "Looks a foot thick. How come a car went through?"

"It went down in a channel," Ben said, walking ahead of us and calling backward so that his voice seemed to drift in and out of the wind. "It went over a pressure ridge, and that's all she wrote."

"Did anyone drown?"

He didn't answer. She ran ahead to catch up to him, slipping, losing her balance, then recovering it. In fact I knew that no one had drowned. My stepfather had told me that the man driving the car had somehow—I wasn't sure how a person did this—pulled himself out through the window. Apparently the front end dropped through the ice first, but the car had stayed up for a few minutes before it gradually eased itself into the lake. The last two nights had been very cold, with lows around fifteen below zero, and by now the hole the car had gone through had iced over.

Both my brother and Stephanie were quite far ahead of me, and I could see them clutching at each other, Stephanie leaning against him, and my brother trying out his military-school peacock walk. I attempted this walk for a moment, then thought better of it. The late-afternoon January light was getting very raw: the sun came out for a few seconds, lighting and coloring what there was, then disappeared again, closing up and leaving us in a kind of sour grayness. I wondered if my brother and Stephanie actually liked each other or whether they were friends because they had to be.

I ran to catch up to them. "We should have brought our skates," I said, but they weren't listening to me. Ben was pointing at some clear ice, and Stephanie was nodding.

"Quiet down," my brother said. "Quiet down and listen."

All three of us stood still. Some cloud or other was beginning to drop snow on us, and from the ice underneath our feet we heard a continual chinging and barking as the ice slowly shifted.

"This is exciting," Stephanie said.

My brother nodded, but instead of looking at her he turned slightly to glance at me. Our eyes met, and he smiled.

"It's over there," he said, after a moment. The index finger of his black leather glove pointed toward a spot in the channel between Eagle Island and Crane Island where the ice was ridged and unnaturally clear. "Come on," he said.

We walked. I was ready at any moment to throw myself flat if the ice broke beneath me. I was a good swimmer—Ben had taught me—but I wasn't sure how well I would swim wearing all my clothes. I was absorbent and would probably sink headfirst, like that car.

"Get down," my brother said.

We watched him lowering himself to his hands and knees, and we followed. This was probably something he had learned in military school, this crawling. "We're ambushing this car," Stephanie said, creeping in front of me.

"There it is," he said. He pointed down.

This new ice was so smooth that it reminded me of the thick glass in the Shedd Aquarium, in Chicago. But instead of seeing a loggerhead turtle or a barracuda I looked through the ice and saw this abandoned car, this two-door Impala. It was wonderful to see—white-painted steel filtered by ice and lake water—and I wanted to laugh out of sheer happiness at the craziness of it. Dimly lit but still visible through the murk, it sat down there, its huge trunk and the sloping fins just a bit green in the algae-colored light. This is a joke, I thought, a practical joke meant to confuse the fish. I could see the car well enough to notice its radio antenna, and the windshield wipers halfway up the front window, and I could see the chrome of the front grille reflecting the dull light that ebbed down to it from where we were lying on our stomachs, ten feet above it.

"That is one unhappy automobile," Stephanie said. "Did anyone get caught inside?"

"No," I said, because no one had, and then my brother said, "Maybe."

I looked at him quickly. As usual, he wasn't looking back at me. "They aren't sure yet," he said. "They won't be able to tell until they bring the tow truck out here and pull it up."

Stephanie said, "Well, either they know or they don't. Someone's down there or not, right?"

Ben shook his head. "Maybe they don't know. Maybe there's a dead body in the backseat of that car. Or in the trunk."

"Oh, no," she said. She began to edge backward.

"I was just fooling you," my brother said. "There's nobody down there."

"What?" She was behind the area where the ice was smooth, and she stood up.

"I was just teasing you," Ben said. "The guy that was in the car got out. He got out through the window."

"Why did you lie to me?" Stephanie asked. Her arms were crossed in front of her chest.

"I just wanted to give you a thrill," he said. He stood up and walked over to where she was standing. He put his arm around her.

"I don't mind normal," she said. "Something could be normal and I'd like that, too." She glanced at me. Then she whispered into my brother's ear for about fifteen seconds, which is a long time if you're watching. Ben nodded and bent forward and whispered something in return, but I swiveled and looked around the bay at all the houses on the shore, and the old amusement park in the distance. Lights were beginning to go on, and, as if that weren't enough, it was snowing. As far as I was concerned, all those houses were guilty, both the houses and the people in them. The whole state of Michigan was guilty—all the adults, anyway—and I wanted to see them locked up.

"Wait here," my brother said. He turned and went quickly off toward the shore of the bay.

"Where's he going?" I asked.

"He's going to get his car," she said.

"What for?"

"He's going to bring it out on the ice. Then he's going to drive me home across the lake."

"That's really stupid!" I said. "That's really one of the dumbest things I ever heard! You'll go through the ice, just like that car down there did."

"No, we won't," she said. "I know we won't."

"How do you know?"

"Your brother understands this lake," she said. "He knows where the pressure ridges are and everything. He just *knows*, Russell. You have to trust him. And he can always get off the ice if he thinks it's not safe. He can always find a road."

"Well, I'm not going with you," I said. She nodded. I looked at her, and I wondered if she might be crazed with the bad judgment my parents had told me all teenagers had. Bad judgment of this kind was starting to interest me; it was a powerful antidote for boredom, which seemed worse.

"You don't want to come?"

"No," I said. "I'll walk home." I gazed up the hill, and in the distance I could see the lights of our house, a twenty-minute walk across the bay.

"Okay," Stephanie said. "I didn't think you'd want to come along." We waited. "Russell, do you think your brother is interested in me?"

"I guess so," I said. I wasn't sure what she meant by "interested." Anybody interested him, up to a point. "He says he likes you."

"That's funny, because I feel like something in the Lost and Found," she said, scratching her boot into the ice. "You know, one of those gloves that don't match anything." She put her hand on my shoulder. "One glove. One left-hand glove, with the thumb missing."

I could hear Ben's car starting, and then I saw it heading down Gallagher's boat landing. I was glad he was driving out toward us, because I didn't want to talk to her this way anymore.

Stephanie was now watching my brother's car. His headlights were on. It was odd to see a car with headlights on out on the ice, where there was no road. I saw my brother accelerate and fishtail the car, then slam on the brakes and do a 360-degree spin. He floored it, revving the back wheels, which made a high, whining sound on the ice, like a buzz saw working through wood. He was having a thrill and soon would give Stephanie another thrill by driving her home across ice that might break at any time. Thrills did it, whatever it was. Thrills led to other thrills.

"Would you look at that," I said.

She turned. After a moment she made a little sound in her throat. I remember that sound. When I see her now, she still makes it— a sign of impatience or worry. After all, she didn't go through the ice in my brother's car on the way home. She and my brother didn't drown, together or separately. Stephanie had two marriages and several children. Recently, she and her second husband adopted a Korean baby. She has the complex dignity of many small-town people who do not resort to alcohol until well after night has fallen. She continues to live in Five Oaks, Michigan, and she works behind the counter at the post office, where I buy stamps from her and gossip, holding up the line, trying to make her smile. She still has an overbite and she still laughs easily, despite the moody expression that comes over her when she relaxes. She has moved back to the same house she grew up in. Even now the exterior paint on that house blisters in cobweb patterns. I keep track of her. She and my brother certainly didn't get married; in fact, they broke up a few weeks after seeing the Chevrolet under ice.

"What are we doing out here?" Stephanie asked. I shook my head. "In the middle of winter, out here on this stupid lake? I'll tell you, Russell, I sure don't know. But I do know that your brother doesn't notice me enough, and I can't love him unless he notices me. You know your brother. You know what he pays attention to. What do I have to do to get him to notice me?"

I was twelve years old. I said, "Take off your shoes."

She stood there, thinking about what I had said, and then, quietly, she bent down and took off her boots, and, putting her hand on my shoulder to balance herself, she took off her brown loafers and her white socks. She stood there in front of me with her bare feet on the ice. I saw in the grayish January light that her toenails were painted. Bare feet with painted toenails on the ice—this was a desperate and beautiful sight, and I shivered and felt my fingers curling inside my gloves.

"How does it feel?" I asked.

"You'll know," she said. "You'll know in a few years."

My brother drove up close to us. He rolled down his window and opened the passenger-side door. He didn't say anything. I watched Stephanie get into the car, carrying her shoes and socks and boots, and then I waved good-bye to them before turning to walk back to our house. I heard the car heading north across the ice. My brother would be looking at Stephanie's bare feet on the floor of his car. He would probably not be saying anything just now.

When I reached our front lawn, I stood out in the dark and looked in through the kitchen window. My mother and stepfather were sitting at the kitchen counter; I couldn't be sure if they were speaking to each other, but then I saw my mother raise her arm in one of her can-you-believe-this gestures. I didn't want to go inside. I wanted to feel cold, so cold that the cold itself became permanently interesting. I took off my overcoat and my gloves.

Tilting my head back, I felt some snow fall onto my face. I thought of the word *exposure* and of how once or twice a year deer hunters in the Upper Peninsula died of it, and I bent down and stuck my hand into the snow and frozen grass and held it there. The cold rose from my hand to my elbow, and when I had counted to forty and couldn't stand another second of it, I picked up my coat and gloves and walked into the bright heat of the front hallway.

EUDORA WELTY | # NO PLACE FOR YOU, MY LOVE

To Elizabeth Bowen

THEY WERE strangers to each other, both fairly well strangers to the place, now seated side by side at luncheon—a party combined in a free-and-easy way when the friends he and she were with recognized each other across Galatoire's. The time was a Sunday in summer—those hours of afternoon that seem Time Out in New Orleans.

The moment he saw her little blunt, fair face, he thought that here was a woman who was having an affair. It was one of those odd meetings when such an impact is felt that it has to be translated at once into some sort of speculation.

With a married man, most likely, he supposed, slipping quickly into a groove—he was long married—and feeling more conventional, then, in his curiosity as she sat there, leaning her cheek on her hand, looking no further before her than the flowers on the table, and wearing that hat.

He did not like her hat, any more than he liked tropical flowers. It was the wrong hat for her, thought this Eastern businessman who had no interest whatever in women's clothes and no eye for them; he thought the unaccustomed thing crossly.

It must stick out all over me, she thought, so people think they can love me or hate me just by looking at me. How did it leave us—the old, safe, slow way people used to know of learning how one another feels, and the privilege that went with it of shying away if it seemed best? People in love like me, I suppose, give away the shortcuts to everybody's secrets.

Something, though, he decided, had been settled about her predicament—for the time being, anyway; the parties to it were all still alive, no doubt. Nevertheless, her predicament was the only one he felt so sure of here, like the only recognizable shadow in that restaurant, where mirrors and fans were busy agitating the light, as the very local talk drawled across and agitated the peace. The shadow lay between her fingers, between her little square hand and her cheek, like something always best carried about the person. Then suddenly, as she took her hand down, the secret fact was still there—it lighted her. It was a bold and full light, shot up under the brim of that hat, as close to them all as the flowers in the center of the table.

Did he dream of making her disloyal to that hopelessness that he saw very well she'd been cultivating down here? He knew very well that he did not. What they amounted to was two Northerners keeping each other company. She glanced up at the big gold clock on the wall and smiled. He didn't smile back. She had that naïve face that he associated, for no good reason, with the Middle West—because it said "Show me," perhaps. It was a serious, now-watch-out-everybody face, which orphaned her entirely in the company of these Southerners. He guessed her age, as he could not guess theirs: thirty-two. He himself was further along.

Of all human moods, deliberate imperviousness may be the most quickly communicated—it may be the most successful, most fatal signal of all. And two people can indulge in imperviousness as well as in anything else. "You're not very hungry either," he said.

The blades of fan shadows came down over their two heads, as he saw inadvertently in the mirror, with himself smiling at her now like a villain. His remark sounded dominant and rude enough for everybody present to listen back a moment; it even sounded like an answer to a question she might have just asked him. The other women glanced at him. The Southern look—Southern mask—of life-is-a-dream irony, which could turn to pure challenge at the drop of a hat, he could wish well away. He liked naïveté better.

"I find the heat down here depressing," she said, with the heart of Ohio in her voice.

"Well—I'm in somewhat of a temper about it, too," he said.

They looked with grateful dignity at each other.

"I have a car here, just down the street," he said to her as the luncheon party was rising to leave, all the others wanting to get back to their houses and sleep. "If it's all right with—Have you ever driven down south of here?"

Out on Bourbon Street, in the bath of July, she asked at his shoulder, "South of New Orleans? I didn't know there was any south to *here*. Does it just go on and on?" She laughed, and adjusted the exasperating hat to her head in a different way. It was more than frivolous, it was conspicuous, with some sort of glitter or flitter tied in a band around the straw and hanging down.

"That's what I'm going to show you."

"Oh—you've been there?"

"No!"

His voice rang out over the uneven, narrow sidewalk and dropped back from the walls. The flaked-off, colored houses were spotted like the hides of beasts faded and shy, and were hot as a wall of growth that seemed to breathe flowerlike down onto them as they walked to the car parked there.

"It's just that it couldn't be any worse—we'll see."

"All right, then," she said. "We will."

So, their actions reduced to amiability, they settled into the car—a faded red Ford convertible with a rather threadbare canvas top, which had been standing in the sun for all those lunch hours.

"It's rented," he explained. "I asked to have the top put down, and was told I'd lost my mind."

"It's out of this world. *Degrading* heat," she said and added, "Doesn't matter."

The stranger in New Orleans always sets out to leave it as though following the clue in a maze. They were threading through the narrow and one-way streets, past the pale violet bloom of tired squares, the brown steeples and statues, the balcony with the live and probably famous black monkey dipping along the railing as over a ballroom floor, past the grillework and the latticework to all the iron swans painted flesh color on the front steps of bungalows outlying.

Driving, he spread his new map and put his finger down on it. At the intersection marked Arabi, where their road led out of the tangle and he took it, a small Negro seated beneath a black umbrella astride a box chalked SHOU SHINE lifted his pink-and-black hand and waved them languidly good-bye. She didn't miss it, and waved back.

Below New Orleans there was a raging of insects from both sides of the concrete highway, not quite together, like the playing of separated marching bands. The river and the levee were still on her side, waste and jungle and some occasional settlements on his—poor houses. Families bigger than housefuls thronged the yards. His nodding, driving head would veer from side to side, looking and almost lowering. As time passed and the distance from New Orleans grew, girls ever darker and younger were disposing themselves over the porches and the porch steps, with jet black hair pulled high, and ragged palm-leaf fans rising and falling like rafts of butterflies. The children running forth were nearly always naked ones.

She watched the road. Crayfish constantly crossed in front of the wheels, looking grim and bonneted, in a great hurry.

"How the Old Woman Got Home," she murmured to herself.

He pointed, as it flew by, at a saucepan full of cut zinnias which stood waiting on the open lid of a mailbox at the roadside, with a little note tied onto the handle.

They rode mostly in silence. The sun bore down. They met fishermen and other men bent on some local pursuits, some in sulphur-colored pants, walking and riding; met wagons, trucks, boats in trucks, autos, boats on top of autos—all coming to meet them, as though something of high moment were doing back where the car came from, and he and she were determined to miss it. There was nearly always a man lying with his shoes off in the bed of any truck otherwise empty—with the raw, red look of a man sleeping in the daytime, being jolted about as he slept. Then there was a sort of dead man's land, where nobody came. He loosened his collar and tie. By rushing through the heat at high speed, they brought themselves the effect of fans turned onto their cheeks. Clearing alternated with jungle and canebrake like something tried, tried again. Little shell roads led off on both sides; now and then a road of planks led into the yellow-green.

"Like a dance floor in there." She pointed.

He informed her, "In there's your oil, I think."

There were thousands, millions of mosquitoes and gnats—a universe of them, and on the increase.

A family of eight or nine people on foot strung along the road in the same direction the car was going, beating themselves with the wild palmettos. Heels, shoulders, knees, breasts, back of the heads, elbows, hands, were touched in turn—like some game, each playing it with himself.

He struck himself on the forehead, and increased their speed. (His wife would not be at her most charitable if he came bringing malaria home to the family.)

More and more crayfish and other shell creatures littered their path, scuttling or dragging. These little samples, little jokes of creation, persisted and sometimes perished, the more of them the deeper down the road went. Terrapins and turtles came up steadily over the horizons of the ditches.

Back there in the margins were worse—crawling hides you could not penetrate with bullets or quite believe, grins that had come down from the primeval mud.

"Wake up." Her Northern nudge was very timely on his arm. They had veered toward the side of the road. Still driving fast, he spread his map.

Like a misplaced sunrise, the light of the river flowed up; they were mounting the levee on a little shell road.

"Shall we cross here?" he asked politely.

He might have been keeping track over years and miles of how long they could keep that tiny ferry waiting. Now skidding down the levee's flank, they were the last-minute car, the last possible car that could squeeze on. Under the sparse shade of one willow tree, the small, amateurish-looking boat slapped the water, as, expertly, he wedged on board.

"Tell him we put him on hubcap!" shouted one of the numerous olive-skinned, dark-eyed young boys standing dressed up in bright shirts at the railing, hugging each other with delight that that last straw was on board. Another boy drew his affectionate initials in the dust of the door on her side.

She opened the door and stepped out, and, after only a moment's standing at bay, started up a little iron stairway. She appeared above the car, on the tiny bridge beneath the captain's window and the whistle.

From there, while the boat still delayed in what seemed a trance—as if it were too full to attempt the start—she could see the panlike deck below, separated by its rusty rim from the tilting, polished water.

The passengers walking and jostling about there appeared oddly amateurish, too—amateur travelers. They were having such a good time. They all knew each other. Beer was being passed around in cans, bets were being loudly settled and new bets made, about local and special subjects on which they all doted. One red-haired man in a burst of wildness even tried to give away his truckload of shrimp to a man on the other side of the boat—nearly all the trucks were full of shrimp—causing taunts and then protests of "They good! They good!" from the giver. The young boys leaned on each other thinking of what next, rolling their eyes absently.

A radio pricked the air behind her. Looking like a great tomcat just above her head, the captain was digesting the news of a fine stolen automobile.

At last a tremendous explosion burst—the whistle. Everything shuddered in outline from the sound, everybody said something—everybody else.

They started with no perceptible motion, but her hat blew off. It went spiraling to the deck below, where he, thank heaven, sprang out of the car and picked it up. Everybody looked frankly up at her now, holding her hands to her head.

The little willow tree receded as its shade was taken away. The heat was like something falling on her head. She held the hot rail before her. It was like riding a stove. Her shoulders dropping, her hair flying, her skirt buffeted by the sudden strong wind, she stood there, thinking they all must see that with her entire self all she did was wait. Her set hands, with the bag that hung from her wrist and rocked back and forth—all three seemed objects bleaching there, belonging to no one; she could not feel a thing in the skin of her face; perhaps she was crying, and not knowing it. She could look down and see him just below her, his black shadow, her hat, and his black hair. His hair in the wind looked unreasonably long and rippling. Little did he know that from here it had a red undergleam like an animal's. When she looked up and outward, a vortex of light drove through and over the brown waves like a star in the water.

He did after all bring the retrieved hat up the stairs to her. She took it back—useless—and held it to her skirt. What they were saying below was more polite than their searchlight faces.

"Where you think he come from, that man?"

"I bet he come from Lafitte."

"Lafitte? What you bet, eh?"—all crouched in the shade of trucks, squatting and laughing.

Now his shadow fell partly across her; the boat had jolted into some other strand of current. Her shaded arm and shaded hand felt pulled out from the blaze of light and water, and she hoped humbly for more shade for her head. It had seemed so natural to climb up and stand in the sun.

The boys had a surprise—an alligator on board. One of them pulled it by a chain around the deck, between the cars and trucks, like a toy—a hide that could walk. He thought, Well they had to catch one sometime. It's Sunday afternoon. So they have him on board now, riding him across the Mississippi River. . . . The playfulness of it beset everybody on the ferry. The hoarseness of the boat whistle, commenting briefly, seemed part of the general appreciation.

"Who want to rassle him? Who want to, eh?" two boys cried, looking up. A boy with shrimp-colored arms capered from side to side, pretending to have been bitten.

What was there so hilarious about jaws that could bite? And what danger was there once in this repulsiveness—so that the last worldly evidence of some old heroic horror of the dragon had to be paraded in capture before the eyes of country clowns?

He noticed that she looked at the alligator without flinching at all. Her distance was set—the number of feet and inches between herself and it mattered to her.

Perhaps her measuring coolness was to him what his bodily shade was to her, while they stood pat up there riding the river, which felt like the sea and looked like the earth under them—full of the red-brown earth, charged with it. Ahead of the boat it was like an exposed vein of ore. The river seemed to swell in the vast middle with the curve of the earth. The sun rolled under them. As if in memory of the size of things, uprooted trees were drawn across their path, sawing at the air and tumbling one over the other.

When they reached the other side, they felt that they had been racing around an arena in their chariot, among lions. The whistle took and shook the stairs as they went down. The young boys, looking taller, had taken out colored combs and were combing their wet hair back in solemn pompadours above their radiant foreheads. They had been bathing in the river themselves not long before.

The cars and trucks, then the foot passengers and the alligator, waddling like a child to school, all disembarked and wound up the weed-sprung levee.

Both respectable and merciful, their hides, she thought, forcing herself to dwell on the alligator as she looked back. Deliver us all from the naked in heart. (As she had been told.)

When they regained their paved road, he heard her give a little sigh and saw her turn her straw-colored head to look back once more. Now that she rode with her hat in her lap, her earrings were conspicuous too. A little metal ball set with small pale stones danced beside each square, faintly downy cheek.

Had she felt a wish for someone else to be riding with them? He thought it was more likely that she would wish for her husband if she had one (his wife's voice) than for the lover in whom he believed. Whatever people liked to think, situations (if not scenes) were usually three-way—there was somebody else always. The one who didn't—couldn't—understand the two made the formidable third.

He glanced down at the map flapping on the seat between them, up at his wristwatch, out at the road. Out there was the incredible brightness of four o'clock.

On this side of the river, the road ran beneath the brow of the levee and followed it. Here was a heat that ran deeper and brighter and more intense than all the rest—its nerve. The road grew one with the heat as it was one with the unseen river. Dead snakes stretched across the concrete like markers—inlaid mosaic bands, dry as feathers, which their tires licked at intervals that began to seem clocklike.

No, the heat faced them—it was ahead. They could see it waving at them, shaken in the air above the white of the road, always at a certain distance ahead, shimmering finely as a cloth, with running edges of green and gold, fire and azure.

"It's never anything like this in Syracuse," he said.

"Or in Toledo, either," she replied with dry lips.

They were driving through greater waste down here, through fewer and even more insignificant towns. There was water under everything. Even where a screen of jungle had been left to stand, splashes could be heard from under the trees. In the vast open, sometimes boats moved inch by inch through what appeared endless meadows of rubbery flowers.

Her eyes overcome with brightness and size, she felt a panic rise, as sudden as nausea. Just how far below questions and answers, concealment and revelation, they were running now—that was still a new question, with a power of its own, waiting. How dear— how costly—could this ride be?

"It looks to me like your road can't go much further," she remarked cheerfully. "Just over there, it's all water."

"Time out," he said, and with that he turned the car into a sudden road of white shells that rushed at them narrowly out of the left.

They bolted over a cattle guard, where some rayed and crested purple flowers burst out of the vines in the ditch, and rolled onto a long, narrow, green, mowed clearing: a churchyard. A paved track ran between two short rows of raised tombs, all neatly whitewashed and now brilliant as faces against the vast flushed sky.

The track was the width of the car with a few inches to spare. He passed between the tombs slowly but in the manner of a feat. Names took their places on the walls slowly at a level with the eye, names as near as the eyes of a person stopping in conversation, and as far away in origin, and in all their music and dead longing, as Spain. At intervals were set packed bouquets of zinnias, oleanders, and some kind of purple flowers, all quite fresh, in fruit jars, like nice welcomes on bureaus.

They moved on into an open plot beyond, of violent green grass, spread before the green-and-white frame church with worked flower beds around it, flowerless poinsettias growing up to the windowsills. Beyond was a house, and left on the doorstep of the house a fresh-caught catfish the size of a baby—a fish wearing whiskers and bleeding. On a clothesline in the yard, a priest's black gown on a hanger hung airing, swaying at man's height, in a vague, trainlike, ladylike sweep along an evening breath that might otherwise have seemed imaginary from the unseen, felt river.

With the motor cut off, with the raging of the insects about them, they sat looking out at the green and white and black and red and pink as they leaned against the sides of the car.

"What is your wife like?" she asked. His right hand came up and spread—iron, wooden, manicured. She lifted her eyes to his face. He looked at her like that hand.

Then he lit a cigarette, and the portrait, and the right-hand testimonial it made, were blown away. She smiled, herself as unaffected as by some stage performance; and he was annoyed in the cemetery. They did not risk going on to her husband—if she had one.

Under the supporting posts of the priest's house, where a boat was, solid ground ended and palmettos and water hyacinths could not wait to begin; suddenly the rays of the sun, from behind the car, reached that lowness and struck the flowers. The priest came out onto the porch in his underwear, stared at the car a moment as if he wondered what time it was, then collected his robe off the line and his fish off the doorstep and returned inside. Vespers was next, for him.

After backing out between the tombs he drove on still south, in the sunset. They caught up with an old man walking in a sprightly way in their direction, all by himself, wearing a clean bright shirt printed with a pair of palm trees fanning green over his chest. It might better be a big colored woman's shirt, but she didn't have it. He flagged the car with gestures like hoops.

"You're coming to the end of the road," the old man told

them. He pointed ahead, tipped his hat to the lady, and pointed again. "End of the road." They didn't understand that he meant, "Take me."

They drove on. "If we do go any further, it'll have to be by water—is that it?" he asked her, hesitating at this odd point.

"You know better than I do," she replied politely.

The road had for some time ceased to be paved; it was made of shells. It was leading into a small, sparse settlement like the others a few miles back, but with even more of the camp about it. On the lip of the clearing, directly before a green willow blaze with the sunset gone behind it, the row of houses and shacks faced out on broad, colored, moving water that stretched to reach the horizon and looked like an arm of the sea. The houses on their shaggy posts, patchily built, some with plank runways instead of steps, were flimsy and alike, and not much bigger than the boats tied up at the landing.

"Venice," she heard him announce, and he dropped the crackling map in her lap.

They coasted down the brief remainder. The end of the road— she could not remember ever seeing a road simply end—was a spoon shape, with a tree stump in the bowl to turn around by.

Around it, he stopped the car, and they stepped out, feeling put down in the midst of a sudden vast pause or subduement that was like a yawn. They made their way on foot toward the water, where at an idle-looking landing men in twos and threes stood with their backs to them.

The nearness of darkness, the still uncut trees, bright water partly under a sheet of flowers, shacks, silence, dark shapes of boats tied up, then the first sounds of people just on the other side of thin walls—all this reached them. Mounds of shells like day old snow, pink-tinted, lay around a central shack with a beer sign on it. An old man up on the porch there sat holding an open newspaper, with a fat white goose sitting opposite him on the floor. Below, in the now shadowless and sunless open, another old man, with a colored pencil bright under his hat brim, was late mending a sail.

When she looked clear around, thinking they had a fire burning somewhere now, out of the heat had risen the full moon. Just beyond the trees, enormous, tangerine-colored, it was going solidly up. Other lights just striking into view, looking farther distant, showed moss shapes hanging, or slipped and broke matchlike on the water that so encroached upon the rim of ground they were standing on.

There was a touch at her arm—his, accidental.

"We're at the jumping-off place," he said.

She laughed, having thought his hand was a bat, while her eyes rushed downward toward a great pale drift of water hyacinths— still partly open, flushed and yet moonlit, level with her feet— through which paths of water for the boats had been hacked. She drew her hands up to her face under the brim of her hat; her own cheeks felt like the hyacinths to her, all her skin still full of too much light and sky, exposed. The harsh vesper bell was ringing.

"I believe there must be something wrong with me, that I came on this excursion to begin with," she said, as if he had already said this and she were merely in hopeful, willing, maddening agreement with him.

He took hold of her arm, and said, "Oh, come on—I see we can get something to drink here, at least."

But there was a beating, muffled sound from over the darkening water. One more boat was coming in, making its way through the tenacious, tough, dark flower traps, by the shaken light of what first appeared to be torches. He and she waited for the boat, as if on each other's patience. As if borne in on a mist of twilight or a breath, a horde of mosquitoes and gnats came singing and striking at them first. The boat bumped, men laughed. Somebody was offering somebody else some shrimp.

Then he might have cocked his dark city head down at her; she did not look up at him, only turned when he did. Now the shell mounds, like the shacks and trees, were solid purple. Lights had appeared in the not-quite-true window squares. A narrow neon sign, the lone sign, had come out in bright blush on the beer shack's roof: BABA'S PLACE. A light was on on the porch.

The barnlike interior was brightly lit and unpainted, looking not quite finished, with a partition dividing this room from what lay behind. One of the four cardplayers at a table in the middle of the floor was the newspaper reader; the paper was in his pants pocket. Midway along the partition was a bar, in the form of a pass-through to the other room, with a varnished, secondhand fretwork overhang. They crossed the floor and sat, alone there, on wooden stools. An eruption of humorous signs, newspaper cutouts and cartoons, razor-blade cards, and personal messages of significance to the owner or his friends decorated the overhang, framing where Baba should have been but wasn't.

Through there came a smell of garlic and cloves and red pepper, a blast of hot cloud escaped from a cauldron they could see now on a stove at the back of the other room. A massive back, presumably female, with a twist of gray hair on top, stood with a ladle akimbo. A young man joined her and with his fingers stole something out of the pot and ate it. At Baba's they were boiling shrimp.

When he got ready to wait on them, Baba strolled out to the counter, young, black-headed, and in very good humor.

"Coldest beer you've got. And food—What will you have?"

"Nothing for me, thank you," she said. "I'm not sure I could eat, after all."

"Well, I could," he said, shoving his jaw out. Baba smiled. "I want a good solid ham sandwich."

"I could have asked him for some water," she said, after he had gone.

While they sat waiting, it seemed very quiet. The bubbling of the shrimp, the distant laughing of Baba, and the slap of cards, like the beating of moths on the screens, seemed to come in fits and starts. The steady breathing they heard came from a big rough dog asleep in the corner. But it was bright. Electric lights were strung riotously over the room from a kind of spider web of old wires in the rafters. One of the written messages tacked before them read, "Joe! At the boyy!!" It looked very yellow, older than Baba's Place. Outside, the world was pure dark.

Two little boys, almost alike, almost the same size, and just cleaned up, dived into the room with a double bang of the screen door, and circled around the card game. They ran their hands into the men's pockets.

"Nickel for some pop!"

"Nickel for some pop!"

"Go 'way and let me play, you!"

They circled around and shrieked at the dog, ran under the lid of the counter and raced through the kitchen and back, and hung over the stools at the bar. One child had a live lizard on his shirt, clinging like a breast pin—like lapis lazuli.

Bringing in a strong odor of geranium talcum, some men had come in now—all in bright shirts. They drew near the counter, or stood and watched the game.

When Baba came out bringing the beer and sandwich, "Could I have some water?" she greeted him.

Baba laughed at everybody. She decided the woman back there must be Baba's mother.

Beside her, he was drinking his beer and eating his sandwich— ham, cheese, tomato, pickle, and mustard. Before he finished, one of the men who had come in beckoned from across the room. It was the old man in the palm-tree shirt.

She lifted her head to watch him leave her, and was looked at, from all over the room. As a minute passed, no cards were laid down. In a far-off way, like accepting the light from Arcturus, she accepted it that she was more beautiful or perhaps more fragile than the women they saw every day of their lives. It was just this thought coming into a woman's face, and at this hour, that seemed familiar to them.

Baba was smiling. He had set an opened, frosted brown bottle before her on the counter, and a thick sandwich, and stood looking at her. Baba made her eat some supper, for what she was.

"What the old fellow wanted," said he when he came back at last, "was to have a friend of his apologize. Seems church is just out. Seems the friend made a remark coming in just now. His pals told him there was a lady present."

"I see you bought him a beer," she said.

"Well, the old man looked like he wanted *something*."

All at once the jukebox interrupted from back in the corner, with the same old song as anywhere. The half-dozen slot machines along the wall were suddenly all run to like Maypoles, and thrown into action—taken over by further battalions of little boys.

There were three little boys to each slot machine. The local custom appeared to be that one pulled the lever for the friend he was holding up to put the nickel in, while the third covered the pictures with the flat of his hand as they fell into place, so as to surprise them all if anything happened.

The dog lay sleeping on in front of the raging jukebox, his ribs working fast as a concertina's. At the side of the room a man with a cap on his white thatch was trying his best to open a side screen door, but it was stuck fast. It was he who had come in with the remark considered ribald; now he was trying to get out the other way. Moths as thick as ingots were trying to get in. The cardplayers broke into shouts of derision, then joy, then tired derision among themselves; they might have been there all afternoon— they were the only ones not cleaned up and shaved. The original pair of little boys ran in once more, with the hyphenated bang. They got nickels this time, then were brushed away from the table like mosquitoes, and they rushed under the counter and on to the cauldron behind, clinging to Baba's mother there. The evening was at the threshold.

They were quite unnoticed now. He was eating another sandwich, and she, having finished part of hers, was fanning her face with her hat. Baba had lifted the flap of the counter and come out into the room. Behind his head there was a sign lettered in orange crayon: SHRIMP DANCE SUN. P.M. That was tonight, still to be.

And suddenly she made a move to slide down from her stool, maybe wishing to walk out into that nowhere down the front steps to be cool a moment. But he had hold of her hand. He got down from his stool, and, patiently, reversing her hand in his own—just as she had had the look of being about to give up, faint—began moving her, leading her. They were dancing.

"I get to thinking this is what we get—what you and I deserve," she whispered, looking past his shoulder into the room. "And all the time, it's real. It's a real place—away off down here. . . ."

They danced gratefully, formally, to some song carried on in what must be the local patois, while no one paid any attention as long as they were together, and the children poured the family nickels steadily into the slot machines, walloping the handles down with regular crashes and troubling nobody with winning.

She said rapidly, as they began moving together too well, "One of those clippings was an account of a shooting right here. I guess they're proud of it. And that awful knife Baba was carrying . . . I wonder what he called me," she whispered in his ear.

"Who?"

"The one who apologized to you."

If they had ever been going to overstep themselves, it would be now as he held her closer and turned her, when she became aware that he could not help but see the bruise at her temple. It would not be six inches from his eyes. She felt it come out like an evil star. (Let it pay him back, then, for the hand he had stuck in her face when she'd tried once to be sympathetic, when she'd asked about his wife.) They danced on still as the record changed, after standing wordless and motionless, linked together in the middle of the room, for the moment between.

Then, they were like a matched team—like professional, Spanish dancers wearing masks—while the slow piece was playing.

Surely even those immune from the world, for the time being, need the touch of one another, or all is lost. Their arms encircling

[263]

each other, their bodies circling the odorous, just-nailed-down floor, they were, at last, imperviousness in motion. They had found it, and had almost missed it: they had had to dance. They were what their separate hearts desired that day, for themselves and each other.

They were so good together that once she looked up and half smiled. "For whose benefit did we have to show off?"

Like people in love, they had a superstition about themselves almost as soon as they came out on the floor, and dared not think the words *happy* or *unhappy*, which might strike them, one or the other, like lightning.

In the thickening heat they danced on while Baba himself sang with the mosquito-voiced singer in the chorus of "Moi pas l'aimez ça," enumerating the *ça's* with a hot shrimp between his fingers. He was counting over the platters the old woman now set out on the counter, each heaped with shrimp in their shells boiled to iridescence, like mounds of honeysuckle flowers.

The goose wandered in from the back room under the lid of the counter and hitched itself around the floor among the table legs and people's legs, never seeing that it was neatly avoided by two dancers—who nevertheless vaguely thought of this goose as learned, having earlier heard an old man read to it. The children called it Mimi, and lured it away. The old thatched man was again drunkenly trying to get out by the stuck side door; now he gave it a kick, but was prevailed on to remain. The sleeping dog shuddered and snored.

It was left up to the dancers to provide nickels for the jukebox; Baba kept a drawerful for every use. They had grown fond of all the selections by now. This was the music you heard out of the distance at night—out of the roadside taverns you fled past, around the late corners in cities half asleep, drifting up from the carnival over the hill, with one odd little strain always managing to repeat itself. This seemed a homey place.

Bathed in sweat, and feeling the false coolness that brings, they stood finally on the porch in the lapping night air for a moment before leaving. The first arrivals of the girls were coming up the steps under the porch light—all flowered fronts, their black pompadours giving out breathlike feelers from sheer abundance. Where they'd resprinkled it since church, the talcum shone like mica on their downy arms. Smelling solidly of geranium, they filed across the porch with short steps and fingers joined, just timed to turn their smiles loose inside the room. He held the door open for them.

"Ready to go?" he asked her.

Going back, the ride was wordless, quiet except for the motor and the insects driving themselves against the car. The windshield was soon blinded. The headlights pulled in two other spinning storms, cones of flying things that, it seemed, might ignite at the last minute. He stopped the car and got out to clean the windshield thoroughly with his brisk, angry motions of driving. Dust lay thick and cratered on the roadside scrub. Under the now ash white moon, the world traveled through very faint stars—very many slow stars, very high, very low.

It was a strange land, amphibious—and whether water-covered or grown with jungle or robbed entirely of water and trees, as now, it had the same loneliness. He regarded the great sweep—like steppes, like moors, like deserts (all of which were imaginary to him); but more than it was like any likeness, it was South. The vast, thin, wide-thrown, pale, unfocused star-sky, with its veils of lightning adrift, hung over this land as it hung over the open sea. Standing out in the night alone, he was struck as powerfully with recognition of the extremity of this place as if all other bearings had vanished—as if snow had suddenly started to fall.

He climbed back inside and drove. When he moved to slap furiously at his shirtsleeves, she shivered in the hot, licking night wind that their speed was making. Once the car lights picked out two people—a Negro couple, sitting on two facing chairs in the yard outside their lonely cabin—half undressed, each battling for self against the hot night, with long white rags in endless, scarflike motions.

In peopleless open places there were lakes of dust, smudge fires burning at their hearts. Cows stood in untended rings around them, motionless in the heat, in the night—their horns standing up sharp against that glow.

At length, he stopped the car again, and this time he put his arm under her shoulder and kissed her—not knowing ever whether gently or harshly. It was the loss of that distinction that told him this was now. Then their faces touched unkissing, unmoving, dark, for a length of time. The heat came inside the car and wrapped them still, and the mosquitoes had begun to coat their arms and even their eyelids.

Later, crossing a large open distance, he saw at the same time two fires. He had the feeling that they had been riding for a long time across a face—great, wide, and upturned. In its eyes and open mouth were those fires they had had glimpses of, where the cattle had drawn together: a face, a head, far down here in the South— south of South, below it. A whole giant body sprawled downward then, on and on, always, constant as a constellation or an angel. Flaming and perhaps falling, he thought.

She appeared to be sound asleep, lying back flat as a child, with her hat in her lap. He drove on with her profile beside his, behind his, for he bent forward to drive faster. The earrings she wore twinkled with their rushing motion in an almost regular beat. They might have spoken like tongues. He looked straight before him and drove on, at a speed that, for the rented, overheated, not at all new Ford car, was demoniac.

It seemed often now that a barnlike shape flashed by, roof and all outlined in lonely neon—a movie house at a crossroads. The long white flat road itself, since they had followed it to the end and turned around to come back, seemed able, this far up, to pull them home.

★ ★ ★

A thing is incredible, if ever, only after it is told—returned to the world it came out of. For their different reasons, he thought, neither of them would tell this (unless something was dragged out of them): that, strangers, they had ridden down into a strange land together and were getting safely back—by a slight margin, perhaps, but margin enough. Over the levee wall now, like an aurora borealis, the sky of New Orleans, across the river, was flickering gently. This time they crossed by bridge, high above everything, merging into a long light-stream of cars turned city-ward.

For a time afterward he was lost in the streets, turning almost at random with the noisy traffic until he found his bearings. When he stopped the car at the next sign and leaned forward frowning to make it out, she sat up straight on her side. It was Arabi. He turned the car right around.

"We're all right now," he muttered, allowing himself a cigarette.

Something that must have been with them all along suddenly, then, was not. In a moment, tall as panic, it rose, cried like a human, and dropped back.

"I never got my water," she said.

She gave him the name of her hotel, he drove her there, and he said good night on the sidewalk. They shook hands.

"Forgive . . ." For, just in time, he saw she expected it of him.

And that was just what she did, forgive him. Indeed, had she waked in time from a deep sleep, she would have told him her story. She disappeared through the revolving door, with a gesture of smoothing her hair, and he thought a figure in the lobby strolled to meet her. He got back in the car and sat there.

He was not leaving for Syracuse until early in the morning. At length, he recalled the reason; his wife had recommended that he stay where he was this extra day so that she could entertain some old, unmarried college friends without him underfoot.

As he started up the car, he recognized in the smell of exhausted, body-warm air in the streets, in which the flow of drink was an inextricable part, the signal that the New Orleans evening was just beginning. In Dickie Grogan's, as he passed, the well-known Josefina at her organ was charging up and down with "Clair de Lune." As he drove the little Ford safely to its garage, he remembered for the first time in years when he was young and brash, a student in New York, and the shriek and horror and unholy smother of the subway had its original meaning for him as the lilt and expectation of love.

RICHARD
BAUSCH

CONSOLATION

LATE one summer afternoon, Milly Harmon and her older
sister, Meg, spend a blessed, uncomplicated hour at a motel pool
in Philadelphia, sitting in the shade of one of the big umbrella
tables. They drink tropical punch from cans, and Milly nurses the
baby, staring out at the impossibly silver agitation of water around
the body of a young, dark swimmer, a boy with Spanish black
hair and eyes. He's the only one in the pool. Across the way, an
enormous woman in a red terry-cloth bikini lies on her stomach
in the sun, her head resting on her folded arms. Milly's sister puts
her own head down for a moment, then looks at Milly. "I feel
fat," she says, low. "I look like that woman over there, I just
know it."

"Be quiet," Milly says. "Your voice carries."

"Nobody can hear us," Meg says. She's always worried about
weight, though she's nothing like the woman across the way. Her
thighs are heavy, her hips wide, but she's big-boned, as their
mother always says; she's not built to be skinny. Milly's the one
who's skinny. When they were growing up, Meg often called her
"stick." Sometimes it was an endearment and sometimes it was a

jibe, depending on the circumstances. These days, Meg calls her "honey" and speaks to her with something like the careful tones of sympathy. Milly's husband was killed last September, when Milly was almost six months pregnant, and the two women have traveled here to see Milly's in-laws, to show them their grandchild, whom they have never seen.

The visit hasn't gone well. Things have been strained and awkward. Milly is exhausted and discouraged, so her sister has worked everything out, making arrangements for the evening, preserving these few hours in the day for the two of them and the baby. In a way, the baby's the problem: Milly would never have suspected that her husband's parents would react so peevishly, with such annoyance, to their only grandson—the only grandchild they will ever have.

Last night, when the baby started crying at dinner, both the Harmons seemed to sulk, and finally Wally's father excused himself and went to bed—went into his bedroom and turned a radio on. His dinner was still steaming on his plate; they hadn't even quite finished passing the food around. The music sounded through the walls of the small house, while Milly, Wally's mother, and Meg sat through the meal trying to be cordial to each other, the baby fussing between them.

Finally Wally's mother said, "Perhaps if you nurse him."

"I just did," Milly told her."

"Well, he wants *something*."

"Babies cry," Meg put in, and the older woman looked at her as though she had said something off-color.

"Hush," Milly said to the baby. "Be quiet." Then there seemed nothing left to say.

Mrs. Harmon's hands trembled over the lace edges of the tablecloth. "Can I get you anything?" she said.

At the end of the evening she took Milly by the elbow and murmured, "I'm afraid you'll have to forgive us, we're just not used to the commotion."

"Commotion," Meg said as they drove back to the motel. "Jesus. Commotion."

Milly looked down into the sleeping face of her son. "My little commotion," she said, feeling tired and sad.

Now Meg turns her head on her arms and gazes at the boy in the pool. "Maybe I'll go for a swim," she says.

"He's too young for you," Milly says.

Meg affects a forlorn sigh, then sits straight again. "You want me to take Zeke for a while?" The baby's name is Wally, after his dead father, but Meg calls him Zeke. She claims she's always called every baby Zeke, boy or girl, but she's especially fond of the name for *this* baby. This baby, she says, looks like a Zeke. Even Milly uses the name occasionally, as an endearment.

"He's not through nursing," Milly says.

It's been a hot day. Even now, at almost six o'clock, the sky is pale blue and crossed with thin, fleecy clouds that look like filaments of steam. Meg wants a tan, or says she does, but she's worn a kimono all afternoon, and hasn't moved out of the shade. She's with Milly these days because her marriage is breaking up. It's an amicable divorce; there are no children. Meg says the whole thing simply collapsed of its own weight. Neither party is interested in anyone else, and there haven't been any ugly scenes or secrets. They just don't want to be married to each other anymore, see no future in it. She talks about how civilized the whole procedure has been, how even the lawyers are remarking on it, but Milly thinks she hears some sorrow in her voice. She thinks of two friends of hers who have split up twice since the warehouse fire that killed Wally, and whose explanations, each time, have seemed to preclude any possibility of reconciliation. Yet they're now living together, and sometimes, when Milly sees them, they seem happy.

"Did I tell you that Jane and Martin are back together?" she asks Meg.

"Again?"

She nods.

"Tied to each other on a rock in space," Meg says.

"What?"

"Come on, let me hold Zeke," Meg reaches for the baby. "He's through, isn't he?"

"He's asleep."

Meg pretends to pout, extending her arm across the table and putting her head down again. She makes a yawning sound. "Where are all the boys? Let's have some fun here anyway—right? Let's get in a festive mood or something."

Milly removes the baby's tight little sucking mouth from her breast and covers herself. The baby sleeps on, still sucking. "Look at this," she says to her sister.

Meg leans toward her to see. "What in the world do you think is wrong with them?"

She's talking about Wally's parents, of course. Milly shrugs. She doesn't feel comfortable discussing them. She wants the baby to have both sets of grandparents, and a part of her feels that this ambition is in some way laudatory—that the strange, stiff people she has brought her child all this way to see ought to appreciate what she's trying to do. She wonders if they harbor some resentment about how before she would marry their son she'd extracted a promise from him about not leaving Illinois, where her parents and her sister live. It's entirely possible that Wally's parents unconsciously blame her for Wally's death, for the fact that his body lies far away in her family's plot in a cemetery in Lincoln, Illinois.

"Hey," Meg says.

"What."

"I asked a question. You drove all the way out here to see them and let them see their grandson, and they act like it's some kind of bother."

"They're just tired," Milly says. "Like we are."

"Seven hundred miles of driving to sit by a motel pool."

"They're not used to having a baby around," Milly says. "It's awkward for them, too." She wishes her sister would stop. "Can't we just not worry it all to death?"

"Hey," Meg says. "It's your show."

Milly says, "We'll see them tonight and then we'll leave in the morning and that'll be that, okay?"

"I wonder what they're doing right now. You think they're watching the four o'clock movie or something? With their only grandson two miles away in a motel?"

In a parking lot in front of a group of low buildings on the other side of the highway, someone sets off a pack of firecrackers—they make a sound like small machine-gun fire.

"All these years of independence," Meg says. "So people like us can have these wonderful private lives."

Milly smiles. It's always been Meg who defined things, who spoke out and offered opinions. Milly thinks of her sister as someone who knows the world, someone with experience she herself lacks, though Meg is only a little more than a year older. So much of her own life seems somehow duplicitous to her, as if the wish to please others and to be well thought of had somehow dulled the edges of her identity and left her with nothing but a set of received impressions. She knows she loves the baby in her lap, and she knows she loved her husband—though during the four years of her marriage she was confused much of the time, and afraid of her own restlessness. It was only in the weeks just before Wally was taken from her that she felt most comfortably in love with him, glad of his presence in the house and worried about the dangerous fire-fighting work that was, in fact, the agency of his death. She doesn't want to think about this now, and she marvels at how a moment of admiration for the expressiveness of her sister could lead to remembering that her husband died just as she was beginning to understand her need for him. She draws a little shuddering breath, and Meg frowns.

"You looked like something hurt you," Meg says. "You were thinking about Wally."

Milly nods.

"Zeke looks like him, don't you think?"

"I wasted so much time wondering if I loved him," Milly says.

"I think he was happy," her sister tells her.

In the pool the boy splashes and dives, disappears; Milly watches the shimmery surface. He comes up on the other side, spits a stream of water, and climbs out. He's wearing tight, dark blue bathing trunks.

"Come on," Meg says, reaching for the baby. "Let me have him."

"I don't want to wake him," Milly says.

Meg walks over to the edge of the pool, takes off her sandals, and dips the toe of one foot in, as though trying to gauge how cold the water is. She comes back, sits down, drops the sandals between her feet and steps into them one by one. "You know what I think it is with the Harmons?" she says. "I think it's the war. I think the war got them. That whole generation."

Milly ignores this, and adjusts, slightly, the weight of the baby in her lap. "Zeke," she says. "Pretty Zeke."

The big woman across the way has labored up off her towel and is making slow progress out of the pool area.

"Wonder if she's married," Meg says. "I think I'll have a pool party when the divorce is final."

The baby stirs in Milly's lap. She moves slightly, rocking her legs.

"We ought to live together permanently," Meg says.

"You want to keep living with us?"

"Sure, why not? Zeke and I get along. A divorced woman and a widow. And one cool baby boy."

They're quiet a while. Somewhere off beyond the trees at the end of the motel parking lot, more firecrackers go off. Meg stands, stretches. "I knew a guy once who swore he got drunk and slept on top of the Tomb of the Unknown Soldier. On Independence Day. Think of it."

"You didn't believe him," Milly says.

"I believed he had the idea. Whole culture's falling apart. Whole goddamn thing."

"Do you really want to stay with us?" Milly asks her.

"I don't know. That's an idea, too." She ambles over to the pool again, then walks around it, out of the gate, to the small stairway leading up to their room. At the door of the room she turns, shrugs, seems to wait. Milly lifts the baby to her shoulder, then rises. Meg is standing at the railing on the second level, her kimono partway open at the legs. Milly, approaching her, thinks she looks wonderful, and tells her so.

"I was just standing here wondering how long it'll take to drive you crazy if we keep living together," Meg says, opening the door to the room. Inside, in the air-conditioning, she flops down on the nearest bed. Milly puts the baby in the Port-a-Crib and turns to see that the telephone message light is on. "Hey, look," she says.

Meg says, "Ten to one it's the Harmons canceling out."

"No bet," Milly says, tucking the baby in. "Oh, I just want to go home, anyway."

Her sister dials the front desk, then sits cross-legged with pillows at her back, listening. "I don't believe this," she says.

It turns out that there are two calls: one from the Harmons, who say they want to come earlier than planned, and one from Meg's estranged husband, Larry, who has apparently traveled here from Champaign, Illinois. When Meg calls the number he left, he answers, and she waves Milly out of the room. Milly takes the baby, who isn't quite awake, and walks back down to the pool. It's empty; the water is perfectly smooth. She sits down, watches the light shift on the surface, clouds moving across it in reflection.

It occurs to her that she might have to spend the rest of the trip on her own, and this thought causes a flutter at the pit of her stomach. She thinks of Larry, pulling this stunt, and she wonders why she didn't imagine that he might show up, her sister's casual talk of the divorce notwithstanding. He's always been prone to the grand gesture: once, after a particularly bad quarrel, he rented a van with loudspeakers and drove up and down the streets of Champaign, proclaiming his love. Milly remembers this, sitting by the empty pool, and feels oddly threatened.

It isn't long before Meg comes out and calls her back. Meg is already trying to make herself presentable. What Larry wants, she tells Milly, what he pleaded for, is only that Meg agree to see him. He came to Philadelphia and began calling all the Harmons in the phone book, and when he got Wally's parents, they gave him the number of the motel. "The whole thing's insane," she says, hurriedly brushing her hair. "I don't get it. We're almost final."

"Meg, I need you now," Milly says.

"Don't be ridiculous," says her sister.

"What're we going to do about the Harmons?"

"Larry says they asked him to say hello to you. Can you feature that? I mean, what in the world is that? It's like they don't expect to see you again."

"Yes," Milly says. "But they're coming."

"He called before, you know."

"Mr. Harmon?"

"No—Larry. He called just before we left. I didn't get it. I mean, he kept hinting around and I just didn't get it. I guess I told him we were coming to Philly."

The baby begins to whine and complain.

"Hey, Zeke," Meg says. She looks in the mirror. "Good Lord, I look like war," and then she's crying. She moves to the bed, sits down, still stroking her hair with the brush.

"Don't cry," Milly says. "You don't want to look all red-eyed, do you?"

"What the hell," Meg says. "I'm telling you, I don't care about it. I mean—I don't care. He's such a baby about everything."

Milly is completely off balance. She has been the one in need on this trip, and now everything's turned around. "Here," she says, offering her sister a Kleenex. "You can't let him see you looking miserable."

"You believe this?" Meg says. "You think I should go with him?"

"He wants to take you somewhere?"

"I don't know."

"What about the Harmons?"

Meg looks at her. "What about them?"

"They're on their way here, too."

"I can't handle the Harmons anymore," Meg tells her.

"Who asked you to handle them?"

"You know what I mean."

"Well—are you just going to go off with Larry?"

"I don't know what he wants."

"Well, for God's sake, Meg. He wouldn't come all this way just to tell you hello."

"That's what he said. He said 'Hello.' "

"Meg."

"I'm telling you, honey, I just don't have a clue."

In a little while Larry arrives, looking sheepish and expectant. Milly lets him in, and accepts his clumsy embrace, explaining that Meg is in the bathroom changing out of her bathing suit.

"Hey," he says, "I brought mine with me."

"She'll be through in a minute."

"Is she mad at me?" he asks.

"She's just changing," Milly tells him.

He looks around the room, walks over to the Port-a-Crib and stands there making little cooing sounds at the baby. "He's smiling at me. Look at that."

"He smiles a lot." She moves to the other side of the crib and watches him make funny faces at the baby.

Larry is a fair, willowy man, and though he's older than Milly, she has always felt a tenderness toward him for his obvious unease with her, for the way Meg orders him around, and for his boyish romantic fragility—which, she realizes now, reminds her a little of Wally. It's in the moment that she wishes he hadn't come here that she thinks of this, and abruptly she has an urge to reach across the crib and touch his wrist, as if to make up for some wrong she's done. He leans down and puts one finger into the baby's hand. "Look at that," he says. "Quite a grip. Boy's going to be a linebacker."

"He's small for his age," Milly tells him.

"It's not the size. It's the strength."

She says nothing. She wishes Meg would come out of the bathroom. Larry pats the baby's forehead, then moves to the windows and, holding the drapes back, looks out.

"Pretty," he says. "Looks like it'll be a nice, clear night for fireworks."

For the past year or so, Larry has worked in a shoe store in Urbana, and he's gone through several other jobs, though he often talks about signing up for English courses at the junior college and getting started on a career. He wants to save money for school, but in five years he hasn't managed to save enough for one course. He explains himself in terms of his appetite for life: he's unable to put off the present, and frugality sometimes suffers. Meg has often talked about him with a kind of wonder at his capacity for pleasure. It's not a thing she would necessarily want to change. He can make her laugh, and he writes poems to her, to women in general, though according to Meg they're not very good poems.

The truth is, he's an amiable, dreamy young man without an ounce of objectivity about himself, and what he wears on this occasion seems to illustrate this. His bohemian dress is embarrassingly like a costume—the bright red scarf and black beret and jeans; the sleeveless turtleneck shirt, its dark colors bleeding into each other across the front.

"So," he says, turning from the windows. "Are the grandparents around?"

She draws in a breath, deciding to tell him about the Harmons, but Meg comes out of the bathroom at last. She's wearing the kimono open, showing the white shorts and blouse she's changed into.

Larry stands straight, clears his throat. "God, Meg. You look great," he says.

Meg flops down on the bed nearest the door and lights a cigarette. "Larry, what're you trying to pull here?"

"Nothing," he says. He hasn't moved. He's standing by the windows. "I just wanted to see you again. I thought Philadelphia on the Fourth might be good."

"Okay," Meg says, drawing on the cigarette.

"You know me," he says. "I have a hard time saying this sort of stuff up close."

"What sort of stuff, Larry?"

"I'll take Zeke for a walk," Milly says.

"I can't believe this," Meg says, blowing smoke.

Milly gathers up the baby, but Larry stops her. "You don't have to go."

"Stay," Meg tells her.

"I thought I'd go out and meet the Harmons."

"Come on, tell me what you're doing here," Meg says to Larry.

"You don't know?"

"What if I need you to tell me anyway," she says.

He hesitates, then reaches into his jeans and brings out a piece of folded paper. "Here."

Meg takes it, but doesn't open it.

"Aren't you going to read it?"

"I can't read it with you watching me like that. Jesus, Larry— what in the world's going through your mind?"

"I started thinking about it being final," he says, looking down. Milly moves to the other side of the room, to her own bed, still holding the baby.

"I won't read it with you standing here," Meg says.

Larry reaches for the door. "I'll be outside," he says.

Milly, turning to sit with her back to them, hears the door close quietly. She looks at Meg, who's sitting against the headboard of the other bed, the folded paper in her lap.

"Aren't you going to read it?"

"I'm embarrassed for him."

Milly recalls her own, secret, embarrassment at the unattractive, hyena-like note poor Wally struck every time he laughed. "It was probably done with love," she says.

Meg offers her the piece of paper across the space between the two beds. "You read it to me."

"I can't do that, Meg. It's private. I shouldn't even be here."

Meg opens the folded paper, and reads silently. "Jesus," she says. "Listen to this."

"Meg," Milly says.

"You're my sister. Listen. 'When I began to think our time was really finally up / My chagrined regretful eyes lumbered tightly shut.' Lumbered, for God's sake."

Milly says nothing.

"My eyes lumbered shut."

And quite suddenly the two of them are laughing. They laugh quietly, or they try to. Milly sets Zeke down on his back, and pulls the pillows of the bed to her face in an attempt to muffle herself, and when she looks up she sees Meg on all fours with her blanket pulled over her head and, beyond her. Larry's faint shadow through the window drapes. He's pacing. He stops and leans on the railing, looking out at the pool.

"Shhh," Meg says, finally. "There's more." She sits straight, composes herself, pushes the hair back from her face, and holds up the now crumpled piece of paper. "Oh," she says. "Ready?"

"Meg, he's right there."

Meg looks. "He can't hear anything."

"Whisper," Milly says.

Meg reads. " 'I cried and sighed under the lids of these lonely eyes / Because I knew I'd miss your lavish thighs.' "

For a few moments they can say nothing. Milly, coughing and sputtering into the cotton smell of the sheets, has a moment of perceiving, by contrast, the unhappiness she's lived with these last few months, how bad it has been—this terrible time—and it occurs to her that she's managed it long enough not to notice it, quite. Everything is suffused in an ache she's grown accustomed to, and now it's as if she's flying in the face of it all. She laughs more deeply than she ever has, laughs even as she thinks of the Harmons, and of her grief. She's woozy from lack of air and breath. At last she sits up, wipes her eyes with part of the pillowcase, still laughing. The baby's fussing, so she works to stop, to gain some control of herself. She realizes that Meg is in the bathroom, running water. Then Meg comes out and offers her a wet washcloth.

"I didn't see you go in there."

"Quiet," Meg says. "Don't get me started again."

Milly holds the baby on one arm. "I have to feed Zeke some more."

"So once more I don't get to hold him."

They look at each other.

"Poor Larry," Meg says. "Married to a philistine. But—just maybe—he did the right thing, coming here."

"You don't suppose he heard us."

"I don't suppose it matters if he did. He'd never believe we could laugh at one of his *poems*."

"Oh, Meg—that's so mean."

"It's the truth. There are some things, honey, that love just won't change."

Now it's as if they are both suddenly aware of another context for these words—both thinking about Wally. They gaze at each other. But then the moment passes. They turn to the window and Meg says, "Is Larry out there? What'll I tell him anyway?" She crosses the room and looks through the little peephole in the door. "God," she says, "the Harmons are here."

Mrs. Harmon is standing in front of the door with Larry, who has apparently begun explaining himself. Larry turns and takes Meg by the arm as she and Milly come out. "All the way from

Champaign to head it off," he says to Mrs. Harmon. "I hope I just avoided making the biggest mistake of my life."

"God," Meg says to him. "If only you had money." She laughs at her own joke. Mrs. Harmon steps around her to take the baby's hand. She looks up at Milly. "I'm afraid we went overboard," she says. "We went shopping for the baby."

Milly nods at her. There's confusion now: Larry and Meg are talking, seem about to argue. Larry wants to know what Meg thinks of the poem, but Milly doesn't hear what she says to him. Mrs. Harmon is apologizing for coming earlier than planned.

"It's only an hour or so," Milly says, and then wonders if that didn't sound somehow ungracious. She can't think of anything else to say. And then she turns to see Mr. Harmon laboring up the stairs. He's carrying a giant teddy bear with a red ribbon wrapped around its thick middle. He has it over his shoulder, like a man lugging a body. The teddy bear is bigger than he is, and the muscles of his neck are straining as he sets it down. "This is for Wally," he says with a smile that seems sad. His eyes are moist. He puts one arm around his wife's puffy midriff and says, "I mean—if it's okay."

"I don't want to be divorced," Larry is saying to Meg.

Milly looks at the Harmons, at the hopeful, nervous expressions on their faces, and then she tries to give them the satisfaction of her best appreciation: she marvels at the size and the softness of the big teddy, and she holds the baby up to it, saying, "See? See?"

"It's quite impractical, of course," says Mr. Harmon.

"We couldn't pass it up," his wife says. "We have some other things in the car."

"I don't know where we'll put it," says Milly.

"We can keep it here," Mrs. Harmon hurries to say. She's holding on to her husband, and her pinched, unhappy features make her look almost frightened. Mr. Harmon raises the hand that had been around her waist and lightly, reassuringly, clasps her shoulder. He stands there, tall and straight in that intentionally ramrod-stiff way of his—the stance, he would say, of an old military man, which happens to be exactly what he is. His wife stands closer to him, murmurs something about the fireworks going off in the distance. It seems to Milly that they're both quite changed; it's as if they've come with bad news and are worried about hurting her with more of it. Then she realizes what it is they are trying to give her, in what is apparently the only way they know how, and she remembers that they have been attempting to get used to the loss of their only child. She feels her throat constrict, and when Larry reaches for her sister, putting his long, boy's arms around Meg, it's as if this embrace is somehow the expression of what they all feel. The Harmons are gazing at the baby now. Still arm in arm.

"Yes," Milly tells them, her voice trembling. "Yes, of course. You—we could keep it here."

Meg and Larry are leaning against the railing, in their embrace. It strikes Milly that she's the only one of these people without a lover, without someone to stand with. She lifts the baby to her shoulder and looks away from them all, but only for a moment. Far off, the sky is turning dusky; it's getting near the time for rockets and exploding blooms of color.

"Dinner for everyone," Mr. Harmon says, his voice full of brave cheerfulness. He leans close to Milly, and speaks to the child. "And you, young fellow, you'll have to wait a while."

"We'll eat at the motel restaurant and then watch the fireworks," says Mrs. Harmon. "We could sit right here on the balcony and see it all."

Meg touches the arm of the teddy bear. "Thing's as big as a *real* bear," she says.

"I feel like fireworks," Larry says.

"They put on quite a show," says Mr. Harmon. "There used to be a big field out this way—before they widened the street. Big field of grass, and people would gather—"

"We brought Wally here when he was a little boy," Mrs. Harmon says. "So many—such good times."

"They still put on a good show," Mr. Harmon says, squeezing his wife's shoulder.

Milly faces him, faces them, fighting back any sadness. In the next moment, without quite thinking about it, she steps forward slightly and offers her child to Mrs. Harmon. Mrs. Harmon tries to speak, but can't. Her husband clears his throat, lifts the big teddy bear as if to show it to everyone again. But he, too, is unable to speak. He sets it down, and seems momentarily confused. Milly lightly grasps his arm above the elbow, and steps forward to watch her mother-in-law cradle the baby. Mrs. Harmon makes a slight swinging motion, looking at her husband, and then at Milly. "Such a pretty baby," she says.

Mr. Harmon says, "A handsome baby."

Meg and Larry move closer. They all stand there on the motel balcony with the enormous teddy bear propped against the railing. They are quiet, almost shy, not quite looking at each other, and for the moment it's as if, like the crowds beginning to gather on the roofs of the low buildings across the street, they have come here only to wait for what will soon be happening in every quarter of the city of brotherly love.

DONALD BARTHELME | # THE BALLOON

THE BALLOON, beginning at a point on Fourteenth Street, the exact location of which I cannot reveal, expanded northward all one night, while people were sleeping, until it reached the Park. There, I stopped it, at dawn the northernmost edges lay over the Plaza, the free-hanging motion was frivolous and gentle. But experiencing a faint irritation at stopping, even to protect the trees, and seeing no reason the balloon should not be allowed to expand upward, over the parts of the city it was already covering, into the "air space" to be found there, I asked the engineers to see to it. This expansion took place throughout the morning, soft imperceptible sighing of gas through the valves. The balloon then covered forty-five blocks north-south and an irregular area east-west, as many as six crosstown blocks on either side of the Avenue in some places. That was the situation, then.

But it is wrong to speak of "situations," implying sets of circumstances leading to some resolution, some escape of tension, there were no situations, simply the balloon hanging there—muted heavy grays and browns for the most part, contrasting with walnut and soft yellows. A deliberate lack of finish, enhanced by skillful installation, gave the surface a rough, forgotten quality, sliding weights on the inside, carefully adjusted, anchored the great, vari-shaped mass at a number of points. Now we have had a flood of original ideas in all media, works of singular beauty as well as significant milestones in the history of inflation, but at that moment there was only *this balloon*, concrete particular, hanging there.

There were reactions. Some people found the balloon "interesting." As a response this seemed inadequate to the immensity of the balloon, the suddenness of its appearance over the city, on the other hand, in the absence of hysteria or other societally induced anxiety, it must be judged a calm, "mature" one. There was a certain amount of initial argumentation about the "meaning" of the balloon, this subsided, because we have learned not to insist on meanings, and they are rarely even looked for now, except in cases involving the simplest, safest phenomena. It was agreed that since the meaning of the balloon could never be known absolutely, extended discussion was pointless, or at least less purposeful than the activities of those who, for example, hung green and blue paper lanterns from the warm gray underside, in certain streets, or seized the occasion to write messages on the surface, announcing their availability for the performance of unnatural acts, or the availability of acquaintances.

Daring children jumped, especially at those points where the balloon hovered close to a building, so that the gap between balloon and building was a matter of a few inches, or points where the balloon actually made contact, exerting an ever-so-slight pressure against the side of a building, so that balloon and building seemed a unity. The upper surface was so structured that a "landscape" was presented, small valleys as well as slight knolls, or mounds, once atop the balloon, a stroll was possible, or even a trip, from one place to another. There was pleasure in being able to run down an incline, then up the opposing slope, both gently graded, or in making a leap from one side to the other. Bouncing was possible, because of the pneumaticity of the surface, and even falling, if that was your wish. That all these varied motions, as well as others, were within one's possibilities, in experiencing the "up" side of the balloon, was extremely exciting for children, accustomed to the city's flat, hard skin. But the purpose of the balloon was not to amuse children.

Too, the number of people, children and adults, who took advantage of the opportunities described was not so large as it might have been: a certain timidity, lack of trust in the balloon, was seen. There was, furthermore, some hostility. Because we had hidden the pumps, which fed helium to the interior, and because the surface was so vast that the authorities could not determine the point of entry—that is, the point at which the gas was injected—a degree of frustration was evidenced by those city officers into whose province such manifestations normally fell. The apparent purposelessness of the balloon was vexing (as was the fact that it was "there" at all). Had we painted, in great letters, LABORATORY TESTS PROVE or 18 PERCENT MORE EFFECTIVE on the sides of the balloon, this difficulty would have been circumvented. But I could not bear to do so. On the whole, these officers were remarkably tolerant, considering the dimensions of the anomaly, this tolerance being the result of, first, secret tests conducted by night that convinced them that little or nothing could be done in the way of removing or destroying the balloon, and, secondly, a public warmth that arose (not uncolored by touches of the aforementioned hostility) toward the balloon, from ordinary citizens.

As a single balloon must stand for a lifetime of thinking about balloons, so each citizen expressed, in the attitude he chose, a complex of attitudes. One man might consider that the balloon had to do with the notion *sullied*, as in the sentence *The big balloon sullied the otherwise clear and radiant Manhattan sky.* That is, the balloon was, in this man's view, an imposture, something inferior to the sky that had formerly been there, something interposed between the people and their "sky." But in fact it was January, the sky was dark and ugly, it was not a sky you could look up into, lying on your back in the street, with pleasure, unless pleasure, for you, proceeded from having been threatened, from having been misused. And the underside of the balloon was a pleasure to look up into, we had seen to that, muted grays and browns for the most part, contrasted with walnut and soft, forgotten yellows. And so, while this man was thinking *sullied,* still there was an admixture of pleasurable cognition in his thinking, struggling with the original perception.

Another man, on the other hand, might view the balloon as if it were part of a system of unanticipated rewards, as when one's employer walks in and says, "Here, Henry, take this package of money I have wrapped for you, because we have been doing so well in the business here, and I admire the way you bruise the tulips, without which bruising your department would not be a success, or at least not the success that it is." For this man the balloon might be a brilliantly heroic "muscle and pluck" experience, even if an experience poorly understood.

Another man might say, "Without the example of ———? it is doubtful that ——— would exist today in its present form, and find many to agree with him, or to argue with him. Ideas of "bloat" and "float" were introduced, as well as concepts of dream and responsibility. Others engaged in remarkably detailed fantasies having to do with a wish either to lose themselves in the balloon, or to engorge it. The private character of these wishes, of their origins, deeply buried and unknown, was such that they were not much spoken of, yet there is evidence that they were widespread. It was also argued that what was important was what you felt when you stood under the balloon, some people claimed that they felt sheltered, warmed, as never before, while enemies of the balloon felt, or reported feeling, constrained, a "heavy" feeling.

Critical opinion was divided:

THE BALLOON

"monstrous pourings"

"harp"

XXXXXXX "certain contrasts with darker portions"

"inner joy"

"large, square corners"

"conservative eclecticism that has so far governed
modern balloon design"

::::::: "abnormal vigor"

"warm, soft lazy passages"

"Has unity been sacrificed for a sprawling quality?"

"*Quelle catastrophe!*"

"munching"

People began, in a curious way, to locate themselves in relation
to aspects of the balloon: "I'll be at that place where it dips down
into Forty-seventh Street almost to the sidewalk, near the Alamo
Chili House," or, "Why don't we go stand on top, and take the
air, and maybe walk about a bit, where it forms a tight, curving
line with the façade of the Gallery of Modern Art—" Marginal
intersections offered entrances within a given time duration, as
well as "warm, soft, lazy passages" in which . . . But it is wrong
to speak of "marginal intersections," each intersection was crucial,
none could be ignored (as if, walking there, you might not find
someone capable of turning your attention, in a flash, from old
exercises to new exercises, risks and escalations). Each intersection
was crucial, meeting of balloon and building, meeting of balloon
and man, meeting of balloon and balloon.

It was suggested that what was admired about the balloon was
finally this: that it was not limited, or defined. Sometimes a bulge,
blister, or subsection would carry all the way east to the river on

its own initiative, in the manner of an army's movements on a map, as seen in a headquarters remote from the fighting. Then that part would be, as it were, thrown back again, or would withdraw into new dispositions; the next morning, that part would have made another sortie, or disappeared altogether. This ability of the balloon to shift its shape, to change, was very pleasing, especially to people whose lives were rather rigidly patterned, persons to whom change, although desired, was not available. The balloon, for the twenty-two days of its existence, offered the possibility, in its randomness, of mislocation of the self, in contradistinction to the grid of precise, rectangular pathways under our feet. The amount of specialized training currently needed, and the consequent desirability of long-term commitments, has been occasioned by the steadily growing importance of complex machinery, in virtually all kinds of operations; as this tendency increases, more and more people will turn, in bewildered inadequacy, to solutions for which the balloon may stand as a prototype, or "rough draft."

I met you under the balloon, on the occasion of your return from Norway, you asked if it was mine, I said it was. The balloon, I said, is a spontaneous autobiographical disclosure, having to do with the unease I felt at your absence, and with sexual deprivation, but now that your visit to Bergen has been terminated, it is no longer necessary or appropriate. Removal of the balloon was easy; trailer trucks carried away the depleted fabric, which is now stored in West Virginia, awaiting some other time of unhappiness, some time, perhaps, when we are angry with one another.

THE STUDENT'S WIFE

HE HAD been reading to her from Rilke, a poet he admired, when she fell asleep with her head on his pillow. He liked reading aloud, and he read well—a confident sonorous voice, now pitched low and somber, now rising, now thrilling. He never looked away from the page when he read and stopped only to reach to the nightstand for a cigarette. It was a rich voice that spilled her into a dream of caravans just setting out from walled cities and bearded men in robes. She had listened to him for a few minutes, then she had closed her eyes and drifted off.

He went on reading aloud. The children had been asleep for hours, and outside a car rubbered by now and then on the wet pavement. After a while he put down the book and turned in the bed to reach for the lamp. She opened her eyes suddenly, as if frightened, and blinked two or three times. Her eyelids looked oddly dark and fleshy to him as they flicked up and down over her fixed glassy eyes. He stared at her.

"Are you dreaming?" he asked.

She nodded and brought her hand up and touched her fingers to the plastic curlers at either side of her head. Tomorrow would be Friday, her day for all the four-to-seven-year-olds in the Wood-lawn Apartments. He kept looking at her, leaning on his elbow, at the same time trying to straighten the spread with his free hand. She had a smooth-skinned face with prominent cheekbones; the cheekbones, she sometimes insisted to friends, were from her father, who had been one-quarter Nez Perce.

Then: "Make me a little sandwich of something, Mike. With butter and lettuce and salt on the bread."

He did nothing and he said nothing because he wanted to go to sleep. But when he opened his eyes she was still awake, watching him.

"Can't you go to sleep, Nan?" he said, very solemnly. "It's late."

"I'd like something to eat first," she said. "My legs and arms hurt for some reason, and I'm hungry."

He groaned extravagantly as he rolled out of bed.

He fixed her the sandwich and brought it in on a saucer. She sat up in bed and smiled when he came into the bedroom, then slipped a pillow behind her back as she took the saucer. He thought she looked like a hospital patient in her white nightgown.

"What a funny little dream I had."

"What were you dreaming?" he said, getting into bed and turning over onto his side away from her. He stared at the nightstand waiting. Then he closed his eyes slowly.

"Do you really want to hear it?" she said.

"Sure," he said.

She settled back comfortably on the pillow and picked a crumb from her lip.

"Well. It seemed like a real long drawn-out kind of dream, you know, with all kinds of relationships going on, but I can't remember everything now. It was all very clear when I woke up, but it's beginning to fade now. How long have I been asleep, Mike? It doesn't really matter, I guess. Anyway, I think it was that we were staying someplace overnight. I don't know where the kids were, but it was just the two of us at some little hotel or something. It was on some lake that wasn't familiar. There was another, older, couple there and they wanted to take us for a ride in their motorboat." She laughed, remembering, and leaned forward off the pillow. "The next thing I recall is we were down at the boat landing. Only the way it turned out, they had just one seat in the boat, a kind of bench up in the front, and it was only big enough for three. You and I started arguing about who was going to sacrifice and sit all cooped up in the back. You said you were, and I said I was. But I finally squeezed in the back of the boat. It was so narrow it hurt my legs, and I was afraid the water was going to come in over the sides. Then I woke up."

"That's some dream," he managed to say and felt drowsily that he should say something more. "You remember Bonnie Travis? Fred Travis's wife? She used to have *color* dreams, she said.

She looked at the sandwich in her hand and took a bite. When she had swallowed, she ran her tongue in behind he lips and balanced the saucer on her lap as she reached behind and plumped up the pillow. Then she smiled and leaned back against the pillow again.

"Do you remember that time we stayed overnight on the Tilton River, Mike? When you caught that big fish the next morning?" She places her hand on his shoulder. "Do you remember that?" she said.

She did. After scarcely thinking about it these last years, it had begun coming back to her lately. It was a month or two after they'd married and gone away for a weekend. They had sat by a little campfire that night, a watermelon in the snow-cold river, and she'd fried Spam and eggs and canned beans for supper and pancakes and Spam and eggs in the same blackened pan the next morning. She had burned the pan both times she cooked, and they could never get the coffee to boil, but it was one of the best times they'd ever had. She remembered he had read to her that night as well: Elizabeth Browning and a few poems from the *Rubáiyát*. They had had so many covers over them that she could hardly turn her feet under all the weight. The next morning he had hooked a big trout, and people stopped their cars on the road across the river to watch him play it in.

"Well? Do you remember or not?" she said, patting him on the shoulder. "Mike?"

"I remember," he said. He shifted a little on his side, opened his eyes. He did not remember very well, he thought. What he did remember was very carefully combed hair and loud half-baked ideas about life and art, and he did not want to remember that.

"That was a long time ago, Nan," he said.

"We'd just got out of high school. You hadn't started to college," she said.

He waited, and then he raised up onto his arm and turned his head to look at her over his shoulder. "You about finished with that sandwich, Nan?" She was still sitting up in the bed.

She nodded and gave him the saucer.

"I'll turn off the light," he said.

"If you want," she said.

Then he pulled down into the bed again and extended his foot until it touched against hers. He lay still for a minute and then tried to relax.

"Mike, you're not asleep, are you?"

"No," he said. "Nothing like that."

"Well, don't go to sleep before me," she said. "I don't want to be awake by myself."

He didn't answer, but he inched a little closer to her on his side. When she put her arm over him and planted her hand flat against his chest, he took her fingers and squeezed them lightly. But in moments his hand dropped away to the bed, and he sighed.

"Mike? Honey? I wish you'd rub my legs. My legs hurt," she said.

"God," he said softly. "I was sound asleep."

"Well, I wish you'd rub my legs and talk to me. My shoulders hurt, too. But my legs especially."

He turned over and began rubbing her legs, then fell asleep again with his hand on her hip.

"Mike?"

"What is it, Nan? Tell me what it *is*."

"I wish you'd rub me all over," she said, turning onto her back. "My legs and arms both hurt tonight." She raised her knees to make a tower with the covers.

He opened his eyes briefly in the dark and then shut them. "Growing pains, huh?"

"Oh God, yes," she said, wiggling her toes, glad she had drawn him out. "When I was ten or eleven years old I was as big then as I am now. You should've seen me! I grew so fast in those days my legs and arms hurt me all the time. Didn't you?"

"Didn't I what?"

"Didn't you ever feel yourself growing?"

"Not that I remember," he said.

At last he raised up on his elbow, struck a match, and looked at the clock. He turned his pillow over to the cooler side and lay down again.

She said, "You're asleep, Mike. I wish you'd want to talk."

"All right," he said, not moving.

"Just hold me and get me off to sleep. I can't go to sleep," she said.

He turned over and put his arm over her shoulder as she turned onto her side to face the wall.

"Mike?"

He tapped his toes against her foot.

"Why don't you tell me all the things you like and the things you don't like."

"Don't know any right now," he said. "Tell me if you want," he said.

"If you promise to tell *me*. Is that a promise?

He tapped her foot again.

"Well . . ." she said and turned onto her back, pleased. "I like good foods, steaks and hash-brown potatoes, things like that. I like good books and magazines, riding on trains at night, and those times I flew in an airplane." She stopped. "Of course none of this is in order of preference. I'd have to think about it if it was in the order of preference. But I like that, flying in airplanes. There's a moment as you leave the ground you feel whatever happens is all right." She put her leg across his ankle. "I like staying up late at night and then staying in bed the next morning. I wish we could do that all the time, not just once in a while. And I like sex. I like to be touched now and then when I'm not expecting it. I like going to movies and drinking beer with friends afterward. I like to have friends. I like Janice Hendricks very much. I'd like to go dancing at least once a week. I'd like to have nice clothes all the time. I'd like to be able to buy the kids nice clothes every time they need it without having to wait. Laurie needs a new little outfit right now for Easter. And I'd like to get Gary a little suit or something. He's old enough. I'd like you to have a new suit, too. You really need a new suit more than he does. And I'd like us to have a place of our own. I'd like to stop moving around every year, or every other year. Most of all, she said, "I'd like us both just to live a good honest life without having to worry about money and bills and things like that. You're asleep," she said.

"I'm not," he said.

"I can't think of anything else. You go now. Tell me what you'd like."

"I don't know. Lots of things," he mumbled.

"Well, tell me. We're just talking aren't we?"

"I wish you'd leave me alone, Nan." He turned over to his side of the bed again and let his arm rest off the edge. She turned too and pressed against him.

"Mike?"

"Jesus," he said. Then: "All right. Let me stretch my legs a minute, then I'll wake up."

In a while she said, "Mike? Are you asleep?" She shook his shoulder gently, but there was no response. She lay there for a time huddled against his body, trying to sleep. She lay quietly at first, without moving, crowded against him and taking only very small, very even breaths. But she could not sleep.

She tried not to listen to his breathing, but it began to make her uncomfortable. There was a sound coming from inside his nose when he breathed. She tried to regulate her breathing so that she could breathe in and out at the same rhythm he did. It was no use. The little sound in his nose made everything no use. There was a webby squeak in his chest too. She turned again and nestled her bottom against his, stretched her arm over to the edge and cautiously put her fingertips against the cold wall. The covers had pulled up at the foot of the bed, and she could feel a draft when she moved her legs. She heard two people coming up the stairs to the apartment next door. Someone gave a throaty laugh before opening the door. Then she heard a chair drag on the floor. She turned again. The toilet flushed next door, and then it flushed again. Again she turned, onto her back this time, and tried to relax. She remembered an article she'd once read in a magazine: If all the bones and muscles and joints in the body could join together in perfect relaxation, sleep would almost certainly come. She took a long breath, closed her eyes, and lay perfectly still, arms straight along her sides. She tried to relax. She tried to imagine her legs suspended, bathed in something gauzelike. She turned onto her stomach. She closed her eyes, then she opened them. She thought of the fingers of her hand lying curled on the sheet in front of her lips. She raised a finger and lowered it to the sheet. She touched the wedding band on her ring finger with her thumb. She turned onto her side and then onto her back again. And then she began to feel afraid, and in one unreasoning moment of longing she prayed to go to sleep.

Please, God, let me go to sleep.

She tried to sleep.

"Mike," she whispered.

There was no answer.

She heard one of the children turn over in the bed and bump against the wall in the next room. She listened and listened but there was no other sound. She laid her hand under her left breast and felt the beat of her heart rising into her fingers. She turned onto her stomach and began to cry, her head off the pillow, her mouth against the sheet. She cried. And then she climbed out over the foot of the bed.

She washed her hands and face in the bathroom. She brushed her teeth. She brushed her teeth and watched her face in the mirror. In the living room she turned up the heat. Then she sat down at the kitchen table, drawing her feet up underneath the nightgown. She cried again. She lit a cigarette from the pack on the table. After a time she walked back to the bedroom and got her robe.

She looked in on the children. She pulled the covers up over her son's shoulders. She went back to the living room and sat in the big chair. She paged through a magazine and tried to read. She gazed at the photographs and then she tried to read again. Now and then a car went by on the street outside and she looked up. As each car passed she waited, listening. And then she looked down at the magazine again. There was a stack of magazines in the rack by the big chair. She paged through them all.

When it began to be light outside she got up. She walked to the window. The cloudless sky over the hills was beginning to turn white. The trees and the row of two-story apartment houses across the street were beginning to take shape as she watched. The sky grew whiter, the light expanding rapidly up from behind the hills. Except for the times she had been up with one or another of the children (which she did not count because she had never looked outside, only hurried back to bed or to the kitchen), she had seen few sunrises in her life and those when she was little. She knew that none of them had been like this. Not in pictures she had seen not in any book she had read had she learned a sunrise was so terrible as this.

She waited and then she moved over to the door and turned the lock and stepped out onto the porch. She closed the robe at her throat. The air was wet and cold. By stages things were becoming very visible. She let her eyes see everything until they fastened on the red winking light atop the radio tower atop the opposite hill.

★ ★ ★

She went through the dim apartment, back into the bedroom. He was knotted up in the center of the bed, the covers bunched over his shoulders, his head half under the pillow. He looked desperate in his heavy sleep, his arms flung out across her side of the bed, his jaws clenched. As she looked, the room grew very light and the pale sheets whitened grossly before her eyes.

She wet her lips with a sticking sound and got down on her knees. She put her hands out on the bed.

"God," she said. "God, will you help us, God?" she said.

JAYNE ANNE
PHILLIPS

SOMETHING THAT HAPPENED

I AM in the basement sorting clothes, whites with whites, colors with colors, delicates with delicates—it's a segregated world—when my youngest child yells down the steps. She yells when I'm in the basement, always, angrily, as if I've slipped below the surface and though she's twenty-one years old she can't believe it.

"Do you know what day it is? I mean do you *know* what day it is, Kay?" It's this new thing of calling me by my first name. She stands groggy-eyed, surveying her mother.

I say, "No, Angela, so what does that make me?" Now my daughter shifts into second, narrows those baby blues I once surveyed in such wonder and prayed *Lord, lord, this is the last.*

"Well, never mind," she says. "I've made you breakfast." And she has, eggs and toast and juice and flowers on the porch. Then she sits and watches me eat it, twirling her fine gold hair.

Halfway through the eggs it dawns on me, my ex–wedding anniversary. Angela, under the eyeliner and blue jeans you're a haunted and ancient presence. When most children can't remember an anniversary, Angela can't forget it. Every year for five years, she has pushed me to the brink of remembrance.

[300]

"The trouble with you," she finally says, "is that you don't care enough about yourself to remember what's been important in your life."

"Angela," I say, "in the first place I haven't been married for five years, so I no longer have a wedding anniversary to remember."

"That doesn't matter" (twirling her hair, not scowling). "It's still something that happened."

Two years ago I had part of an ulcerated stomach removed and I said to the kids, "Look, I can't worry for you anymore. If you get into trouble, don't call me. If you want someone to take care of you, take care of each other." So the three older girls packed Angela off to college and her brother drove her there. Since then I've gradually resumed my duties. Except that I was inconspicuously absent from my daughters' weddings. I say inconspicuously because, thank God, all of them were hippies who got married in fields without benefit of aunts and uncles. Or mothers. But Angela reads *Glamour*, and she'll ask me to her wedding. Though Mr. Charm has yet to appear in any permanent guise, she's already gearing up for it. Pleadings. Remonstrations. Perhaps a few tears near the end. But I shall hold firm, I hate sacrificial offerings of my own flesh. "I can't help it," I'll joke, "I have a weak stomach, only half of it is there."

Angela sighs, perhaps foreseeing it all. The phone is ringing. And slowly, there she goes. By the time she picks it up, cradles the receiver to her brown neck, her voice is normal. Penny-bright, and she spends it fast. I look out the screened porch on the alley and the clean garbage cans. It seems to me that I remembered everything before the kids were born. I say kids as though they appeared collectively in a giant egg, my stomach. When actually there were two years, then one year, then two, then three between them. The Child-Bearing Years, as though you stand there like a blossomed pear tree and the fruit plops off. Eaten or rotted to seed to start the whole thing all over again.

★ ★ ★

Angela has fixed too much food for me. She often does. I don't digest large amounts so I eat small portions six times a day. The dog drags his basset ears to my feet, waits for the plate. And I give it to him, urging him on so he'll gobble it fast and silent before Angela comes back.

Dear children, I always confused my stomach with my womb. Lulled into confusion by nearly four pregnant years I heard them say, "Oh, you're eating for two," as if the two organs were directly · connected by a small tube. In the hospital I was convinced they had removed my uterus along with half of my stomach. The doctors, at an end of patience, labeled my decision an anxiety reaction. And I reacted anxiously by demanding an X ray so I could see that my womb was still there.

Angela returns, looks at the plate, which I have forgotten to pick up, looks at the dog, puts her hand on my shoulder.

"I'm sorry," she says.

"Well," I say.

Angela twists her long fingers, her fine thin fingers with their smooth knuckles, twists the diamond ring her father gave her when she was sixteen.

"Richard," I'd said to my husband, "she's your daughter, not your fiancée."

"Kay," intoned the husband, the insurance agent, the successful adjuster of claims, "she's only sixteen once. This ring is a gift, our love for Angela. She's beautiful, she's blossoming."

"Richard," I said, shuffling Maalox bottles and planning my bland lunch, "diamonds are not for blossoms. They're for those who need a piece of the rock." At which Richard laughed heartily, always amused at my cynicism regarding the business that principally buttered my bread. Buttered his bread, because by then I couldn't eat butter.

"What is it you're afraid to face?" asked Richard. "What is it in your life you can't control? You're eating yourself alive. You're dissolving your own stomach."

"Richard," I said, "it's a tired old story. I have this husband who wants to marry his daughter."

"I want you to see a psychiatrist," said Richard, tightening his expertly knotted tie. "That's what you need, Kay, a chance to talk it over with someone who's objective."

"I'm not interested in objectives," I said. "I'm interested in shrimp and butter sauce, Tabasco, hot chilis, and an end of pain."

"Pain never ends," said Richard.

"Oh, Richard," I said, "no wonder you're the King of the Southeast Division."

"Look," he said, "I'm trying to put four kids through college and one wife through graduate school. I'm starting five investment plans now so when our kids get married no one has to wait twenty-five years to finish a dissertation on George Eliot like you did. Really, am I such a bad guy? I don't remember forcing you into any of this. And your goddamn stomach has to quit digesting itself. I want you to see a psychiatrist."

"Richard," I said, "if our daughters have five children in eight years—which most of them won't, being members of Zero Population Growth who quote *Diet for a Small Planet* every Thanksgiving—they may still be slow with Ph.Ds despite your investment plans."

Richard untied his tie and tied it again. "Listen," he said. "Plenty of women with five children have Ph.Ds."

"Really," I said. "I'd like to see those statistics."

"I suppose you resent your children's births," he said, straightening his collar. "Well, just remember, the last one was your miscalculation."

"And the first one was yours," I said.

It's true. We got pregnant, as Richard affectionately referred to it, in a borrowed bunk bed on Fire Island. It was the eighth time we'd slept together. Richard gasped that of course he'd take care of things, had he ever failed me? But I had my first orgasm and no one remembered anything.

After the fourth pregnancy and first son, Richard was satisfied. Angela, you were born in a bad year. You were expensive, your father was starting in insurance after five years as a high school principal. He wanted the rock, all of it. I had a rock in my belly we thought three times was dead. So he swore his love to you, with that ring he thee guiltily wed. Sweet Sixteen, does she remember? She never forgets.

Angela pasted sugar cubes to pink ribbons for a week, Sweet Sixteen party favors she read about in *Seventeen*, while the older girls shook their sad heads. Home from colleges in Ann Arbor, Boston, Berkeley, they stared aghast at their golden-haired baby sister, her Villager suits, the ladybug stickpin in her blouses. Angela owned no blue jeans; her boyfriend opened the car door for her and carried her books home. They weren't heavy, he was a halfback. Older sister no. 3: "Don't you have arms?" Older sister no. 2: "He'll take it out of your hide, wait and see." Older sister no. 1: "The nuclear family lives off women's guts. Your mother has ulcers, Angela, she can't eat gravy with your daddy."

At which point Richard slapped oldest sister, his miscalculation, and she flew back to Berkeley, having cried in my hands and begged me to come with her. She missed the Sweet Sixteen party. She missed Thanksgiving and Christmas for the next two years.

Angela's jaw set hard. I saw her reject politics, feminism, and everyone's miscalculations. I hung sugar cubes from the ceiling for her party until the room looked like the picture in the magazine. I ironed sixteen pink satin ribbons she twisted in her hair. I applauded with everyone else, including the smiling halfback, when her father slipped the diamond on her finger. Then I filed for divorce.

The day Richard moved out of the house, my son switched his major to pre-med at NYU. He said it was the only way to get out of selling insurance. The last sound of the marriage was Richard being nervously sick in the kitchen sink. Angela gave hi[m] washcloth and took me out to dinner at Señor Miguel's w[hile] stacked up his boxes and drove them away. I ate chilis rel[l] guacamole chips in sour cream, cheese enchiladas, Mexican bread, and three green chili burritos. Then I ate tranquilizers bouillon for two weeks.

Angela was frightened.

"Mother," she said, "I wish you could be happy."

"Angela," I answered, "I'm glad you married your father, I couldn't do it anymore."

Angela finished high school the next year and twelve copies each of *Ingenue*, *Cosmopolitan*, *Mademoiselle*. She also read the Bible alone at night in her room.

"Because I'm nervous," she said, "and it helps me sleep. All the trees and fruit, the figs, begat and begat going down like the multiplication tables."

"Angela," I said, "are you thinking of making love to someone?"

"No, Mother," she said, "I think I'll wait. I think I'll wait a long time."

Angela quit eating meat and blinked her mascaraed eyes at the glistening fried liver I slid onto her plate.

"It's so brown," she said. "It's just something's guts."

"You've always loved it," I said, and she tried to eat it, glancing at my midriff, glancing at my milk and cottage cheese.

When her father took over the Midwest and married a widow, Angela declined to go with him. When I went to the hospital to have my stomach reduced by half, Angela declined my invitations to visit and went on a fast. She grew wan and romantic, said she wished I taught at her college instead of City, she'd read about Sylvia Plath in *Mademoiselle*. We talked on the telephone while I watched the hospital grounds go dark in my square window. It was summer and the trees were so heavy.

I thought about Angela, I thought about my miscalculations. I

a cold
hile he
enos,
ried
nd

ınd white mucous coatings. About
first baby, skinny in his turned-
ending roses every birth, American
ping in the washbasin, tiny wriggling
their translucent heads. And starting or-
piercing thick skins with a fingernail so the
.em. After a while, I didn't want to watch the
.o the white ragged coat beneath.

comes home in the summers, halfway through business,
.ary education, or home ec. She doesn't want to climb
.ockies or go to India. She wants to show houses to wives,
.al estate, and feed me mashed potatoes, cherry pie, avocados,
and artichokes. Today she not only fixes breakfast for my ex–
anniversary, she fixes lunch and dinner. She wants to pile up my
plate and see me eat everything. If I eat, surely something good
will happen. She won't remember what's been important enough
in my life to make me forget everything. She is spooning breaded
clams, french fries, nuts, and anchovy salad onto my plate.

"Angela, it's too much."

"That's OK, we'll save what you don't want."

"Angela, save it for who?"

She puts down her fork. "For anyone," she says. "For any time
they want it."

In a moment, she slides my plate onto her empty one and begins
to eat.